Grimms' Fairy Tales

JACOB AND WILHELM GRIMM

Published by Paperview (2004)
ISBN: 2-87427-087-3
www.paperviewgroup.com

CONTENTS

1 The Frog-King, or Iron Henry

In old times when wishing still helped one, there lived a king whose daughters were all beautiful, but the youngest was so beautiful that the sun itself, which has seen so much, was astonished whenever it shone in her face. Close by the King's castle lay a great dark forest, and under an old lime-tree in the forest was a well, and when the day was very warm, the King's child went out into the forest and sat down by the side of the cool fountain, and when she was dull she took a golden ball, and threw it up on high and caught it, and this ball was her favourite plaything.

Now it so happened that on one occasion the princess's golden ball did not fall into the little hand which she was holding up for it, but on to the ground beyond, and rolled straight into the water. The King's daughter followed it with her eyes, but it vanished, and the well was deep, so deep that the bottom could not be seen. On this she began to cry, and cried louder and louder, and could not be comforted. And as she thus lamented someone said to her, "What ails thee, King's daughter? Thou weepest so that even a stone would show pity."

She looked round to the side from whence the voice came, and saw a frog stretching forth its thick, ugly head from the water. "Ah! old water-splasher, is it thou?" said she; "I am weeping for my golden ball, which has fallen into the well."

"Be quiet, and do not weep," answered the frog, "I can help thee, but what wilt thou give me if I bring thy plaything up again?"

"Whatever thou wilt have, dear frog," said she—" My clothes, my pearls and jewels, and even the golden crown which I am wearing."

The frog answered, "I do not care for thy clothes, thy pearls and jewels, or thy golden crown, but if thou wilt love me and let me be thy companion and play-fellow, and sit by thee at thy little table, and eat off thy little golden plate, and drink out of thy little cup, and sleep in thy little bed—if thou wilt promise me this I will go down below, and bring thee thy golden ball up again."

"Oh yes," said she, "I promise thee all thou wishest, if thou wilt but bring me my ball back again." She, however, thought, "How the silly frog does talk! He lives in the water with the other frogs, and croaks, and can be no companion to any human being!"

But the frog when he had received this promise, put his head into the water and sank down, and in a short while came swimming up again with the ball in his mouth, and threw it on the grass. The King's daughter was delighted to see her pretty plaything once more, and picked it up, and ran away with it. "Wait, wait," said the frog. "Take me with thee. I can't run as thou canst." But what did it avail him to scream his croak, croak, after her, as loudly as he could? She did not listen to it, but ran home and soon forgot the poor frog, who was forced to go back into his well again.

The next day when she had seated herself at table with the King and all the courtiers, and was eating from her little golden plate, something came creeping *splish, splash, splish, splash*, up the marble staircase, and when it had got to the top, it knocked at the door and cried, "Princess, youngest princess, open the door for me." She ran to see who was outside, but when she opened the door, there sat the frog in front of it. Then she slammed the door to, in great haste, sat down to dinner again, and was quite frightened. The King saw plainly that her heart was beating violently, and said, "My child, what art thou so afraid of? Is there perchance a giant outside who wants to carry thee away?"

"Ah, no," replied she. "It is no giant but a disgusting frog."

"What does a frog want with thee?"

"Ah, dear father, yesterday as I was in the forest sitting by the well, playing, my golden ball fell into the water. And because I cried so, the frog brought it out again for me, and because he so insisted, I promised him he should be my companion, but I never thought he would be able to come out of his water! And now he is outside there, and wants to come in for me."

In the meantime it knocked a second time, and cried:

> "Princess! youngest princess!
> Open the door for me!
> Dost thou not know what thou saidst to me
> Yesterday by the cool waters of the fountain?
> Princess, youngest princess!
> Open the door for me!"

Then said the King, "That which thou hast promised must thou perform. Go and let him in."

She went and opened the door, and the frog hopped in and followed her, step by step, to her chair. There he sat and cried, "Lift me up beside thee."

She delayed, until at last the King commanded her to do it. When the frog was once on the chair he wanted to be on the table, and when he was on the table he said, "Now, push thy lit-

7

tle golden plate nearer to me that we may eat together." She did this, but it was easy to see that she did not do it willingly. The frog enjoyed what he ate, but almost every mouthful she took choked her. At length he said, "I have eaten and am satisfied; now I am tired, carry me into thy little room and make thy little silken bed ready, and we will both lie down and go to sleep."

The King's daughter began to cry, for she was afraid of the cold frog which she did not like to touch, and which was now to sleep in her pretty, clean little bed. But the King grew angry and said, "He who helped thee when thou wert in trouble ought not afterwards to be despised by thee." So she took hold of the frog with two fingers, carried him upstairs, and put him in a corner. But when she was in bed he crept to her and said, "I am tired, I want to sleep as well as thou, lift me up or I will tell thy father." Then she was terribly angry, and took him up and threw him with all her might against the wall. "Now, thou wilt be quiet, odious frog," said she. But when he fell down he was no frog but a King's son with beautiful kind eyes. He by her father's will was now her dear companion and husband. Then he told her how he had been bewitched by a wicked witch, and how no one could have delivered him from the well but herself, and that tomorrow they would go together into his kingdom. Then they went to sleep, and next morning when the sun awoke them, a carriage came driving up with eight white horses, which had white ostrich feathers on their heads, and were harnessed with golden chains, and behind stood the young King's servant Faithful Henry. Faithful Henry had been so unhappy when his master was changed into a frog, that he had caused three iron bands to be laid round his heart, lest it should burst with grief and sadness. The carriage was to conduct the young King into his Kingdom. Faithful Henry helped them both in, and placed himself behind again, and was full of joy because of this deliverance. And when they had driven a part of the way the King's son heard a cracking behind him as if something had broken. So he turned round and cried, "Henry, the carriage is breaking."

"No, master, it is not the carriage. It is a band from my heart, which was put there in my great pain when you were a frog and imprisoned in the well." Again and once again while they were on their way something cracked, and each time the King's son thought the carriage was breaking; but it was only the bands which were springing from the heart of faithful Henry because his master was set free and was happy.

2 The Cat and the Mouse in Partnership

A certain cat had made the acquaintance of a mouse, and had said so much to her about the great love and friendship she felt for her, that at length the mouse agreed that they should live and keep house together. "But we must make a provision for winter, or else we shall suffer from hunger," said the cat, "and you, little mouse, cannot venture everywhere, or you will be caught in a trap some day." The good advice was followed, and a pot of fat was bought, but they did not know where to put it. At length, after much consideration, the cat said, "I know no place where it will be better stored up than in the church, for no one dares take anything away from there. We will set it beneath the altar, and not touch it until we are really in need of it." So the pot was placed in safety, but it was not long before the cat had a great yearning for it, and said to the mouse, "I want to tell you something, little mouse; my cousin has brought a little son into the world, and has asked me to be godmother; he is white with brown spots, and I am to hold him over the font at the christening. Let me go out today, and you look after the house by yourself."

"Yes, yes," answered the mouse, "by all means go, and if you get anything

very good, think of me, I should like a drop of sweet red christening wine too." All this, however, was untrue; the cat had no
cousin, and had not been asked to be godmother. She went
straight to the church, stole to the pot of fat, began to lick at it,
and licked the top of the fat off. Then she took a walk upon the
roofs of the town, looked out for opportunities, and then
stretched herself in the sun, and licked her lips whenever she
thought of the pot of fat, and not until it was evening did she
return home. "Well, here you are again," said the mouse, "no
doubt you have had a merry day."

"All went off well," answered the cat.

"What name did they give the child?"

"Top off!" said the cat quite coolly.

"Top off!" cried the mouse, "that is a very odd and uncommon name, is it a usual one in your family?"

"What does it mean?" said the cat, "it is no worse than
Crumb-stealer, as your godchildren are called."

Before long the cat was seized by another fit of longing. She
said to the mouse, "You must do me a favour, and once more
manage the house for a day alone. I am again asked to be godmother, and, as the child has a white ring round its neck, I cannot refuse." The good mouse consented, but the cat crept behind
the town walls to the church, and devoured half the pot of fat.
"Nothing ever seems so good as what one keeps to oneself," said
she, and was quite satisfied with her day's work. When she went
home the mouse inquired, "And what was this child christened?"

"Half-done," answered the cat.

"Half-done! What are you saying? I never heard the name in
my life, I'll wager anything it is not in the calendar!"

The cat's mouth soon began to water for some more licking.
"All good things go in threes," said she, "I am asked to stand
godmother again. The child is quite black, only it has white
paws, but with that exception, it has not a single white hair on
its whole body; this only happens once every few years, you will
let me go, won't you?"

"Top-off! Half-done!" answered the mouse, "they are such odd names, they make me very thoughtful."

"You sit at home," said the cat, "in your dark-grey fur coat and long tail, and are filled with fancies, that's because you do not go out in the daytime." During the cat's absence the mouse cleaned the house, and put it in order, but the greedy cat entirely emptied the pot of fat. "When everything is eaten up one has some peace," said she to herself, and well filled and fat she did not return home till night. The mouse at once asked what name had been given to the third child. "It will not please you more than the others," said the cat. "He is called All-gone."

"All gone," cried the mouse, "that is the most suspicious name of all! I have never seen it in print. All gone; what can that mean?" and she shook her head, curled herself up, and lay down to sleep. From this time forth no one invited the cat to be godmother, but when the winter had come and there was no longer anything to be found outside, the mouse thought of their provision, and said, "Come cat, we will go to our pot of fat which we have stored up for ourselves—we shall enjoy that."

"Yes," answered the cat, "you will enjoy it as much as you would enjoy sticking that dainty tongue of yours out of the window." They set out on their way, but when they arrived, the pot of fat certainly was still in its place, but it was empty. "Alas!" said the mouse, "now I see what has happened, now it comes to light! You are a true friend! You have devoured all when you were standing godmother. First top off, then half-done, then—."

"Will you hold your tongue," cried the cat, "one word more and I will eat you too."

"All gone" was already on the poor mouse's lips; scarcely had she spoken it before the cat sprang on her, seized her, and swallowed her down. Truly, that is the way of the world.

3 The Wolf and the Seven Little Kids

There was once upon a time an old goat who had seven little kids, and loved them with all the love of a mother for her children. One day she wanted to go into the forest and fetch some food. So she called all seven to her and said, "Dear children, I have to go into the forest, be on your guard against the wolf; if he come in, he will devour you all—skin, hair, and all. The wretch often disguises himself, but you will know him at once by his rough voice and his black feet." The kids said, "Dear mother, we will take good care of ourselves; you may go away without any anxiety." Then the old one bleated, and went on her way with an easy mind.

It was not long before some one knocked at the house-door and called, "Open the door, dear children; your mother is here, and has brought something back with her for each of you." But the little kids knew that it was the wolf, by the rough voice; "We will not open the door," cried they, "thou art not our mother. She has a soft, pleasant voice, but thy voice is rough; thou art the wolf!" Then the wolf went away to a shopkeeper and bought himself a great lump of chalk, ate this and made his voice soft with it. Then he came back, knocked at the door of the house, and cried, "Open the door, dear children, your mother is here and has brought something back with her for each of you." But the wolf had laid his black paws against the window, and the children saw them and cried, "We will not open the door, our mother has not black feet like thee; thou art the wolf." Then the wolf ran to a baker and said, "I have hurt my feet, rub some dough over them for me." And when the baker had rubbed his feet over, he ran to the miller and said, "Strew some white meal over my feet for me." The miller thought to himself, "The wolf wants to deceive someone," and refused; but the wolf said, "If thou wilt not do it, I will devour thee." Then the miller was afraid, and made his paws white for him. Truly men are like that.

So now the wretch went for the third time to the house-door, knocked at it and said, "Open the door for me, children, your dear little mother has come home, and has brought every one of you something back from the forest with her." The little kids cried, "First show us thy paws that we may know if thou art our dear little mother." Then he put his paws in through the window, and when the kids saw that they were white, they believed that all he said was true, and opened the door. But who should come in but the wolf! They were terrified and wanted to hide themselves. One sprang under the table, the second into the bed, the third into the stove, the fourth into the kitchen, the fifth into the cupboard, the sixth under the washing-bowl, and the seventh into the clock-case. But the wolf found them all, and used no great ceremony; one after the other he swallowed them down his throat. The youngest, who was in the clock-case, was the only one he did not find. When the wolf had satisfied his appetite he took himself off, laid himself down under a tree in the green meadow outside, and began to sleep.

Soon afterwards the old goat came home again from the forest. Ah! What a sight she saw there! The house-door stood wide open. The table, chairs, and benches were thrown down, the washing-bowl lay broken to pieces, and the quilts and pillows were pulled off the bed. She sought her children, but they were nowhere to be found. She called them one after another by name, but no one answered. At last, when she came to the youngest, a soft voice cried, "Dear mother, I am in the clock-case." She took the kid out, and it told her that the wolf had come and had eaten all the others. Then you may imagine how she wept over her poor children.

At length in her grief she went out, and the youngest kid ran with her. When they came to the meadow, there lay the wolf by the tree and snoring so loudly that the branches shook. She looked at him on every side and saw that something was moving and struggling in his gorged belly. "Ah, heavens," said she, "is it possible that my poor children whom he has swallowed down for his supper, can be still alive?" Then the kid had to run home and fetch scissors, and a needle and thread, and the goat cut open the monster's stomach, and hardly had she made one cut, than one little kid thrust its head out, and when she cut farther, all six sprang out one after another, and were all still alive, and had suffered no injury whatever, for in his greediness the monster had swallowed them down whole. What rejoicing there was! They embraced their dear mother, and jumped like a sailor at his wedding. The mother, however, said, "Now go and look for some big stones, and we will fill the wicked beast's stomach with them while he is still asleep." Then the seven kids dragged the stones thither with all speed, and put as many of them into his stomach as they could get in; and the mother sewed him up again in the greatest haste, so that he was not aware of anything and never once stirred.

When the wolf at length had had his sleep out, he got on his legs, and as the stones in his stomach made him very thirsty, he wanted to go to a well to drink. But when he began to walk and move about, the stones in his stomach knocked against each other and rattled. Then cried he:

> "What rumbles and tumbles
>   Against my poor bones?
> I thought 't was six kids,
>   But it's naught but big stones."

And when he got to the well and stooped over the water and was just about to drink, the heavy stones made him fall in, and there was no help, but he had to drown miserably. When the seven kids saw that, they came running to the spot and cried aloud, "The wolf is dead! The wolf is dead!" and danced for joy round about the well with their mother.

4 The Wonderful Musician

There was once a wonderful musician, who went quite alone through a forest and thought of all manner of things, and when nothing was left for him to think about, he said to himself, "Time is beginning to pass heavily with me here in the forest, I will fetch hither a good companion for myself." Then he took his fiddle from his back, and played so that it echoed through the trees. It was not long before a wolf came trotting through the thicket towards him. "Ah, here is a wolf coming! I have no desire for him!" said the musician; but the wolf came nearer and said to him, "Ah, dear musician, how beautifully thou dost play. I should like to learn that, too."

"It is soon learnt," the musician replied, "thou hast only to do all that I bid thee."

"Oh, musician," said the wolf, "I will obey thee as a scholar obeys his master." The musician bade him follow, and when they had gone part of the way together, they came to an old oak-tree which was hollow inside, and cleft in the middle. "Look," said the musician, "if thou wilt learn to fiddle, put thy fore paws into this crevice." The wolf obeyed, but the musician quickly picked up a stone and with one blow wedged his two paws so fast that he was forced to stay there like a prisoner. "Stay there until I come back again," said the musician, and went his way.

After a while he again said to himself, "Time is beginning to pass heavily with me here in the forest, I will fetch hither another companion," and took his fiddle and again played in the forest. It was not long before a fox came creeping through the trees towards him. "Ah, there's a fox coming!" said the musician. "I have no desire for him." The fox came up to him and said, "Oh, dear musician, how beautifully thou dost play! I should like to learn that too."

"That is soon learnt," said the musician. "Thou hast only to do everything that I bid thee."

"Oh, musician," then said the fox, "I will obey thee as a scholar obeys his master."

"Follow me," said the musician; and when they had walked a part of the way, they came to a footpath, with high bushes on both sides of it. There the musician stood still, and from one side bent a young hazel-bush down to the ground, and put his foot on the top of it, then he bent down a young tree from the other side as well, and said, "Now little fox, if thou wilt learn something, give me thy left front paw." The fox obeyed, and the musician fastened his paw to the left bough. "Little fox," said he, "now reach me thy right paw" and he tied it to the right bough. When he had examined whether they were firm enough, he let go, and the bushes sprang up again, and jerked up the little fox, so that it hung struggling in the air. "Wait there till I come back again," said the musician, and went his way.

Again he said to himself, "Time is beginning to pass heavily with me here in the forest, I will fetch hither another companion," so he took his fiddle, and the sound echoed through the forest. Then a little hare came springing towards him. "Why, a hare is coming," said the musician, "I do not want him."

"Ah, dear musician," said the hare, "how beautifully thou dost fiddle; I too, should like to learn that."

"That is soon learnt," said the musician, "thou hast only to do everything that I bid thee."

"Oh, musician," replied the little hare, "I will obey thee as a scholar obeys his master." They went a part of the way together until they came to an open space in the forest, where stood an aspen tree. The musician tied a long string round the little hare's neck, the other end of which he fastened to the tree. "Now briskly, little hare, run twenty times round the tree!" cried the musician, and the little hare obeyed, and when it had run round twenty times, it had twisted the string twenty times round the trunk of the tree, and the little hare was caught, and let it pull and tug as it liked, it only made the string cut into its tender neck. "Wait there till I come back," said the musician, and went onwards.

The wolf, in the meantime, had pushed and pulled and bitten at the stone, and had worked so long that he had set his feet at liberty and had drawn them once more out of the cleft. Full of anger and rage he hurried after the musician and wanted to tear him to pieces. When the fox saw him running, he began to lament, and cried with all his might, "Brother wolf, come to my help, the musician has betrayed me!" The wolf drew down the little tree, bit the cord in two, and freed the fox, who went with him to take revenge on the musician. They found the tied-up hare, whom likewise they delivered, and then they all sought the enemy together.

The musician had once more played his fiddle as he went on his way, and this time he had been more fortunate. The sound reached the ears of a poor wood-cutter, who instantly, whether he would or no, gave up his work and came with his hatchet under his arm to listen to the music. "At last comes the right companion," said the musician, "for I was seeking a human being, and no wild beast." And he began and played so beautifully and delightfully that the poor man stood there as if bewitched, and his heart leaped with gladness. And as he thus stood, the wolf, the fox, and the hare came up, and he saw well that they had some evil design. So he raised his glittering axe and placed himself before the musician, as if to say, "Whoso wishes to touch him let him beware, for he will have to do with me!" Then the beasts were terrified and ran back into the forest. The musician, however, played once more to the man out of gratitude, and then went onwards.

19

5 The Pack of Ragamuffins

The cock once said to the hen, "It is now the time when our nuts are ripe, so let us go to the hill together and for once eat our fill before the squirrel takes them all away."

"Yes," replied the hen, "come, we will have some pleasure together." Then they went away to the hill, and as it was a bright day they stayed till evening. Now I do not know whether it was that they had eaten till they were too fat, or whether they had become proud, but they would not go home on foot, and the cock had to build a little carriage of nut-shells. When it was ready, the little hen seated herself in it and said to the cock, "Thou canst just harness thyself to it."

"I like that!" said the cock, "I would rather go home on foot than let myself be harnessed to it; no, that is not our bargain. I do not mind being coachman and sitting on the box, but drag it myself I will not."

As they were thus disputing, a duck quacked to them, "You thieving folks, who bade you go to my nut-hill? Well, you shall suffer for it!" and ran with open beak at the cock. But the cock also was not idle, and fell boldly on the duck, and at last wounded her so with his spurs that she also begged for mercy, and willingly let herself be harnessed to the carriage as a punishment. The little cock now seated himself on the box and was coachman, and thereupon they went off in a gallop, with "Duck, go as fast as thou canst." When they had driven a part of the way they met two foot-passengers, a pin and a needle. They cried, "Stop! stop!" and said that it would soon be as dark as pitch, and then they could not go a step further, and that it was so dirty on the road, and asked if they could not get into the carriage for a while. They had been at the tailor's public-house by the gate, and had stayed too long over the beer. As they were thin people, who did not take up much room, the cock let them both get in, but they had to promise him and his little hen not to step on their feet. Late in the evening they came to an inn, and as they did not like to go further by night, and as the duck also was not strong on her feet, and fell from one side to the other, they went in. The host at first made many objections, his house was already full, besides he thought they could not be very distinguished persons; but at last, as they made pleasant speeches, and told him that he should have the egg which the little hen has laid on the way, and should likewise keep the duck, which laid one every day, he at length said that they might stay the night. And now they had themselves well served, and feasted and rioted. Early in the morning, when day was breaking, and every one was asleep, the cock awoke the hen, brought the egg, pecked it open, and they ate it together, but they threw the shell on the hearth. Then they went to the needle which was still asleep, took it by the head and stuck it into the cushion of the landlord's chair, and put the pin in his towel, and at the last without more ado they flew away over the heath. The duck who liked to sleep in the open air and had stayed in the yard, heard them going away, made herself merry and found a stream, down which she swam, which was a much quicker way of travelling than being harnessed to a carriage. The host did not get out of bed for two hours after this; he washed himself and wanted to dry himself, then the pin went over his face and made a red streak from one ear to the other. After this he went into the kitchen and wanted to light a pipe, but when he came to the hearth the egg-shell darted into his eyes. "This morning everything attacks my head," said he, and angrily sat down on his grandfather's chair, but he quickly started up again and cried, "Woe is me", for the needle had pricked him still worse than the pin, and not in the head. Now he was thoroughly angry, and suspected the guests who had come so late the night before, and when he went and looked about for them, they were gone. Then he made a vow to take no more ragamuffins into his house, for they consume much, pay for nothing, and play mischievous tricks into the bargain by way of gratitude.

6 Little Brother and Little Sister

Little brother took his little sister by the hand and said, "Since our mother died we have had no happiness; our step-mother beats us every day, and if we come near her she kicks us away with her foot. Our meals are the hard crusts of bread that are left over; and the little dog under the table is better off, for she often throws it a nice bit. May Heaven pity us. If our mother only knew! Come, we will go forth together into the wide world."

They walked the whole day over meadows, fields, and stony places; and when it rained the little sister said, "Heaven and our hearts are weeping together." In the evening they came to a large forest, and they were so weary with sorrow and hunger and the long walk, that they lay down in a hollow tree and fell asleep.

The next day when they awoke, the sun was already high in the sky, and shone down hot into the tree. Then the brother said, "Sister, I am thirsty; if I knew of a little brook I would go and just take a drink; I think I hear one running." The brother got up and took the little sister by the hand, and they set off to find the brook.

But the wicked step-mother was a witch, and had seen how the two children had gone away, and had crept after them privily, as witches do creep, and had bewitched all the brooks in the forest.

Now when they found a little brook leaping brightly over the stones, the brother was going to drink out of it, but the sister heard how it said as it ran, "Who drinks of me will be a tiger; who drinks of me will be a tiger." Then the sister cried, "Pray, dear brother, do not drink, or you will become a wild beast, and tear me to pieces." The brother did not drink, although he was so thirsty, but said, "I will wait for the next spring."

When they came to the next brook the sister heard this also say, "Who drinks of me will be a wolf; who drinks of me will be a wolf." Then the sister cried out, "Pray, dear brother, do not drink, or you will become a wolf, and devour me." The brother did not drink, and said, "I will wait until we come to the next spring, but then I must drink, say what you like; for my thirst is too great."

It said as it ran, "Who drinks of me will be a deer; who drinks of me will be a deer." The sister said, "Oh, I pray you, dear brother, do not drink, or you will become a deer, and run away from me." But the brother had knelt down at once by the brook, and had bent down and drunk some of the water, and as soon as the first drops touched his lips he lay there a young fawn.

And now the sister wept over her poor bewitched brother, and the little fawn wept also, and sat sorrowfully near to her. But at last the girl said, "Be quiet, dear little fawn, I will never, never leave you."

Then she untied her golden garter and put it round the fawn's neck, and she plucked rushes and wove them into a soft cord. With this she tied the little beast and led it on, and she walked deeper and deeper into the forest.

And when they had gone a very long way they came at last to a little house, and the girl looked in; and as it was empty, she thought, "We can stay here and live." Then she sought for leaves and moss to make a soft bed for the fawn; and every morning she went out and gathered roots and berries and nuts for herself, and brought tender grass for the fawn, who ate out of her hand, and was content and played round about her. In the evening, when the sister was tired, and had said her prayer, she laid her head upon the fawn's back: that was her pillow, and she slept softly on it. And if only the brother had had his human form it would have been a delightful life.

For some time they were alone like this in the wilderness. But it happened that the King of the country held a great hunt in the forest. Then the blasts of the horns, the barking of dogs, and the merry shouts of the huntsmen rang through the trees, and the fawn heard all, and was only too anxious to be there. "Oh," said he, to his sister, "let me be off to the hunt, I cannot bear it any longer;" and he begged so much that at last she agreed. "But," said she to him, "come back to me in the evening; I must shut my door for fear of the rough huntsmen, so knock and say, 'My little sister, let me in!' that I may know you; and if you do not say that, I shall not open the door." Then the young fawn sprang away; so happy was he and so merry in the open air.

The King and the huntsmen saw the pretty creature, and started after him, but they could not catch him, and when they thought that they surely had him, away he sprang through the bushes and could not be seen. When it was dark he ran to the cottage, knocked, and said, "My little sister, let me in." Then the door was opened for him, and he jumped in, and rested himself the whole night through upon his soft bed.

The next day the hunt went on afresh, and when the fawn again heard the bugle-horn, and the *tally-ho!* of the huntsmen, he had no peace, but said, "Sister, let me out, I must be off." His sister opened the door for him, and said, "But you must be here again in the evening and say your pass-word."

When the King and his huntsmen again saw the young fawn with the golden collar, they all chased him, but he was too quick and nimble for them. This went on for the whole day, but at last by the evening the huntsmen had surrounded him, and one of them wounded him a little in the foot, so that he limped and ran slowly. Then a hunter crept after him to the cottage and heard how he said, "My little sister, let me in," and saw that the door was opened for him, and was shut again at once. The huntsman took notice of it all, and went to the King and told him what he had seen and heard. Then the King said, "Tomorrow we will hunt once more."

The little sister, however, was dreadfully frightened when she saw that her fawn was hurt. She washed the blood off him, laid herbs on the wound, and said, "Go to your bed, dear fawn, that you may get well again." But the wound was so slight that the fawn, next morning, did not feel it any more. And when he again heard the sport outside, he said, "I cannot bear it, I must be there; they shall not find it so easy to catch me." The sister cried, and said, "This time they will kill you, and here am I alone in the forest and forsaken by all the world. I will not let you out."

"Then you will have me die of grief," answered the fawn; "when I hear the bugle-horns I feel as if I must jump out of my skin." Then the sister could not do otherwise, but opened the door for him with a heavy heart, and the fawn, full of health and joy, bounded into the forest.

When the King saw him, he said to his huntsmen, "Now chase him all day long till night-fall, but take care that no one does him any harm."

As soon as the sun had set, the King said to the huntsman, "Now come and show me the cottage in the wood;" and when he was at the door, he knocked and called out, "Dear little sister, let me in." Then the door opened, and the King walked in, and there stood a maiden more lovely than any he had ever seen. The maiden was frightened when she saw, not her little fawn, but a man come in who wore a golden crown upon his head. But the King looked kindly at her, stretched out his hand, and said, "Will you go with me to my palace and be my dear wife?"

"Yes, indeed," answered the maiden, "but the little fawn must go with me, I cannot leave him." The King said, "It shall stay with you as long as you live, and shall want nothing." Just then he came running in, and the sister again tied him with the cord of rushes, took it in her own hand, and went away with the King from the cottage.

The King took the lovely maiden upon his horse and carried her to his palace, where the wedding was held with great pomp. She was now the Queen, and they lived for a long time happily together; the fawn was tended and cherished, and ran about in the palace-garden.

But the wicked step-mother, because of whom the children had gone out into the world, thought all the time that the sister had been torn to pieces by the wild beasts in the wood, and that the brother had been shot for a fawn by the huntsmen. Now when she heard that they were so happy, and so well off, envy and hatred rose in her heart and left her no peace, and she thought of nothing but how she could bring them again to misfortune. Her own daughter, who was ugly as sin, and had only one eye, grumbled at her and said, "A Queen! that ought to have been my luck."

"Only be quiet," answered the old woman, and comforted her by saying, "when the time comes I shall be ready."

As time went on, the Queen had a pretty little boy, and it happened that the King was out hunting; so the old witch took the form of the chamber-maid, went into the room where the Queen lay, and said to her, "Come, the bath is ready; it will do you good, and give you fresh strength; make haste before it gets cold."

The daughter also was close by; so they carried the weakly

Queen into the bathroom, and put her into the bath; then they shut the door and ran away. But in the bathroom they had made a fire of such deadly heat that the beautiful young Queen was soon suffocated.

When this was done the old woman took her daughter, put a nightcap on her head, and laid her in bed in place of the Queen. She gave her too the shape and the look of the Queen, only she could not make good the lost eye. But in order that the King might not see it, she was to lie on the side on which she had no eye.

In the evening when he came home and heard that he had a son he was heartily glad, and was going to the bed of his dear wife to see how she was. But the old woman quickly called out, "For your life leave the curtains closed; the Queen ought not to see the light yet, and must have rest." The King went away, and did not find out that a false Queen was lying in the bed.

But at midnight, when all slept, the nurse, who was sitting in the nursery by the cradle, and who was the only person awake, saw the door open and the true Queen walk in. She took the child out of the cradle, laid it on her arm, and suckled it. Then she shook up its pillow, laid the child down again, and covered it with the little quilt. And she did not forget the fawn, but went into the corner where it lay, and stroked its back. Then she went quite silently out of the door again. The next morning the nurse asked the guards whether anyone had come into the palace during the night, but they answered, "No, we have seen no one."

She came thus many nights and never spoke a word: the nurse always saw her, but she did not dare to tell anyone about it. When some time had passed in this manner, the Queen began to speak in the night, and said—

"How fares my child, how fares my fawn?

Twice shall I come, then never more."

The nurse did not answer, but when the Queen had gone again, went to the King and told him all. The King said, "Ah, heavens! What is this? Tomorrow night I will watch by the child." In the evening he went into the nursery, and at midnight the Queen again appeared and said—

> "How fares my child, how fares my fawn?
> Once will I come, then never more."

And she nursed the child as she usually did before she disappeared. The King dared not speak to her, but on the next night he watched again. Then she said—

> "How fares my child, how fares my fawn?
> This time I come, then never more."

Then the King could not restrain himself; he sprang towards her, and said, "You can be none other than my dear wife." She answered, "Yes, I am your dear wife," and at the same moment she received life again, and by God's grace became fresh, rosy, and full of health.

Then she told the King the evil deed which the wicked witch and her daughter had been guilty of towards her. The King ordered both to be led before the judge, and judgment was delivered against them. The daughter was taken into the forest where she was torn to pieces by wild beasts, but the witch was cast into the fire and miserably burnt. And as soon as she was burnt the fawn changed his shape, and received his human form again, so the sister and brother lived happily together all their lives.

7 Rapunzel

There were once a man and a woman who had long in vain wished for a child. At length the woman hoped that God was about to grant her desire. These people had a little window at the back of their house from which a splendid garden could be seen, which was full of the most beautiful flowers and herbs. It was, however, surrounded by a high wall, and no one dared to go into it because it belonged to an enchantress, who had great power and was dreaded by all the world. One day the woman was standing by this window and looking down into the garden, when she saw a bed which was planted with the most beautiful rampion (rapunzel), and it looked so fresh and green that she longed for it, and had the greatest desire to eat some. This desire increased every day, and as she knew that she could not get any of it, she quite pined away, and looked pale and miserable. Then her husband was alarmed, and asked, "What aileth thee, dear wife?"

"Ah," she replied, "if I can't get some of the rampion, which is in the garden behind our house, to eat, I shall die." The man, who loved her, thought, "Sooner than let thy wife die, bring her some of the rampion thyself, let it cost thee what it will." In the twilight of the evening, he clambered down over the wall into the garden of the enchantress, hastily clutched a handful of rampion, and took it to his wife. She at once made herself a salad of it, and ate it with much relish. She, however, liked it so much—so very much, that the next day she longed for it three times as much as before. If he was to have any rest, her husband must once more descend into the garden. In the gloom of evening, therefore, he let himself down again; but when he had clambered down the wall he was terribly afraid, for he saw the enchantress standing before him. "How canst thou dare," said she with angry look, "to descend into my garden and steal my rampion like a thief? Thou shalt suffer for it!"

"Ah," answered he, "let mercy take the place of justice, I only made up my mind to do it out of necessity. My wife saw your rampion from the window, and felt such a longing for it that she would have died if she had not got some to eat." Then the enchantress allowed her anger to be softened, and said to him, "If the case be as thou sayest, I will allow thee to take away with thee as much rampion as thou wilt, only I make one condition, thou must give me the child which thy wife will bring into the world; it shall be well treated, and I will care for it like a mother." The man in his terror consented to everything, and when the woman was brought to bed, the enchantress appeared at once, gave the child the name of Rapunzel, and took it away with her.

Rapunzel grew into the most beautiful child beneath the sun. When she was twelve years old, the enchantress shut her into a tower, which lay in a forest, and had neither stairs nor door, but quite at the top was a little window. When the enchantress wanted to go in, she placed herself beneath it and cried:

> "Rapunzel, Rapunzel,
> Let down thy hair to me."

Rapunzel had magnificent long hair, fine as spun gold, and when she heard the voice of the enchantress she unfastened her braided tresses, wound them round one of the hooks of the window above, and then the hair fell twenty ells down, and the enchantress climbed up by it.

After a year or two, it came to pass that the King's son rode through the forest and went by the tower. Then he heard a song, which was so charming that he stood still and listened. This was Rapunzel, who in her solitude passed her time in letting her sweet voice resound. The King's son wanted to climb up to her, and looked for the door of the tower, but none was to be found. He rode home, but the singing had so deeply touched his heart, that every day he went out into the forest and listened to it. Once when he was thus standing behind a tree, he saw that an enchantress came there, and he heard how she cried:

> "Rapunzel, Rapunzel,
> Let down thy hair."

Then Rapunzel let down the braids of her hair, and the enchantress climbed up to her. "If that is the ladder by which one mounts, I will for once try my fortune," said he, and the next day when it began to grow dark, he went to the tower and cried:

> "Rapunzel, Rapunzel,
> Let down thy hair."

Immediately the hair fell down and the King's son climbed up. At first Rapunzel was terribly frightened when a man such as her eyes had never yet beheld, came to her; but the King's son began to talk to her quite like a friend, and told her that his heart had been so stirred that it had let him have no rest, and he had been forced to see her. Then Rapunzel lost her fear, and when he asked her if she would take him for her husband, and she saw that he was young and handsome, she thought, "He will love me more than old Dame Gothel does;" and she said yes, and laid her hand in his. She said, "I will willingly go away with thee, but I do not know how to get down. Bring with thee a skein of silk every time that thou comest, and I will weave a ladder with it, and when that is ready I will descend, and thou wilt take me on thy horse." They agreed that until that time he should come to her every evening, for the old woman came by day. The enchantress remarked nothing of this, until once Rapunzel said to her, "Tell me, Dame Gothel, how it happens that you are so much heavier for me to draw up than the young King's son—he is with me in a moment."

"Ah! thou wicked child," cried the enchantress."What do I hear thee say! I thought I had separated thee from all the world, and yet thou hast deceived me. In her anger she clutched Rapunzel's beautiful tresses, wrapped them twice round her left hand, seized a pair of scissors with the right, and snip, snap, they were cut off, and the lovely braids lay on the ground. And she was so pitiless that she took poor Rapunzel into a desert where she had to live in great grief and misery.

On the same day, however, that she cast out Rapunzel, the enchantress in the evening fastened the braids of hair which she had cut off, to the hook of the window, and when the King's son came and cried:

> "Rapunzel, Rapunzel,
> Let down thy hair,"

she let the hair down. The King's son ascended, but he did not find his dearest Rapunzel above, but the enchantress, who gazed at him with wicked and venomous looks. "Aha!" she cried mockingly, "Thou wouldst fetch thy dearest, but the beautiful bird sits no longer singing in the nest; the cat has got it, and will scratch out thy eyes as well. Rapunzel is lost to thee; thou wilt never see her more." The King's son was beside himself with pain, and in his despair he leapt down from the tower. He escaped with his life, but the thorns into which he fell, pierced his eyes. Then he wandered quite blind about the forest, ate nothing but roots and berries, and did nothing but lament and weep over the loss of his dearest wife. Thus he roamed about in misery for some years, and at length came to the desert where Rapunzel, with the twins to which she had given birth, a boy and a girl, lived in wretchedness. He heard a voice, and it seemed so familiar to him that he went towards it, and when he approached, Rapunzel knew him and fell on his neck and wept. Two of her tears wetted his eyes and they grew clear again, and he could see with them as before. He led her to his kingdom where he was joyfully received, and they lived for a long time afterwards, happy and contented.

8 The Three Spinners

There was once a girl who was idle and would not spin, and let her mother say what she would, she could not bring her to it. At last the mother was once so overcome with anger and impatience, that she beat her, on which the girl began to weep loudly. Now at this very moment the Queen drove by, and when she heard the weeping she stopped her carriage, went into the house and asked the mother why she was beating her daughter so that the cries could be heard out on the road. Then the woman was ashamed to reveal the laziness of her daughter and said, "I cannot get her to leave off spinning. She insists on spinning for ever and ever, and I am poor, and cannot procure the flax." Then answered the Queen, "There is nothing that I like better to hear than spinning, and I am never happier than when the wheels are humming. Let me have your daughter with me in the palace. I have flax enough, and there she shall spin as much as she likes." The mother was heartily satisfied with this, and the Queen took the girl with her. When they had arrived at the palace, she led her up into three rooms which were filled from the bottom to the top with the finest flax. "Now spin me this flax," said she, "and when thou hast done it, thou shalt have my eldest son for a husband, even if thou art poor. I care not for that, thy indefatigable industry is dowry enough." The girl was secretly terrified, for she could not have spun the flax, no, not if she had lived till she was three hundred years old, and had sat at it every day from morning till night. When therefore she was alone, she began to weep, and sat thus for three days without moving a finger. On the third day came the Queen, and when she saw that nothing had been spun yet, she was surprised; but the girl excused herself by saying that she had not been able to begin because of her great distress at leaving her mother's house. The queen was satisfied with this, but said when she was going away," Tomorrow thou must begin to work."

When the girl was alone again, she did not know what to do, and in her distress went to the window. Then she saw three women coming towards her, the first of whom had a broad flat foot, the second had such a great underlip that it hung down over her chin, and the third had a immense thumb. They remained standing before the window, looked up, and asked the girl what was amiss with her. She complained of her trouble, and they offered her their help and said, "If thou wilt invite us to the wedding, not be ashamed of us, and wilt call us thine aunts, and likewise wilt place us at thy table, we will spin up the flax for thee, and that in a very short time."

"With all my heart," she replied, "do but come in and begin the work at once." Then she let in the three strange women, and cleared a place in the first room, where they seated themselves and began their spinning. The one drew the thread and trod the wheel, the other wetted the thread, the third twisted it, and struck the table with her finger, and as often as she struck it, a skein of thread fell to the ground that was spun in the finest manner possible. The girl concealed the three spinners from the Queen, and showed her whenever she came the great quantity of spun thread, until the latter could not praise her enough. When the first room was empty she went to the second, and at last to the third, and that too was quickly cleared. Then the three women took leave and said to the girl, "Do not forget what thou hast promised us,—it will make thy fortune."

When the maiden showed the Queen the empty rooms, and the great heap of yarn, she gave orders for the wedding, and the bridegroom rejoiced that he was to have such a clever and industrious wife, and praised her mightily. "I have three aunts," said the girl, "and as they have been very kind to me, I should not like to forget them in my good fortune; allow me to invite them to the wedding, and let them sit with us at table." The Queen and the bridegroom said, "Why should we not allow that?" Therefore when the feast began, the three women entered in strange apparel, and the bride said, "Welcome, dear aunts."

"Ah," said the bridegroom, "how comest thou by these odious friends?" Thereupon he went to the one with the broad flat foot, and said, "How do you come by such a broad foot?"

"By treading," she answered, "by treading."' Then the bridegroom went to the second, and said, "How do you come by your falling lip?"

"By licking," she answered, "by licking." Then he asked the third, "How do you come by your broad thumb?"

"By twisting the thread," she answered, "by twisting the thread." On this the King's son was alarmed and said, "Neither now nor ever shall my beautiful bride touch a spinning-wheel." And thus she got rid of the hateful task of flax-spinning.

9 Hansel and Gretel

Hard by a great forest dwelt a poor wood-cutter with his wife and his two children. The boy was called Hansel and the girl Gretel. He did not have much food, and once when great famine fell on the land, he could no longer procure daily bread. Now when he thought over this by night in his bed, and tossed about in his anxiety, he groaned and said to his wife, "What is to become of us? How are we to feed our poor children, when we no longer have anything even for ourselves?"

"I'll tell you what, husband," answered the woman, "Early tomorrow morning we will take the children out into the forest to where it is the thickest, there we will light a fire for them, and give each of them one piece of bread more, and then we will go to our work and leave them alone. They will not find the way home again, and we shall be rid of them."

"No, wife," said the man, "I will not do that; how can I bear to leave my children alone in the forest? The wild animals would soon come and tear them to pieces."

"O, thou fool!" said she, "Then we must all four die of hunger, thou mayest as well plane the planks for our coffins," and she left him no peace until he consented. "But I feel very sorry for the poor children, all the same," said the man.

The two children had also not been able to sleep for hunger, and had heard what their step-mother had said to their father. Gretel wept bitter tears, and said to Hansel, "Now all is over with us."

"Be quiet, Gretel," said Hansel, "do not distress thyself, I will soon find a way to help us." And when the old folks had fallen asleep, he got up, put on his little coat, opened the door below, and crept outside. The moon shone brightly, and the white pebbles which lay in front of the house glittered like real silver pennies. Hansel stooped and put as many of them in the little pocket of his coat as he could possibly get in. Then he went back and said to Gretel, "Be comforted, dear little sister, and sleep in peace, God will not forsake us," and he lay down again in his bed. When day dawned, but before the sun had risen, the woman came and awoke the two children, saying "Get up, you sluggards! We are going into the forest to fetch wood." She gave each a little piece of bread, and said, "There is something for your dinner, but do not eat it up before then, for you will get nothing else." Gretel took the bread under her apron, as Hansel had the stones in his pocket. Then they all set out together on the way to the forest. When they had walked a short time, Hansel stood still and peeped back at the house, and did so again and again. His father said, "Hansel, what art thou looking at there and staying behind for? Mind what thou art about, and do not forget how to use thy legs."

"Ah, father," said Hansel, "I am looking at my little white cat, which is sitting up on the roof, and wants to say good-bye to me." The wife said, "Fool, that is not thy little cat, that is the morning sun which is shining on the chimneys." Hansel, however, had not been looking back at the cat, but had been constantly throwing one of the white pebble-stones out of his pocket on the road.

When they had reached the middle of the forest, the father said, "Now, children, pile up some wood, and I will light a fire that you may not be cold." Hansel and Gretel gathered brushwood together, as high as a little hill. The brushwood was lighted, and when the flames were burning very high, the woman said, "Now, children, lay yourselves down by the fire and rest, we will go into the forest and cut some wood. When we have done, we will come back and fetch you away."

Hansel and Gretel sat by the fire, and when noon came, each ate a little piece of bread, and as they heard the strokes of the wood-axe they believed that their father was near. It was not, however, the axe, it was a branch which he had fastened to a withered tree which the wind was blowing backwards and forwards. And as they had been sitting such a long time, their eyes shut with fatigue, and they fell fast asleep. When at last they awoke, it was already dark night. Gretel began to cry and said, "How are we to get out of the forest now?" But Hansel comforted her and said, "Just wait a little, until the moon has risen, and then we will soon find the way." And when the full moon had risen, Hansel took his little sister by the hand, and followed the pebbles which shone like newly-coined silver pieces, and showed them the way.

They walked the whole night long, and by break of day came once more to their father's house. They knocked at the door, and when the woman opened it and saw that it was Hansel and Gretel, she said, "You naughty children, why have you slept so long in the forest?—We thought you were never coming back at all!" The father, however, rejoiced, for it had cut him to the heart to leave them behind alone.

Not long afterwards, there was once more great faine in all parts, and the children heard their mother saying at night to their father, "Everything is eaten again, we have one half loaf left, and after that we will have no more food. The children must go, we will take them farther into the wood, so that they will not find their way out again; there is no other means of saving ourselves!" The man's heart was heavy, and he thought "it would be better for thee to share the last mouthful with thy children." The woman, however, would listen to nothing that he had to say, but scolded and reproached him. Once you give an inch, people take a mile, and as he had yielded the first time, he had to do so a second time also.

The children were, however, still awake and had heard the conversation. When the old folks were asleep, Hansel again got up, and wanted to go out and pick up pebbles as he had done before, but the woman had locked the door, and Hansel could not get out. Nevertheless he comforted his little sister, and said, "Do not cry, Gretel, go to sleep quietly, the good God will help us."

Early in the morning came the woman, and took the children out of their beds. Their bit of bread was given to them, but it was still smaller than the time before. On the way into the forest Hansel crumbled his in his pocket, and often stood still and threw a morsel on the ground. "Hansel, why dost thou stop and look round?" said the father, "go on."

"I am looking back at my little pigeon which is sitting on the roof, and wants to say good-bye to me," answered Hansel. "Simpleton!" said the woman, "that is not thy little pigeon, that is the morning sun that is shining on the chimney." Hansel, however, little by little, threw all the crumbs on the path.

The woman led the children still deeper into the forest, where they had never in their lives been before. Then a great fire was again made, and the mother said, "Just sit there, you children, and when you are tired you may sleep a little; we are going into the forest to cut wood, and in the evening when we are done, we will come and fetch you away." When it was noon, Gretel shared her piece of bread with Hansel, who had scattered his by the way. Then they fell asleep and evening came and went, but no one came to the poor children. They did not awake until it was dark night, and Hansel comforted his little sister and said, "Just wait, Gretel, until the moon rises, and then we shall see the crumbs of bread which I have strewn about, they will show us our way home again." When the moon came they set out, but they found no crumbs, for the many thousands of birds which fly about in the woods and fields had picked them all up. Hansel said to Gretel, "We shall soon find the way," but they did not find it. They walked the whole night and all the next day too from morning till evening, but they did not get out of the forest, and were very hungry, for they had nothing to eat but two or three berries, which grew on the ground. And as they were so weary that their legs would carry them no longer, they lay down beneath a tree and fell asleep.

It was now three mornings since they had left their father's house. They began to walk again, but they always got deeper into the forest, and if help did not come soon, they must die of hunger and weariness. When it was mid-day, they saw a beautiful snow-white bird sitting on a bough, which sang so delightfully that they stood still and listened to it. And when it had finished its song, it spread its wings and flew away before them, and they followed it until they reached a little house, on the roof of which it alighted; and when they came quite up to the little house they saw that it was built of bread and covered with cakes, but that the windows were of clear sugar. "We will set to work on that," said Hansel, "and have a good meal. I will eat a bit of the roof, and thou, Gretel, canst eat some of the window, it will taste sweet." Hansel reached up above, and broke off a little of the roof to see how it tasted, and Gretel leant against the window and nibbled at the panes. Then a soft voice cried from the room:

> "Nibble, nibble, I hear a mouse,
> Who is that nibbling at my little house?"

The children answered:

> "The wind, the wind, it's very mild,
> Blowing like the heavenly child,"

and went on eating without disturbing themselves. Hansel, who thought the roof tasted very nice, tore down a great piece of it, and Gretel pushed out the whole of one round window-pane, sat down, and enjoyed herself with it. Suddenly the door opened, and a very, very old woman, who supported herself on crutches, came creeping out. Hansel and Gretel were so terribly frightened that they dropped what they had in their hands. The old woman, however, nodded her head, and said, "Oh, you dear children, who has brought you here? Do come in, and stay with me. No harm shall happen to you." She took them both by the hand, and led them into her little house. Then good food was set before them, milk and pancakes, with sugar, apples, and nuts. Afterwards two pretty little beds were covered with clean white linen, and Hansel and Gretel lay down in them, and thought they were in heaven.

The old woman had only pretended to be so kind; she was in reality a wicked witch, who lay in wait for children, and had only built the little house of bread in order to entice them there. When a child fell into her power, she killed it, cooked and ate it, and that was a feast day with her. Witches have red eyes, and cannot see far, but they have a keen scent like animals, and are aware when human beings draw near. When Hansel and Gretel came into her neighbourhood, she laughed maliciously, and said mockingly, "I have them, they shall not escape me again!" Early in the morning before the children were awake, she was already up, and when she saw both of them sleeping and looking so pretty, with their plump red cheeks, she muttered to herself, "That will be a dainty mouthful!" Then she seized Hansel with her shrivelled hand, carried him into a little stable, and shut him in with a grated door. He might scream as he liked, that was of no use. Then she went to Gretel, shook her till she awoke, and cried, "Get up, lazy bones, fetch some water, and cook something good for thy brother, he is in the stable outside, and is to be made fat. When he is fat, I will eat him." Gretel began to weep bitterly, but it was all in vain, she was forced to do what the wicked witch ordered her.

And now the best food was cooked for poor Hansel, but Gretel got nothing but crab-shells. Every morning the woman crept to the little stable, and cried, "Hansel, stretch out thy finger that I may feel if thou wilt soon be fat." Hansel, however, stretched out a little bone to her, and the old woman, who had dim eyes, could not see it, and thought it was Hansel's finger, and was astonished that there was no way of fattening him. When four weeks had gone by, and Hansel still continued thin, she was seized with impatience and would not wait any longer. "Get there, Gretel," she cried to the girl, "be active, and bring some water. Let Hansel be fat or lean, tomorrow I will kill him, and cook him." Oh, how the poor little sister wailed when she had to fetch the water, and how her tears flowed down over her cheeks! "Dear God, help us," she cried. "If the wild beasts in the forest had but devoured us, we should at any rate have died together."

"Just keep thy noise to thyself," said the old woman, "all that won't help thee at all."

Early in the morning, Gretel had to go out and hang up the cauldron with the water, and light the fire. "We will bake first," said the old woman, "I have already heated the oven, and kneaded the dough." She pushed poor Gretel out to the oven, from which flames were already darting. "Creep in," said the witch, "and see if it is properly heated, so that we can shut the bread in." And once Gretel was inside, she intended to shut the oven and let her bake in it, and then she would eat her, too. But Gretel saw what she had in her mind, and said, "I do not know how I am to do it; how do you get in?"

"Silly goose," said the old woman, "The door is big enough; just look, I can get in myself!" and she crept up and thrust her head into the oven. Then Gretel gave her a push that drove her far into it, and shut the iron door, and fastened the bolt. Oh! Then she began to howl quite horribly, but Gretel ran away, and the godless witch was miserably burnt to death.

Gretel, however, ran like lightning to Hansel, opened his little stable, and cried, "Hansel, we are saved! The old witch is dead!" Then Hansel sprang out like a bird from its cage when the door is opened for it. How they did rejoice and embrace each other, and dance about and kiss each other! And as they had no longer any need to fear her, they went into the witch's house, and in every corner there stood chests full of pearls and jewels. "These are far better than pebbles!" said Hansel, and thrust into his pockets whatever could be got in, and Gretel said, "I, too, will take something home with me," and filled her pinafore full. "But now we will go away." said Hansel, "that we may get out of the witch's forest."

When they had walked for two hours, they came to a great river. "We cannot get over," said Hansel, "I see no foot-plank, and no bridge."

"And no boat crosses either," answered Gretel, "but a white duck is swimming there; if I ask her, she will help us over." Then she cried:

> "Help us, help us, little duck,
> We're Hansel and Gretel, out of luck.
> We can't get over, try as we may.
> Please take us over right away!"

The duck came to them, and Hansel seated himself on its back, and told his sister to sit by him. "No," replied Gretel, "that will be too heavy for the little duck; she shall take us across, one after the other." The good little duck did so, and when they were safely across and had walked for a short time, the forest seemed to be more and more familiar to them, and at length they saw from afar their father's house. Then they began to run, rushed into the parlour, and threw themselves into their father's arms. The man had not known one happy hour since he had left the children in the forest; the woman, however, was dead. Gretel emptied her pinafore until pearls and precious stones ran about the room, and Hansel threw one handful after another out of his pocket to add to them. Then all anxiety was at an end, and they lived together in perfect happiness. My tale is done, there runs a mouse, whosoever catches it, may make himself a great big cap out of it's fur.

10 The White Snake

A long time ago there lived a king who was famed for his wisdom through all the land. Nothing was hidden from him, and it seemed as if news of the most secret things was brought to him through the air. But he had a strange custom; every day after dinner, when the table was cleared, and no one else was present, a trusty servant had to bring him one more dish. It was covered, however, and even the servant did not know what was in it, neither did anyone know, for the King never took off the cover to eat of it until he was quite alone.

This had gone on for a long time, when one day the servant, who took away the dish, was overcome with such curiosity that he could not help carrying the dish into his room. When he had carefully locked the door, he lifted up the cover, and saw a white snake lying on the dish. But when he saw it he could not deny himself the pleasure of tasting it, so he cut off a little bit and put it into his mouth. No sooner had it touched his tongue than he heard a strange whispering of little voices outside his window. He went and listened, and then noticed that it was the sparrows who were chattering together, and telling one another of all kinds of things which they had seen in the fields and woods. Eating the snake had given him power of understanding the language of animals.

Now it so happened that on this very day the Queen lost her most beautiful ring, and suspicion of having stolen it fell upon this trusty servant, who was allowed to go everywhere. The King ordered the man to be brought before him, and threatened with angry words that unless he could before the morrow point out the thief, he himself should be looked upon as guilty and executed. In vain he declared his innocence; he was dismissed with no better answer.

In his trouble and fear he went down into the courtyard and

thought about how to help himself out of his trouble. Now some ducks were sitting together quietly by a brook and taking their rest; and, whilst they were making their feathers smooth with their bills, they were having a confidential conversation together. The servant stood by and listened. They were telling one another of all the places where they had been waddling about all the morning, and what good food they had found, and one said in a pitiful tone, "Something lies heavy on my stomach; as I was eating in haste I swallowed a ring which lay under the Queen's window." The servant at once seized her by the neck, carried her to the kitchen, and said to the cook, "Here is a fine duck; pray, kill her."

"Yes," said the cook, and weighed her in his hand; "she has spared no trouble to fatten herself, and has been waiting to be roasted long enough." So he cut off her head, and as she was being dressed for the spit, the Queen's ring was found inside her.

The servant could now easily prove his innocence; and the King, to make amends for the wrong, allowed him to ask a favour, and promised him the best place in the court that he could wish for. The servant refused everything, and only asked for a horse and some money for travelling, as he had a mind to see the world and go about a little.

When his request was granted he set out on his way, and one day came to a pond, where he saw three fishes caught in the reeds and gasping for water. Now, though it is said that fishes are dumb, he heard them lamenting that they must perish so miserably, and, as he had a kind heart, he got off his horse and put the three prisoners back into the water. They quivered with delight, put out their heads, and cried to him, "We will remember you and repay you for saving us!"

He rode on, and after a while it seemed to him that he heard a voice in the sand at his feet. He listened, and heard an ant-king complain, "Why cannot folks, with their clumsy beasts, keep off our bodies? That stupid horse, with his heavy hoofs, has been treading down my people without mercy!" So he turned on to a side path and the ant-king cried out to him, 'We will remember you—one good turn deserves another!"

The path led him into a wood, and here he saw two old ravens standing by their nest, and throwing out their young ones. "Out with you, you idle, good-for-nothing creatures!" cried they; "we cannot find food for you any longer; you are big enough, and can provide for yourselves." But the poor young ravens lay upon the ground, flapping their wings, and crying, "Oh, what helpless chicks we are! We must shift for ourselves, and yet we cannot fly! What can we do, but lie here and starve?" So the good young fellow alighted and killed his horse with his sword, and gave it to them for food. Then they came hopping up to it, satisfied their hunger, and cried, "We will remember you— one good turn deserves another!"

And now he had to use his own legs, and when he had walked a long way, he came to a large city. There was a great noise and crowd in the streets, and a man rode up on horseback, crying aloud, "The King's daughter wants a husband; but who-ever sues for her hand must perform a hard task, and if he does not succeed he will forfeit his life." Many had already made the attempt, but in vain; nevertheless when the youth saw the King's daughter he was so overcome by her great beauty that he forgot all danger, went before the King, and declared himself a suitor.

So he was led out to the sea, and a gold ring was thrown into it, in his sight; then the King ordered him to fetch this ring up from the bottom of the sea, and added, "If you come up again without it you will be thrown in again and again until you per-ish amid the waves." All the people grieved for the handsome youth; then they went away, leaving him alone by the sea.

He stood on the shore and considered what he should do, when suddenly he saw three fishes come swimming towards him, and they were the very fishes whose lives he had saved. The one in the middle held a mussel in its mouth, which it laid on the shore at the youth's feet, and when he had taken it up and opened it, there lay the gold ring in the shell. Full of joy he took it to the King, and expected that he would grant him the promised reward.

But when the proud princess perceived that he was not her equal in birth, she scorned him, and required him first to perform another task. She went down into the garden and strewed with her own hands ten sacks-full of millet-seed on the grass; then she said, "Tomorrow morning before sunrise these must be picked up, and not a single grain be wanting."

The youth sat down in the garden and considered how it might be possible to perform this task, but he could think of nothing, and there he sat sorrowfully awaiting the break of day, when he should be led to death. But as soon as the first rays of the sun shone into the garden he saw all the ten sacks standing side by side, quite full, and not a single grain was missing. The ant-king had come in the night with thousands and thousands of ants, and the grateful creatures had by great industry picked up all the millet-seed and gathered them into the sacks.

Presently the King's daughter herself came down into the garden, and was amazed to see that the young man had done the task she had given him. But she could not yet conquer her proud heart, and said, "Although he has performed both the tasks, he shall not be my husband until he has brought me an apple from the Tree of Life."

The youth did not know where the Tree of Life stood, but he set out, and would have gone on for ever, as long as his legs would carry him, though he had no hope of finding it. After he had wandered through three kingdoms, he came one evening to a wood, and lay down under a tree to sleep. But he heard a rustling in the branches, and a golden apple fell into his hand. At the same time three ravens flew down to him, perched themselves upon his knee, and said, "We are the three young ravens whom you saved from starving; when we had grown big, and heard that you were seeking the Golden Apple, we flew over the sea to the end of the world, where the Tree of Life stands, and have brought you the apple."

The youth, full of joy, set out homewards, and took the Golden Apple to the King's beautiful daughter, who had no more excuses left to make. They cut the Apple of Life in two and ate it together; and then her heart became full of love for him, and they lived in undisturbed happiness to a great age.

11 The Straw, the Coal, and the Bean

In a village dwelt a poor old woman, who had gathered together a dish of beans and wanted to cook them. So she made a fire on her hearth, and that it might burn the quicker, she lighted it with a handful of straw. When she was emptying the beans into the pan, one dropped without her observing it, and lay on the ground beside a straw, and soon afterwards a burning coal from the fire leapt down to the two. Then the straw said, "Dear friends, from whence do you come here?" The coal replied, "I fortunately sprang out of the fire, and if I had not escaped by main force, my death would have been certain,—I should have been burnt to ashes." The bean said, "I too have escaped with a whole skin, but if the old woman had got me into the pan, I should have been made into broth without any mercy, like my comrades."

"And would a better fate have fallen to my lot?" said the straw. "The old woman has destroyed all my brethren in fire and smoke; she seized sixty of them at once, and took their lives. I luckily slipped through her fingers."

"But what are we to do now?" said the coal.

"I think," answered the bean, "that as we have so fortunately escaped death, we should keep together like good companions, and lest a new mischance should overtake us here, we should go away together, and repair to a foreign country."

The proposition pleased the two others, and they set out on their way in company. Soon, however, they came to a little brook, and as there was no bridge or foot-plank, they did not know how they were to get over it. The straw hit on a good idea, and said, "I will lay myself straight across, and then you can walk over on me as on a bridge." The straw therefore stretched itself from one bank to the other, and the coal, who was of a fiery disposition, tripped quite boldly on to the newly-built bridge. But when she had reached the middle, and heard the water rushing beneath her, she was, after all, afraid, and stood still, and ventured no farther. The straw, however, began to burn, broke in two pieces, and fell into the stream. The coal slipped after her, hissed when she got into the water, and breathed her last. The bean, who had prudently stayed behind on the shore, could not but laugh at the event, was unable to stop, and laughed so heartily that she burst. It would have been all over with her, likewise, if, by good fortune, a tailor who was travelling in search of work, had not sat down to rest by the brook. As he had a compassionate heart he pulled out his needle and thread, and sewed her together. The bean thanked him most prettily, but as the tailor used black thread, all beans since then have a black seam.

12 The Fisherman and His Wife

There was once upon a time a fisherman who lived with his wife in a miserable hovel close by the sea, and every day he went out fishing. And once as he was sitting with his rod, looking at the clear water, his line suddenly went down, far down below, and when he drew it up again he brought out a large flounder. Then the flounder said to him, "Hark, you fisherman, I pray you, let me live, I am no flounder really, but an enchanted prince. What good will it do you to kill me? I should not be good to eat, put me in the water again, and let me go."

"Come," said the fisherman, "there is no need for so many words about it—a fish that can talk I should certainly let go, anyhow," with that he put him back again into the clear water, and the flounder went to the bottom, leaving a long streak of blood behind him. Then the fisherman got up and went home to his wife in the hovel.

"Husband," said the woman, "have you caught nothing today?"

"No," said the man, "I did catch a flounder, who said he was an enchanted prince, so I let him go again."

"Did you not wish for anything first?" said the woman. "No," said the man; "what should I wish for?"

"Ah," said the woman, "it is surely hard to have to live always in this dirty hovel; you might have wished for a small cottage for us. Go back and call him. Tell him we want to have a small cottage, he will certainly give us that."

"Ah," said the man, "why should I go there again?"

"Why," said the woman, "you did catch him, and you let him go again; he is sure to do it. Go at once." The man still did not quite like to go, but did not like to oppose his wife, and went to the sea.

When he got there the sea was all green and yellow, and no

longer so smooth; so he stood still and said:

> "Flounder, flounder in the sea,
> Come, I pray thee, here to me;
> For my wife, good Ilsabil,
> Wills not as I'd have her will."

Then the flounder came swimming to him and said, "Well what does she want, then?"

"Ah," said the man, "I did catch you, and my wife says I really ought to have wished for something. She does not like to live in a wretched hovel any longer. She would like to have a cottage."

"Go, then," said the flounder, "she has it already."

When the man went home, his wife was no longer in the hovel, but instead of it there stood a small cottage, and she was sitting on a bench before the door. Then she took him by the hand and said to him, "Just come inside, look, now isn't this a great deal better?" So they went in, and there was a small porch, and a pretty little parlour and bedroom, and a kitchen and pantry, with the best of furniture, and fitted up with the most beautiful things made of tin and brass, whatsoever was wanted. And behind the cottage there was a small yard, with hens and ducks, and a little garden with flowers and fruit. "Look," said the wife, "isn't that nice!"

"Yes," said the husband, "and so we must always think it,—now we will live quite contented."

"We will think about that," said the wife. With that they ate something and went to bed.

Everything went well for a week or a fortnight, and then the woman said, "Hark you, husband, this cottage is far too small for us, and the garden and yard are little; the flounder might just as well have given us a larger house. I should like to live in a great stone castle; go to the flounder, and tell him to give us a castle."

"Ah, wife," said the man, "the cottage is quite good enough; why should we live in a castle?"

"What!" said the woman; "just go there, the flounder can always do that."

"No, wife," said the man, "the flounder has just given us the cottage, I do not like to go back so soon, it might make him angry."

"Go," said the woman, "he can do it quite easily, and will be glad to do it; just you go to him."

The man's heart grew heavy, and he would not go. He said to himself, "It is not right," and yet he went. And when he came to the sea the water was quite purple and dark-blue, and grey and thick, and no longer so green and yellow, but it was still quiet. And he stood there and said—

> "Flounder, flounder in the sea,
> Come, I pray thee, here to me;
> For my wife, good Ilsabil,
> Wills not as I'd have her will."

"Well, what does she want, then?" said the flounder. "Alas," said the man, half scared, "she wants to live in a great stone castle."

"Go to it, then, she is standing before the door," said the flounder.

Then the man went away, intending to go home, but when he got there, he found a great stone palace, and his wife was just standing on the steps going in, and she took him by the hand and said, "Come in." So he went in with her, and in the castle was a great hall paved with marble, and many servants, who flung wide the doors; And the walls were all bright with beautiful hangings, and in the rooms were chairs and tables of pure gold, and crystal chandeliers hung from the ceiling, and all the rooms and bedrooms had carpets, and food and wine of the very best were standing on all the tables, so that they nearly broke down beneath it. Behind the house, too, there was a great courtyard, with stables for horses and cows, and the very best of carriages; there was a magnificent large garden, too, with the most beautiful flowers and fruit-trees, and a park quite half a mile long, in which were stags, deer, and hares, and everything that could be desired. "Come," said the woman, "isn't that beautiful?"

"Yes, indeed," said the man, "now let it be; and we will live in this beautiful castle and be content."

"We will consider about that," said the woman, "and sleep upon it;" thereupon they went to bed.

Next morning the wife awoke first, and it was just daybreak, and from her bed she saw the beautiful country lying before her. Her husband was still stretching himself, so she poked him in the side with her elbow, and said, "Get up, husband, and just peep out of the window. Look you, couldn't we be the king over all that land? Go to the flounder, we will be the king."

"Ah, wife," said the man, "why should we be king? I do not want to be king."

"Well," said the wife, "if you won't be king, I will; go to the flounder, for I will be king."

"Ah, wife," said the man, "why do you want to be king? I do not like to say that to him."

"Why not?" said the woman; "go to him this instant; I must be king!" So the man went, and was quite unhappy because his wife wished to be king. "It is not right; it is not right," thought he. He did not wish to go, but yet he went.

And when he came to the sea, it was quite dark-grey, and the water heaved up from below, and smelt putrid. Then he went and stood by it, and said:

> "Flounder, flounder in the sea,
> Come, I pray thee, here to me;
> For my wife, good Ilsabil,
> Wills not as I'd have her will"

"Well, what does she want, then?" said the flounder. "Alas," said the man, "she wants to be king."

"Go to her; she is king already."

So the man went, and when he came to the palace, the castle had become much larger, and had a great tower and magnificent ornaments, and the sentinel was standing before the door, and there were numbers of soldiers with kettle-drums and trumpets. And when he went inside the house, everything was of real marble and gold, with velvet covers and great golden tassels. Then the doors of the hall were opened, and there was the court in all its splendour, and his wife was sitting on a high throne of gold and diamonds, with a great crown of gold on her head, and a sceptre of pure gold and jewels in her hand, and on both sides of her stood her maids-in-waiting in a row, each of them always one head shorter than the last.

Then he went and stood before her, and said, "Ah, wife, and now you are king."

"Yes," said the woman, "now I am king." So he stood and looked at her, and when he had looked at her thus for some time, he said, "And now that you are king, let all else be, now we will wish for nothing more."

"Nay, husband," said the woman, quite anxiously, "I find time pass very heavily, I can bear it no longer; go to the flounder—I am king, but I must be emperor, too."

"Alas, wife, why do you wish to be emperor?"

"Husband," said she, "go to the flounder. I will be emperor."

"Alas, wife," said the man, "he cannot make you emperor; I may not say that to the fish. There is only one emperor in the land. An emperor the flounder cannot make you! I assure you he cannot."

"What!" said the woman, "I am the king, and you are nothing but my husband; will you go this moment? Go at once! If he can make a king he can make an emperor. I will be emperor; go instantly." So he was forced to go. As the man went, however, he was troubled in mind, and thought to himself, "It will not end well; it will not end well! Emperor is too shameless! The flounder will at last be tired out."

With that he reached the sea, and the sea was quite black and thick, and began to boil up from below, so that it threw up bubbles, and such a sharp wind blew over it that it curdled, and the man was afraid. Then he went and stood by it, and said:

> "Flounder, flounder in the sea,
> Come, I pray thee, here to me;
> For my wife, good Ilsabil,
> Wills not as I'd have her will."

"Well, what does she want, then?" said the flounder. "Alas, flounder," said he, "my wife wants to be emperor."

"Go to her," said the flounder; "she is emperor already."

So the man went, and when he got there the whole palace was made of polished marble with alabaster figures and golden ornaments, and soldiers were marching before the door blowing trumpets, and beating cymbals and drums; and in the house, barons, and counts, and dukes were going about as servants. Then they opened the doors to him, which were of pure gold. And when he entered, there sat his wife on a throne, which was made of one piece of gold, and was quite two miles high; and she wore a great golden crown that was three yards high, and set with diamonds and carbuncles, and in one hand she had the sceptre, and in the other the imperial orb; and on both sides of her stood the yeomen of the guard in two rows, each being smaller than the one before him, from the biggest giant, who was two miles high, to the very smallest dwarf, just as big as my little finger. And before it stood a number of princes and dukes.

Then the man went and stood among them, and said, "Wife, are you emperor now?"

"Yes," said she, "now I am emperor." Then he stood and looked at her well, and when he had looked at her thus for some time, he said, "Ah, wife, be content, now that you are emperor."

"Husband," said she, "why are you standing there? Now, I am emperor, but I will be pope too; go to the flounder."

"Alas, wife," said the man, "what will you not wish for? You cannot be pope. There is but one in Christendom. He cannot make you pope."

"Husband," said she, "I will be pope; go immediately, I must be pope this very day."

"No, wife," said the man, "I do not like to say that to him; that would not do, it is too much; the flounder can't make you pope."

"Husband," said she, "what nonsense! If he can make an emperor he can make a pope. Go to him directly. I am emperor, and you are nothing but my husband; will you go at once?"

Then he was afraid and went; but he was quite faint, and shivered and shook, and his knees and legs trembled. And a high wind blew over the land, and the clouds flew, and towards evening all grew dark, and the leaves fell from the trees, and the water rose and roared as if it were boiling, and splashed upon the shore. And in the distance he saw ships which were firing guns in their sore need, pitching and tossing on the waves. And yet in the midst of the sky there was still a small bit of blue, though on every side it was as red as in a heavy storm. So, full of despair, he went and stood in much fear and said:

> "Flounder, flounder in the sea,
> Come, I pray thee, here to me;"
> For my wife, good Ilsabil,
> Wills not as I'd have her will.

"Well, what does she want, then?" said the flounder. "Alas," said the man, "she wants to be pope."

"Go to her then," said the flounder; "she is pope already."

So he went, and when he got there, he saw what seemed to be a large church surrounded by palaces. He pushed his way through the crowd. Inside, however, everything was lighted up with thousands and thousands of candles, and his wife was clad in gold, and she was sitting on a much higher throne, and had three great golden crowns on, and round about her there was much ecclesiastical splendour; and on both sides of her was a row of candles the largest of which was as tall as the very tallest tower, down to the very smallest kitchen candle, and all the emperors and kings were on their knees before her, kissing her shoe. "Wife," said the man, and looked attentively at her, "are you now pope?"

"Yes," said she, "I am pope." So he stood and looked at her, and it was just as if he was looking at the bright sun. When he had stood looking at her thus for a short time, he said, "Ah, wife, if you are pope, do let well alone!" But she looked as stiff as a post, and did not move or show any signs of life. Then said he, "Wife, now that you are pope, be satisfied, you cannot become anything greater now."

"I will consider about that," said the woman. Thereupon they both went to bed, but she was not satisfied, and greediness let her have no sleep, for she was continually thinking what there was left for her to be.

The man slept well and soundly, for he had run about a great deal during the day; but the woman could not fall asleep at all, and flung herself from one side to the other the whole night through, thinking always what more was left for her to be, but unable to call to mind anything else. At length the sun began to rise, and when the woman saw the red of dawn, she sat up in bed and looked at it. And when, through the window, she saw the sun thus rising, she said, "Cannot I, too, order the sun and moon to rise?"

"Husband," she said, poking him in the ribs with her elbows, "wake up! go to the flounder, for I wish to be even as God is." The man was still half asleep, but he was so horrified that he fell out of bed. He thought he must have heard amiss, and rubbed his eyes, and said, "Alas, wife, what are you saying?"

"Husband," said she, "if I can't order the sun and moon to rise, and have to look on and see the sun and moon rising, I can't bear it. I shall not know what it is to have another happy hour, unless I can make them rise myself." Then she looked at him so terribly that a shudder ran over him, and said, "Go at once; I wish to be like God."

"Alas, wife," said the man, falling on his knees before her, "the flounder cannot do that; he can make an emperor and a pope; I beseech you, go on as you are, and be pope." Then she fell into a rage, and her hair flew wildly about her head, and she cried, "I will not endure this, I'll not bear it any longer; wilt thou go?" Then he put on his trousers and ran away like a madman. But outside a great storm was raging, and blowing so hard that he could scarcely keep his feet; houses and trees toppled over, the mountains trembled, rocks rolled into the sea the sky was pitch black, and it thundered and lightened, and the sea came in with black waves as high as church-towers and mountains, and all with crests of white foam at the top. Then he cried, but could not hear his own words:

> "Flounder, flounder in the sea,
> Come, I pray thee, here to me;
> For my wife, good Ilsabil,
> Wills not as I'd have her will."

"Well, what does she want, then?" said the flounder. "Alas," said he, "she wants to be like God."

"Go to her, and you will find her back again in the dirty hovel." And there they are living still at this very time.

13 The Valiant Little Tailor

One summer's morning a little tailor was sitting on his table by the window; he was in good spirits, and sewed with all his might. Then came a peasant woman down the street crying, "Good jams, cheap! Good jams, cheap!" This rang pleasantly in the tailor's ears; he stretched his delicate head out of the window, and called, "Come up here, dear woman; here you will get rid of your goods." The woman came up the three steps to the tailor with her heavy basket, and he made her unpack the whole of the pots for him. He inspected all of them, lifted them up, put his nose to them, and at length said, "The jam seems to me to be good, so weigh me out four ounces, dear woman, and if it is a quarter of a pound that is of no consequence." The woman who had hoped to find a good sale, gave him what he desired, but went away quite angry and grumbling. "Now, God bless the jam to my use," cried the little tailor, "and give me health and strength;" so he brought the bread out of the cupboard, cut himself a piece right across the loaf and spread the jam over it. "This won't taste bitter," said he, "but I will just finish the jacket before I take a bite." He laid the bread near him, sewed on, and in his joy, made bigger and bigger stitches. In the meantime the smell of the sweet jam ascended so to the wall, where the flies were sitting in great numbers, that they were attracted and descended on it in hosts. "Hola! who invited you?" said the little tailor, and drove the unbidden guests away. The flies, however, who understood no German, would not be turned away, but came back again in ever-increasing companies. The little tailor at last lost all patience, and got a bit of cloth from the hole under his work-table, and saying, "Wait, and I will give it to you," struck it mercilessly on them. When he drew it away and counted, there lay before him no fewer than seven, dead and with legs stretched out. "Art thou a fellow of that sort?" said he, and could not help admiring his own bravery. "The whole town shall know of this!" And the little tailor hastened to cut himself a girdle, stitched it, and embroidered on it in large letters, "Seven at one stroke!"

"Why just the town!" he continued, "The whole world shall hear of it!" and his heart wagged with joy like a lamb's tail. The tailor put on the girdle, and resolved to go forth into the world, because he thought his workshop was too small for his valour. Before he went away, he sought about in the house to see if there was anything which he could take with him; however, he found nothing but an old cheese, and that he put in his pocket. In front of the door he observed a bird which had caught itself in the thicket. It had to go into his pocket with the cheese. Now he took to the road boldly, and as he was light and nimble, he felt no fatigue. The road led him up a mountain, and when he had reached the highest point of it, there sat a powerful giant looking about him quite comfortably. The little tailor went bravely up, spoke to him, and said, "Good day, comrade, so thou art sitting there overlooking the wide-spread world! I am just on my way thither, and want to try my luck. Hast thou any inclination to go with me?" The giant looked contemptuously at the tailor, and said, "Thou ragamuffin! Thou miserable creature!"

"Oh, indeed?" answered the little tailor, and unbuttoned his coat, and showed the giant the girdle, "There mayst thou read what kind of a man I am!" The giant read, "Seven at one stroke," and thought that they had been men whom the tailor had killed, and began to feel a little respect for the tiny fellow. Nevertheless, he wished to try him first, and took a stone in his hand and squeezed it together so that water dropped out of it. "Do that likewise," said the giant, "if thou hast strength?"

"Is that all?" said the tailor, "that is child's play with us!" and put his hand into his pocket, brought out the soft cheese, and pressed it until the liquid ran out of it. "Faith," said he, "that was a little better, wasn't it?" The giant did not know what to say, and could not believe it of the little man. Then the giant picked up a stone and threw it so high that the eye could scarcely follow it. "Now, little mite of a man, do that likewise."

"Well thrown," said the tailor, "but after all the stone came down to earth again; I will throw you one which shall never come back at all." And he put his hand into his pocket, took out the bird, and threw it into the air. The bird, delighted with its liberty, rose, flew away and did not come back. "How does that shot please you, comrade?" asked the tailor. "Thou canst certainly throw," said the giant, "but now we will see if thou art able to carry anything properly." He took the little tailor to a mighty oak tree which lay there felled on the ground, and said, "If thou art strong enough, help me to carry the tree out of the forest."

"Readily," answered the little man; "take thou the trunk on thy shoulders, and I will raise up the branches and twigs; after all, they are the heaviest." The giant took the trunk on his shoulder, but the tailor seated himself on a branch, and the giant who could not look round, had to carry away the whole tree, and the little tailor into the bargain: he behind, was quite merry and happy, and whistled the song, "Three tailors rode forth from the gate," as if carrying the tree were child's play. The giant, after he had dragged the heavy burden part of the way, could go no further, and cried, "Hark you, I shall have to let the tree fall!" The tailor sprang nimbly down, seized the tree with both arms as if he had been carrying it, and said to the giant, "Thou art such a great fellow, and yet canst not even carry the tree!"

They went on together, and as they passed a cherry-tree, the giant laid hold of the top of the tree where the ripest fruit was hanging, bent it down, gave it into the tailor's hand, and bade him eat. But the little tailor was much too weak to hold the tree, and when the giant let it go, it sprang back again, and the tailor was hurried into the air with it. When he had fallen down again without injury, the giant said, "What is this? Hast thou not strength enough to hold the weak twig?"

"There is no lack of strength," answered the little tailor. "Dost thou think that could be anything to a man who has struck down seven at one blow? I leapt over the tree because the huntsmen are shooting down there in the thicket. Jump as I did, if thou canst do it." The giant made the attempt, but could not get over the tree, and remained hanging in the branches, so that in this also the tailor kept the upper hand.

The giant said, "If thou art such a valiant fellow, come with me into our cavern and spend the night with us." The little tailor was willing, and followed him. When they went into the cave, other giants were sitting there by the fire, and each of them had a roasted sheep in his hand and was eating it. The little tailor looked round and thought, "It is much more spacious here than in my workshop." The giant showed him a bed, and said he was to lie down in it and sleep. The bed, however, was too big for the little tailor; he did not lie down in it, but crept into a corner. When it was midnight, and the giant thought that the little tailor was lying in a sound sleep, he got up, took a great iron bar, cut through the bed with one blow, and thought he had given the grasshopper his finishing stroke. With the earliest dawn the giants went into the forest, and had quite forgotten the little tailor, when all at once he walked up to them quite merrily and boldly. The giants were terrified, they were afraid that he would strike them all dead, and ran away in a great hurry.

The little tailor went onwards, always following his own pointed nose. After he had walked for a long time, he came to the courtyard of a royal palace, and as he felt weary, he lay down on the grass and fell asleep. Whilst he lay there, the people came and inspected him on all sides, and read on his girdle, "Seven at one stroke."

"Ah," said they, "What does the great warrior here in the midst of peace? He must be a mighty lord." They went and announced him to the King, and gave it as their opinion that if war should break out, this would be a weighty and useful man who ought on no account to be allowed to depart. The counsel pleased the King, and he sent one of his courtiers to the little tailor to offer him military service when he awoke. The ambassador remained standing by the sleeper, waited until he stretched his limbs and opened his eyes, and then conveyed to him this proposal. "For this very reason have I come here," the tailor replied, "I am ready to enter the King's service." He was therefore honourably received and a special dwelling was assigned him.

The soldiers, however, were set against the little tailor, and wished him a thousand miles away. "What is to be the end of this?" they said amongst themselves. "If we quarrel with him, and he strikes about him, seven of us will fall at every blow; not one of us can stand against him." They came therefore to a decision, betook themselves in a body to the King, and begged for their dismissal. "We are not prepared," said they, "to stay with a man who kills seven at one stroke." The King was sorry that for the sake of one he should lose all his faithful servants, wished that he had never set eyes on the tailor, and would willingly have been rid of him again. But he did not venture to give him his dismissal, for he dreaded lest he should strike him and all his people dead, and place himself on the royal throne. He thought about it for a long time, and at last found good counsel. He sent to the little tailor and caused him to be informed that as he was such a great warrior, he had one request to make to him. In a forest of his country lived two giants who caused great mischief with their robbing, murdering, ravaging, and burning, and no one could approach them without putting himself in danger of death. If the tailor conquered and killed these two giants, he would give him his only daughter to wife, and half of his kingdom as a dowry, likewise one hundred horsemen should go with him to assist him. "That would indeed be a fine thing for a man like me!" thought the little tailor. "One is not offered a beautiful princess and half a kingdom every day of one's life!"

"Oh, yes," he replied, "I will soon subdue the giants, and do not require the help of the hundred horsemen to do it; he who can hit seven with one blow has no need to be afraid of two."

The little tailor went forth, and the hundred horsemen followed him. When he came to the outskirts of the forest, he said to his followers, "Just stay waiting here, I alone will soon finish off the giants." Then he bounded into the forest and looked about right and left. After a while he perceived both giants. They lay sleeping under a tree, and snored so that the branches waved up and down. The little tailor, not idle, gathered two pocketsful of stones, and with these climbed up the tree. When he was half-way up, he slipped down by a branch, until he sat just above the sleepers, and then let one stone after another fall on the breast of one of the giants. For a long time the giant felt nothing, but at last he awoke, pushed his comrade, and said, "Why art thou knocking me?"

"Thou must be dreaming," said the other, "I am not knocking thee." They laid themselves down to sleep again, and then the tailor threw a stone down on the second. "What is the meaning of this?" cried the other. "Why art thou pelting me?"

"I am not pelting thee," answered the first, growling. They disputed about it for a time, but as they were weary they let the matter rest, and their eyes closed once more. The little tailor began his game again, picked out the biggest stone, and threw it with all his might on the breast of the first giant. "That is too bad!" cried he, and sprang up like a madman, and pushed his companion against the tree until it shook. The other paid him back in the same coin, and they got into such a rage that they tore up trees and belaboured each other so long, that at last they both fell down dead on the ground at the same time. Then the little tailor leapt down. "It is a lucky thing," said he, "that they did not tear up the tree on which I was sitting, or I should have had to spring on to another like a squirrel; but we tailors are nimble." He drew out his sword and gave each of them a couple of thrusts in the breast, and then went out to the horsemen and said, "The work is done; I have given both of them their finishing stroke, but it was hard work! They tore up trees in their sore need, and defended themselves with them, but all that is to no purpose when a man like myself comes, who can kill seven at one blow."

"But are you not wounded?" asked the horsemen. "You need not concern yourself about that," answered the tailor, "They have not bent one hair of mine." The horsemen would not believe him, and rode into the forest; there they found the giants swimming in their blood, and all round about lay the torn-up trees.

The little tailor demanded of the King the promised reward; he, however, repented of his promise, and again bethought himself how he could get rid of the hero. "Before thou receivest my daughter, and the half of my kingdom," said he to him, "thou must perform one more heroic deed. In the forest roams a unicorn which does great harm, and thou must catch it first."

"I fear one unicorn still less than two giants. Seven at one blow, is my kind of affair." He took a rope and an axe with him, went forth into the forest, and again bade those who were sent with him to wait outside. He had to seek long. The unicorn soon came towards him, and rushed directly on the tailor, as if it would spit him on his horn without more ceremony. "Softly, softly; it can't be done as quickly as that," said he, and stood still and waited until the animal was quite close, and then sprang nimbly behind the tree. The unicorn ran against the tree with all its strength, and struck its horn so fast in the trunk that it had not strength enough to draw it out again, and thus it was caught. "Now, I have got the bird," said the tailor, and came out from behind the tree and put the rope round its neck, and then with his axe he hewed the horn out of the tree, and when all was ready he led the beast away and took it to the King.

The King still would not give him the promised reward, and made a third demand. Before the wedding the tailor was to catch him a wild boar that made great havoc in the forest, and the huntsmen should give him their help. "Willingly," said the tailor, "that is child's play!" He did not take the huntsmen with him into the forest, and they were well pleased that he did not, for the wild boar had several times received them in such a manner that they had no inclination to lie in wait for him. When the boar perceived the tailor, it ran on him with foaming mouth and whetted tusks, and was about to throw him to the ground, but the active hero sprang into a chapel which was near, and up to the window at once, and in one bound out again. The boar ran in after him, but the tailor ran round outside and shut the door behind it, and then the raging beast, which was much too heavy and awkward to leap out of the window, was caught. The little tailor called the huntsmen thither that they might see the prisoner with their own eyes. The hero, however went to the King, who was now, whether he liked it or not, obliged to keep his promise, and gave him his daughter and the half of his kingdom. Had he known that it was no warlike hero, but a little tailor who was standing before him, it would have gone to his heart still more than it did. The wedding was held with great magnificence and small joy, and out of a tailor a King was made.

After some time the young Queen heard her husband say in his dreams at night, "Boy, make me the doublet, and patch the pantaloons, or else I will rap the yard-measure over thine ears." Then she discovered in what state of life the young lord had been born, and next morning complained of her wrongs to her father, and begged him to help her to get rid of her husband, who was nothing else but a tailor. The King comforted her and said, "Leave thy bed-room door open this night, and my servants shall stand outside, and when he has fallen asleep shall go in, bind him, and take him on board a ship which shall carry him into the wide world." The woman was satisfied with this; but the King's armour-bearer, who had heard all, was friendly with the young lord, and informed him of the whole plot. "I'll put a screw into that business," said the little tailor. At night he went to bed with his wife at the usual time, and when she thought that he had fallen asleep, she got up, opened the door, and then lay down again. The little tailor, who was only pretending to be asleep, began to cry out in a clear voice, "Boy, make me the doublet and patch me the pantaloons, or I will rap the yard-measure over thine ears. I smote seven at one blow. I killed two giants, I brought away one unicorn and caught a wild boar, and am I to fear those who are standing outside the room." When these men heard the tailor speaking thus, they were overcome by a great dread, and ran as if the wild huntsman were behind them, and none of them would venture anything further against him. So the little tailor was a King and remained one, to the end of his life.

14 Cinderella

The wife of a rich man fell sick, and as she felt that her end was drawing near, she called her only daughter to her bedside and said, "Dear child, be good and pious, and then the good God will always protect thee, and I will look down on thee from heaven and be near thee." Thereupon she closed her eyes and departed. Every day the maiden went out to her mother's grave, and wept, and she remained pious and good. When winter came the snow spread a white sheet over the grave, and when the spring sun had drawn it off again, the man had taken another wife.

The woman had brought two daughters into the house with her, who were beautiful and fair of face, but vile and black of heart. Now began a bad time for the poor step-child. "Is the stupid goose to sit in the parlour with us?" said they. "He who wants to eat bread must earn it; out with the kitchen-wench." They took her pretty clothes away from her, put an old grey bedgown on her, and gave her wooden shoes. "Just look at the proud princess, how decked out she is!" they cried, and laughed, and led her into the kitchen. There she had to do hard work from morning till night, get up before daybreak, carry water, light fires, cook and wash. Besides this, the sisters did her every imaginable injury—they mocked her and emptied her peas and lentils into the ashes, so that she was forced to sit and pick them out again. In the evening when she had worked till she was weary she had no bed to go to, but had to sleep by the fireside in the ashes. And as on that account she always looked dusty and dirty, they called her Cinderella. It happened that the father was once going to the fair, and he asked his two step-daughters what he should bring back for them. "Beautiful dresses," said one, "Pearls and jewels," said the second. "And thou, Cinderella," said he, "what wilt thou have?"

"Father, break off for me the first branch which knocks

against your hat on your way home." So he bought beautiful dresses, pearls and jewels for his two step-daughters, and on his way home, as he was riding through a green thicket, a hazel twig brushed against him and knocked off his hat. Then he broke off the branch and took it with him. When he reached home he gave his step-daughters the things which they had wished for, and to Cinderella he gave the branch from the hazel-bush. Cinderella thanked him, went to her mother's grave and planted the branch on it, and wept so much that the tears fell down on it and watered it. And it grew, however, and became a handsome tree. Thrice a day Cinderella went and sat beneath it, and wept and prayed, and a little white bird always came on the tree, and if Cinderella expressed a wish, the bird threw down to her what she had wished for.

It happened, however, that the King appointed a festival which was to last three days, and to which all the beautiful young girls in the country were invited, in order that his son might choose himself a bride. When the two step-sisters heard that they too were to appear among the number, they were delighted, called Cinderella and said, "Comb our hair for us, brush our shoes and fasten our buckles, for we are going to the festival at the King's palace." Cinderella obeyed, but wept, because she too would have liked to go with them to the dance, and begged her step-mother to allow her to do so. "Thou go, Cinderella!" said she; "Thou art dusty and dirty and wouldst go to the festival? Thou hast no clothes and shoes, and yet wouldst dance!" As, however, Cinderella went on asking, the step-mother at last said, "I have emptied a dish of lentils into the ashes for thee, if thou hast picked them out again in two hours, thou shalt go with us." The maiden went through the back-door into the garden, and called, "You tame pigeons, you turtle-doves, and all you birds beneath the sky, come and help me to pick

> The good into the pot,
> The bad into the crop.

JACOB AND WILHELM GRIMM

Then two white pigeons came in by the kitchen-window, and afterwards the turtle-doves, and at last all the birds beneath the sky, came whirring and crowding in, and alighted amongst the ashes. And the pigeons nodded with their heads and began pick, pick, pick, pick, and the rest began also pick, pick, pick, pick, and gathered all the good grains into the dish. Hardly had one hour passed before they had finished, and all flew out again. Then the girl took the dish to her step-mother, and was glad, and believed that now she would be allowed to go with them to the festival. But the step-mother said, "No, Cinderella, thou hast no clothes and thou canst not dance; thou wouldst only be laughed at." And as Cinderella wept at this, the step-mother said, "If thou canst pick two dishes of lentils out of the ashes for me in one hour, thou shalt go with us." And she thought to herself, "That she most certainly cannot do." When the step-mother had emptied the two dishes of lentils amongst the ashes, the maiden went through the back-door into the garden and cried, "You tame pigeons, you turtle-doves, and all you birds under heaven, come and help me to pick

The good into the pot,
The bad into the crop.

Then two white pigeons came in by the kitchen-window, and afterwards the turtle-doves, and at length all the birds beneath the sky, came whirring and crowding in, and alighted amongst the ashes. And the doves nodded with their heads and began pick, pick, pick, pick, and the others began also pick, pick, pick, pick, and gathered all the good seeds into the dishes, and before half an hour was over they had already finished, and all flew out again. Then the maiden carried the dishes to the step-mother and was delighted, and believed that she might now go with them to the festival. But the step-mother said, "All this will not help thee; thou goest not with us, for thou hast no clothes and canst not dance; we should be ashamed of thee!" On this she turned her back on Cinderella, and hurried away with her two proud daughters.

As no one was now at home, Cinderella went to her mother's grave beneath the hazel-tree, and cried:

> Shiver and quiver, little tree,
> Silver and gold throw down over me.

Then the bird threw a gold and silver dress down to her, and slippers embroidered with silk and silver. She put on the dress with all speed, and went to the festival. Her step-sisters and the step-mother however did not know her, and thought she must be a foreign princess, for she looked so beautiful in the golden dress. They never once thought of Cinderella, and believed that she was sitting at home in the dirt, picking lentils out of the ashes. The prince went to meet her, took her by the hand and danced with her. He would dance with no other maiden, and never left loose of her hand, and if any one else came to invite her, he said, "This is my partner."

She danced till it was evening, and then she wanted to go home. But the King's son said, "I will go with thee and bear thee company," for he wished to see to whom the beautiful maiden belonged. She escaped from him, however, and sprang into the pigeon-house. The King's son waited until her father came, and then he told him that the stranger maiden had leapt into the pigeon-house. The old man thought, "Can it be Cinderella?" and they had to bring him an axe and a pickaxe that he might hew the pigeon-house to pieces, but no one was inside it. And when they got home Cinderella lay in her dirty clothes among the ashes, and a dim little oil-lamp was burning on the mantle-piece, for Cinderella had jumped quickly down from the back of the pigeon-house and had run to the little hazel-tree, and there she had taken off her beautiful clothes and laid them on the grave, and the bird had taken them away again, and then she had placed herself in the kitchen amongst the ashes in her grey gown.

Next day when the festival began afresh, and her parents and the step-sisters had gone once more, Cinderella went to the hazel-tree and said—

> Shiver and quiver, my little tree,
> Silver and gold throw down over me.

Then the bird threw down a much more beautiful dress than on the preceding day. And when Cinderella appeared at the festival in this dress, every one was astonished at her beauty.

The King's son had waited until she came, and instantly took her by the hand and danced with no one but her. When others came and invited her, he said, "She is my partner." When evening came she wished to leave, and the King's son followed her and wanted to see into which house she went. But she sprang away from him, and into the garden behind the house. Therein stood a beautiful tall tree on which hung the most magnificent pears. She clambered so nimbly between the branches like a squirrel that the King's son did not know where she was gone. He waited until her father came, and said to him, "The stranger-maiden has escaped from me, and I believe she has climbed up the pear-tree." The father thought, "Can it be Cinderella?" and had an axe brought and cut the tree down, but no one was on it. And when they got into the kitchen, Cinderella lay there amongst the ashes, as usual, for she had jumped down on the other side of the tree, had taken the beautiful dress to the bird on the little hazel-tree, and put on her grey gown.

On the third day, when the parents and sisters had gone away, Cinderella went once more to her mother's grave and said to the little tree—

> Shiver and quiver, my little tree,
> Silver and gold throw down over me.

And now the bird threw down to her a dress which was more splendid and magnificent than any she had yet had, and the slippers were golden. And when she went to the festival in the dress, no one knew how to speak for astonishment. The King's son danced with her only, and if any one invited her to dance, he said, "She is my partner."

When evening came, Cinderella wished to leave, and the King's son was anxious to go with her, but she escaped from him so quickly that he could not follow her. The King's son had, however, used a stratagem, and had caused the whole staircase to be smeared with pitch, and there, when she ran down, had the maiden's left slipper remained sticking. The King's son picked it up, and it was small and dainty, and all golden. Next morning, he went with it to the father, and said to him, "No one shall be my wife but she whose foot this golden slipper fits." Then were the two sisters glad, for they had pretty feet. The eldest went with the shoe into her room and wanted to try it on, and her mother stood by. But she could not get her big toe into it, and the shoe was too small for her. Then her mother gave her a knife and said, "Cut the toe off; when thou art Queen thou wilt have no more need to go on foot." The maiden cut the toe off, forced the foot into the shoe, swallowed the pain, and went out to the King's son. Then he took her on his horse as his bride and rode away with her. They were, however, obliged to pass the grave, and there, on the hazel-tree, sat the two pigeons and cried:

> "Turn and peep, turn and peep,
> There's blood within the shoe.
> The shoe it is too small for her,
> The true bride waits for you."

Then he looked at her foot and saw how the blood was streaming from it. He turned his horse round and took the false bride home again, and said she was not the true one, and that the other sister was to put the shoe on. Then this one went into her chamber and got her toes safely into the shoe, but her heel was too large. So her mother gave her a knife and said, "Cut a bit off thy heel; when thou art Queen thou wilt have no more need to go on foot." The maiden cut a bit off her heel, forced her foot into the shoe, swallowed the pain, and went out to the King's son. He took her on his horse as his bride, and rode away with her, but when they passed by the hazel-tree, two little pigeons sat on it and cried:

> Turn and peep, turn and peep,
> There's blood within the shoe
> The shoe it is too small for her,
> The true bride waits for you.

He looked down at her foot and saw how the blood was running out of her shoe, and how it had stained her white stocking. Then he turned his horse and took the false bride home again. "This also is not the right one," said he, "have you no other daughter?"

"No," said the man, "There is still a little stunted kitchen-wench which my late wife left behind her, but she cannot possibly be the bride." The King's son said he was to send her up to him; but the mother answered, "Oh, no, she is much too dirty, she cannot show herself!" He absolutely insisted on it, and Cinderella had to be called. She first washed her hands and face clean, and then went and bowed down before the King's son, who gave her the golden shoe. Then she seated herself on a stool, drew her foot out of the heavy wooden shoe, and put it into the slipper, which fitted like a glove. And when she rose up and the King's son looked at her face he recognised the beautiful maiden who had danced with him and cried, "That is the true bride!" The step-mother and the two sisters were terrified and became pale with rage; he, however, took Cinderella on his horse and rode away with her. As they passed by the hazel-tree, the two white doves cried—"Turn and peep, turn and peep, No blood is in the shoe, The shoe is not too small for her, The true bride rides with you," and when they had cried that, the two came flying down and placed themselves on Cinderella's shoulders, one on the right, the other on the left, and remained sitting there.

When the wedding with the King's son had to be celebrated, the two false sisters came and wanted to get into favour with Cinderella and share her good fortune. When the betrothed couple went to church, the elder was at the right side and the younger at the left, and the pigeons pecked out one eye of each of them. Afterwards as they came back, the elder was at the left, and the younger at the right, and then the pigeons pecked out the other eye of each. And thus, for their wickedness and falsehood, they were punished with blindness as long as they lived.

15 The Riddle

There was once a King's son who was seized with a desire to travel about the world, and took no one with him but a faithful servant. One day he came to a great forest, and when darkness overtook him he could find no shelter, and knew not where to pass the night. Then he saw a girl who was going towards a small house, and when he came nearer, he saw that the maiden was young and beautiful. He spoke to her, and said, "Dear child, can I and my servant find shelter for the night in the little house?"

"Oh, yes," said the girl in a sad voice, "that you certainly can, but I do not advise you to venture it. Do not go in."

"Why not?" asked the King's son. The maiden sighed and said, "My step-mother practises wicked arts; she is ill-disposed toward strangers." Then he saw very well that he had come to the house of a witch, but as it was dark, and he could not go farther, and also was not afraid, he entered. The old woman was sitting in an armchair by the fire, and looked at the stranger with her red eyes. "Good evening," growled she, and pretended to be quite friendly. "Take a seat and rest yourselves." She blew up the fire on which she was cooking something in a small pot. The daughter warned the two to be prudent, to eat nothing, and drink nothing, for the old woman brewed evil drinks. They slept quietly until early morning. When they were making ready for their departure, and the King's son was already seated on his horse, the old woman said, "Stop a moment, I will first hand you a parting draught." Whilst she fetched it, the King's son rode away, and the servant who had to buckle his saddle tight, was the only one present when the wicked witch came with the drink. "Take that to your master," said she. But at that instant the glass broke and the poison spirted on the horse, and it was so strong that the animal immediately fell down dead. The servant ran after his master and told him what had happened, but would not leave his saddle behind him, and ran back to fetch it. When, however, he came to the dead horse a raven was already sitting on it devouring it. "Who knows whether we shall find anything better today?" said the servant; so he killed the raven, and took it with him. And now they journeyed onwards into the forest the whole day, but could not get out of it. By nightfall they found an inn and entered it. The servant gave the raven to the innkeeper to make ready for supper. They had, however, stumbled on a den of murderers, and during the darkness twelve of these came, intending to kill the strangers and rob them. Before they set about this work, they sat down to supper, and the innkeeper and the witch sat down with them, and together they ate a dish of soup in which was cut up the flesh of the raven. Hardly, however, had they swallowed a couple of mouthfuls, before they all fell down dead, for the raven had communicated to them the poison from the horse-flesh. There was no one else left in the house but the innkeeper's daughter, who was honest, and had taken no part in their godless deeds. She opened all doors to the stranger and showed him the heaped-up treasures. But the King's son said she might keep everything, he would have none of it, and rode onwards with his servant.

After they had travelled about for a long time, they came to a town in which was a beautiful but proud princess, who had caused it to be proclaimed that whosoever should set her a riddle which she could not guess, that man should be her husband; but if she guessed it, his head must be cut off. She had three days to guess it in, but was so clever that she always found the answer to the riddle given her, before the appointed time. Nine suitors had already perished in this manner, when the King's son arrived, and blinded by her great beauty, was willing to stake his life for it. Then he went to her and laid his riddle before her.

"What is this?" said he, "One slew none, and yet slew twelve." She did not know what that was, she thought and thought, but she could not find out, she opened her riddlebooks, but it was not in them—in short, her wisdom was at an end. As she did not know how to help herself, she ordered her maid to creep into the lord's sleeping-chamber, and listen to his dreams, and thought that he would perhaps speak in his sleep and discover the riddle. But the clever servant had placed himself in the bed instead of his master, and when the maid came there, he tore off from her the mantle in which she had wrapped herself, and chased her out with rods. The second night the King's daughter sent her maid-in-waiting, who was to see if she could succeed better in listening, but the servant took her mantle also away from her, and hunted her out with rods. Now the master believed himself safe for the third night, and lay down in his own bed. Then came the princess herself, and she had put on a misty-grey mantle, and she seated herself near him. And when she thought that he was asleep and dreaming, she spoke to him, and hoped that he would answer in his sleep, as many do, but he was awake, and understood and heard everything quite well. Then she asked, "One slew none, what is that?" He replied, "A raven, which ate of a dead and poisoned horse, and died of it." She inquired further, "And yet slew twelve, what is that?" He answered, "That means twelve murderers, who ate the raven and died of it."

When she knew the answer to the riddle she wanted to steal away, but he held her mantle so fast that she was forced to leave it behind her. Next morning, the King's daughter announced that she had guessed the riddle, and sent for the twelve judges and expounded it before them. But the youth begged for a hearing, and said, "She stole into my room in the night and questioned me, otherwise she could not have discovered it." The judges said, "Bring us a proof of this." Then were the three mantles brought thither by the servant, and when the judges saw the misty-grey one which the King's daughter usually wore, they said, "Let the mantle be embroidered with gold and silver, and then it will be your wedding-mantle.

16 The Mouse, the Bird, and the Sausage

Once upon a time a mouse, a bird, and a sausage became companions, kept house together, lived well and happily with each other, and wonderfully increased their possessions. The bird's work was to fly every day into the forest and bring back wood. The mouse had to carry water, light the fire, and lay the table, but the sausage had to cook.

He who is too well off is always longing for something new. One day, therefore, the bird met with another bird, on the way, to whom it related its excellent circumstances and boasted of them. The other bird, however, called it a poor simpleton for his hard work, but said that the two at home had good times. For when the mouse had made her fire and carried her water, she went into her little room to rest until they called her to lay the table. The sausage stayed by the pot, saw that the food was cooking well, and, when it was nearly time for dinner, it rolled itself once or twice through the broth or vegetables and then they were buttered, salted, and ready. When the bird came home and laid his burden down, they sat down to dinner, and after they had had their meal, they slept their fill till next morning, and that was a splendid life.

Next day the bird, prompted by the other bird, would go no more into the wood, saying that he had been servant long enough, and had been made a fool of by them, and that they must change about for once, and try to arrange it in another way. And, though the mouse and the sausage also begged most earnestly, the bird would have his way, and said it must be tried. They cast lots about it, and the lot fell on the sausage who was to carry wood, the mouse became cook, and the bird was to fetch water.

What happened? The little sausage went out towards the wood, the little bird lighted the fire, the mouse stayed by the pot and waited alone until little sausage came home and brought wood for the next day. But the little sausage stayed so long on the road that they both feared something was amiss, and the bird flew out a little way in the air to meet it. Not far off, however, it met a dog on the road who had fallen on the poor sausage as lawful booty, and had seized and swallowed it. The bird charged the dog with an act of barefaced robbery, but it was in vain to speak, for the dog said he had found forged letters on the sausage, on which account its life was forfeited to him.

The bird sadly took up the wood, flew home, and related what he had seen and heard. They were much troubled, but agreed to do their best and remain together. The bird therefore laid the cloth, and the mouse made ready the food, and wanted to dress it, and to get into the pot as the sausage used to do, and roll and creep amongst the vegetables to mix them; but before she got into the midst of them she was stopped, and lost her skin and hair and life in the attempt.

When the bird came to carry up the dinner, no cook was there. In its distress the bird threw the wood here and there, called and searched, but no cook was to be found! Owing to his carelessness the wood caught fire, so that a conflagration ensued, the bird hastened to fetch water, and then the bucket dropped from his claws into the well, and he fell down with it, and could not recover himself, but had to drown there.

17 Little Red Riding Hood

Once upon a time there was a dear little girl who was loved by every one who looked at her, but most of all by her grandmother, and there was nothing that she would not have given to the child. Once she gave her a little cap of red velvet, which suited her so well that she would never wear anything else; so she was always called "Little Riding Hood."

One day her mother said to her, "Come, Little Riding Hood, here is a piece of cake and a bottle of wine; take them to your grandmother, she is ill and weak, and they will do her good. Set out before it gets hot, and when you are going, walk nicely and quietly and do not run off the path, or you may fall and break the bottle, and then your grandmother will get nothing; and when you go into her room, don't forget to say, 'Good-morning,' and don't peep into every corner before you do it."

"I will take great care," said Little Riding Hood to her mother, and gave her hand on it.

The grandmother lived out in the wood, half a league from the village, and just as Little Riding Hood entered the wood, a wolf met her. Riding Hood did not know what a wicked creature he was, and was not at all afraid of him.

"Good-day, Little Riding Hood," said he.

"Thank you kindly, wolf."

"Whither away so early, Little Riding Hood?"

"To my grandmother's."

"What have you got in your apron?"

"Cake and wine; yesterday was baking-day, so poor sick grandmother is to have something good, to make her stronger."

"Where does your grandmother live, Little Riding Hood?"

"A good quarter of a league farther on in the wood; her house stands under the three large oak-trees, the nut-trees are just below; you surely must know it," replied Little Riding

Hood.

The wolf thought to himself, "What a tender young creature! What a nice plump mouthful—she will be better to eat than the

old woman. I must act craftily, so as to catch both." So he walked for a short time by the side of Little Riding Hood, and then he said, "See Little Riding Hood, how pretty the flowers are about here—why do you not look round? I believe, too, that you do not hear how sweetly the little birds are singing; you walk gravely along as if you were going to school, while everything else out here in the wood is merry."

Little Riding Hood raised her eyes, and when she saw the sunbeams dancing here and there through the trees, and pretty flowers growing everywhere, she thought, "Suppose I take grandmother a fresh nosegay; that would please her too. It is so early in the day that I shall still get there in good time." and so she ran from the path into the wood to look for flowers. And whenever she had picked one, she fancied that she saw a still prettier one farther on, and ran after it, and so got deeper and deeper into the wood.

Meanwhile the wolf ran straight to the grandmother's house and knocked at the door.

"Who is there?"

"Little Riding Hood," replied the wolf. "She is bringing cake and wine; open the door."

"Lift the latch," called out the grandmother, "I am too weak, and cannot get up."

The wolf lifted the latch, the door flew open, and without saying a word he went straight to the grandmother's bed, and devoured her. Then he put on her clothes, dressed himself in her cap, laid himself in bed and drew the curtains.

Little Riding Hood, however, had been running about picking flowers, and when she had gathered so many that she could carry no more, she remembered her grandmother, and set out on the way to her.

She was surprised to find the cottage-door standing open, and when she went into the room, she had such a strange feeling that she said to herself, "Oh dear! how uneasy I feel today, and at other times I like being with grandmother so much." She called out, "Good morning," but received no answer; so she went to the bed and drew back the curtains. There lay her grandmother with her cap pulled far over her face, and looking very strange.

"Oh! grandmother," she said, "what big ears you have!"

"The better to hear you with, my child," was the reply.

"But, grandmother, what big eyes you have!" she said.

"The better to see you with, my dear."

"But, grandmother, what large hands you have!"

"The better to hug you with."

"Oh! but, grandmother, what a terrible big mouth you have!"

"The better to eat you with!"

And scarcely had the wolf said this, than with one bound he was out of bed and swallowed up Riding Hood.

When the wolf had appeased his appetite, he lay down again in the bed, fell asleep and began to snore very loud. The huntsman was just passing the house, and thought to himself, "How the old woman is snoring! I must just see if she wants anything." So he went into the room, and when he came to the bed, he saw that the wolf was lying in it. "Do I find thee here, thou old sinner!" said he. "I have long sought thee!" Then just as he was going to fire at him, it occurred to him that the wolf might have devoured the grandmother, and that she might still be saved, so he did not fire, but took a pair of scissors, and began to cut open the stomach of the sleeping wolf. When he had made two snips, he saw the little Riding Hood shining, and then he made two snips more, and the little girl sprang out, crying, "Ah, how frightened I have been! How dark it was inside the wolf"; and after that the aged grandmother came out alive also, but scarcely able to breathe. Riding Hood, however, quickly fetched great stones with which they filled the wolf's body, and when he awoke, he wanted to run away, but the stones were so heavy that he fell down at once, and fell dead.

Then all three were delighted. The huntsman drew off the wolf's skin and went home with it; the grandmother ate the cake and drank the wine which Riding Hood had brought, and revived, but Riding Hood thought to herself, "As long as I live, I will never by myself leave the path, to run into the wood, when my mother has forbidden me to do so."

*   *   *   *   *   *   *

It is also related that once when Riding Hood was again taking cakes to the old grandmother, another wolf spoke to her, and tried to entice her from the path. Riding Hood, however, was on her guard, and went straight forward on her way, and told her grandmother that she had met the wolf, and that he had said "good-morning" to her, but with such a wicked look in his eyes, that if they had not been on the public road she was certain he would have eaten her up. "Well," said the grandmother, "we will shut the door, that he may not come in." Soon afterwards the wolf knocked, and cried, "Open the door, grandmother, I am little Riding Hood, and am fetching you some cakes." But they did not speak, or open the door, so the grey-beard stole twice or thrice round the house, and at last jumped on the roof, intending to wait until Riding Hood went home in the evening, and then to steal after her and devour her in the darkness. But the grandmother saw what was in his thoughts. In front of the house was a great stone trough, so she said to the child, "Take the pail, Riding Hood; I made some sausages yesterday, so carry the water in which I boiled them to the trough." Riding Hood carried until the great trough was quite full. Then the smell of the sausages reached the wolf, and he sniffed and peeped down, and at last stretched out his neck so far that he could no longer keep his footing and began to slip, and slipped down from the roof straight into the great trough, and was drowned. But Riding Hood went joyously home, and never did anything to harm any one.

18 The Devil With the Three Golden Hairs

There was once a poor woman who gave birth to a little son; and as he came into the world with a caul on, it was predicted that in his fourteenth year he would have the King's daughter for his wife. It happened that soon afterwards the King came into the village, and no one knew that he was the King, and when he asked the people what news there was, they answered, "A child has just been born with a caul on; whatever any one so born undertakes turns out well. It is prophesied, too, that in his fourteenth year he will have the King's daughter for his wife."

The King, who had a bad heart, and was angry about the prophecy, went to the parents, and, seeming quite friendly, said, "You poor people, let me have your child, and I will take care of it." At first they refused, but when the stranger offered them a large amount of gold for it, and they thought, "It is a luck-child, and everything must turn out well for it," they at last consented, and gave him the child.

The King put it in a box and rode away with it until he came to a deep piece of water; then he threw the box into it and thought, "I have freed my daughter from her unlooked-for suitor."

The box, however, did not sink, but floated like a boat, and not a drop of water made its way into it. And it floated to within two miles of the King's chief city, where there was a mill, and it came to a stand-still at the mill-dam. A miller's boy, who by good luck was standing there, noticed it and pulled it out with a hook, thinking that he had found a great treasure, but when he opened it there lay a pretty boy inside, quite fresh and lively. He took him to the miller and his wife, and as they had no children they were glad, and said, "God has given him to us." They took great care of the foundling, and he grew up in all goodness.

It happened that once in a storm, the King went into the mill, and he asked the mill-folk if the tall youth was their son. "No," answered they, "he's a foundling. Fourteen years ago he floated down to the mill-dam in a box, and the mill-boy pulled him out of the water."

Then the King knew that it was none other than the luck-child which he had thrown into the water, and he said, "My good people, could not the youth take a letter to the Queen; I will give him two gold pieces as a reward?"

"Just as the King commands," answered they, and they told the boy to hold himself in readiness. Then the King wrote a letter to the Queen, wherein he said, "As soon as the boy arrives with this letter, let him be killed and buried, and all must be done before I come home."

The boy set out with this letter; but he lost his way, and in the evening came to a large forest. In the darkness he saw a small light; he went towards it and reached a cottage. When he went in, an old woman was sitting by the fire quite alone. She started when she saw the boy, and said, "Whence do you come, and whither are you going?"

"I come from the mill," he answered, "and wish to go to the Queen, to whom I am taking a letter; but as I have lost my way in the forest I should like to stay here over night."

"You poor boy," said the woman, "you have come into a den of thieves, and when they come home they will kill you."

"Let them come," said the boy, "I am not afraid; but I am so tired that I cannot go any farther:" and he stretched himself upon a bench and fell asleep.

Soon afterwards the robbers came, and angrily asked what strange boy was lying there. "Ah," said the old woman, "it is an innocent child who has lost himself in the forest, and out of pity I have let him come in; he has to take a letter to the Queen." The robbers opened the letter and read it, and in it was written that the boy as soon as he arrived should be put to death. Then the hard-hearted robbers felt pity, and their leader tore up the letter and wrote another, saying, that as soon as the boy came, he should be married at once to the King's daughter. Then they let him lie quietly on the bench until the next morning, and when he awoke they gave him the letter, and showed him the right way.

And the Queen, when she had received the letter and read it, did as was written in it, and had a splendid wedding-feast prepared, and the King's daughter was married to the luck-child, and as the youth was handsome and agreeable she lived with him in joy and contentment.

After some time the King returned to his palace and saw that the prophecy was fulfilled, and the luck-child married to his daughter. "How has that come to pass?" said he; "I gave quite another order in my letter."

So the Queen gave him the letter, and said that he might see for himself what was written in it. The King read the letter and saw quite well that it had been exchanged for the other. He asked the youth what had become of the letter entrusted to him, and why he had brought another instead of it. "I know nothing about it," answered he; "it must have been changed in the night, when I slept in the forest." The King said in a passion, "You shall not have everything quite so much your own way; whosoever marries my daughter must fetch me from hell three golden hairs from the head of the devil; bring me what I want, and you shall keep my daughter." In this way the King hoped to be rid of him for ever. But the luck-child answered, "I will fetch the golden hairs, I am not afraid of the Devil;" thereupon he took leave of them and began his journey.

The road led him to a large town, where the watchman by the gates asked him what his trade was, and what he knew. "I know everything," answered the luck-child. "Then you can do us a favour," said the watchman, "if you will tell us why our market-fountain, which once flowed with wine has become dry, and no longer gives even water?"

"That you shall know," answered he; "only wait until I come back."

Then he went farther and came to another town, and there also the gatekeeper asked him what was his trade, and what he knew. "I know everything," answered he. "Then you can do us a favour and tell us why a tree in our town which once bore golden apples now does not even put forth leaves?"

"You shall know that," answered he; "only wait until I come back."

Then he went on and came to a wide river over which he must go. The ferryman asked him what his trade was, and what he knew. "I know everything," answered he. "Then you can do me a favour," said the ferryman, "and tell me why I must always be rowing backwards and forwards, and am never set free?"

"You shall know that," answered he; "only wait until I come back."

When he had crossed the water he found the entrance to Hell. It was black and sooty within, and the Devil was not at home, but his grandmother was sitting in a large arm-chair. "What do you want?" said she to him, but she did not look so very wicked. "I should like to have three golden hairs from the devil's head," answered he, "else I cannot keep my wife."

"That is a good deal to ask for," said she; "if the devil comes home and finds you, it will cost you your life; but as I pity you, I will see if I cannot help you."

She changed him into an ant and said, "Creep into the folds of my dress, you will be safe there."

"Yes," answered he, "so far, so good; but there are three things besides that I want to know: why a fountain which once flowed with wine has become dry, and no longer gives even water; why a tree which once bore golden apples does not even put forth leaves; and why a ferry-man must always be going backwards and forwards, and is never set free?"

"Those are difficult questions," answered she, "but only be silent and quiet and pay attention to what the devil says when I pull out the three golden hairs."

As the evening came on, the devil returned home. No sooner had he entered than he noticed that the air was not pure. "I smell man's flesh," said he; "all is not right here." Then he pried into every corner, and searched, but could not find anything. His grandmother scolded him. "It has just been swept," said she, "and everything put in order, and now you are upsetting it again; you have always got man's flesh in your nose. Sit down and eat your supper."

When he had eaten and drunk he was tired, and laid his head in his grandmother's lap, and before long he was fast asleep, snoring and breathing heavily. Then the old woman took hold of a golden hair, pulled it out, and laid it down near her. "Oh!" cried the devil, "what are you doing?"

"I have had a bad dream," answered the grandmother, "so I seized hold of your hair."

"What did you dream then?" said the devil. "I dreamed that a fountain in a market-place from which wine once flowed was dried up, and not even water would flow out of it; what is the cause of it?"

"Oh, ho! if they did but know it," answered the devil; "there is a toad sitting under a stone in the well; if they killed it, the wine would flow again."

He went to sleep again and snored until the windows shook. Then she pulled the second hair out. "Ha! what are you doing?" cried the devil angrily. "Do not take it ill," said she, "I did it in a dream."

"What have you dreamt this time?" asked he. "I dreamt that in a certain kingdom there stood an apple-tree which had once borne golden apples, but now would not even bear leaves. What, think you, was the reason?"

"Oh! if they did but know," answered the devil. "A mouse is gnawing at the root; if they killed this they would have golden apples again, but if it gnaws much longer the tree will wither altogether. But leave me alone with your dreams: if you disturb me in my sleep again you will get a box on the ear."

The grandmother spoke gently to him until he fell asleep again and snored. Then she took hold of the third golden hair and pulled it out. The devil jumped up, roared out, and would have treated her ill if she had not quieted him once more and said, "Who can help bad dreams?"

"What was the dream, then?" asked he, and was quite curious in spite of himself. "I dreamt of a ferry-man who complained that he must always ferry from one side to the other, and was never released. What is the cause of it?"

"Ah! the fool," answered the devil; "when any one comes and wants to go across he must put the oar in his hand, and the other man will have to ferry and he will be free." As the grandmother had plucked out the three golden hairs, and the three questions were answered, she let the old serpent alone, and he slept until daybreak.

When the devil had gone out again the old woman took the ant out of the folds of her dress, and gave the luck-child his human shape again. "There are the three golden hairs for you," said she. "What the Devil said to your three questions, I suppose you heard?"

"Yes," answered he, "I heard, and will take care to remember."

"You have what you want," said she, "and now you can go your way." He thanked the old woman for helping him in his need, and left hell well content that everything had turned out so fortunately.

When he came to the ferry-man he was expected to give the promised answer. "Ferry me across first," said the luck-child, "and then I will tell you how you can be set free," and when he reached the opposite shore he gave him the devil's advice: "Next time any one comes, who wants to be ferried over, just put the oar in his hand."

He went on and came to the town wherein stood the unfruitful tree, and there too the watchman wanted an answer. So he told him what he had heard from the devil: "Kill the mouse which is gnawing at its root, and it will again bear golden apples." Then the watchman thanked him, and gave him as a reward two donkeys laden with gold, which followed him.

At last he came to the town whose well was dry. He told the watchman what the devil had said: "A toad is in the well beneath a stone; you must find it and kill it, and the well will again give wine in plenty." The watchman thanked him, and also gave him two donkeys laden with gold.

At last the luck-child got home to his wife, who was heartily glad to see him again, and to hear how well he had prospered in everything. To the King he took what he had asked for, the devil's three golden hairs, and when the King saw the four asses laden with gold he was quite content, and said, "Now all the conditions are fulfilled, and you can keep my daughter. But tell me, dear son-in-law, where did all that gold come from? this is tremendous wealth!"

"I was rowed across a river," answered he, "and got it there; it lies on the shore instead of sand."

"Can I too fetch some of it?" said the King; and he was quite eager about it. "As much as you like," answered he. "There is a ferry-man on the river; let him ferry you over, and you can fill your sacks on the other side." The greedy King set out in all haste, and when he came to the river he beckoned to the ferry-man to put him across. The ferry-man came and bade him get in, and when they got to the other shore he put the oar in his hand and sprang out. But from this time forth the King had to ferry, as a punishment for his sins. Perhaps he is ferrying still? If he is, it is because no one has taken the oar from him.

18 The Louse and the Flea

A louse and a flea kept house together and were brewing beer in an egg-shell. Then the little louse fell in and burnt herself. On this the little flea began to scream loudly. Then the little door to the room asked, "Little flea, why art thou screaming?"

"Because the louse has burnt herself."

Then the little door began to creak. On this a little broom in the corner said, "Why art thou creaking, little door?"

"Have I not reason to creak?"

> "The little louse has burnt herself,
> the little flea is weeping."

So the little broom began to sweep frantically. Then a little cart passed by and said, "Why art thou sweeping, little broom?"

"Have I not reason to sweep?"

> "The little louse has burnt herself,
> the little flea is weeping,
> the little door is creaking."

So the little cart said, "Then I will run," and began to run wildly. Then said the ash-heap by which it ran, "Why art thou running so, little cart?"

"Have I not reason to run?"

> "The little louse has burnt herself,
> the little flea is weeping,
> the little door is creaking,
> he little broom is sweeping."

The ash-heap said, "Then I will burn furiously," and began to burn in clear flames. A little tree stood near the ash-heap and said, "Ash-heap, why art thou burning?"

"Have I not reason to burn?"

> "The little louse has burnt herself,
> the little flea is weeping,
> the little door is creaking,
> the little broom is sweeping,
> the little cart is running."

The little tree said, "Then I will shake myself," and began to shake herself so that all her leaves fell off; a girl who came up with her water-pitcher saw that, and said, "Little tree, why art thou shaking thyself?"

"Have I not reason to shake myself?"

> "The little louse has burnt herself,
> the little flea is weeping,
> the little door is creaking,
> the little broom is sweeping,
> the little cart is running,
> the little ash-heap is burning."

On this the girl said, "Then I will break my little water-pitcher," and she broke her little water-pitcher. Then said the little spring from which ran the water, "Girl, why art thou breaking thy water-jug?"

"Have I not reason to break my water-jug?"

> "The little louse has burnt herself,
> the little flea is weeping,
> the little door is creaking,
> the little broom is sweeping,
> the little cart is running,
> The little ash-heap is burning,
> the little tree is shaking itself."

"Oh, ho!" said the spring, "then I will begin to flow," and began to flow violently. And in the water everything was drowned, the girl, the little tree, the little ash-heap, the little cart, the broom, the little door, the little flea, the little louse, all together.

97

20 The Elves

A shoemaker, by no fault of his own, had become so poor that at last he had nothing left but leather for one pair of shoes. So in the evening, he cut out the shoes which he wished to begin to make the next morning, and as he had a good conscience, he lay down quietly in his bed, commended himself to God, and fell asleep. In the morning, after he had said his prayers, and was just going to sit down to work, the two shoes stood quite finished on his table. He was so astounded by this that he didn't know what to say. He took the shoes in his hands to observe them closer, and they were so neatly made that there was not one bad stitch in them, just as if they were intended as a masterpiece. Soon after, a buyer came in, and as the shoes pleased him so well, he paid more for them than was customary, and, with the money, the shoemaker was able to purchase leather for two pairs of shoes. He cut them out at night, and next morning was about to set to work with fresh courage; but he had no need to do so, for, when he got up, they were already made, and buyers also were not wanting, who gave him money enough to buy leather for four pairs of shoes. The following morning, too, he found the four pairs made; and so it went on constantly, what he cut out in the evening was finished by the morning, so that he soon had his honest independence again, and at last became a wealthy man. Now it befell that one evening not long before Christmas, when the man had been cutting out, he said to his wife, before going to bed, "What think you if we were to stay up tonight to see who it is that lends us this helping hand?" The woman liked the idea, and lighted a candle, and then they hid themselves in a corner of the room, behind some clothes which were hanging up there, and watched. When it was midnight, two pretty little naked elves came, sat down by the shoemaker's table, took all the work which was cut out before them and began to stitch, and sew, and hammer so skilfully and so quickly with their little fingers that the shoemaker could not turn away his eyes for astonishment. They did not stop until all was done, and stood finished on the table, and they ran quickly away.

Next morning the woman said, "The little elves have made us rich, and we really must show that we are grateful for it. They run about so, and have nothing on, and must be cold. I'll tell thee what I'll do: I will make them little shirts, and coats, and vests, and trousers, and knit both of them a pair of stockings, and do thou, too, make them two little pairs of shoes." The man said, "I shall be very glad to do it;" and one night, when everything was ready, they laid their presents all together on the table instead of the cut-out work, and then concealed themselves to see how the little elves would behave. At midnight they came bounding in, and wanted to get to work at once, but as they did not find any leather cut out, but only the pretty little articles of clothing, they were at first astonished, and then they showed intense delight. They dressed themselves with the greatest rapidity, putting the pretty clothes on, and singing, "Now we are boys so fine to see, Why should we longer cobblers be?"

Then they danced and skipped and leapt over chairs and benches. At last they danced out of doors. From that time forth they came no more, but as long as the shoemaker lived all went well with him, and all his undertakings prospered.

SECOND STORY

There was once a poor servant-girl, who was industrious and cleanly, and swept the house every day, and emptied her sweepings on the great heap in front of the door. One morning when she was just going back to her work, she found a letter on this heap, and as she could not read, she put her broom in the corner, and took the letter to her master and mistress, and behold it was an invitation from the elves, who asked the girl to hold a child for them at its christening. The girl did not know what to do, but at length, after much persuasion, and as they told her that it was not right to refuse an invitation of this kind, she consented. Then three elves came and conducted her to a hollow mountain, where the little folks lived. Everything there was small, but more elegant and beautiful than can be described. The baby's mother lay in a bed of black ebony ornamented with pearls, the coverlids were embroidered with gold, the cradle was of ivory, the bath of gold. The girl stood as godmother, and then wanted to go home again, but the little elves urgently entreated her to stay three days with them. So she stayed, and passed the time in pleasure and gaiety, and the little folks did all they could to make her happy. At last she set out on her way home. Then first they filled her pockets quite full of money, and after that they led her out of the mountain again. When she got home, she wanted to begin her work, and took the broom, which was still standing in the corner, in her hand and began to sweep. Then some strangers came out of the house, who asked her who she was, and what business she had there. And she had not, as she thought, been three days with the little men in the mountains, but seven years, and in the meantime her former masters had died.

THIRD STORY

A certain mother's child had been taken away out of its cradle by the elves, and a changeling with a large head and staring eyes, which would do nothing but eat and drink, laid in its place. In her trouble she went to her neighbour, and asked her advice. The neighbour said that she was to carry the changeling into the kitchen, set it down on the hearth, light a fire, and boil some water in two egg-shells, which would make the changeling laugh, and if he laughed, all would be over with him. The woman did everything that her neighbour bade her. When she put the egg-shells with water on the fire, the imp said, "I am as old now as the Wester forest, but never yet have I seen any one boil anything in an egg-shell!" And he began to laugh at it. Whilst he was laughing, suddenly came a host of little elves, who brought the right child, set it down on the hearth, and took the changeling away with them.

21 The Robber Bridegroom

There was once upon a time a miller, who had a beautiful daughter, and as she was grown up, he wished that she was provided for, and well married. He thought, "If any good suitor comes and asks for her, I will give her to him." Not long afterwards, a suitor came, who appeared to be very rich, and as the miller had no fault to find with him, he promised his daughter to him. The maiden, however, did not like him quite so much as a girl should like the man to whom she is engaged, and had no confidence in him. Whenever she saw, or thought of him, she felt a secret horror. Once he said to her, "Thou art my betrothed, and yet thou hast never once paid me a visit." The maiden replied, "I know not where thy house is." Then said the bridegroom, "My house is out there in the dark forest." She tried to excuse herself and said she could not find the way there. The bridegroom said, "Next Sunday thou must come out there to me; I have already invited the guests, and I will strew ashes in order that thou mayst find thy way through the forest." When Sunday came, and the maiden had to set out on her way, she became very uneasy, she herself knew not exactly why, and to mark her way she filled both her pockets full of peas and lentils. Ashes were strewn at the entrance of the forest, and these she followed, but at every step she threw a couple of peas on the ground. She walked almost the whole day until she reached the middle of the forest, where it was the darkest, and there stood a solitary house, which she did not like, for it looked so dark and dismal. She went inside it, but no one was within, and the most absolute stillness reigned. Suddenly a voice cried:

> "Turn back, turn back, young maiden dear,
> 'Tis a murderer's house you enter here."

The maiden looked up, and saw that the voice came from a bird, which was hanging in a cage on the wall. Again it cried:

> "Turn back, turn back, young maiden dear,
> 'tis a murderer's house you enter here."

Then the young maiden went on farther from one room to another, and walked through the whole house, but it was entirely empty and not one human being was to be found. At last she came to the the cellar, and there sat an extremely aged woman, whose head shook constantly. "Can you not tell me," said the maiden, "if my betrothed lives here?"

"Alas, poor child," replied the old woman, "whither hast thou come? Thou art in a murderer's den. Thou thinkest thou art a bride soon to be married, but thou wilt keep thy wedding with death. Look, I have been forced to put a great kettle on there, with water in it, and when they have thee in their power, they will cut thee to pieces without mercy, will cook thee, and eat thee, for they are eaters of human flesh. If I do not have compassion on thee, and save thee, thou art lost".

Thereupon the old woman led her behind a great hogshead where she could not be seen. "Be as still as a mouse," said she, "do not make a sound, or move, or all will be over with thee. At night, when the robbers are asleep, we will escape; I have long waited for an opportunity." Hardly was this done, than the godless crew came home. They dragged with them another young girl. They were drunk, and paid no heed to her screams and lamentations. They gave her wine to drink, three glasses full, one glass of white wine, one glass of red, and a glass of yellow, and with this her heart burst in twain. Thereupon they tore off her delicate raiment, laid her on a table, cut her beautiful body in pieces and strewed salt thereon. The poor bride behind the cask trembled and shook, for she saw right well what fate the robbers had destined for her. One of them noticed a gold ring on the little finger of the murdered girl, and as it would not come off at once, he took an axe and cut the finger off, but it sprang up in the air, away over the cask and fell straight into the bride's bosom. The robber took a candle and wanted to look for it, but could not find it. Then another of them said, "Hast thou looked behind the great hogshead?" But the old woman cried, "Come and get something to eat, and leave off looking till the morning, the finger won't run away from you."

Then the robbers said, "The old woman is right," and gave up their search, and sat down to eat, and the old woman poured a sleeping-draught in their wine, so that they soon lay down in the cellar, and slept and snored. When the bride heard that, she came out from behind the hogshead, and had to step over the sleepers, for they lay in rows on the ground, and great was her terror lest she should waken one of them. But God helped her, and she got safely over. The old woman went up with her, opened the doors, and they hurried out of the murderers' den with all the speed in their power. The wind had blown away the strewn ashes, but the peas and lentils had sprouted and grown up, and showed them the way in the moonlight. They walked the whole night, until in the morning they arrived at the mill, and then the maiden told her father everything exactly as it had happened.

When the day came when the wedding was to be celebrated, the bridegroom appeared, and the Miller had invited all his relations and friends. As they sat at table, each was bidden to relate something. The bride sat still, and said nothing. Then said the bridegroom to the bride, "Come, my darling, dost thou know nothing? Relate something to us like the rest." She replied, "Then I will relate a dream. I was walking alone through a wood, and at last I came to a house, in which no living soul was, but on the wall there was a bird in a cage which cried:

"Turn back, turn back, young maiden dear,

'tis a murderer's house you enter here."

"And this it cried once more.(My darling, I only dreamt this.) Then I went through all the rooms, and they were all empty, and there was something so horrible about them! At last I went down into the cellar, and there sat a very very old woman, whose head shook; I asked her, "Does my bridegroom live in this house?"

She answered, "Alas poor child, thou hast got into a murderer's den, thy bridegroom does live here, but he will hew thee in pieces, and kill thee, and then he will cook thee, and eat thee.' (My darling, I only dreamt this.) But the old woman hid me behind a great hogshead, and, scarcely was I hidden, when the robbers came home, dragging a maiden with them, to whom they gave three kinds of wine to drink, white, red, and yellow, with which her heart broke in twain. (My darling, I only dreamt this.) Thereupon they pulled off her pretty clothes, and hewed her fair body into pieces on a table, and sprinkled them with salt. (My darling, I only dreamt this). And one of the robbers saw that there was still a ring on her little finger, and as it was hard to draw off, he took an axe and cut it off, but the finger sprang up in the air, and sprang behind the great hogshead, and fell in my bosom. And there is the finger with the ring!" And with these words she drew it forth, and showed it to those present.

The robber, who had during this story become as pale as ashes, leapt up and wanted to escape, but the guests held him fast, and delivered him over to justice. Then he and his whole troop were executed for their infamous deeds.

22 The Girl Without Hands

A certain miller had little by little fallen into poverty, and had nothing left but his mill and a large apple-tree behind it. Once when he had gone into the forest to fetch wood, an old man stepped up to him whom he had never seen before, and said, "Why dost thou plague thyself with cutting wood, I will make thee rich, if thou wilt promise me what is standing behind thy mill."

"What can that be but my apple-tree?" thought the miller, and said, "Yes," and gave a written promise to the stranger. He, however, laughed mockingly and said, "When three years have passed, I will come and carry away what belongs to me," and then he went. When the miller got home, his wife came to meet him and said, "Tell me, miller, from whence comes this sudden wealth into our house? All at once every box and chest was filled; no one brought it in, and I know not how it happened." He answered, "It comes from a stranger who met me in the forest, and promised me great treasure. I, in return, have promised him what stands behind the mill; we can very well give him the big apple-tree for it."

"Ah, husband," said the terrified wife, "that must have been the devil! He did not mean the apple-tree, but our daughter, who was standing behind the mill sweeping the yard."

The miller's daughter was a beautiful, pious girl, and lived through the three years in the fear of God and without sin. When therefore the time was over, and the day came when the Evil One was to fetch her, she washed herself clean, and made a circle round herself with chalk. The devil appeared quite early, but he could not come near to her. Angrily, he said to the miller, "Take all water away from her, that she may no longer be able to wash herself, for otherwise I have no power over her." The miller was afraid, and did so. The next morning the devil came again, but she had wept on her hands, and they were quite clean. Again he could not get near her, and furiously said to the miller, "Cut her hands off, or else I cannot get the better of her." The miller was shocked and answered, "How could I cut off my own child's hands?" Then the Evil One threatened him and said, "If thou dost not do it thou art mine, and I will take thee thyself." The father became alarmed, and promised to obey him. So he went to the girl and said, "My child, if I do not cut off both thine hands, the devil will carry me away, and in my terror I have promised to do it. Help me in my need, and forgive me the harm I do thee." She replied, "Dear father, do with me what you will, I am your child." Thereupon she laid down both her hands, and let them be cut off. The devil came for the third time, but she had wept so long and so much on the stumps, that after all they were quite clean. Then he had to give in, and had lost all right over her.

The miller said to her, "I have by means of thee received such great wealth that I will keep thee most delicately as long as thou livest." But she replied, "Here I cannot stay, I will go forth, compassionate people will give me as much as I require." Thereupon she caused her maimed arms to be bound to her back, and by sunrise she set out on her way, and walked the whole day until night fell. Then she came to a royal garden, and by the shimmering of the moon she saw that trees covered with beautiful fruits grew in it, but she could not enter, for there was much water round about it. And as she had walked the whole day and not eaten one mouthful, and hunger tormented her, she thought, "Ah, if I were but inside, that I might eat of the fruit, else must I die of hunger!" Then she knelt down, called on God the Lord, and prayed. And suddenly an angel came towards her, who made a dam in the water, so that the moat became dry and she could walk through it. And now she went into the garden and the angel went with her. She saw a tree covered with beautiful pears, but they were all counted. Then she went to them, and to still her hunger, ate one with her mouth from the tree, but no more. The gardener was watching; but as the angel was standing by, he was afraid and thought the maiden was a spirit, and was silent, neither did he dare to cry out, or to speak to the spirit. When she had eaten the pear, she was satisfied, and went and concealed herself among the bushes. The King to whom the garden belonged, came down to it next morning, and counted, and saw that one of the pears was missing, and asked the gardener what had become of it, as it was not lying beneath the tree, but was gone. Then answered the gardener, "Last night, a spirit came in, who had no hands, and ate off one of the pears with its mouth." The King said, "How did the spirit get over the water, and where did it go after it had eaten the pear?" The gardener answered, "Some one came in a snow-white garment from heaven who made a dam, and kept back the water, that the spirit might walk through the moat. And as it must have been an angel, I was afraid, and asked no questions, and did not cry out. When the spirit had eaten the pear, it went back again." The King said, "If it be as thou sayest, I will watch with thee tonight."

When it grew dark the King came into the garden and brought a priest with him, who was to speak to the spirit. All three seated themselves beneath the tree and watched. At midnight the maiden came creeping out of the thicket, went to the tree, and again ate one pear off it with her mouth, and beside her stood the angel in white garments. Then the priest went out to them and said, "Comest thou from heaven or from earth? Art thou a spirit, or a human being?" She replied, "I am no spirit, but an unhappy mortal deserted by all but God." The King said, "If thou art forsaken by all the world, yet will I not forsake thee." He took her with him into his royal palace, and as she was so beautiful and good, he loved her with all his heart, had silver hands made for her, and took her for his wife.

After a year the King had to take the field, so he commended his young Queen to the care of his mother and said, "If she is brought to bed take care of her, nurse her well, and tell me of it at once in a letter." Then she gave birth to a fine boy. So the old mother made haste to write and announce the joyful news to him. But the messenger rested by a brook on the way, and as he was fatigued by the great distance, he fell asleep. Then came the Devil, who was always seeking to injure the good Queen, and exchanged the letter for another, in which was written that the Queen had brought a monster into the world. When the King read the letter he was shocked and much troubled, but he wrote in answer that they were to take great care of the Queen and nurse her well until his arrival. The messenger went back with the letter, but rested at the same place and again fell asleep. Then came the Devil once more, and put a different letter in his pocket, in which it was written that they were to put the Queen and her child to death. The old mother was terribly shocked when she received the letter, and could not believe it. She wrote back again to the King, but received no other answer, because each time the Devil substituted a false letter, and in the last letter it was also written that she was to preserve the Queen's tongue and eyes as a token that she had obeyed.

But the old mother wept to think such innocent blood was to be shed, and had a hind brought by night and cut out her tongue and eyes, and kept them. Then said she to the Queen, "I cannot have thee killed as the King commands, but here thou mayst stay no longer. Go forth into the wide world with thy child, and never come here again." The poor woman tied her child on her back, and went away with eyes full of tears. She came into a great wild forest, and then she fell on her knees and prayed to God, and the angel of the Lord appeared to her and led her to a little house on which was a sign with the words, "Here all dwell free." A snow-white maiden came out of the little house and said, "Welcome, Lady Queen," and conducted her inside. Then they unbound the little boy from her back, and held him to her breast that he might feed, and laid him in a beautifully-made little bed. Then said the poor woman, "From whence knowest thou that I was a queen?" The white maiden answered, "I am an angel sent by God, to watch over thee and thy child." The Queen stayed seven years in the little house, and was well cared for, and by God's grace, because of her piety, her hands which had been cut off, grew once more.

At last the King came home again from the war, and his first wish was to see his wife and the child. Then his aged mother began to weep and said, "Thou wicked man, why didst thou write to me that I was to take those two innocent lives?" and she showed him the two letters which the Evil One had forged, and then continued, "I did as thou badest me," and she showed the tokens, the tongue and eyes. Then the King began to weep for his poor wife and his little son so much more bitterly than she was doing, that the aged mother had compassion on him and said, "Be at peace, she still lives; I secretly caused a hind to be killed, and took these tokens from it; but I bound the child to thy wife's back and bade her go forth into the wide world, and made her promise never to come back here again, because thou wert so angry with her." Then spoke the King, "I will go as far as the sky is blue, and will neither eat nor drink until I have found again my dear wife and my child, if in the meantime they have not been killed, or died of hunger."

Thereupon the King travelled about for seven long years, and sought her in every cleft of the rocks and in every cave, but he found her not, and thought she had died of want. During the whole of this time he neither ate nor drank, but God supported him. At length he came into a great forest, and found therein the little house whose sign was, "Here all dwell free." Then forth came the white maiden, took him by the hand, led him in, and said, "Welcome, Lord King," and asked him from whence he came. He answered, "Soon shall I have travelled about for the space of seven years, and I seek my wife and her child, but cannot find them." The angel offered him meat and drink, but he did not take anything, and only wished to rest a little. Then he lay down to sleep, and put a handkerchief over his face.

Thereupon the angel went into the chamber where the Queen

sat with her son, whom she usually called "Sorrowful," and said to her, "Go out with thy child, thy husband hath come." So she went to the place where he lay, and the handkerchief fell from his face. Then said she, "Sorrowful, pick up thy father's hand-kerchief, and cover his face again." The child picked it up, and put it over his face again. The King in his sleep heard what passed, and had pleasure in letting the handkerchief fall once more. But the child grew impatient, and said, "Dear mother, how can I cover my father's face when I have no father in this world? I have learnt to say the prayer, 'Our Father, which art in Heaven,' thou hast told me that my father was in Heaven, and was the good God, and how can I know a wild man like this? He is not my father." When the King heard that, he got up, and asked who they were. Then said she, "I am thy wife, and that is thy son, Sorrowful." And he saw her living hands, and said, "My wife had silver hands." She answered, "The good God has caused my natural hands to grow again;" and the angel went into the inner room, and brought the silver hands, and showed them to him. Hereupon he knew for a certainty that it was his dear wife and his dear child, and he kissed them, and was glad, and said, "A heavy stone has fallen from off mine heart." Then the angel of God gave them one meal with her, and after that they went home to the King's aged mother. There were great rejoic-ings everywhere, and the King and Queen were married again, and lived contentedly to their happy end.

23 The Six Swans

Once upon a time, a certain King was hunting in a great forest, and he chased a wild beast so eagerly that none of his attendants could follow him. When evening drew near he stopped and looked around him, and then he saw that he had lost his way. He sought a way out, but could find none. Then he perceived an aged woman with a head which nodded perpetually, who came towards him, but she was a witch. "Good woman," said he to her, "Can you not show me the way through the forest?"

"Oh, yes, Lord King," she answered, "that I certainly can, but on one condition, and if you do not fulfil that, you will never get out of the forest, and will die of hunger in it."

"What kind of condition is it?" asked the King.

"I have a daughter," said the old woman, "who is as beautiful as any one in the world, and well deserves to be your consort, and if you will make her your Queen, I will show you the way out of the forest." In the anguish of his heart the King consented, and the old woman led him to her little hut, where her daughter was sitting by the fire. She received the King as if she had been expecting him, and he saw that she was very beautiful, but still she did not please him, and he could not look at her without secret horror. After he had taken the maiden up on his horse, the old woman showed him the way, and the King reached his royal palace again, where the wedding was celebrated.

The King had already been married once, and had by his first wife, seven children, six boys and a girl, whom he loved better than anything else in the world. As he now feared that the step-mother might not treat them well, and even do them some injury, he took them to a lonely castle which stood in the midst of a forest. It lay so concealed, and the way was so difficult to find that he himself would not have found it, if a wise woman had not given him a ball of yarn with wonderful properties. When he threw it down before him, it unrolled itself and showed him his path. The King, however, went so frequently away to his dear children that the Queen observed his absence; she was curious and wanted to know what he did when he was quite alone in the forest. She gave a great deal of money to his servants, and they betrayed the secret to her, and told her likewise of the ball which alone could point out the way. And now she knew no rest until she had learnt where the King kept the ball of yarn, and then she made little shirts of white silk, and as she had learnt the art of witchcraft from her mother, she sewed a charm inside them. And once when the King had ridden forth to hunt, she took the little shirts and went into the forest, and the ball showed her the way. The children, who saw from a distance that some one was approaching, thought that their dear father was coming to them, and full of joy, ran to meet him. Then she threw one of the little shirts over each of them, and no sooner had the shirts touched their bodies than they were changed into swans, and flew away over the forest. The Queen went home quite delighted, and thought she had got rid of her step-children, but the girl had not run out with her brothers, and the Queen knew nothing about her. Next day the King went to visit his children, but he found no one but the little girl. "Where are thy brothers?' asked the King. "Alas, dear father," she answered, "they have gone away and left me alone!" and she told him that she had seen from her little window how her brothers had flown away over the forest in the shape of swans, and she showed him the feathers, which they had let fall in the courtyard, and which she had picked up. The King mourned, but he did not think that the Queen had done this wicked deed, and as he feared that the girl would also be stolen away from him, he wanted to take her away with him. But she was afraid of her step-mother, and entreated the King to let her stay just this one night more in the forest castle.

The poor girl thought, "I can no longer stay here. I will go and seek my brothers." And when night came, she ran away, and went straight into the forest. She walked the whole night long, and next day also without stopping, until she could go no farther for weariness. Then she saw a forest-hut, and went into it, and found a room with six little beds, but she did not venture to get into one of them, but crept under one, and lay down on the hard ground, intending to pass the night there. Just before sunset, however, she heard a rustling, and saw six swans come flying in at the window. They alighted on the ground and blew at each other, and blew all the feathers off, and their swan's skins stripped off like a shirt. Then the maiden looked at them and recognised her brothers, was glad and crept forth from beneath the bed. The brothers were not less delighted to see their little sister, but their joy was of short duration. "Here canst thou not abide," they said to her. "This is a shelter for robbers, if they come home and find thee, they will kill thee."

"But can you not protect me?" asked the little sister. "No," they replied, "only for one quarter of an hour each evening can we lay aside our swan's skins and have during that time our human form; after that, we are once more turned into swans." The little sister wept and said, "Can you not be set free?"

"Alas, no," they answered, "the conditions are too hard! For six years thou mayst neither speak nor laugh, and in that time thou must sew together six little shirts of starwort for us. And if one single word falls from thy lips, all thy work will be lost." And when the brothers had said this, the quarter of an hour was over, and they flew out of the window again as swans.

The maiden, however, firmly resolved to deliver her brothers, even if it should cost her her life. She left the hut, went into the midst of the forest, seated herself on a tree, and there passed the night. Next morning she went out and gathered starwort and began to sew. She could not speak to any one, and she had no inclination to laugh; she sat there and looked at nothing but her work. When she had already spent a long time there it came to pass that the King of the country was hunting in the forest, and his huntsmen came to the tree on which the maiden was sitting.

They called to her and said, "Who art thou?" But she made no answer. "Come down to us," said they. "We will not do thee any harm." She only shook her head. As they pressed her further with questions she threw her golden necklace down to them, and thought to content them thus. They, however, did not cease, and then she threw her girdle down to them, and as this also was to no purpose, her garters, and by degrees everything that she had on that she could do without until she had nothing left but her shift. The huntsmen, however, did not let themselves be turned aside by that, but climbed the tree and fetched the maiden down and led her before the King. The King asked, "Who art thou? What art thou doing on the tree?" But she did not answer. He put the question in every language that he knew, but she remained as mute as a fish. As she was so beautiful, the King's heart was touched, and he was smitten with a great love for her. He put his mantle on her, took her before him on his horse, and carried her to his castle. Then he caused her to be dressed in rich garments, and she shone in her beauty like bright daylight, but no word could be drawn from her. He placed her by his side at table, and her modest bearing and courtesy pleased him so much that he said, "She is the one whom I wish to marry, and no other woman in the world." And after some days he united himself to her.

The King, however, had a wicked mother who was dissatisfied with this marriage and spoke ill of the young Queen. "Who knows," said she, "from whence the creature who can't speak, comes? She is not worthy of a king!" After a year had passed, when the Queen brought her first child into the world, the old woman took it away from her, and smeared her mouth with blood as she slept. Then she went to the King and accused the Queen of being a man-eater. The King would not believe it, and would not suffer any one to do her any injury. She, however, sat continually sewing at the shirts, and cared for nothing else. The next time, when she again bore a beautiful boy, the false step-mother used the same treachery, but the King could not bring himself to give credit to her words. He said, "She is too pious and good to do anything of that kind; if she were not dumb, and could defend herself, her innocence would come to light." But when the old woman stole away the newly-born child for the third time, and accused the Queen, who did not utter one word of defence, the King could do no otherwise than deliver her over to justice, and she was sentenced to suffer death by fire.

When the day came for the sentence to be executed, it was the last day of the six years during which she was not to speak or laugh, and she had delivered her dear brothers from the power of the enchantment. The six shirts were ready, only the left sleeve of the sixth was wanting. When, therefore, she was led to the stake, she laid the shirts on her arm, and when she stood on high and the fire was just going to be lighted, she looked around and six swans came flying through the air towards her. Then she saw that her deliverance was near, and her heart leapt with joy. The swans swept towards her and sank down so that she could throw the shirts over them, and as they were touched by them, their swan's skins fell off, and her brothers stood in their own bodily form before her, and were vigorous and handsome. The youngest only lacked his left arm, and had in the place of it a swan's wing on his shoulder. They embraced and kissed each other, and the Queen went to the King, who was greatly moved, and she began to speak and said, "Dearest husband, now I may speak and declare to thee that I am innocent, and falsely accused." And she told him of the treachery of the old woman who had taken away her three children and hidden them. Then to the great joy of the King they were brought thither, and as a punishment, the wicked step-mother was bound to the stake, and burnt to ashes. But the King and the Queen with their six brothers lived many years in happiness and peace.

24 Snow White

Once upon a time in the middle of winter, when the flakes of snow were falling like feathers from the sky, a queen sat at a window sewing, and the frame of the window was made of black ebony. And whilst she was sewing and looking out of the window at the snow, she pricked her finger with the needle, and three drops of blood fell upon the snow. And the red looked pretty upon the white snow, and she thought to herself, "Would that I had a child as white as snow, as red as blood, and as black as the wood of the window-frame."

Soon after that she had a little daughter, who was as white as snow, and as red as blood, and her hair was as black as ebony; and she was therefore called Little Snow White. And when the child was born, the Queen died.

After a year had passed the King took to himself another wife. She was a beautiful woman, but proud and haughty, and she could not bear that anyone else should surpass her in beauty. She had a wonderful looking-glass, and when she stood in front of it and looked at herself in it, and said—

> "Looking-glass, Looking-glass, on the wall,
> Who in this land is the fairest of all?"

the looking-glass answered—

> "Thou, O Queen, art the fairest of all!"

Then she was satisfied, for she knew that the looking-glass spoke the truth.

But Snow White was growing up, and grew more and more beautiful; and when she was seven years old she was as beautiful as the day, and more beautiful than the Queen herself. And once when the Queen asked her looking-glass—

> "Looking-glass, Looking-glass, on the wall,
> Who in this land is the fairest of all?"

it answered—

> "Thou art fairer than all who are here, Lady Queen.
> But more beautiful still is Snow White, as I ween."

Then the Queen was shocked, and turned yellow and green with envy. From that hour, whenever she looked at Snow White, her heart heaved in her breast, she hated the girl so much.

And envy and pride grew higher and higher in her heart like a weed, so that she had no peace day or night. She called a huntsman, and said, "Take the child away into the forest; I will no longer have her in my sight. Kill her, and bring me back her heart as a token." The huntsman obeyed, and took her away; but when he had drawn his knife, and was about to pierce Snow White's innocent heart, she began to weep, and said, "Ah dear huntsman, leave me my life! I will run away into the wild forest, and never come home again." And as she was so beautiful the huntsman had pity on her and said, "Run away, then, you poor child."

"The wild beasts will soon have devoured you," thought he, and yet it seemed as if a stone had been rolled from his heart since it was no longer needful for him to kill her. And as a young boar just then came running by he stabbed it, and cut out its heart and took it to the Queen as proof that the child was dead. The cook had to salt this, and the wicked Queen ate it, and thought she had eaten the heart of Snow White.

But now the poor child was all alone in the great forest, and so terrified that she looked at every leaf of every tree, and did not know what to do. Then she began to run, and ran over sharp stones and through thorns, and the wild beasts ran past her, but did her no harm.

She ran as long as her feet would go until it was almost evening; then she saw a little cottage and went into it to rest herself. Everything in the cottage was small, but neater and cleaner than can be told. There was a table on which was a white cover, and seven little plates, and on each plate a little spoon; moreover, there were seven little knives and forks, and seven little mugs. Against the wall stood seven little beds side by side, and covered with snow-white counterpanes.

Little Snow White was so hungry and thirsty that she ate some vegetables and bread from each plate and drank a drop of wine out of each mug, for she did not wish to take all from one only. Then, as she was so tired, she laid herself down on one of the little beds, but none of them suited her; one was too long, another too short, but at last she found that the seventh one was right, and so she remained in it, said a prayer and went to sleep.

When it was quite dark the owners of the cottage came back; they were seven dwarfs who dug and delved in the mountains for ore. They lit their seven candles, and as it was now light within the cottage they saw that someone had been there, for everything was not in the same order in which they had left it.

The first said, "Who has been sitting on my chair?"

The second, "Who has been eating off my plate?"

The third, "Who has been taking some of my bread?"

The fourth, "Who has been eating my vegetables?"

The fifth, "Who has been using my fork?"

The sixth, "Who has been cutting with my knife?"

The seventh, "Who has been drinking out of my mug?"

Then the first looked round and saw that there was a little hole on his bed, and he said, "Who has been getting into my bed?" The others came up and each called out, "Somebody has been lying in my bed too." But the seventh when he looked at his bed saw little Snow White, who was lying asleep therein. And he called the others, who came running up, and they cried out with astonishment, and brought their seven little candles and let the light fall on little Snow White. "Oh, heavens! oh, heavens!" cried they, "what a lovely child!" and they were so glad that they did not wake her up, but let her sleep on in the bed. And the seventh dwarf slept with his companions, one hour with each, and so got through the night.

When it was morning little Snow White awoke, and was frightened when she saw the seven dwarfs. But they were friendly and asked her what her name was. "My name is Snow White," she answered. "How have you come to our house?" said the dwarfs. Then she told them that her step-mother had wished to have her killed, but that the huntsman had spared her life, and that she had run for the whole day, until at last she had found their dwelling. The dwarfs said, "If you will take care of our house, cook, make the beds, wash, sew, and knit, and if you will keep everything neat and clean, you can stay with us and you shall want for nothing."

"Yes," said Snow White, "with all my heart," and she stayed with them. She kept the house in order for them; in the mornings they went to the mountains and looked for copper and gold, in the evenings they came back, and then their supper had to be ready. The girl was alone the whole day, so the good dwarfs warned her and said, "Beware of your step-mother, she will soon know that you are here; be sure to let no one come in."

But the Queen, believing that she had eaten Snow White's heart, could not but think that she was again the first and most beautiful of all; and she went to her looking-glass and said—

> "Looking-glass, Looking-glass, on the wall,
> Who in this land is the fairest of all?"

and the glass answered—

> "Oh, Queen, thou art fairest of all I see,
> But over the hills, where the seven dwarfs dwell,
> Snow White is still alive and well,
> And none is so fair as she."

Then she was astounded, for she knew that the looking-glass never spoke falsely, and she knew that the huntsman had betrayed her, and that little Snow White was still alive.

And so she thought and thought again how she might kill

her, for so long as she was not the fairest in the whole land, envy let her have no rest. And when she had at last thought of something to do, she painted her face, and dressed herself like an old pedler-woman, and no one could have known her. In this disguise she went over the seven mountains to the seven dwarfs, and knocked at the door and cried, "Pretty things to sell, very cheap, very cheap." Little Snow White looked out of the window and called out, "Good-day my good woman, what have you to sell?"

"Good things, pretty things," she answered; "stay-laces of all colours," and she pulled out one which was woven of bright-coloured silk. "I may let the worthy old woman in," thought Snow White, and she unbolted the door and bought the pretty laces. "Child," said the old woman, "what a fright you look; come, I will lace you properly for once." Snow White had no suspicion, but stood before her, and let herself be laced with the new laces. But the old woman laced so quickly and so tightly that Snow White lost her breath and fell down as if dead. "Now I am the most beautiful," said the Queen to herself, and ran away.

Not long afterwards, in the evening, the seven dwarfs came home, but how shocked they were when they saw their dear little Snow White lying on the ground, and that she neither stirred nor moved, and seemed to be dead. They lifted her up, and, as they saw that she was laced too tightly, they cut the laces; then she began to breathe a little, and after a while came to life again. When the dwarfs heard what had happened they said, "The old pedler-woman was no one else than the wicked Queen; take care and let no one come in when we are not with you."

But the wicked woman when she had reached home went in front of the glass and asked—

> "Looking-glass, Looking-glass, on the wall,
> Who in this land is the fairest of all?"

and it answered as before—

> "Oh, Queen, thou art fairest of all I see,
> But over the hills, where the seven dwarfs dwell,
> Snow White is still alive and well,
> And none is so fair as she."

When she heard that, all her blood rushed to her heart with fear, for she saw plainly that little Snow White was again alive. "But now," she said, "I will think of something that shall put an end to you," and by the help of witchcraft, which she understood, she made a poisonous comb. Then she disguised herself and took the shape of another old woman. So she went over the seven mountains to the seven dwarfs, knocked at the door, and cried, "Good things to sell, cheap, cheap!" Little Snow White looked out and said, "Go away; I cannot let any one come in."

"I suppose you can look," said the old woman, and pulled the poisonous comb out and held it up. It pleased the girl so well that she let herself be beguiled, and opened the door. When they had made a bargain the old woman said, "Now I will comb you properly for once." Poor little Snow White had no suspicion, and let the old woman do as she pleased, but hardly had she put the comb in her hair than the poison in it took effect, and the girl fell down senseless. "You paragon of beauty," said the wicked woman, "you are done for now," and she went away.

But fortunately it was almost evening, when the seven dwarfs came home. When they saw Snow White lying as if dead upon the ground they at once suspected the step-mother, and they looked and found the poisoned comb. Scarcely had they taken it out when Snow White came to herself, and told them what had happened. Then they warned her once more to be upon her guard and to open the door to no one.

The Queen, at home, went in front of the glass and said—

> "Looking-glass, Looking-glass, on the wall,
> Who in this land is the fairest of all?"

then it answered as before—

> "Oh, Queen, thou art fairest of all I see,
> But over the hills, where the seven dwarfs dwell,
> Snow White is still alive and well,
> And none is so fair as she."

When she heard the glass speak thus she trembled and shook with rage. "Snow White shall die," she cried, "even if it costs me my life!"

Thereupon she went into a quite secret, lonely room, where no one ever came, and there she made a very poisonous apple. Outside it looked pretty, white with a red cheek, so that everyone who saw it longed for it; but whoever ate a piece of it must surely die.

When the apple was ready she painted her face, and dressed herself up as a country-woman, and so she went over the seven mountains to the seven dwarfs. She knocked at the door. Snow White put her head out of the window and said, "I cannot let any one in; the seven dwarfs have forbidden me."

"It is all the same to me," answered the woman, "I shall soon get rid of my apples. There, I will give you one."

"No," said Snow White, "I dare not take anything."

"Are you afraid of poison?" said the old woman; "look, I will cut the apple in two pieces; you eat the red cheek, and I will eat the white." The apple was so cunningly made that only the red cheek was poisoned. Snow White longed for the fine apple, and when she saw that the woman ate part of it she could resist no longer, and stretched out her hand and took the poisonous half. But hardly had she a bit of it in her mouth than she fell down dead. Then the Queen looked at her with a dreadful look, and laughed aloud and said, "White as snow, red as blood, black as ebony-wood! this time the dwarfs cannot wake you up again."

And when she asked of the Looking-glass at home—

> "Looking-glass, Looking-glass, on the wall,
> Who in this land is the fairest of all?"

it answered at last—

> "Oh, Queen, in this land thou art fairest of all."

Then her envious heart had rest, so far as an envious heart can have rest.

The dwarfs, when they came home in the evening, found Snow White lying upon the ground; she breathed no longer and was dead. They lifted her up, looked to see whether they could find anything poisonous, unlaced her, combed her hair, washed her with water and wine, but it was all of no use; the poor child was dead, and remained dead. They laid her upon a bier, and all seven of them sat round it and wept for her, and wept three days long.

Then they were going to bury her, but she still looked as if she were living, and still had her pretty red cheeks. They said, "We could not bury her in the dark ground," and they had a transparent coffin of glass made, so that she could be seen from all sides, and they laid her in it, and wrote her name upon it in golden letters, and that she was a king's daughter. Then they put the coffin out upon the mountain, and one of them always stayed by it and watched it. And birds came too, and wept for Snow

White; first an owl, then a raven, and last a dove.

And now Snow White lay a long, long time in the coffin, and she did not change, but looked as if she were asleep; for she was as white as snow, as red as blood, and her hair was as black as ebony.

It happened, however, that a king's son came into the forest, and went to the dwarfs' house to spend the night. He saw the coffin on the mountain, and the beautiful Snow White within it, and read what was written upon it in golden letters. Then he said to the dwarfs, "Let me have the coffin, I will give you whatever you want for it." But the dwarfs answered, "We will not part with it for all the gold in the world." Then he said, "Let me have it as a gift, for I cannot live without seeing Snow White. I will honour and prize her as my dearest possession." As he spoke in this way the good dwarfs took pity upon him, and gave him the coffin.

And now the King's son had it carried away by his servants on their shoulders. And it happened that they stumbled over a tree-stump, and with the shock the poisonous piece of apple which Snow White had bitten off came out of her throat. And before long she opened her eyes, lifted up the lid of the coffin, sat up, and was once more alive. "Oh, heavens, where am I?" she cried. The King's son, full of joy, said, "You are with me," and told her what had happened, and said, "I love you more than everything in the world; come with me to my father's palace, you shall be my wife."

And Snow White was willing, and went with him, and their wedding was held with great show and splendour. But Snow White's wicked step-mother was also bidden to the feast. When she had arrayed herself in beautiful clothes she went before the Looking-glass, and said—

> "Looking-glass, Looking-glass, on the wall,
> Who in this land is the fairest of all?"

the glass answered—

"Oh, Queen, of all here the fairest art thou,
But the young Queen is fairer by far as I trow."

Then the wicked woman uttered a curse, and was so wretched, so utterly wretched, that she knew not what to do. At first she would not go to the wedding at all, but she had no peace, and must go to see the young Queen. And when she went in she knew Snow White; and she stood still with rage and fear, and could not stir. But iron slippers had already been put upon the fire, and they were brought in with tongs, and set before her. Then she was forced to put on the red-hot shoes, and dance until she dropped down dead.

25 Rumpelstiltskin

Once there was a miller who was poor, but who had a beautiful daughter. Now it happened that he had to go and speak to the King, and in order to make himself appear important he said to him, "I have a daughter who can spin straw into gold." The King said to the miller, "That is an art which pleases me well; if your daughter is as clever as you say, bring her tomorrow to my palace, and I will try what she can do."

And when the girl was brought to him he took her into a room which was quite full of straw, gave her a spinning-wheel and a reel, and said, "Now set to work, and if by tomorrow morning early you have not spun this straw into gold during the night, you must die." Thereupon he himself locked up the room, and left her in it alone. So there sat the poor miller's daughter, and for the life of her could not tell what to do; she had no idea how straw could be spun into gold, and she grew more and more miserable, until at last she began to weep.

But all at once the door opened, and in came a little man, and said, "Good evening, Mistress Miller; why are you crying so?"

"Alas!" answered the girl, "I have to spin straw into gold, and I do not know how to do it."

"What will you give me," said the manikin, "if I do it for you?"

"My necklace," said the girl. The little man took the necklace, seated himself in front of the wheel, and "whirr, whirr, whirr," three turns, and the reel was full; then he put another on, and whirr, whirr, whirr, three times round, and the second was full too. And so it went on until the morning, when all the straw was spun, and all the reels were full of gold. By daybreak the King was already there, and when he saw the gold he was astonished and delighted, but his heart became only more greedy. He had the miller's daughter taken into another room full of straw,

127

which was much larger, and commanded her to spin that also in one night if she valued her life. The girl knew not how to help herself, and was crying, when the door again opened, and the little man appeared, and said, "What will you give me if I spin that straw into gold for you?"

"The ring on my finger," answered the girl. The little man took the ring, again began to turn the wheel, and by morning had spun all the straw into glittering gold.

The King rejoiced beyond measure at the sight, but still he had not gold enough; and he had the miller's daughter taken into a still larger room full of straw, and said, "You must spin this, too, in the course of this night; but if you succeed, you shall be my wife."

"Even if she be a miller's daughter," thought he, "I could not find a richer wife in the whole world."

When the girl was alone the manikin came again for the third time, and said, "What will you give me if I spin the straw for you this time also?"

"I have nothing left that I could give," answered the girl. "Then promise me, if you should become Queen, your first child."

"Who knows whether that will ever happen?" thought the miller's daughter; and, not knowing how else to help herself in this strait, she promised the manikin what he wanted, and for that he once more span the straw into gold.

And when the King came in the morning, and found all as he had wished, he took her in marriage, and the pretty miller's daughter became a Queen.

A year after, she had a beautiful child, and she never gave a thought to the manikin. But suddenly he came into her room, and said, "Now give me what you promised." The Queen was horror-struck, and offered the manikin all the riches of the kingdom if he would leave her the child. But the manikin said, "No, something that is living is dearer to me than all the treasures in the world." Then the Queen began to weep and cry, so that the manikin pitied her. "I will give you three days' time," said he, "if by that time you find out my name, then shall you keep your child."

So the Queen thought the whole night of all the names that she had ever heard, and she sent a messenger over the country to inquire, far and wide, for any other names that there might be. When the manikin came the next day, she began with Caspar, Melchior, Balthazar, and said all the names she knew, one after another; but to every one the little man said, "That is not my name." On the second day she had inquiries made in the neighbourhood as to the names of the people there, and she repeated to the manikin the most uncommon and curious. "Perhaps your name is Shortribs, or Sheepshanks, or Laceleg?" but he always answered, "That is not my name."

On the third day the messenger came back again, and said, "I have not been able to find a single new name, but as I came to a high mountain at the end of the forest, where the fox and the hare bid each other good night, there I saw a little house, and before the house a fire was burning, and round about the fire quite a ridiculous little man was jumping: he hopped upon onc leg, and shouted—

> "Today I bake, tomorrow brew,
> The next I'll have the young Queen's child.
> Ha! glad am I that no one knew
> That Rumpelstiltskin I am styled."

You may think how glad the Queen was when she heard the name! And when soon afterwards the little man came in, and asked, "Now, Mistress Queen, what is my name?" at first she said, "Is your name Conrad?"

"No."

"Is your name Harry?"

"No."

"Perhaps your name is Rumpelstiltskin?"

"The devil has told you that! the devil has told you that!" cried the little man, and in his anger he plunged his right foot so deep into the earth that his whole leg went in; and then in rage he pulled at his right leg so hard with both hands that he tore himself in two.

25 Clever Hans

The mother of Hans said, "Whither away, Hans?" Hans answered, "To Gretel."

"Behave well, Hans."

"Oh, I'll behave well. Good-bye, mother."

"Good-bye, Hans." Hans comes to Gretel, "Good day, Gretel."

"Good day, Hans. What dost thou bring that is good?"

"I bring nothing, I want to have something given me." Gretel presents Hans with a needle. Hans says, "Good-bye, Gretel."

"Good-bye, Hans."

Hans takes the needle, sticks it into a hay-cart, and follows the cart home. "Good evening, mother."

"Good evening, Hans. Where hast thou been?"

"With Gretel."

"What didst thou take from her?"

"Took nothing; had something given me."

"What did Gretel give thee?"

"Gave me a needle."

"Where is the needle, Hans?"

"Stuck it in the hay-cart."

"That was ill done, Hans. Thou shouldst have stuck the needle in thy sleeve."

"Never mind, I'll do better next time."

"Whither away, Hans?"

"To Gretel, mother."

"Behave well, Hans."

"Oh, I'll behave well. Good-bye, mother."

"Good-bye, Hans."

Hans comes to Gretel. "Good day, Gretel."

"Good day, Hans. What dost thou bring that is good?"

"I bring nothing; I want to have something given to me."

Gretel presents Hans with a knife. "Good-bye, Gretel."

"Good-bye Hans." Hans takes the knife, sticks it in his sleeve, and goes home. "Good evening, mother."

"Good evening, Hans. Where hast thou been?"

"With Gretel."

"What didst thou take from her?"

"Took nothing, she gave me something."

"What did Gretel give thee?"

"Gave me a knife."

"Where is the knife, Hans?"

"Stuck in my sleeve."

"That's ill done, Hans, thou shouldst have put the knife in thy pocket."

"Never mind, will do better next time."

"Whither away, Hans?"

"To Gretel, mother. "

"Behave well, Hans."

"Oh, I'll behave well. Good-bye, mother."

"Good-bye, Hans."

Hans comes to Gretel. "Good day, Gretel."

"Good day, Hans. What good thing dost thou bring?"

"I bring nothing, I want something given me." Gretel presents Hans with a young goat. "Good-bye, Gretel."

"Good-bye, Hans." Hans takes the goat, ties its legs, and puts it in his pocket. When he gets home it is suffocated. "Good evening, mother."

"Good evening, Hans. Where hast thou been?"

"With Gretel."

"What didst thou take from her?"

"Took nothing, she gave me something."

"What did Gretel give thee?"

"She gave me a goat."

"Where is the goat, Hans?"

"Put it in my pocket."

"That was ill done, Hans, thou shouldst have put a rope

round the goat's neck."

"Never mind, will do better next time."

"Whither away, Hans,?"

"To Gretel, mother."

"Behave well, Hans."

"Oh, I'll behave well. Good-bye, mother."

"Good-bye, Hans." Hans comes to Gretel. "Good day, Gretel."

"Good day, Hans. What good thing dost thou bring?"

"I bring nothing, I want something given me." Gretel presents Hans with a piece of bacon. "Good-bye, Gretel."

"Good-bye, Hans."

Hans takes the bacon, ties it to a rope, and drags it away behind him. The dogs come and devour the bacon. When he gets home, he has the rope in his hand, and there is no longer anything hanging to it. "Good evening, mother."

"Good evening, Hans."

"Where hast thou been?"

"With Gretel." What didst thou take from her?"

"I took nothing, she gave me something."

"What did Gretel give thee?"

"Gave me a bit of bacon."

"Where is the bacon, Hans?"

"I tied it to a rope, brought it home, dogs took it."

"That was ill done, Hans, thou shouldst have carried the bacon on thy head."

"Never mind, will do better next time."

"Whither away, Hans?"

"To Gretel, mother."

"Behave well, Hans."

"I'll behave well. Good-bye, mother."

"Good-bye, Hans."

Hans comes to Gretel. "Good day, Gretel."

"Good day, Hans."

"What good thing dost thou bring?"

"I bring nothing, but would have something given." Gretel presents Hans with a calf. "Good-bye, Gretel."

"Good-bye, Hans."

Hans takes the calf, puts it on his head, and the calf kicks his face. Good evening, mother."

"Good evening, Hans. Where hast thou been?"

"With Gretel."

"What didst thou take from her?"

"I took nothing, but had something given me."

"What did Gretel give thee?"

"A calf."

"Where hast thou the calf, Hans?"

"I set it on my head and it kicked my face."

"That was ill done, Hans, thou shouldst have led the calf, and put it in the stall."

"Never mind, will do better next time."

"Whither away, Hans?"

"To Gretel, mother."

"Behave well, Hans."

"I'll behave well. Good-bye, mother."

"Good-bye, Hans."

Hans comes to Gretel. "Good day, Gretel."

"Good day, Hans. What good thing dost thou bring?"

"I bring nothing, but would have something given." Gretel says to Hans, "I will go with thee."

Hans takes Gretel, ties her to a rope, leads her to the rack and binds her fast. Then Hans goes to his mother. "Good evening, mother."

"Good evening, Hans. Where hast thou been?"

"With Gretel."

"What didst thou take from her?"

"I took nothing."

"What did Gretel give thee?"

"She gave me nothing, she came with me."

"Where hast thou left Gretel?"

"I led her by the rope, tied her to the rack, and scattered some grass for her."

"That was ill done, Hans, thou shouldst have cast friendly eyes on her."

"Never mind, will do better."

Hans went into the stable, cut out all the calves', and sheep's eyes, and threw them in Gretel's face. Then Gretel became angry, tore herself loose and ran away, and that is how Hans lost his bride.

27 Clever Elsie

There was once a man who had a daughter who was called Clever Elsie. And when she had grown up her father said, "We will get her married."

"Yes," said the mother, "if only any one would come who would have her." At length a man came from a distance and wooed her, who was called Hans; but he stipulated that Clever Elsie should be really wise. "Oh," said the father, "she's sharp enough;" and the mother said, "Oh, she can see the wind coming up the street, and hear the flies coughing."

"Well," said Hans, "if she is not really wise, I won't have her." When they were sitting at dinner and had eaten, the mother said, "Elsie, go into the cellar and fetch some beer." Then Clever Elsie took the pitcher from the wall, went into the cellar, and tapped the lid briskly as she went, so that the time might not appear long. When she was below she fetched herself a chair, and set it before the barrel so that she had no need to stoop, and did not hurt her back or do herself any unexpected injury. Then she placed the can before her, and turned the tap, and while the beer was running she would not let her eyes be idle, but looked up at the wall, and after much peering here and there, saw a pick-axe exactly above her, which the masons had accidentally left there.

Then Clever Elsie began to weep, and said, "If I get Hans, and we have a child, and he grows big, and we send him into the cellar here to draw beer, then the pick-axe will fall on his head and kill him." Then she sat and wept and screamed with all the strength of her body, over the misfortune which lay before her. Those upstairs waited for the drink, but Clever Elsie still did not come. Then the woman said to the servant, "Just go down into the cellar and see where Elsie is." The maid went and found her sitting in front of the barrel, screaming loudly. "Elsie, why weepest thou?" asked the maid. "Ah," she answered, "have I not reason to weep? If I get Hans, and we have a child, and he grows big, and has to draw beer here, the pick-axe will perhaps fall on his head, and kill him." Then said the maid, "What a clever Elsie we have!" and sat down beside her and began loudly to weep over the misfortune. After a while, as the maid did not come back, those upstairs were thirsty for the beer, the man said to the boy, "Just go down into the cellar and see where Elsie and the girl are." The boy went down, and there sat Clever Elsie and the girl both weeping together. Then he asked, "Why are ye weeping?"

"Ah," said Elsie, "have I not reason to weep? If I get Hans, and we have a child, and he grows big, and has to draw beer here, the pick-axe will fall on his head and kill him." Then said the boy, "What a clever Elsie we have!" and sat down by her, and likewise began to howl loudly. Upstairs they waited for the boy, but as he still did not return, the man said to the woman, "Just go down into the cellar and see where Elsie is!" The woman went down, and found all three in the midst of their lamentations, and inquired what was the cause; then Elsie told her also that her future child was to be killed by the pick-axe, when it grew big and had to draw beer, and the pick-axe fell down. Then said the mother likewise, "What a clever Elsie we have!" and sat down and wept with them. The man upstairs waited a short time, but as his wife did not come back and his thirst grew ever greater, he said, "I must go into the cellar myself and see where Elsie is." But when he got into the cellar, and they were all sitting together crying, and he heard the reason, and that Elsie's child was the cause, and that Elsie might perhaps bring one into the world some day, and that it might be killed by the pick-axe, if it should happen to be sitting beneath it, drawing beer just at the very time when it fell down, he cried, "Oh, what a clever Elsie!" and sat down, and likewise wept with them. The bridegroom stayed upstairs alone for a long time; then as no one would come back he thought, "They must be waiting for me

below; I too must go there and see what they are about." When
he got down, five of them were sitting screaming and lamenting
quite piteously, each out-doing the other. "What misfortune has
happened then?" he asked. "Ah, dear Hans," said Elsie, "if we
marry each other and have a child, and he is big, and we perhaps
send him here to draw something to drink, then the pick-axe
which has been left up there might dash his brains out if it were
to fall down, so have we not reason to weep?"

"Come," said Hans, "more understanding than that is not
needed for my household, as thou art such a clever Elsie, I will
have thee," and he seized her hand, took her upstairs with him,
and married her.

After Hans had had her some time, he said, "Wife, I am
going out to work and earn some money for us; go into the field
and cut the corn that we may have some bread."

"Yes, dear Hans, I will do that." After Hans had gone away,
she cooked herself some good broth and took it into the field
with her. When she came to the field she said to herself, "What
shall I do; shall I shear first, or shall I eat first? Oh, I will eat
first." Then she emptied her basin of broth, and when she was
fully satisfied, she once more said, "What shall I do? Shall I
shear first, or shall I sleep first? I will sleep first." Then she lay
down among the corn and fell asleep. Hans had been at home
for a long time, but Elsie did not come; then said he, "What a
clever Elsie I have; she is so industrious that she does not even
come home to eat." As, however, she still stayed away, and it was
evening, Hans went out to see what she had cut, but nothing was
cut, and she was lying among the corn asleep. Then Hans hastened home and brought a fowler's net with little bells and hung
it round about her, and she still went on sleeping. Then he ran
home, shut the house-door, and sat down in his chair and
worked. At length, when it was quite dark, Clever Elsie awoke
and when she got up there was a jingling all round about her,
and the bells rang at each step which she took. Then she was
alarmed, and became uncertain whether she really was Clever

Elsie or not, and said, "Is it I, or is it not I?" But she knew not what answer to make to this, and stood for a time in doubt; at length she thought, "I will go home and ask if it be I, or if it be not I, they will be sure to know." She ran to the door of her own house, but it was shut; then she knocked at the window and cried, "Hans, is Elsie within?"

"Yes," answered Hans, "she is within." Hereupon she was terrified, and said, "Ah, heavens! Then it is not I," and went to another door; but when the people heard the jingling of the bells they would not open it, and she could get in nowhere. Then she ran out of the village, and no one has seen her since.

28 The Wedding of Mrs. Fox

There was once upon a time an old fox with nine tails, who believed that his wife was not faithful to him, and wished to try her. He stretched himself out under the bench, did not move a limb, and behaved as if he were stone dead. Mrs. Fox went up to her room, shut herself in, and her maid, Miss Cat, sat by the fire, and did the cooking. When it became known that the old fox was dead, wooers presented themselves. The maid heard some one standing at the house-door, knocking. She went and opened it, and it was a young fox, who said:

> "What may you be about, Miss Cat?
> Do you sleep or do you wake?"

She answered:

> "I am not sleeping, I am waking,
> Wouldst thou know what I am making?
> I am boiling warm beer with butter so nice,
> Will the gentleman enter and drink some likewise?"

"No, thank you, miss," said the fox, "what is Mrs. Fox doing?" The maid replied:

> "She sits all alone,
> And makes her moan,
> Weeping her little eyes quite red,
> Because old Mr. Fox is dead."

"Do just tell her, miss, that a young fox is here, who would like to woo her."
"Certainly, young sir."

> The cat goes up the stairs trip, trap,
> The door she knocks at tap, tap, tap,
> "Mistress Fox, are you inside?"

"Oh yes, my little cat," she cried.
"A wooer he stands at the door out there."
"Tell me what he is like, my dear?"

"But has he nine as beautiful tails as the late Mr. Fox?"

"Oh, no," answered the cat, "he has only one."

"Then I will not have him." Miss Cat went downstairs and sent the wooer away. Soon afterwards there was another knock, and another fox was at the door who wished to woo Mrs. Fox. He had two tails, but he did not fare better than the first. After this still more came, each with one tail more than the other, but they were all turned away, until at last one came who had nine tails, like old Mr. Fox. When the widow heard that, she said joyfully to the cat:

"Now open the gates and doors all wide, And carry old Mr. Fox outside."

But just as the wedding was going to be solemnised, old Mr. Fox stirred under the bench, and cudgelled all the rabble, and drove them and Mrs. Fox out of the house.

SECOND STORY

When old Mr. Fox was dead, the wolf came as a wooer, and knocked at the door, and the cat who was servant to Mrs. Fox, opened it for him. The wolf greeted her, and said:

"Good day, Mrs. Cat of Kehrewit,
How comes it that alone you sit?"

What are you making good?"
The cat replied:

"In milk I'm breaking bread so sweet,
Will the gentleman please come in and eat?"

"No, thank you, Mrs. Cat," answered the wolf. "Is Mrs. Fox not at home?"

The cat said:

"She sits upstairs in her room,
Bewailing her sorrowful doom,
Bewailing her trouble so sore,
For old Mr. Fox is no more."

The wolf answered:

"If she's in want of a husband now,
Then will it please her to step below?"
The cat runs quickly up the stair,
And lets her tail fly here and there,
Until she comes to the parlour door.
With her five gold rings at the door she knocks,
"Are you within, good Mistress Fox?
If you're in want of a husband now,
Then will it please you to step below?"

Mrs. Fox asked, "Has the gentleman red stockings on and has he a pointed mouth?"

"No," answered the cat. "Then he won't do for me."

When the wolf was gone, came a dog, a stag, a hare, a bear, a lion, and all the beasts of the forest, one after the other. But one of the good points which old Mr. Fox had possessed, was always lacking, and the cat had continually to send the wooers away. At length came a young fox. Then Mrs. Fox said, "Has the gentleman red stockings on, and has he a little pointed mouth?"

"Yes," said the cat, "he has."

"Then let him come upstairs," said Mrs. Fox, and ordered the servant to prepare the wedding-feast.

"Sweep me the room as clean as you can,
Up with the window, fling out my old man?
For many a fine fat mouse he brought,
Yet of his wife he never thought,
But ate up every one he caught."

Then the wedding was solemnised with young Mr. Fox, and there was much rejoicing and dancing; and if they have not left off, they are dancing still.

29 Fitcher's Bird

There was once a wizard who used to take the form of a poor man, and went to houses and begged, and caught pretty girls. No one knew whither he carried them, for they were never seen more. One day he appeared before the door of a man who had three pretty daughters; he looked like a poor weak beggar, and carried a basket on his back, as if he meant to collect charitable gifts in it. He begged for a little food, and when the eldest daughter came out and was just reaching him a piece of bread, he did but touch her, and she was forced to jump into his basket. Thereupon he hurried away with long strides, and carried her away into a dark forest to his house, which stood in the midst of it. Everything in the house was magnificent; he gave her whatsoever she could possibly desire, and said, "My darling, thou wilt certainly be happy with me, for thou hast everything thy heart can wish for." This lasted a few days, and then he said, "I must journey forth, and leave thee alone for a short time; there are the keys of the house; thou mayst go everywhere and look at everything except into one room, which this little key here opens, and there I forbid thee to go on pain of death." He likewise gave her an egg and said, "Preserve the egg carefully for me, and carry it continually about with thee, for a great misfortune would arise from the loss of it."

She took the keys and the egg, and promised to obey him in everything. When he was gone, she went all round the house from the bottom to the top, and examined everything. The rooms shone with silver and gold, and she thought she had never seen such great splendour. At length she came to the forbidden door; she wished to pass it by, but curiosity let her have no rest. She examined the key, it looked just like any other; she put it in the keyhole and turned it a little, and the door sprang open. But what did she see when she went in? A great bloody basin stood in the middle of the room, and therein lay human beings, dead and hewn to pieces, and hard by was a block of wood, and a gleaming axe lay upon it. She was so terribly alarmed that the egg which she held in her hand fell into the basin. She got it out and washed the blood off, but in vain, it appeared again in a moment. She washed and scrubbed, but she could not get it out.

It was not long before the man came back from his journey, and the first things which he asked for were the key and the egg. She gave them to him, but she trembled as she did so, and he saw at once by the red spots that she had been in the bloody chamber. "Since thou hast gone into the room against my will," said he, "thou shalt go back into it against thine own. Thy life is ended." He threw her down, dragged her thither by her hair, cut her head off on the block, and hewed her in pieces so that her blood ran on the ground. Then he threw her into the basin with the rest.

"Now I will fetch myself the second," said the wizard, and again he went to the house in the shape of a poor man, and begged. Then the second daughter brought him a piece of bread; he caught her like the first, by simply touching her, and carried her away. She did not fare better than her sister. She allowed herself to be led away by her curiosity, opened the door of the bloody chamber, looked in, and had to atone for it with her life on the wizard's return. Then he went and brought the third sister, but she was clever and crafty. When he had given her the keys and the egg, and had left her, she first put the egg away with great care, and then she examined the house, and at last went into the forbidden room. Alas, what did she behold! Both her sisters lay there in the basin, cruelly murdered, and cut in pieces. But she began to gather their limbs together and put them in order, head, body, arms and legs. And when nothing further was wanting the limbs began to move and unite themselves together, and both the maidens opened their eyes and were once more alive. Then they rejoiced and kissed and caressed each other.

On his arrival, the man at once demanded the keys and the egg, and as he could perceive no trace of any blood on it, he said, "Thou hast stood the test, thou shalt be my bride." He now had no longer any power over her, and was forced to do whatsoever she desired. "Oh, very well," said she, "thou shalt first take a basketful of gold to my father and mother, and carry it thyself on thy back; in the meantime I will prepare for the wedding." Then she ran to her sisters, whom she had hidden in a little chamber, and said, "The moment has come when I can save you. The wretch shall himself carry you home again, but as soon as you are at home send help to me." She put both of them in a basket and covered them quite over with gold, so that nothing of them was to be seen, then she called in the wizard and said to him, "Now carry the basket away, but I shall look through my little window and watch to see if thou stoppest on the way to stand or to rest."

The wizard raised the basket on his back and went away with it, but it weighed him down so heavily that the perspiration streamed from his face. Then he sat down and wanted to rest awhile, but immediately one of the girls in the basket cried, "I am looking through my little window, and I see that thou art resting. Wilt thou go on at once?" He thought it was his bride who was calling that to him; and got up on his legs again. Once more he was going to sit down, but instantly she cried, "I am looking through my little window, and I see that thou art resting. Wilt thou go on directly?" And whenever he stood still, she cried this, and then he was forced to go onwards, until at last, groaning and out of breath, he took the basket with the gold and the two maidens into their parents' house. At home, however, the bride prepared the marriage-feast, and sent invitations to the friends of the wizard. Then she took a skull with grinning teeth, put some ornaments on it and a wreath of flowers, carried it upstairs to the garret-window, and let it look out from thence. When all was ready, she got into a barrel of honey, and then cut the feather-bed open and rolled herself in it, until she looked like a wondrous bird, and no one could recognise her. Then she went out of the house, and on her way she met some of the wedding-guests, who asked:

> "O, Fitcher's bird, how com'st thou here?"
> "I come from Fitcher's house quite near."
> "And what may the young bride be doing?"
> "From cellar to garret she's swept all clean,
> And now from the window she's peeping, I ween."

At last she met the bridegroom, who was coming slowly back. He, like the others, asked:

> "O, Fitcher's bird, how com'st thou here?"
> "I come from Fitcher's house quite near."
> "And what may the young bride be doing?
> "From cellar to garret she's swept all clean,
> And now from the window she's peeping, I ween."

The bridegroom looked up, saw the decked-out skull, thought it was his bride, and nodded to her, greeting her kindly. But when he and his guests had all gone into the house, the brothers and kinsmen of the bride, who had been sent to rescue her, arrived. They locked all the doors of the house, that no one might escape, set fire to it, and the wizard and all his crew had to burn.

30 The Juniper Tree

It is now long ago, quite two thousand years, since there was a rich man who had a beautiful and pious wife, and they loved each other dearly. They had, however, no children, though they wished for them very much, and the woman prayed for them day and night, but still they had none. Now there was a courtyard in front of their house in which was a juniper tree, and one day in winter the woman was standing beneath it, paring herself an apple, and while she was paring herself the apple she cut her finger, and the blood fell on the snow. "Ah," said the woman, and sighed right heavily, and looked at the blood before her, and was most unhappy, "ah, if I had but a child as red as blood and as white as snow!" And while she thus spake, she became quite happy in her mind, and felt just as if that were going to happen. Then she went into the house and a month went by and the snow was gone, and two months, and then everything was green, and three months, and then all the flowers came out of the earth, and four months, and then all the trees in the wood grew thicker, and the green branches were all closely entwined, and the birds sang until the wood resounded and the blossoms fell from the trees, then the fifth month passed away and she stood under the juniper tree, which smelt so sweetly that her heart leapt, and she fell on her knees and was beside herself with joy, and when the sixth month was over the fruit was large and fine, and then she was quite still, and the seventh month she snatched at the juniper-berries and ate them greedily, then she grew sick and sorrowful, then the eighth month passed, and she called her husband to her, and wept and said, "If I die then bury me beneath the juniper tree." Then she was quite comforted and happy until the next month was over, and then she had a child as white as snow and as red as blood, and when she beheld it she was so delighted that she died.

Then her husband buried her beneath the juniper tree, and he began to weep sore; after some time he was more at ease, and though he still wept he could bear it, and after some time longer he took another wife.

By the second wife he had a daughter, but the first wife's child was a little son, and he was as red as blood and as white as snow. When the woman looked at her daughter she loved her very much, but then she looked at the little boy and it seemed to cut her to the heart, for the thought came into her mind that he would always stand in her way, and she was for ever thinking how she could get all the fortune for her daughter, and the Evil One filled her mind with this till she was quite angry with the little boy, and slapped him here and cuffed him there, until the unhappy child was in continual terror, for when he came out of school he had no peace in any place.

One day the woman had gone upstairs to her room, and her little daughter went up too, and said, "Mother, give me an apple."

"Yes, my child," said the woman, and gave her a fine apple out of the chest, but the chest had a great heavy lid with a great sharp iron lock. "Mother," said the little daughter, "is brother not to have one too?" This made the woman angry, but she said, "Yes, when he comes out of school." And when she saw from the window that he was coming, it was just as if the Devil entered into her, and she snatched at the apple and took it away again from her daughter, and said, "Thou shalt not have one before thy brother." Then she threw the apple into the chest, and shut it. Then the little boy came in at the door, and the Devil made her say to him kindly, "My son, wilt thou have an apple?" and she looked wickedly at him. "Mother," said the little boy, "how dreadful you look! Yes, give me an apple." Then it seemed to her as if she were forced to say to him, "Come with me," and she opened the lid of the chest and said, "Take out an apple for thyself," and while the little boy was stooping inside, the Devil prompted her, and crash! she shut the lid down, and his head flew off and fell among the red apples. Then she was over-whelmed with terror, and thought, "If I could but make them think that it was not done by me!" So she went upstairs to her room to her chest of drawers, and took a white handkerchief out of the top drawer, and set the head on the neck again, and fold-ed the handkerchief so that nothing could be seen, and she set him on a chair in front of the door, and put the apple in his hand.

After this Marlinchen came into the kitchen to her mother, who was standing by the fire with a pan of hot water before her which she was constantly stirring round. "Mother," said Marlinchen, "brother is sitting at the door, and he looks quite white and has an apple in his hand. I asked him to give me the apple, but he did not answer me, and I was quite frightened."

"Go back to him," said her mother, "and if he will not answer thee, give him a box on the ear." So Marlinchen went to him and said, "Brother, give me the apple." But he was silent, and she gave him a box on the ear, on which his head fell down. Marlinchen was terrified, and began crying and screaming, and ran to her mother, and said, "Alas, mother, I have knocked my brother's head off!" and she wept and wept and could not be comforted. "Marlinchen," said the mother, "what hast thou done? but be quiet and let no one know it; it cannot be helped now, we will make him into black-puddings." Then the mother took the little boy and chopped him in pieces, put him into the pan and made him into black puddings; but Marlinchen stood by weeping and weeping, and all her tears fell into the pan and there was no need of any salt.

Then the father came home, and sat down to dinner and said, "But where is my son?" And the mother served up a great dish of black-puddings, and Marlinchen wept and could not leave off. Then the father again said, "But where is my son?"

"Ah," said the mother, "he has gone across the country to his mother's great uncle; he will stay there awhile."

"And what is he going to do there? He did not even say good-bye to me."

149

"Oh, he wanted to go, and asked me if he might stay six weeks, he is well taken care of there."

"Ah," said the man, "I feel so unhappy lest all should not be right. He ought to have said good-bye to me." With that he began to eat and said, "Marlinchen, why art thou crying? Thy brother will certainly come back." Then he said, "Ah, wife, how delicious this food is, give me some more." And the more he ate the more he wanted to have, and he said, "Give me some more, you shall have none of it. It seems to me as if it were all mine." And he ate and ate and threw all the bones under the table, until he had finished the whole. But Marlinchen went away to her chest of drawers, and took her best silk handkerchief out of the bottom drawer, and got all the bones from beneath the table, and tied them up in her silk handkerchief, and carried them outside the door, weeping tears of blood. Then the juniper tree began to stir itself, and the branches parted asunder, and moved together again, just as if some one was rejoicing and clapping his hands. At the same time a mist seemed to arise from the tree, and in the centre of this mist it burned like a fire, and a beautiful bird flew out of the fire singing magnificently, and he flew high up in the air, and when he was gone, the juniper tree was just as it had been before, and the handkerchief with the bones was no longer there. Marlinchen, however, was as gay and happy as if her brother were still alive. And she went merrily into the house, and sat down to dinner and ate.

But the bird flew away and lighted on a goldsmith's house, and began to sing:

> "My mother she killed me,
> My father he ate me,
> My sister, little Marlinchen,
> Gathered together all my bones,
> Tied them in a silken handkerchief,
> Laid them beneath the juniper tree,
> Kywitt, kywitt, what a beautiful bird am I!"

The goldsmith was sitting in his workshop making a gold

chain, when he heard the bird which was sitting singing on his roof, and very beautiful the song seemed to him. He stood up, but as he crossed the threshold he lost one of his slippers. But he went away right up the middle of the street with one shoe on and one sock; he had his apron on, and in one hand he had the gold chain and in the other the pincers, and the sun was shining brightly on the street. Then he went right on and stood still, and said to the bird, "Bird," said he then, "how beautifully thou canst sing! Sing me that piece again."

"No," said the bird, "I'll not sing it twice for nothing! Give me the golden chain, and then I will sing it again for thee."

"There," said the goldsmith, "there is the golden chain for thee, now sing me that song again." Then the bird came and took the golden chain in his right claw, and went and sat in front of the goldsmith, and sang:

> "My mother she killed me,
> My father he ate me,
> My sister, little Marlinchen,
> Gathered together all my bones,
> Tied them in a silken handkerchief,
> Laid them beneath the juniper tree,
> Kywitt, kywitt, what a beautiful bird am I!"

Then the bird flew away to a shoemaker, and lighted on his roof and sang:

> "My mother she killed me,
> My father he ate me,
> My sister, little Marlinchen,
> Gathered together all my bones,
> Tied them in a silken handkerchief,
> Laid them beneath the juniper tree,
> Kywitt, kywitt, what a beautiful bird am I!"

The shoemaker heard that and ran out of doors in his shirt sleeves, and looked up at his roof, and was forced to hold his hand before his eyes lest the sun should blind him. "Bird," said he, "how beautifully thou canst sing!" Then he called in at his door, "Wife, just come outside, there is a bird, look at that bird, he can sing really well." Then he called his daughter and children, and apprentices, boys and girls, and they all came up the street and looked at the bird and saw how beautiful he was, and what fine red and green feathers he had, and how like real gold his neck was, and how the eyes in his head shone like stars. "Bird," said the shoemaker, "now sing me that song again."

"Nay," said the bird, "I do not sing twice for nothing; thou must give me something."

"Wife," said the man, "go to the garret, upon the top shelf there stands a pair of red shoes, bring them down." Then the wife went and brought the shoes. "There, bird," said the man, "now sing me that piece again." Then the bird came and took the shoes in his left claw, and flew back on the roof, and sang:

> "My mother she killed me,
> My father he ate me,
> My sister, little Marlinchen,
> Gathered together all my bones,
> Tied them in a silken handkerchief,
> Laid them beneath the juniper tree,
> Kywitt, kywitt, what a beautiful bird am I!"

And when he had sung the whole he flew away. In his right claw he had the chain and the shoes in his left, and he flew far away to a mill, and the mill went, "klipp klapp, klipp klapp, klipp klapp," and in the mill sat twenty miller's men hewing a stone, and cutting, hick hack, hick hack, hick hack, and the mill went klipp klapp, klipp klapp, klipp klapp. Then the bird went and sat on a lime-tree which stood in front of the mill, and sang:

"My mother she killed me," Then one of them stopped working:

"My father he ate me."

Then two more stopped working and listened to that:

"My sister, little Marlinchen," Then four more stopped:

"Gathered together all my bones, Tied them in a silken handkerchief," Now eight only were hewing:

"Laid them beneath"

Now only five,

"The juniper tree," And now only one,

"Kywitt, kywitt, what a beautiful bird am I!"

Then the last stopped also, and heard the last words. "Bird," said he, "how beautifully thou singest! Let me, too, hear that. Sing that once more for me."

"Nay," said the bird, "I will not sing twice for nothing. Give me the millstone, and then I will sing it again."

"Yes," said he, "if it belonged to me only, thou shouldst have it."

"Yes," said the others, "if he sings again he shall have it." Then the bird came down, and the twenty millers all set to work with a beam and raised the stone up. And the bird stuck his neck through the hole, and put the stone on as if it were a collar, and flew on to the tree again, and sang,

> "My mother she killed me,
> My father he ate me,
> My sister, little Marlinchen,
> Gathered together all my bones,
> Tied them in a silken handkerchief,
> Laid them beneath the juniper tree,
> Kywitt, kywitt, what a beautiful bird am I!"

And when he had done singing, he spread his wings, and in his right claw he had the chain, and in his left the shoes, and round his neck the millstone, and he flew far away to his father's house.

In the room sat the father, the mother, and Marlinchen at dinner, and the father said, "How light-hearted I feel, how happy I am!"

"Nay," said the mother, "I feel so uneasy, just as if a heavy storm were coming." Marlinchen, however, sat weeping and weeping, and then came the bird flying, and as it seated itself on the roof the father said, "Ah, I feel so truly happy, and the sun is shining so beautifully outside, I feel just as if I were about to see some old friend again."

"Nay," said the woman, "I feel so anxious, my teeth chatter, and I seem to have fire in my veins." And she tore her stays open, but Marlinchen sat in a corner crying, and held her plate before her eyes and cried till it was quite wet. Then the bird sat on the juniper tree, and sang,

"My mother she killed me," Then the mother stopped her ears, and shut her eyes, and would not see or hear, but there was a roaring in her ears like the most violent storm, and her eyes burnt and flashed like lightning,

"My father he ate me," "Ah, mother," says the man, "that is a beautiful bird! He sings so splendidly, and the sun shines so warm, and there is a smell just like cinnamon."

"My sister, little Marlinchen," Then Marlinchen laid her head on her knees and wept without ceasing, but the man said, "I am going out, I must see the bird quite close."

"Oh, don't go," said the woman, "I feel as if the whole house were shaking and on fire." But the man went out and looked at the bird:

"Gathered together all my bones, Tied them in a silken handkerchief, Laid them beneath the juniper tree, Kywitt, kywitt, what a beautiful bird am I!"

On this the bird let the golden chain fall, and it fell exactly round the man's neck, and so exactly round it that it fitted beautifully. Then he went in and said, "Just look what a fine bird that is, and what a handsome gold chain he has given me, and how pretty he is!" But the woman was terrified, and fell down on the floor in the room, and her cap fell off her head. Then sang the bird once more,

"My mother she killed me."

"Would that I were a thousand feet beneath the earth so as not to hear that!"

"My father he ate me,"

Then the woman fell down again as if dead.

"My sister, little Marlinchen,"

"Ah," said Marlinchen, "I too will go out and see if the bird will give me anything," and she went out.

"Gathered together all my bones, Tied them in a silken handkerchief," Then he threw down the shoes to her.

"Laid them beneath the juniper tree, Kywitt, kywitt, what a beautiful bird am I!"

Then she was light-hearted and joyous, and she put on the new red shoes, and danced and leaped into the house. "Ah," said she, "I was so sad when I went out and now I am so light-hearted; that is a splendid bird, he has given me a pair of red shoes!"

"Well," said the woman, and sprang to her feet and her hair stood up like flames of fire, "I feel as if the world were coming to an end! I, too, will go out and see if my heart feels lighter." And as she went out at the door, crash! the bird threw down the millstone on her head, and she was entirely crushed by it. The father and Marlinchen heard what had happened and went out, and smoke, flames, and fire were rising from the place, and when that was over, there stood the little brother, and he took his father and Marlinchen by the hand, and all three were right glad, and they went into the house to dinner, and ate.

31 Old Sultan

A farmer once had a faithful dog called Sultan, who had grown old, and lost all his teeth, so that he could no longer hold anything fast. One day the farmer was standing with his wife before the house-door, and said, "Tomorrow I intend to shoot Old Sultan, he is no longer of any use."

His wife, who felt pity for the faithful beast, answered, "He has served us so long, and been so faithful, that we might well give him his keep."

"Eh! what?" said the man. "You are not very sharp. He has not a tooth left in his mouth, and not a thief is afraid of him; now he may be off. If he has served us, he has had good feeding for it."

The poor dog, who was lying stretched out in the sun not far off, had heard everything, and was sorry that the morrow was to be his last day. He had a good friend, the wolf, and he crept out in the evening into the forest to him, and complained of the fate that awaited him. "Hark ye, gossip," said the wolf, "be of good cheer, I will help you out of your trouble. I have thought of something. Tomorrow, early in the morning, your master is going with his wife to make hay, and they will take their little child with them, for no one will be left behind in the house. They are wont, during work-time, to lay the child under the hedge in the shade; you lay yourself there too, just as if you wished to guard it. Then I will come out of the wood, and carry off the child. You must rush swiftly after me, as if you would seize it again from me. I will let it fall, and you will take it back to its parents, who will think that you have saved it, and will be far too grateful to do you any harm; on the contrary, you will be in high favor, and they will never let you want for anything again."

The plan pleased the dog, and it was carried out just as it was

JACOB AND WILHELM GRIMM

arranged. The father screamed when he saw the Wolf running across the field with his child, but when Old Sultan brought it back, then he was full of joy, and stroked him and said, "Not a hair of yours shall be hurt, you shall eat my bread free as long as you live." And to his wife he said, "Go home at once and make Old Sultan some bread-sop that he will not have to bite, and bring the pillow out of my bed, I will give him that to lie upon."

Henceforth Old Sultan was as well off as he could wish to be.

Soon afterwards the wolf visited him, and was pleased that everything had succeeded so well. "But, gossip," said he, "you will just wink an eye if when I have a chance, I carry off one of your master's fat sheep."

"Do not reckon upon that," answered the dog; "I will remain true to my master; I cannot agree to that." The wolf, who thought that this could not be spoken in earnest, came creeping about in the night and was going to take away the sheep. But the farmer, to whom the faithful Sultan had told the wolf's plan, caught him and dressed his hide soundly with a flail. The wolf had to pack off, but he cried out to the dog, "Wait a bit, you scoundrel, you shall pay for this."

The next morning the wolf sent the boar to challenge the dog to come out into the forest so that they might settle the affair. Old Sultan could find no one to stand by him but a cat with only three legs, and as they went out together the poor cat limped along, and at the same time stretched out her tail into the air with pain.

The wolf and his friend were already on the spot appointed, but when they saw their enemy coming they thought that he was bringing a sabre with him, for they mistook the outstretched tail of the cat for one. And when the poor beast hopped on its three legs, they could only think every time that it was picking up a stone to throw at them. So they were both afraid; the wild boar crept into the under-wood and the wolf jumped up a tree.

The dog and the cat, when they came up, wondered that there was no one to be seen. The wild boar, however, had not been able to hide himself altogether; and one of his ears was still to be seen. Whilst the cat was looking carefully about, the boar moved his ear; the cat, who thought it was a mouse moving there, jumped upon it and bit it hard. The boar made a fearful noise and ran away, crying out, "The guilty one is up in the tree." The dog and cat looked up and saw the wolf, who was ashamed of having shown himself so timid, and made friends with the dog.

31 Briar-Rose

A long time ago there were a King and Queen who said every day, "Ah, if only we had a child!" but they never had one. But it happened that once when the Queen was bathing, a frog crept out of the water on to the land, and said to her, "Your wish shall be fulfilled; before a year has gone by, you shall have a daughter."

What the frog had said came true, and the Queen had a little girl who was so pretty that the King could not contain himself for joy, and ordered a great feast. He invited not only his kindred, friends and acquaintance, but also the Wise Women, in order that they might be kind and well-disposed towards the child. There were thirteen of them in his kingdom, but, as he had only twelve golden plates for them to eat out of, one of them had to be left at home.

The feast was held with all manner of splendour and when it came to an end the Wise Women bestowed their magic gifts upon the baby: one gave virtue, another beauty, a third riches, and so on with everything in the world that one can wish for.

When eleven of them had made their promises, suddenly the thirteenth came in. She wished to avenge herself for not having been invited, and without greeting, or even looking at any one, she cried with a loud voice, "The King's daughter shall in her fifteenth year prick herself with a spindle, and fall down dead." And, without saying a word more, she turned round and left the room.

They were all shocked; but the twelfth, whose good wish still remained unspoken, came forward, and as she could not undo the evil sentence, but only soften it, she said, "It shall not be death, but a deep sleep of a hundred years, into which the princess shall fall."

The King, who would fain keep his dear child from the misfortune, gave orders that every spindle in the whole kingdom should be burnt. Meanwhile the gifts of the Wise Women were plenteously fulfilled on the young girl, for she was so beautiful, modest, good-natured, and wise, that everyone who saw her was bound to love her.

It happened that on the very day when she was fifteen years old, the King and Queen were not at home, and the maiden was left in the palace quite alone. So she went round into all sorts of places, looked into rooms and bed-chambers just as she liked, and at last came to an old tower. She climbed up the narrow winding-staircase, and reached a little door. A rusty key was in the lock, and when she turned it the door sprang open, and there in a little room sat an old woman with a spindle, busily spinning her flax.

"Good day, old dame," said the King's daughter; "what are you doing there?"

"I am spinning," said the old woman, and nodded her head. "What sort of thing is that, that rattles round so merrily?" said the girl, and she took the spindle and wanted to spin too. But scarcely had she touched the spindle when the magic decree was fulfilled, and she pricked her finger with it.

And, in the very moment when she felt the prick, she fell down upon the bed that stood there, and lay in a deep sleep. And this sleep extended over the whole palace; the King and Queen who had just come home, and had entered the great hall, began to go to sleep, and the whole of the court with them. The horses, too, went to sleep in the stable, the dogs in the yard, the pigeons upon the roof, the flies on the wall; even the fire that was flaming on the hearth became quiet and slept, the roast meat left off frizzling, and the cook, who was just going to pull the hair of the scullery boy, because he had forgotten something, let him go, and went to sleep. And the wind fell, and on the trees before the castle not a leaf moved again.

But round about the castle there began to grow a hedge of thorns, which every year became higher, and at last grew close up round the castle and all over it, so that there was nothing of it to be seen, not even the flag upon the roof. But the story of the beautiful sleeping "Briar-rose," for so the princess was named, went about the country, so that from time to time kings' sons came and tried to get through the thorny hedge into the castle.

But they found it impossible, for the thorns held fast together, as if they had hands, and the youths were caught in them, could not get loose again, and died a miserable death.

After long, long years a King's son came again to that country, and heard an old man talking about the thorn-hedge, and that a castle was said to stand behind it in which a wonderfully beautiful princess, named Briar-rose, had been asleep for a hundred years; and that the King and Queen and the whole court were asleep likewise. He had heard, too, from his grandfather, that many kings' sons had already come, and had tried to get through the thorny hedge, but they had remained sticking fast in it, and had died a pitiful death. Then the youth said, "I am not afraid, I will go and see the beautiful Briar-rose." The good old man might dissuade him as he would, he did not listen to his words.

But by this time the hundred years had just passed, and the day had come when Briar-rose was to awake again. When the King's son came near to the thorn-hedge, it was nothing but large and beautiful flowers, which parted from each other of their own accord, and let him pass unhurt, then they closed again behind him like a hedge. In the castle-yard he saw the horses and the spotted hounds lying asleep; on the roof sat the pigeons with their heads under their wings. And when he entered the house, the flies were asleep upon the wall, the cook in the kitchen was still holding out his hand to seize the boy, and the maid was sitting by the black hen which she was going to pluck.

He went on farther, and in the great hall he saw the whole of the court lying asleep, and up by the throne lay the King and Queen.

Then he went on still farther, and all was so quiet that a breath could be heard, and at last he came to the tower, and opened the door into the little room where Briar-rose was sleeping. There she lay, so beautiful that he could not turn his eyes away; and he stooped down and gave her a kiss. But as soon as he kissed her, Briar-rose opened her eyes and awoke, and looked at him quite sweetly.

Then they went down together, and the King awoke, and the Queen, and the whole court, and looked at each other in great astonishment. And the horses in the court-yard stood up and shook themselves; the hounds jumped up and wagged their tails; the pigeons upon the roof pulled out their heads from under their wings, looked round, and flew into the open country; the flies on the wall crept again; the fire in the kitchen burned up and flickered and cooked the meat; the joint began to turn and frizzle again, and the cook gave the boy such a box on the ear that he screamed, and the maid plucked the fowl ready for the spit.

And then the marriage of the King's son with Briar-rose was celebrated with all splendour, and they lived contented to the end of their days.

33 Fundevogel (Bird-foundling)

There was once a forester who went into the forest to hunt, and as he entered it he heard a sound of screaming as if a little child were there. He followed the sound, and at last came to a high tree, and at the top of this a little child was sitting, for the mother had fallen asleep under the tree with the child, and a bird of prey had seen it in her arms, had flown down, snatched it away, and set it on the high tree.

The forester climbed up, brought the child down, and thought to himself, "Thou wilt take him home with thee, and bring him up with thy Lina." He took it home, therefore, and the two children grew up together. The one, however, which he had found on a tree was called Fundevogel, because a bird had carried it away. Fundevogel and Lina loved each other so dearly that when they did not see each other they were sad.

The forester, however, had an old cook, who one evening took two pails and began to fetch water, and did not go once only, but many times, out to the spring. Lina saw this and said, "Hark you, old Sanna, why are you fetching so much water?"

"If thou wilt never repeat it to anyone, I will tell thee why." So Lina said, no, she would never repeat it to anyone, and then the cook said, "Early tomorrow morning, when the forester is out hunting, I will heat the water, and when it is boiling in the kettle, I will throw in Fundevogel, and will boil him in it."

Betimes next morning the forester got up and went out hunting, and when he was gone the children were still in bed. Then Lina said to Fundevogel, "If thou wilt never leave me, I too will never leave thee." Fundevogel said, "Neither now, nor ever will I leave thee." Then said Lina, "Then I will tell thee. Last night, old Sanna carried so many buckets of water into the house that I asked her why she was doing that, and she said that if I would promise not to tell any one she would tell me, and I said I would be sure not to tell any one, and she said that early tomorrow morning when father was out hunting, she would set the kettle full of water, throw thee into it and boil thee; but we will get up quickly, dress ourselves, and go away together."

The two children therefore got up, dressed themselves quickly, and went away. When the water in the kettle was boiling, the cook went into the bed-room to fetch Fundevogel and throw him into it. But when she came in, and went to the beds, both the children were gone. Then she was terribly alarmed, and she said to herself, "What shall I say now when the forester comes home and sees that the children are gone? They must be followed instantly to get them back again."

Then the cook sent three servants after them, who were to run and overtake the children. The children, however, were sitting outside the forest, and when they saw from afar the three servants running, Lina said to Fundevogel, "Never leave me, and I will never leave thee." Fundevogel said, "Neither now, nor ever." Then said Lina, "Do thou become a rose-tree, and I the rose upon it." When the three servants came to the forest, nothing was there but a rose-tree and one rose on it, but the children were nowhere. Then said they, "There is nothing to be done here," and they went home and told the cook that they had seen nothing in the forest but a little rose-bush with one rose on it. Then the old cook scolded and said, "You simpletons, you should have cut the rose-bush in two, and have broken off the rose and brought it home with you; go, and do it at once." They had therefore to go out and look for the second time. The children, however, saw them coming from a distance. Then Lina said, "Fundevogel, never leave me, and I will never leave thee." Fundevogel said, "Neither now, nor ever." Said Lina, "Then do thou become a church, and I'll be the chandelier in it." So when the three servants came, nothing was there but a church, with a chandelier in it. They said therefore to each other, "What can we do here, let us go home." When they got home, the cook asked if they had not found them; so they said no, they had found nothing but a church, and that there was a chandelier in it. And the cook scolded them and said, "You fools! why did you not pull the church to pieces, and bring the chandelier home with you?" And now the old cook herself got on her legs, and went with the three servants in pursuit of the children. The children, however, saw from afar that the three servants were coming, and the cook waddling after them. Then said Lina, "Fundevogel, never leave me, and I will never leave thee." Then said Fundevogel, "Neither now, nor ever." Said Lina, "Be a fishpond, and I will be the duck upon it." The cook, however, came up to them, and when she saw the pond she lay down by it, and was about to drink it up. But the duck swam quickly to her, seized her head in its beak and drew her into the water, and there the old witch had to drown. Then the children went home together, and were heartily delighted, and if they are not dead, they are living still.

33 King Thrushbeard

A King had a daughter who was beautiful beyond all measure, but so proud and haughty withal that no suitor was good enough for her. She sent away one after the other, and ridiculed them as well.

Once the King made a great feast and invited thereto, from far and near, all the young men likely to marry. They were all marshalled in a row according to their rank and standing; first came the kings, then the grand-dukes, then the princes, the earls, the barons, and the gentry. Then the King's daughter was led through the ranks, but to every one she had some objection to make; one was too fat, "The wine-cask," she said. Another was too tall, "Long and thin has little in." The third was too short, "Short and thick is never quick." The fourth was too pale, "As pale as death." The fifth too red, "A fighting-cock." The sixth was not straight enough, "A green log dried behind the stove."

So she had something to say against every one, but she made herself especially merry over a good king who stood quite high up in the row, and whose chin had grown a little crooked. "Well," she cried and laughed, "he has a chin like a thrush's beak!" and from that time he got the name of King Thrushbeard.

But the old King, when he saw that his daugher did nothing but mock the people, and despised all the suitors who were gathered there, was very angry, and swore that she should have for her husband the very first beggar that came to his doors.

A few days afterwards a fiddler came and sang beneath the windows, trying to earn a small alms. When the King heard him he said, "Let him come up." So the fiddler came in, in his dirty, ragged clothes, and sang before the King and his daughter, and when he had ended he asked for a trifling gift. The King said, "Your song has pleased me so well that I will give you my daughter there, for wife."

The King's daughter shuddered, but the King said, "I have taken an oath to give you to the very first beggar-man, and I will keep it." All she could say was in vain; the priest was brought, and she had to let herself be wedded to the fiddler on the spot. When that was done the King said, "Now it is not proper for you, a beggar-woman, to stay any longer in my palace, you may just go away with your husband."

The beggar-man led her out by the hand, and she was obliged to walk away on foot with him. When they came to a large forest she asked, "To whom does that beautiful forest belong?"

"It belongs to King Thrushbeard; if you had taken him, it would have been yours."

"Ah, unhappy girl that I am, if I had but taken King Thrushbeard!"

Afterwards they came to a meadow, and she asked again, "To whom does this beautiful green meadow belong?"

"It belongs to King Thrushbeard; if you had taken him, it would have been yours."

"Ah, unhappy girl that I am, if I had but taken King Thrushbeard!"

Then they came to a large town, and she asked again, "To whom does this fine large town belong?"

"It belongs to King Thrushbeard; if you had taken him, it would have been yours."

"Ah, unhappy girl that I am, if I had but taken King Thrushbeard!"

"It does not please me," said the fiddler, "to hear you always wishing for another husband; am I not good enough for you?" At last they came to a very little hut, and she said, "Oh goodness! what a small house; to whom does this miserable, mean hovel belong?" The fiddler answered, "That is my house and yours, where we shall live together."

She had to stoop in order to go in at the low door. "Where are the servants?" said the King's daughter. "What servants?"

answered the beggar-man; "you must yourself do what you wish to have done. Just make a fire at once, and set on water to cook my supper, I am quite tired." But the King's daughter knew nothing about lighting fires or cooking, and the beggar-man had to lend a hand himself to get anything fairly done. When they had finished their scanty meal they went to bed; but he forced her to get up quite early in the morning in order to look after the house.

For a few days they lived in this way as well as might be, and came to the end of all their provisions. Then the man said, "Wife, we cannot go on any longer eating and drinking here and earning nothing. You weave baskets." He went out, cut some willows, and brought them home. Then she began to weave, but the tough willows wounded her delicate hands.

"I see that this will not do," said the man; "you had better spin, perhaps you can do that better." She sat down and tried to spin, but the hard thread soon cut her soft fingers so that the blood ran down. "See," said the man, "you are fit for no sort of work; I have made a bad bargain with you. Now I will try to make a business with pots and earthenware; you must sit in the market-place and sell the ware."

"Alas," thought she, "if any of the people from my father's kingdom come to the market and see me sitting there, selling, how they will mock me." But it was of no use, she had to yield unless she chose to die of hunger.

For the first time she succeeded well, for the people were glad to buy the woman's wares because she was good-looking, and they paid her what she asked; many even gave her the money and left the pots with her as well. So they lived on what she had earned as long as it lasted, then the husband bought a lot of new crockery. With this she sat down at the corner of the market-place, and set it out round about her ready for sale. But suddenly there came a drunken hussar galloping along, and he rode right amongst the pots so that they were all broken into a thousand bits. She began to weep, and did now know what to do for fear. "Alas! what will happen to me?" cried she; "what will my husband say to this?"

She ran home and told him of the misfortune. "Who would seat herself at a corner of the market-place with crockery?" said the man; "leave off crying, I see very well that you cannot do any ordinary work, so I have been to our King's palace and have asked whether they cannot find a place for a kitchen-maid, and they have promised me to take you, in that way you will get your food for nothing."

The King's daughter was now a kitchen-maid, and had to be at the cook's beck and call, and do the dirtiest work. In both her pockets she fastened a little jar, in which she took home her share of the leavings, and upon this they lived.

It happened that the wedding of the King's eldest son was to be celebrated, so the poor woman went up and placed herself by the door of the hall to look on. When all the candles were lit, and people, each more beautiful than the other, entered, and all was full of pomp and splendour, she thought of her lot with a sad heart, and cursed the pride and haughtiness which had humbled her and brought her to so great poverty.

The smell of the delicious dishes which were being taken in and out reached her, and now and then the servants threw her a few morsels of them: these she put in her jars to take home.

All at once the King's son entered, clothed in velvet and silk, with gold chains about his neck. And when he saw the beautiful woman standing by the door he seized her by the hand, and would have danced with her; but she refused and shrank with fear, for she saw that it was King Thrushbeard, her suitor whom she had driven away with scorn. Her struggles were of no avail, he drew her into the hall; but the string by which her pockets were hung broke, the pots fell down, the soup ran out, and the scraps were scattered all about. And when the people saw it, there arose general laughter and derision, and she was so ashamed that she would rather have been a thousand fathoms below the ground. She sprang to the door and would have run away, but on the stairs a man caught her and brought her back; and when she looked at him it was King Thrushbeard again. He said to her kindly, "Do not be afraid, I and the fiddler who has been living with you in that wretched hovel are one. For love of you I disguised myself so; and I also was the hussar who rode through your crockery. This was all done to humble your proud spirit, and to punish you for the insolence with which you mocked me."

Then she wept bitterly and said, "I have done great wrong, and am not worthy to be your wife." But he said, "Be comforted, the evil days are past; now we will celebrate our wedding." Then the maids-in-waiting came and put on her the most splendid clothing, and her father and his whole court came and wished her happiness in her marriage with King Thrushbeard, and the joy now began in earnest. I wish you and I had been there too.

35 Sweetheart Roland

There was once upon a time a woman who was a real witch and had two daughters, one ugly and wicked, and this one she loved because she was her own daughter, and one beautiful and good, and this one she hated, because she was her step-daughter. The step-daughter once had a pretty apron, which the other fancied so much that she became envious, and told her mother that she must and would have that apron. "Be quiet, my child," said the old woman, "and thou shalt have it. Thy step-sister has long deserved death, tonight when she is asleep I will come and cut her head off. Only be careful that thou art at the far-side of the bed, and push her well to the front." It would have been all over with the poor girl if she had not just then been standing in a corner, and heard everything. All day long she dared not go out of doors, and when bed-time had come, the witch's daughter got into bed first, so as to lie at the far side, but when she was asleep, the other pushed her gently to the front, and took for herself the place at the back, close by the wall. In the night, the old woman came creeping in, she held an axe in her right hand, and felt with her left to see if anyone was lying at the outside, and then she grasped the axe with both hands, and cut her own child's head off.

When she had gone away, the girl got up and went to her sweetheart, who was called Roland, and knocked at his door. When he came out, she said to him, "Hear me, dearest Roland, we must fly in all haste; my step-mother wanted to kill me, but has struck her own child. When daylight comes, and she sees what she has done, we shall be lost."

"But," said Roland, "I counsel thee first to take away her magic wand, or we cannot escape if she pursues us." The maiden fetched the magic wand, and she took the dead girl's head and dropped three drops of blood on the ground, one in front of the bed, one in the kitchen, and one on the stairs. Then she hurried away with her lover. When the old witch got up next morning, she called her daughter, and wanted to give her the apron, but she did not come. Then the witch cried, "Where art thou?"

"Here, on the stairs, I am sweeping," answered the first drop of blood. The old woman went out, but saw no one on the stairs, and cried again, "Where art thou?"

"Here in the kitchen, I am warming myself," cried the second drop of blood. She went into the kitchen, but found no one. Then she cried again, "Where art thou?"

"Ah, here in the bed, I am sleeping." cried the third drop of blood. She went into the room to the bed. What did she see there? Her own child, whose head she had cut off, bathed in her blood. The witch fell into a passion, sprang to the window, and as she could look forth quite far into the world, she perceived her step-daughter hurrying away with her sweetheart Roland. "That shall not serve you," cried she, "even if you have got a long way off, you shall still not escape me." She put on her many league boots, in which went an hour's walk at every step, and it was not long before she overtook them. The girl, however, when she saw the old woman striding towards her, changed, with her magic wand, her sweetheart Roland into a lake, and herself into a duck swimming in the middle of it. The witch placed herself on the shore, threw bread-crumbs in, and gave herself every possible trouble to entice the duck; but the duck did not let herself be enticed, and the old woman had to go home at night as she had come. On this the girl and her sweetheart Roland resumed their natural shapes again, and they walked on the whole night until daybreak. Then the maiden changed herself into a beautiful flower which stood in the midst of a briar hedge, and her sweetheart Roland into a fiddler. It was not long before the witch came striding up towards them, and said to the musician, "Dear musician, may I pluck that beautiful flower for myself?"

"Oh, yes," he replied, "I will play to you while you do it." As she was hastily creeping into the hedge and was just going to pluck the flower, for she well knew who the flower was, he began to play, and whether she would or not, she was forced to dance, for it was a magical melody. The quicker he played, the more violent springs was she forced to make, and the thorns tore her clothes from her body, and pricked her and wounded her till she bled, and as he did not stop, she had to dance till she lay dead on the ground.

When they were delivered, Roland said, "Now I will go to my father and arrange for the wedding."

"Then in the meantime I will stay here and wait for thee," said the girl, "and that no one may recognise me, I will change myself into a red stone land-mark." Then Roland went away, and the girl stood like a red land-mark in the field and waited for her beloved. But when Roland got home, he fell into the snares of another, who prevailed on him so far that he forgot the maiden. The poor girl remained there a long time, but at length, as he did not return at all, she was sad, and changed herself into a flower, and thought, "Some one will surely come this way, and trample me down."

It befell, however, that a shepherd kept his sheep in the field, and saw the flower, and as it was so pretty, plucked it, took it with him, and laid it away in his chest. From that time forth, strange things happened in the shepherd's house. When he arose in the morning, all the work was already done, the room was swept, the table and benches cleaned, the fire on the hearth was lighted, and the water was fetched, and at noon, when he came home, the table was laid, and a good dinner served. He could not conceive how this came to pass, for he never saw a human being in his house, and no one could have concealed himself in it. He was certainly pleased with this good attendance, but still at last he was so afraid that he went to a wise woman and asked for her advice. The wise woman said, "There is some enchantment behind it, listen very early some morning if anything is moving in the room, and if thou seest anything, let it be what it may, throw a white cloth over it, and then the magic will be stopped."

The shepherd did as she bade him, and next morning just as day dawned, he saw the chest open, and the flower come out. Swiftly he sprang towards it, and threw a white cloth over it. Instantly the transformation came to an end, and a beautiful girl stood before him, who owned to him that she had been the flower, and that up to this time she had attended to his housekeeping. She told him her story, and as she pleased him he asked her if she would marry him, but she answered, "No," for she wanted to remain faithful to her sweetheart Roland, although he had deserted her, but she promised not to go away, but to keep house for the shepherd for the future.

And now the time drew near when Roland's wedding was to be celebrated, and then, according to an old custom in the country, it was announced that all the girls were to be present at it, and sing in honour of the bridal pair. When the faithful maiden heard of this, she grew so sad that she thought her heart would break, and she would not go thither, but the other girls came and took her. When it came to her turn to sing, she stepped back, until at last she was the only one left, and then she could not refuse. But when she began her song, and it reached Roland's ears, he sprang up and cried, "I know the voice, that is the true bride, I will have no other!" Everything he had forgotten, and which had vanished from his mind, had suddenly come home again to his heart. Then the faithful maiden held her wedding with her sweetheart Roland, and grief came to an end and joy began.

36 The Golden Bird

In the olden time there was a king, who had behind his palace a beautiful pleasure-garden in which there was a tree that bore golden apples. When the apples were getting ripe they were counted, but on the very next morning one was missing. This was told to the King, and he ordered that a watch should be kept every night beneath the tree.

The King had three sons, the eldest of whom he sent, as soon as night came on, into the garden; but when midnight came he could not keep himself from sleeping, and next morning again an apple was gone.

The following night the second son had to keep watch, it fared no better with him; as soon as twelve o'clock had struck he fell asleep, and in the morning an apple was gone.

Now it came to the turn of the third son to watch; and he was quite ready, but the King had not much trust in him, and thought that he would be of less use even than his brothers; but at last he let him go. The youth lay down beneath the tree, but kept awake, and did not let sleep master him. When it struck twelve, something rustled through the air, and in the moonlight he saw a bird coming whose feathers were all shining with gold. The bird alighted on the tree, and had just plucked off an apple, when the youth shot an arrow at him. The bird flew off, but the arrow had struck his plumage, and one of his golden feathers fell down. The youth picked it up, and the next morning took it to the King and told him what he had seen in the night. The King called his council together, and everyone declared that a feather like this was worth more than the whole kingdom. "If the feather is so precious," declared the King, "one alone will not do for me; I must and will have the whole bird!"

The eldest son set out; he trusted to his cleverness, and thought that he would easily find the Golden Bird. When he had gone some distance he saw a fox sitting at the edge of a wood, so he cocked his gun and took aim at him. The fox cried, "Do not shoot me! and in return I will give you some good counsel. You are on the way to the Golden Bird; and this evening you will come to a village in which stand two inns opposite to one another. One of them is lighted up brightly, and all goes on merrily within, but do not go into it; go rather into the other, even though it seems a bad one."

"How can such a silly beast give wise advice?" thought the King's son, and he pulled the trigger. But he missed the fox, who stretched out his tail and ran quickly into the wood.

So he pursued his way, and by evening came to the village where the two inns were; in one they were singing and dancing; the other had a poor, miserable look. "I should be a fool, indeed," he thought, "if I were to go into the shabby tavern, and pass by the good one." So he went into the cheerful one, lived there in riot and revel, and forgot the bird and his father, and all good counsels.

When some time had passed, and the eldest son for month after month did not come back home, the second set out, wishing to find the Golden Bird. The fox met him as he had met the eldest, and gave him the good advice of which he took no heed. He came to the two inns, and his brother was standing at the window of the one from which came the music, and called out to him. He could not resist, but went inside and lived only for pleasure.

Again some time passed, and then the King's youngest son wanted to set off and try his luck, but his father would not allow it. "It is of no use," said he, "he will find the Golden Bird still less than his brothers, and if a mishap were to befall him he knows not how to help himself; he is a little wanting at the best." But at last, as he had no peace, he let him go.

Again the fox was sitting outside the wood, and begged for his life, and offered his good advice. The youth was good-natured, and said, "Be easy, little fox, I will do you no harm."

"You shall not repent it," answered the fox; "and that you may get on more quickly, get up behind on my tail." And scarcely had he seated himself when the fox began to run, and away he went over stock and stone till his hair whistled in the wind. When they came to the village the youth got off; he followed the good advice, and without looking round turned into the little inn, where he spent the night quietly.

The next morning, as soon as he got into the open country, there sat the fox already, and said, "I will tell you further what you have to do. Go on quite straight, and at last you will come to a castle, in front of which a whole regiment of soldiers is lying, but do not trouble yourself about them, for they will all be asleep and snoring. Go through the midst of them straight into the castle, and go through all the rooms, till at last you will come to a chamber where a Golden Bird is hanging in a wooden cage. Close by, there stands an empty gold cage for show, but beware of taking the bird out of the common cage and putting it into the fine one, or it may go badly with you." With these words the fox again stretched out his tail, and the King's son seated himself upon it, and away he went over stock and stone till his hair whistled in the wind.

When he came to the castle he found everything as the fox had said. The King's son went into the chamber where the Golden Bird was shut up in a wooden cage, whilst a golden one stood hard by; and the three golden apples lay about the room. "But," thought he, "it would be absurd if I were to leave the beautiful bird in the common and ugly cage," so he opened the door, laid hold of it, and put it into the golden cage. But at the same moment the bird uttered a shrill cry. The soldiers awoke, rushed in, and took him off to prison. The next morning he was taken before a court of justice, and as he confessed everything, was sentenced to death.

The King, however, said that he would grant him his life on one condition namely, if he brought him the Golden Horse which ran faster than the wind; and in that case he should receive, over and above, as a reward, the Golden Bird.

The King's son set off, but he sighed and was sorrowful, for how was he to find the Golden Horse? But all at once he saw his old friend the fox sitting on the road. "Look you," said the fox, "this has happened because you did not give heed to me. However, be of good courage. I will give you my help, and tell you how to get to the Golden Horse. You must go straight on, and you will come to a castle, where in the stable stands the horse. The grooms will be lying in front of the stable; but they will be asleep and snoring, and you can quietly lead out the Golden Horse. But of one thing you must take heed; put on him the common saddle of wood and leather, and not the golden one, which hangs close by, else it will go ill with you." Then the fox stretched out his tail, the King's son seated himself upon it, and away he went over stock and stone until his hair whistled in the wind.

Everything happened just as the fox had said; the prince came to the stable in which the Golden Horse was standing, but just as he was going to put the common saddle upon him, he thought, "It will be a shame to such a beautiful beast, if I do not give him the good saddle which belongs to him by right." But scarcely had the golden saddle touched the horse than he began to neigh loudly. The grooms awoke, seized the youth, and threw him into prison. The next morning he was sentenced by the court to death; but the King promised to grant him his life, and the Golden Horse as well, if he could bring back the beautiful princess from the Golden Castle.

With a heavy heart the youth set out; yet luckily for him he soon found the trusty fox. "I ought only to leave you to your ill-luck," said the fox, "but I pity you, and will help you once more out of your trouble. This road takes you straight to the Golden Castle, you will reach it by eventide; and at night when every-thing is quiet the beautiful princess goes to the bathing-house to bathe. When she enters it, run up to her and give her a kiss, then she will follow you, and you can take her away with you; only do not allow her to take leave of her parents first, or it will go ill with you."

Then the fox stretched out his tail, the King's son seated himself upon it, and away the fox went, over stock and stone, till his hair whistled in the wind.

When he reached the Golden Castle it was just as the fox had said. He waited until midnight, when everything lay in deep sleep, and the beautiful princess was going to the bathing-house. Then he sprang out and gave her a kiss. She said that she would like to go with him, but she asked him pitifully, and with tears, to allow her first to take leave of her parents. At first he withstood her prayer, but when she wept more and more, and fell at his feet, he at last gave in. But no sooner had the maiden reached the bedside of her father than he and all the rest in the castle awoke, and the youth was laid hold of and put into prison.

The next morning the King said to him, "Your life is forfeited, and you can only find mercy if you take away the hill which stands in front of my windows, and prevents my seeing beyond it; and you must finish it all within eight days. If you do that you shall have my daughter as your reward."

The King's son began, and dug and shovelled without leaving off, but when after seven days he saw how little he had done, and how all his work was as good as nothing, he fell into great sorrow and gave up all hope. But on the evening of the seventh day the fox appeared and said, 'You do not deserve that I should take any trouble about you; but just go away and lie down to sleep, and I will do the work for you."

The next morning when he awoke and looked out of the window the hill had gone. The youth ran, full of joy, to the King, and told him that the task was fulfilled, and whether he liked it or not, the King had to hold to his word and give him his daughter.

So the two set forth together, and it was not long before the trusty fox came up with them. "You have certainly got what is best," said he, "but the Golden Horse also belongs to the maiden of the Golden Castle."

"How shall I get it?" asked the youth. "That I will tell you," answered the fox; "first take the beautiful maiden to the King who sent you to the Golden Castle. There will be unheard-of rejoicing; they will gladly give you the Golden Horse, and will bring it out to you. Mount it as soon as possible, and offer your hand to all in farewell; last of all to the beautiful maiden. And as soon as you have taken her hand swing her up on to the horse, and gallop away, and no one will be able to bring you back, for the horse runs faster than the wind."

All was carried out successfully, and the King's son carried off the beautiful princess on the Golden Horse.

The fox did not remain behind, and he said to the youth, "Now I will help you to get the Golden Bird. When you come near to the castle where the Golden Bird is to be found, let the maiden get down, and I will take her into my care. Then ride with the Golden Horse into the castle-yard; there will be great rejoicing at the sight, and they will bring out the Golden Bird for you. As soon as you have the cage in your hand gallop back to us, and take the maiden away again.

When the plan had succeeded, and the King's son was about to ride home with his treasures, the fox said, "Now you shall reward me for my help."

"What do you require for it?" asked the youth. "When you get into the wood yonder, shoot me dead, and chop off my head and feet."

"That would be fine gratitude," said the King's son. "I cannot possibly do that for you."

The fox said, "If you will not do it I must leave you, but before I go away I will give you a piece of good advice. Be careful about two things. Buy no gallows'-flesh, and do not sit at the edge of any well." And then he ran into the wood.

The youth thought, "That is a wonderful beast, he has strange whims; who is going to buy gallows'-flesh? and the desire to sit at the edge of a well has never yet seized me."

He rode on with the beautiful maiden, and his road took him

again through the village in which his two brothers had remained. There was a great stir and noise, and, when he asked what was going on, he was told that two men were going to be hanged. As he came nearer to the place he saw that they were his brothers, who had been playing all kinds of wicked pranks, and had squandered all their wealth. He inquired whether they could not be set free. "If you will pay for them," answered the people; "but why should you waste your money on wicked men, and buy them free." He did not think twice about it, but paid for them, and when they were set free they all went on their way together.

They came to the wood where the fox had first met them, as it was cool and pleasant within it, the two brothers said, "Let us rest a little by the well, and eat and drink." He agreed, and whilst they were talking he forgot himself, and sat down upon the edge of the well without thinking of any evil. But the two brothers threw him backwards into the well, took the maiden, the Horse, and the Bird, and went home to their father. "Here we bring you not only the Golden Bird," said they; "we have won the Golden Horse also, and the maiden from the Golden Castle." Then was there great joy; but the Horse would not eat, the Bird would not sing, and the maiden sat and wept.

But the youngest brother was not dead. By good fortune the well was dry, and he fell upon soft moss without being hurt, but he could not get out again. Even in this strait the faithful fox did not leave him: it came and leapt down to him, and upbraided him for having forgotten its advice. "But yet I cannot give it up so," he said; "I will help you up again into daylight." He bade him grasp his tail and keep tight hold of it; and then he pulled him up.

"You are not out of all danger yet," said the fox. "Your brothers were not sure of your death, and have surrounded the wood with watchers, who are to kill you if you let yourself be seen." But a poor man was sitting upon the road, with whom the youth changed clothes, and in this way he got to the King's palace.

No one knew him, but the Bird began to sing, the Horse

began to eat, and the beautiful maiden left off weeping. The King, astonished, asked, "What does this mean?" Then the maiden said, "I do not know, but I have been so sorrowful and now I am so happy! I feel as if my true bridegroom had come." She told him all that had happened, although the other brothers had threatened her with death if she were to betray anything.

The King commanded that all people who were in his castle should be brought before him; and amongst them came the youth in his ragged clothes; but the maiden knew him at once and fell upon his neck. The wicked brothers were seized and put to death, but he was married to the beautiful maiden and declared heir to the King.

But how did it fare with the poor fox? Long afterwards the King's son was once again walking in the wood, when the fox met him and said, "You have everything now that you can wish for, but there is never an end to my misery, and yet it is in your power to free me," and again he asked him with tears to shoot him dead and chop off his head and feet. So he did it, and scarcely was it done when the fox was changed into a man, and was no other than the brother of the beautiful princess, who at last was freed from the magic charm which had been laid upon him. And now nothing more was wanting to their happiness as long as they lived.

37 The Dog and the Sparrow

A sheep-dog had not a good master, but, on the contrary, one who let him suffer hunger. As he could stay no longer with him, he went quite sadly away. On the road he met a sparrow who said, "Brother dog, why art thou so sad?" The dog replied, "I am hungry, and have nothing to eat." Then said the sparrow, "Dear brother, come into the town with me, and I will satisfy thy hunger." So they went into the town together, and when they came in front of a butcher's shop the sparrow said to the dog, "Stay there, and I will pick a bit of meat down for thee," and he alighted on the stall, looked about him to see that no one was observing him, and pecked and pulled and tore so long at a piece which lay on the edge, that it slipped down. Then the dog seized it, ran into a corner, and devoured it. The sparrow said, "Now come with me to another shop, and then I will get thee one more piece that thou mayst be satisfied." When the dog had devoured the second piece as well, the sparrow asked, "Brother dog, hast thou now had enough?"

"Yes, I have had meat enough," he answered, "but I have had no bread yet." Said the sparrow, "Thou shalt have that also, come with me." Then he took him to a baker's shop, and pecked at a couple of little buns till they rolled down, and as the dog wanted still more, he led him to another stall, and again got bread for him. When that was consumed, the sparrow said, "Brother dog, hast thou now had enough?"

"Yes," he replied, "now we will walk awhile outside the town." Then they both went out on to the highway. It was, however, warm weather, and when they had walked a little way the dog said, "I am tired, and would like to sleep."

"Well, do sleep," answered the sparrow, "and in the meantime I will seat myself on a branch." So the dog lay down on the road, and fell fast asleep. Whilst he lay sleeping there, a waggoner came driving by, who had a cart with three horses, laden with two barrels of wine. The sparrow, however, saw that he was not going to turn aside, but was staying in the wheel track in which the dog was lying, so it cried, "Waggoner, don't do it, or I will make thee poor." The waggoner, however, growled to himself, "Thou wilt not make me poor," and cracked his whip and drove the cart over the dog, and the wheels killed him. Then the sparrow cried, "Thou hast run over my brother dog and killed him, it shall cost thee thy cart and horses."

"Cart and horses indeed!" said the waggoner. "What harm canst thou do me?" and drove onwards. Then the sparrow crept under the cover of the cart, and pecked so long at the same bung-hole that he got the bung out, and then all the wine ran out without the driver noticing it. But once when he was looking behind him he saw that the cart was dripping, and looked at the barrels and saw that one of them was empty.

"Unfortunate fellow that I am," cried he. "Not unfortunate enough yet," said the sparrow, and flew on to the head of one of the horses and pecked his eyes out. When the driver saw that, he drew out his axe and wanted to hit the sparrow, but the sparrow flew into the air, and he hit his horse on the head, and it fell down dead. "Oh, what an unfortunate man I am," cried he. "Not unfortunate enough yet," said the sparrow, and when the driver drove on with the two horses, the sparrow again crept under the cover, and pecked the bung out of the second cask, so all the wine was spilt. When the driver became aware of it, he again cried, "Oh, what an unfortunate man I am," but the sparrow replied, "Not unfortunate enough yet," and seated himself on the head of the second horse, and pecked his eyes out. The driver ran up to it and raised his axe to strike, but the sparrow flew into the air and the blow struck the horse, which fell. "Oh, what an unfortunate man I am."

"Not unfortunate enough yet," said the sparrow, and lighted on the third horse's head, and pecked out his eyes. The driver, in his rage, struck at the sparrow without looking round, and did not hit him but killed his third horse likewise. "Oh, what an unfortunate man I am," cried he. "Not unfortunate enough yet," answered the sparrow. "Now will I make thee unfortunate in thy home," and flew away.

The driver had to leave the waggon standing, and full of anger and vexation went home. "Ah," said he to his wife, "what misfortunes I have had! My wine has run out, and the horses are all three dead!"

"Alas, husband," she answered, "what a malicious bird has come into the house! It has gathered together every bird there is in the world, and they have fallen on our corn up there, and are devouring it." Then he went upstairs, and thousands and thousands of birds were sitting in the loft and had eaten up all the corn, and the sparrow was sitting in the midst of them. Then the driver cried, "Oh, what an unfortunate man I am?"

"Not unfortunate enough yet!" answered the sparrow; "waggoner, it shall cost thee thy life as well," and flew out.

Then the waggoner had lost all his property, and he went downstairs into the room, sat down behind the stove and was quite furious and bitter. But the sparrow sat outside in front of the window, and cried, "Waggoner, it shall cost thee thy life." Then the waggoner snatched the axe and threw it at the sparrow, but it only broke the window, and did not hit the bird. The sparrow now hopped in, placed itself on the stove and cried, "Waggoner, it shall cost thee thy life." The latter, quite mad and blind with rage, smote the stove in twain, and as the sparrow flew from one place to another so it fared with all his household furniture, looking-glass, benches, table, and at last the walls of his house, and yet he could not hit the bird. At length, however, he caught it with his hand. Then his wife said, "Shall I kill it?"

"No," cried he, "that would be too merciful. It shall die much more cruelly," and he took it and swallowed it whole. The sparrow, however, began to flutter about in his body, and fluttered up again into the man's mouth; then it stretched out its head, and cried, "Waggoner, it shall still cost thee thy life." The driver gave the axe to his wife, and said, "Wife, kill the bird in my mouth for me." The woman struck, but missed her blow, and hit the waggoner right on his head, so that he fell dead. But the sparrow flew up and away.

38 Frederick and Catherine

There was once on a time a man who was called Frederick and a woman called Catherine, who had married each other and lived together as young married folks. One day Frederick said, "I will now go and plough, Catherine; when I come back, there must be some roast meat on the table for hunger, and a fresh draught for thirst."

"Just go, Frederick," answered Kate, "just go, I will have all ready for you." Therefore when dinner-time drew near she got a sausage out of the chimney, put it in the frying-pan, put some butter to it, and set it on the fire. The sausage began to fry and to hiss, Catherine stood beside it and held the handle of the pan, and had her own thoughts as she was doing it. Then it occurred to her, "While the sausage is getting done thou couldst go into the cellar and draw beer." So she set the frying-pan safely on the fire, took a can, and went down into the cellar to draw beer. The beer ran into the can and Kate watched it, and then she thought, "Oh, dear! The dog upstairs is not fastened up, it might get the sausage out of the pan. Well thought of." And in a trice she was up the cellar-steps again, but the Spitz had the sausage in its mouth already, and trailed it away on the ground. But Catherine, who was not idle, set out after it, and chased it a long way into the field; the dog, however, was swifter than Catherine and did not let the sausage journey easily, but skipped over the furrows with it. "What's gone is gone!" said Kate, and turned round, and as she had run till she was weary, she walked quietly and com-fortably, and cooled herself. During this time the beer was still running out of the cask, for Kate had not turned the tap. And when the can was full and there was no other place for it, it ran into the cellar and did not stop until the whole cask was empty. As soon as Kate was on the steps she saw the mischance. "Good gracious!" she cried. "What shall I do now to stop Frederick knowing it!" She thought for a while, and at last she remembered that up in the garret was still standing a sack of the finest wheat flour from the last fair, and she would fetch that down and strew it over the beer. "Yes," said she, "he who saves a thing when he ought, has it afterwards when he needs it," and she climbed up to the garret and carried the sack below, and threw it straight down on the can of beer, which she knocked over, and Frederick's draught swam also in the cellar. "It is all right," said Kate, "where the one is the other ought to be also," and she strewed the meal over the whole cellar. When it was done she was heartily delighted with her work, and said, "How clean and wholesome it does look here!" At mid-day home came Frederick: "Now, wife, what have you ready for me?"

"Ah, Freddy," she answered, "I was frying a sausage for you, but whilst I was drawing the beer to drink with it, the dog took it away out of the pan, and whilst I was running after the dog, all the beer ran out, and whilst I was drying up the beer with the flour, I knocked over the can as well, but be easy, the cellar is quite dry again." Said Frederick, "Kate, Kate, you should not have done that! to let the sausage be carried off and the beer run out of the cask, and throw out all our flour into the bargain!"

"Indeed, Frederick, I did not know that, you should have told me." The man thought, "If my wife is like this, I must look after things more." Now he had got together a good number of thalers which he changed into gold, and said to Catherine, "Look, these are counters for playing games; I will put them in a pot and bury them in the stable under the cow's manger, but mind you keep away from them, or it will be the worse for you." Said she, "Oh, no, Frederick, I certainly will not go." And when Frederick was gone some pedlars came into the village who had cheap earthen-bowls and pots, and asked the young woman if there was nothing she wanted to bargain with them for. "Oh, dear people," said Catherine, "I have no money and can buy nothing, but if you have any use for yellow counters I will buy of you."

"Yellow counters, why not? But just let us see them."

"Then go into the stable and dig under the cow's manger, and you will find the yellow counters. I am not allowed to go there." The rogues went thither, dug and found pure gold. Then they laid hold of it, ran away, and left their pots and bowls behind in the house. Catherine though she must use her new things, and as she had no lack in the kitchen already without these, she knocked the bottom out of every pot, and set them all as ornaments on the paling which went round about the house. When Frederick came and saw the new decorations, he said, "Catherine, what have you been about?"

"I have bought them, Frederick, for the counters which were under the cow's manger. I did not go there myself, the pedlars had to dig them out for themselves."

"Ah, wife," said Frederick, "what have you done? Those were not counters, but pure gold, and all our wealth; you should not have done that."

"Indeed, Frederick," said she, "I did not know that, you should have forewarned me."

Catherine stood for a while and bethought to herself; then she said, "Listen, Frederick, we will soon get the gold back again, we will run after the thieves."

"Come, then," said Frederick, "we will try it; but take with you some butter and cheese that we may have something to eat on the way."

"Yes, Frederick, I will take them." They set out, and as Frederick was the better walker, Catherine followed him. "It is to my advantage," thought she, "when we turn back I shall be a little way in advance." Then she came to a hill where there were deep ruts on both sides of the road. "There one can see," said Catherine, "how they have torn and skinned and galled the poor earth, it will never be whole again as long as it lives," and in her heart's compassion she took her butter and smeared the ruts right and left, that they might not be so hurt by the wheels, and as she was thus bending down in her charity, one of the cheeses rolled out of her pocket down the hill. Said Catherine, "I have made my way once up here, I will not go down again; another may run and fetch it back." So she took another cheese and rolled it down. But the cheeses did not come back, so she let a third run down, thinking. "Perhaps they are waiting for company, and do not like to walk alone." As all three stayed away she said, "I do not know what that can mean, but it may perhaps be that the third has not found the way, and has gone wrong, I will just send the fourth to call it." But the fourth did no better than the third. Then Catherine was angry, and threw down the fifth and sixth as well, and these were her last. She remained standing for some time watching for their coming, but when they still did not come, she said, "Oh, you are good folks to send in search of death, you stay a fine long time away! Do you think I will wait any longer for you? I shall go my way, you may run after me; you have younger legs than I." Catherine went on and found Frederick, who was standing waiting for her because he wanted something to eat. "Now just let us have what you have brought with you," said he. She gave him the dry bread. "Where have you the butter and the cheeses?" asked the man. "Ah, Freddy," said Catherine, "I smeared the cart-ruts with the butter and the cheeses will come soon; one ran away from me, so I sent the others after to call it." Said Frederick, "You should not have done that, Catherine, to smear the butter on the road, and let the cheeses run down the hill!"

"Really, Frederick, you should have told me." Then they ate the dry bread together, and Frederick said, "Catherine, did you make the house safe when you came away?"

"No, Frederick, you should have told me to do it before."

"Then go home again, and make the house safe before we go any farther, and bring with you something else to eat. I will wait here for you." Catherine went back and thought, "Frederick wants something more to eat, he does not like butter and cheese, so I will take with me a handkerchief full of dried pears and a pitcher of vinegar for him to drink." Then she bolted the upper half of the door fast, but unhinged the lower door, and took it on her back, believing that when she had placed the door in security the house must be well taken care of. Catherine took her time on the way, and thought, "Frederick will rest himself so much the longer." When she had once reached him she said, "Here is the house-door for you, Frederick, and now you can take care of the house yourself."

"Oh, heavens," said he, "what a wise wife I have! She takes the under-door off the hinges that everything may run in, and bolts the upper one. It is now too late to go back home again, but since you have brought the door here, you shall just carry it farther."

"I will carry the door, Frederick, but the dried pears and the vinegar-jug will be too heavy for me, I will hang them on the door, it may carry them."

And now they went into the forest, and sought the rogues, but did not find them. At length as it grew dark they climbed into a tree and resolved to spend the night there. Scarcely, however, had they sat down at the top of it than the rascals came thither who carry away with them what does not want to go, and find things before they are lost. They sat down under the very tree in which Frederick and Catherine were sitting, lighted a fire, and were about to share their loot. Frederick got down on the other side and collected some stones together. Then he climbed up again with them, and wished to throw them at the thieves and kill them. The stones, however, did not hit them, and the knaves cried, "It will soon be morning, the wind is shaking down the fir-apples. Catherine still had the door on her back, and as it pressed so heavily on her, she thought it was the fault of the dried pears, and said, "Frederick, I must throw the pears down."

"No, Catherine, not now," he replied, "they might betray us."

"Oh, but, Frederick, I must! They weigh me down far too much."

"Do it, then, and be hanged!" Then the dried pears rolled down between the branches, and the rascals below said, "The leaves are falling."

A short time afterwards, as the door was still heavy, Catherine said, "Ah, Frederick, I must pour out the vinegar."

"No, Catherine, you must not, it might betray us."

"Ah, but, Frederick, I must, it weighs me down far too much."

"Then do it and be hanged!" So she emptied out the vinegar, and it besprinkled the robbers. They said amongst themselves, "The dew is already falling." At length Catherine thought, "Can it really be the door which weighs me down so?" and said, "Frederick, I must throw the door down."

"No, not now, Catherine, it might discover us."

"Oh, but, Frederick, I must. It weighs me down far too much."

"Oh, no, Catherine, do hold it fast."

"Ah, Frederick, I am letting it fall!"

"Let it go, then, in the devil's name." Then it fell down with a violent clatter, and the rascals below cried, "The devil is coming down the tree!" and they ran away and left everything behind them. Early next morning, when the two came down they found all their gold again, and carried it home.

When they were once more at home, Frederick said, "And now, Catherine, you, too, must be industrious and work."

"Yes, Frederick, I will soon do that, I will go into the field and cut corn." When Catherine got into the field, she said to herself, "Shall I eat before I cut, or shall I sleep before I cut? Oh, I will eat first." Then Catherine ate and eating made her sleepy, and she began to cut, and half in a dream cut all her clothes to pieces, her apron, her gown, and her shift. When Catherine awoke again after a long sleep she was standing there half-naked, and said to herself, "Is it I, or is it not I? Alas, it is not I." In the meantime night came, and Catherine ran into the village, knocked at her husband's window, and cried, "Frederick."

"What is the matter?"

"I should very much like to know if Catherine is in?"

"Yes, yes," replied Frederick, "she must be in and asleep."

Said she, "'Tis well, then I am certainly at home already," and ran away.

Outside Catherine found some vagabonds who were going to steal. Then she went to them and said, "I will help you to steal." The rascals thought that she knew the situation of the place, and were willing. Catherine went in front of the houses, and cried, "Good folks, have you anything? We want to steal." The thieves thought to themselves, "That's a fine way of doing things," and wished themselves once more rid of Catherine. Then they said to her, "Outside the village the pastor has some turnips in the field. Go there and pull up some turnips for us." Catherine went to the ground, and began to pull them up, but was so idle that she did not gather them together. Then a man came by, saw her, and stood still and thought that it was the devil who was thus rooting amongst the turnips.

He ran away into the village to the pastor, and said, "Mr. Pastor, the devil is in your turnip-ground, rooting up turnips."

"Ah, heavens," answered the pastor, "I have a lame foot, I cannot go out and drive him away." Said the man, "Then I will carry you on my back," and he carried him out on his back. And when they came to the ground, Catherine arose and stood up her full height. "Ah, the devil!" cried the pastor, and both hurried away, and in his great fright the pastor could run better with his lame foot than the man who had carried him on his back could do with his sound one.

39 The Queen Bee

Two kings' sons once went out in search of adventures, and fell into a wild, disorderly way of living, so that they never came home again. The youngest, who was called Simpleton, set out to seek his brothers, but when at length he found them they mocked him for thinking that he with his simplicity could get through the world, when they two could not make their way, and yet were so much cleverer. They all three travelled away together, and came to an ant-hill. The two elder wanted to destroy it, to see the little ants creeping about in their terror, and carrying their eggs away, but Simpleton said, "Leave the creatures in peace; I will not allow you to disturb them." Then they went onwards and came to a lake, on which a great number of ducks were swimming. The two brothers wanted to catch a couple and roast them, but Simpleton would not permit it, and said, " Leave the creatures in peace, I will not suffer you to kill them." At length they came to a bee's nest, in which there was so much honey that it ran out of the trunk of the tree where it was. The two wanted to make a fire beneath the tree, and suffocate the bees in order to take away the honey, but Simpleton again stopped them and said, "Leave the creatures in peace, I will not allow you to burn them." At length the three brothers arrived at a castle where stone horses were standing in the stables, and no human being was to be seen, and they went through all the halls until, quite at the end, they came to a door in which were three locks. In the middle of the door, however, there was a little pane, through which they could see into the room. There they saw a little grey man, who was sitting at a table. They called him, once, twice, but he did not hear; at last they called him for the third time, when he got up, opened the locks, and came out. He said nothing, however, but conducted them to a handsomely-spread table, and when they had eaten and drunk, he took each of them to a bedroom. Next morning the little grey man came to the eldest, beckoned to him, and conducted him to a stone table, on which were inscribed three tasks, by the performance of which the castle could be delivered. The first was that in the forest, beneath the moss, lay the princess's pearls, a thousand in number, which must be picked up, and if by sunset one single pearl was wanting, he who had looked for them would be turned into stone. The eldest went thither, and sought the whole day, but when it came to an end, he had only found one hundred, and what was written on the table came to pass, and he was changed into stone. Next day, the second brother undertook the adventure; it did not, however, fare much better with him than with the eldest; he did not find more than two hundred pearls, and was changed to stone. At last the turn came to Simpleton also, who sought in the moss. It was, however, so hard to find the pearls, and he got on so slowly, that he seated himself on a stone, and wept. And while he was thus sitting, the King of the ants whose life he had once saved, came with five thousand ants, and before long the little creatures had got all the pearls together, and laid them in a heap. The second task, however, was to fetch out of the lake the key of the King's daughter's bed-chamber. When Simpleton came to the lake, the ducks which he had saved, swam up to him, dived down, and brought the key out of the water. But the third task was the most difficult; from amongst the three sleeping daughters of the King was the youngest and dearest to be sought out. They, however, resembled each other exactly, and were only to be distinguished by their having eaten different sweetmeats before they fell asleep; the eldest a bit of sugar; the second a little syrup; and the youngest a spoonful of honey. Then the Queen of the bees, which Simpleton had protected from the fire, came and tasted the lips of all three, and at last she remained sitting on the mouth which had eaten honey, and thus the King's son recognised the right princess. Then the enchantment was at an end; everything was released from sleep, and those who had been turned to stone received once more

their natural forms. Simpleton married the youngest and sweetest princess, and after her father's death became King, and his
two brothers received the two other sisters.

40 The Three Feathers

There was once upon a time a King who had three sons, of whom two were clever and wise, but the third did not speak much, and was simple, and was called the Simpleton. When the King had become old and weak, and was thinking of his end, he did not know which of his sons should inherit the kingdom after him. Then he said to them, "Go forth, and he who brings me the most beautiful carpet shall be King after my death." And that there should be no dispute amongst them, he took them outside his castle, blew three feathers in the air, and said, "You shall go as they fly." One feather flew to the east, the other to the west, but the third flew straight up and did not fly far, but soon fell to the ground. And now one brother went to the right, and the other to the left, and they mocked Simpleton, who was forced to stay where the third feather had fallen. He sat down and was sad, then all at once he saw that there was a trap-door close by the feather. He raised it up, found some steps, and went down them, and then he came to another door, knocked at it, and heard somebody inside calling:

> "Little green maiden small,
> Hopping hither and thither;
> Hop to the door,
> And quickly see who is there."

The door opened, and he saw a great, fat toad sitting, and round about her a crowd of little toads. The fat toad asked what he wanted. He answered, "I should like to have the prettiest and finest carpet in the world." Then she called a young one and said:

> "Little green maiden small,
> Hopping hither and thither,
> Hop quickly and bring me the great box here."

The young toad brought the box, and the fat toad opened it, and gave Simpleton a carpet out of it, so beautiful and so fine, that on the earth above, none could have been woven like it. Then he thanked her, and ascended again. The two others had, however, looked on their youngest brother as so stupid that they believed he would find and bring nothing at all. "Why should we give ourselves a great deal of trouble to search?" said they, and got some coarse handkerchiefs from the first shepherds' wives whom they met, and carried them home to the King. At the same time Simpleton also came back, and brought his beautiful carpet, and when the King saw it he was astonished, and said, "If justice be done, the kingdom belongs to the youngest." But the two others let their father have no peace, and said that it was impossible that Simpleton, who in everything lacked understanding, should be King, and entreated him to make a new agreement with them. Then the father said, "He who brings me the most beautiful ring shall inherit the kingdom," and led the three brothers out, and blew into the air three feathers, which they were to follow. Those of the two eldest again went east and west, and Simpleton's feather flew straight up, and fell down near the door into the earth. Then he went down again to the fat toad, and told her that he wanted the most beautiful ring. She at once ordered her great box to be brought, and gave him a ring out of it, which sparkled with jewels, and was so beautiful that no goldsmith on earth would have been able to make it. The two eldest laughed at Simpleton for going to seek a golden ring. They gave themselves no trouble, but knocked the nails out of an old carriage-ring, and took it to the King; but when Simpleton produced his golden ring, his father again said, "The kingdom belongs to him." The two eldest did not cease from tormenting the King until he made a third condition, and declared that the one who brought the most beautiful woman home, should have the kingdom. He again blew the three feathers into the air, and they flew as before.

Then Simpleton without more ado went down to the fat toad,

and said, "I am to take home the most beautiful woman!"

"Oh," answered the toad, "the most beautiful woman! She is not at hand at the moment, but still thou shalt have her." She gave him a yellow turnip which had been hollowed out, to which six mice were harnessed. Then Simpleton said quite mournfully, "What am I to do with that?" The toad answered, "Just put one of my little toads into it." Then he seized one at random out of the circle, and put her into the yellow coach, but hardly was she seated inside it than she turned into a wonderfully beautiful maiden, and the turnip into a coach, and the six mice into horses. So he kissed her, and drove off quickly with the horses, and took her to the King. His brothers came afterwards; they had given themselves no trouble at all to seek beautiful girls, but had brought with them the first peasant women they chanced to meet. When the King saw them he said, "After my death the kingdom belongs to my youngest son." But the two eldest deafened the King's ears afresh with their clamour, "We cannot consent to Simpleton's being King," and demanded that the one whose wife could leap through a ring which hung in the centre of the hall should have the preference. They thought, "The peasant women can do that easily; they are strong enough, but the delicate maiden will jump herself to death." The aged King agreed likewise to this. Then the two peasant women jumped, and jumped through the ring, but were so stout that they fell, and their coarse arms and legs broke in two. And then the pretty maiden whom Simpleton had brought with him, sprang, and sprang through as lightly as a deer, and all opposition had to cease. So he received the crown, and has ruled wisely for a length of time.

41 The Golden Goose

There was a man who had three sons, the youngest of whom was called Dummling, and was despised, mocked, and put down on every occasion.

It happened that the eldest wanted to go into the forest to hew wood, and before he went his mother gave him a beautiful sweet cake and a bottle of wine in order that he might not suffer from hunger or thirst.

When he entered the forest there met him a little grey-haired old man who bade him good-day, and said, "Do give me a piece of cake out of your pocket, and let me have a draught of your wine; I am so hungry and thirsty." But the prudent youth answered, "If I give you my cake and wine, I shall have none for myself; be off with you," and he left the little man standing and went on.

But when he began to hew down a tree, it was not long before he made a false stroke, and the axe cut him in the arm, so that he had to go home and have it bound up. And this was the little grey man's doing.

After this the second son went into the forest, and his mother gave him, like the eldest, a cake and a bottle of wine. The little old grey man met him likewise, and asked him for a piece of cake and a drink of wine. But the second son, too, said with much reason, "What I give you will be taken away from myself; be off!" and he left the little man standing and went on. His punishment, however, was not delayed; when he had made a few strokes at the tree he struck himself in the leg, so that he had to be carried home.

Then Dummling said, "Father, do let me go and cut wood." The father answered, "Your brothers have hurt themselves with it, leave it alone, you do not understand anything about it." But Dummling begged so long that at last he said, "Just go then, you will get wiser by hurting yourself." His mother gave him a cake made with water and baked in the cinders, and with it a bottle of sour beer.

When he came to the forest the little old grey man met him likewise, and greeting him, said, "Give me a piece of your cake and a drink out of your bottle; I am so hungry and thirsty." Dummling answered, "I have only cinder-cake and sour beer; if that pleases you, we will sit down and eat." So they sat down, and when Dummling pulled out his cinder-cake, it was a fine sweet cake, and the sour beer had become good wine. So they ate and drank, and after that the little man said, "Since you have a good heart, and are willing to divide what you have, I will give you good luck. There stands an old tree, cut it down, and you will find something at the roots." Then the little man took leave of him.

Dummling went and cut down the tree, and when it fell there was a goose sitting in the roots with feathers of pure gold. He lifted her up, and taking her with him, went to an inn where he thought he would stay the night. Now the host had three daughters, who saw the goose and were curious to know what such a wonderful bird might be, and would have liked to have one of its golden feathers.

The eldest thought, "I shall soon find an opportunity of pulling out a feather," and as soon as Dummling had gone out she seized the goose by the wing, but her finger and hand remained sticking fast to it.

The second came soon afterwards, thinking only of how she might get a feather for herself, but she had scarcely touched her sister than she was held fast.

At last the third also came with the like intent, and the others screamed out, "Keep away; for goodness' sake keep away!" But she did not understand why she was to keep away. "The others are there," she thought, "I may as well be there too," and ran to them; but as soon as she had touched her sister, she remained sticking fast to her. So they had to spend the night with the goose.

The next morning Dummling took the goose under his arm and set out, without troubling himself about the three girls who were hanging on to it. They were obliged to run after him continually, now left, now right, just as he was inclined to go.

In the middle of the fields the parson met them, and when he saw the procession he said, "For shame, you good-for-nothing girls, why are you running across the fields after this young man? Is that seemly?" At the same time he seized the youngest by the hand in order to pull her away, but as soon as he touched her he likewise stuck fast, and was himself obliged to run behind.

Before long the sexton came by and saw his master, the parson, running behind three girls. He was astonished at this and called out, "Hi, your reverence, whither away so quickly? Do not forget that we have a christening today!" and running after him he took him by the sleeve, but was also held fast to it.

Whilst the five were trotting thus one behind the other, two labourers came with their hoes from the fields; the parson called out to them and begged that they would set him and the sexton free. But they had scarcely touched the sexton when they were held fast, and now there were seven of them running behind Dummling and the goose.

Soon afterwards he came to a city, where a king ruled who had a daughter who was so serious that no one could make her laugh. So he had put forth a decree that whosoever should be able to make her laugh should marry her. When Dummling heard this, he went with his goose and all her train before the King's daughter, and as soon as she saw the seven people running on and on, one behind the other, she began to laugh quite loudly, and as if she would never leave off. Thereupon Dummling asked to have her for his wife, and the wedding was celebrated. After the King's death, Dummling inherited the kingdom and lived a long time contentedly with his wife.

42 Lucky Hans

Hans had served his master for seven years, so he said to him, "Master, my time is up; now I should be glad to go back home to my mother; give me my wages." The master answered, "You have served me faithfully and honestly, as the service was so shall the reward be"; and he gave Hans a piece of gold as big as his head. Hans pulled his handkerchief out of his pocket, wrapped up the lump in it, put it on his shoulder, and set out on the way home.

As he went on, always putting one foot before the other, he saw a horseman trotting quickly and merrily by on a lively horse. "Ah!" said Hans quite loud, "what a fine thing it is to ride! There you sit as on a chair; you stumble over no stones, you save your shoes, and get on, you don't know how."

The rider, who had heard him, stopped and called out, "Hullo! Hans, why do you go on foot, then?"

"I must," answered he, "for I have this lump to carry home; it is true that it is gold, but I cannot hold my head straight for it, and it hurts my shoulder."

"I will tell you what," said the rider, "we will exchange: I will give you my horse, and you can give me your lump."

"With all my heart," said Hans, "but I can tell you, you will have to crawl along with it."

The rider got down, took the gold, and helped Hans up; then gave him the bridle tight in his hands and said, "If you want to go at a really good pace, you must click your tongue and call out, "Jup! Jup!"

Hans was heartily delighted as he sat upon the horse and rode away so bold and free. After a little while he thought that it ought to go faster, and he began to click with his tongue and call out, "Jup! Jup!" The horse put himself into a sharp trot, and before Hans knew where he was, he was thrown off and lying in a ditch which separated the field from the highway. The horse would have gone off too if it had not been stopped by a countryman, who was coming along the road and driving a cow before him.

Hans got his limbs together and stood up on his legs again, but he was vexed, and said to the countryman, "It is a poor joke, this riding, especially when one gets hold of a mare like this, that kicks and throws one off, so that one has a chance of breaking one's neck. Never again will I mount it. Now I like your cow, for one can walk quietly behind her, and have, over and above, one's milk, butter and cheese every day without fail. What would I not give to have such a cow."

"Well," said the countryman, "if it would give you so much pleasure, I do not mind giving the cow for the horse." Hans agreed with the greatest delight; the countryman jumped upon the horse, and rode quickly away.

Hans drove his cow quietly before him, and thought over his lucky bargain. "If only I have a morsel of bread—and that can hardly fail me—I can eat butter and cheese with it as often as I like; if I am thirsty, I can milk my cow and drink the milk. Good heart, what more can I want?"

When he came to an inn he made a halt, and in his great content ate up what he had with him—his dinner and supper—and all he had, and with his last few farthings had half a glass of beer. Then he drove his cow onwards along the road to his mother's village.

As it drew nearer mid-day, the heat was more oppressive, and Hans found himself upon a moor which it took about an hour to cross. He felt it very hot and his tongue clave to the roof of his mouth with thirst. "I can find a cure for this," thought Hans; "I will milk the cow now and refresh myself with the milk." He tied her to a withered tree, and as he had no pail he put his leather cap underneath; but try as he would, not a drop of milk came. And as he set himself to work in a clumsy way, the impatient beast at last gave him such a blow on his head with its hind foot, that he fell on the ground, and for a long time could not think where he was.

By good fortune a butcher just then came along the road with a wheel-barrow, in which lay a young pig. "What sort of a trick is this?" cried he, and helped the good Hans up. Hans told him what had happened. The butcher gave him his flask and said, "Take a drink and refresh yourself. The cow will certainly give no milk, it is an old beast; at the best it is only fit for the plough, or for the butcher."

"Well, well," said Hans, as he stroked his hair down on his head, "who would have thought it? Certainly it is a fine thing when one can kill a beast like that at home; what meat one has! But I do not care much for beef, it is not juicy enough for me. A young pig like that now is the thing to have, it tastes quite different; and then there are the sausages!"

"Hark ye, Hans," said the butcher, "out of love for you I will exchange, and will let you have the pig for the cow."

"Heaven repay you for your kindness!" said Hans as he gave up the cow, whilst the pig was unbound from the barrow, and the cord by which it was tied was put in his hand.

Hans went on, and thought to himself how everything was going just as he wished; if he did meet with any vexation it was immediately set right. Presently there joined him a lad who was carrying a fine white goose under his arm. They said good morning to each other, and Hans began to tell of his good luck, and how he had always made such good bargains. The boy told him that he was taking the goose to a christening-feast. "Just lift her," added he, and laid hold of her by the wings; "how heavy she is—she has been fattened up for the last eight weeks. Whoever has a bit of her when she is roasted will have to wipe the fat from both sides of his mouth."

"Yes," said Hans, as he weighed her in one hand, "she is a good weight, but my pig is no bad one."

Meanwhile the lad looked suspiciously from one side to the other, and shook his head. "Look here," he said at length, "it may not be all right with your pig. In the village through which I passed, the Mayor himself had just had one stolen out of its sty. I fear—I fear that you have got hold of it there. They have sent out some people and it would be a bad business if they caught you with the pig; at the very least, you would be shut up in the dark hole."

The good Hans was terrified. "Goodness!" he said, "help me out of this fix; you know more about this place than I do, take my pig and leave me your goose."

"I shall risk something at that game," answered the lad, "but I will not be the cause of your getting into trouble." So he took the cord in his hand, and drove away the pig quickly along a by-path.

The good Hans, free from care, went homewards with the goose under his arm. "When I think over it properly," said he to himself, "I have even gained by the exchange; first there is the good roast-meat, then the quantity of fat which will drip from it, and which will give me dripping for my bread for a quarter of a year, and lastly the beautiful white feathers; I will have my pillow stuffed with them, and then indeed I shall go to sleep without rocking. How glad my mother will be!"

As he was going through the last village, there stood a scissors-grinder with his barrow; as his wheel whirred he sang—

> "I sharpen scissors and quickly grind,
> My coat blows out in the wind behind."

Hans stood still and looked at him; at last he spoke to him and said, "All's well with you, as you are so merry with your grinding."

"Yes," answered the scissors-grinder, "the trade has a golden foundation. A real grinder is a man who as often as he puts his hand into his pocket finds gold in it. But where did you buy that fine goose?"

"I did not buy it, but exchanged my pig for it."

"And the pig?"

"That I got for a cow."

"And the cow?"

"I took that instead of a horse."

"And the horse?"

"For that I gave a lump of gold as big as my head."

"And the gold?"

"Well, that was my wages for seven years' service."

"You have known how to look after yourself each time," said the grinder. "If you can only get on so far as to hear the money jingle in your pocket whenever you stand up, you will have made your fortune."

"How shall I manage that?" said Hans. "You must be a grinder, as I am; nothing particular is wanted for it but a grind-stone, the rest finds itself. I have one here; it is certainly a little worn, but you need not give me anything for it but your goose; will you do it?"

"How can you ask?" answered Hans. "I shall be the luckiest fellow on earth; if I have money whenever I put my hand in my pocket, what need I trouble about any longer?" and he handed him the goose and received the grindstone in exchange. "Now," said the grinder, as he took up an ordinary heavy stone that lay by him, "here is a strong stone for you into the bargain; you can hammer well upon it, and straighten your old nails. Take it with you and keep it carefully."

Hans loaded himself with the stones, and went on with a contented heart; his eyes shone with joy. "I must have been born with a caul," he cried; "everything I want happens to me just as if I were a Sunday-child."

Meanwhile, as he had been on his legs since daybreak, he began to feel tired. Hunger also tormented him, for in his joy at the bargain by which he got the cow he had eaten up all his store of food at once. At last he could only go on with great trouble, and was forced to stop every minute; the stones, too, weighed him down dreadfully. Then he could not help thinking how nice it would be if he had not to carry them just then.

He crept like a snail to a well in a field, and there he thought that he would rest and refresh himself with a cool draught of water, but in order that he might not injure the stones in sitting down, he laid them carefully by his side on the edge of the well. Then he sat down on it, and was to stoop and drink, when he made a slip, pushed against the stones, and both of them fell into the water. When Hans saw them with his own eyes sinking to the bottom, he jumped for joy, and then knelt down, and with tears in his eyes thanked God for having shown him this favour also, and delivered him in so good a way, and without his having any need to reproach himself, from those heavy stones which had been the only things that troubled him.

"There is no man under the sun so fortunate as I," he cried out. With a light heart and free from every burden he now ran on until he was with his mother at home.

43 The Young Giant

Once upon a time a countryman had a son who was as big as a thumb, and did not become any bigger, and during several years did not grow one hair's breadth. Once when the father was going out to plough, the little one said, "Father, I will go out with you."

"Thou wouldst go out with me?" said the father. "Stay here, thou wilt be of no use out there, besides thou mightest get lost!" Then Thumbling began to cry, and for the sake of peace his father put him in his pocket, and took him with him. When he was outside in the field, he took him out again, and set him in a freshly-cut furrow. Whilst he was there, a great giant came over the hill. "Do thou see that great bogey man?" said the father, for he wanted to frighten the little fellow to make him good; "he is coming to fetch thee." The giant, however, had scarcely taken two steps with his long legs before he was in the furrow. He took up little Thumbling carefully with two fingers, examined him, and without saying one word went away with him. His father stood by, but could not utter a sound for terror, and he thought nothing else but that his child was lost, and that as long as he lived he should never set eyes on him again.

The giant, however, carried him home, suckled him, and Thumbling grew and became tall and strong after the manner of giants. When two years had passed, the old giant took him into the forest, wanted to try him, and said, "Pull up a stick for thyself." Then the boy was already so strong that he tore up a young tree out of the earth by the roots. But the giant thought, "We must do better than that," took him back again, and suckled him two years longer. When he tried him, his strength had increased so much that he could tear an old tree out of the ground.

That was still not enough for the giant; he again suckled him for two years, and when he then went with him into the forest and said, "Now just tear up a proper stick for me," the boy tore up the strongest oak-tree from the earth, so that it split, and that was a mere trifle to him. "Now that will do," said the giant, "thou art perfect," and took him back to the field from whence he had brought him. His father was there following the plough. The young giant went up to him, and said, "Does my father see what a fine man his son has grown into?"

The farmer was alarmed, and said, "No, thou art not my son; I don't want thee leave me!"

"Truly I am your son; allow me to do your work, I can plough as well as you, nay better."

"No, no, thou art not my son; and thou canst not plough go away!" However, as he was afraid of this great man, he let go of the plough, stepped back and stood at one side of the piece of land. Then the youth took the plough, and just pressed it with one hand, but his grasp was so strong that the plough went deep into the earth. The farmer could not bear to see that, and called to him, "If thou art determined to plough, thou must not press so hard on it, that makes bad work." The youth, however, unharnessed the horses, and drew the plough himself, saying, "Just go home, father, and bid my mother make ready a large dish of food, and in the meantime I will go over the field." Then the farmer went home, and ordered his wife to prepare the food; but the youth ploughed the field which was two acres large, quite alone, and then he harnessed himself to the harrow, and harrowed the whole of the land, using two harrows at once. When he had done it, he went into the forest, and pulled up two oak-trees, laid them across his shoulders, and hung on them one harrow behind and one before, and also one horse behind and one before, and carried all as if it had been a bundle of straw, to his parents' house. When he entered the yard, his mother did not recognise him, and asked, "Who is that horrible tall man?" The farmer said, "That is our son." She said, "No that cannot be our son, we never had such a tall one, ours was a little thing." She called to him, "Go away, we do not want thee!" The youth was silent, but led his horses to the stable, gave them some oats and hay, and all that they wanted. When he had done this, he went into the parlour, sat down on the bench and said, "Mother, now I should like something to eat, will it soon be ready?" Then she said, "Yes," and brought in two immense dishes full of food, which would have been enough to satisfy herself and her husband for a week. The youth, however, ate the whole of it himself, and asked if she had nothing more to set before him. "No," she replied, "that is all we have."

"But that was only a taste, I must have more." She did not dare to oppose him, and went and put a huge caldron full of food on the fire, and when it was ready, carried it in. "At length come a few crumbs," said he, and ate all there was, but it was still not sufficient to appease his hunger. Then said he, "Father, I see well that with you I shall never have food enough; if you will get me an iron staff which is strong, and which I cannot break against my knees, I will go out into the world." The farmer was glad, put his two horses in his cart, and fetched from the smith a staff so large and thick, that the two horses could only just bring it away. The youth laid it across his knees, and snap! he broke it in two in the middle like a bean-stalk, and threw it away. The father then harnessed four horses, and brought a bar which was so long and thick, that the four horses could only just drag it. The son snapped this also in twain against his knees, threw it away, and said, "Father, this can be of no use to me, you must harness more horses, and bring a stronger staff." So the father harnessed eight horses, and brought one which was so long and thick, that the eight horses could only just carry it. When the son took it in his hand, he broke off a bit from the top of it also, and said, "Father, I see that you will not be able to procure me any such staff as I want, I will remain no longer with you."

So he went away, and gave out that he was a smith's apprentice. He arrived at a village, wherein lived a smith who was a greedy fellow, who never did a kindness to any one, but wanted everything for himself. The youth went into the smithy and asked if he needed a journeyman. "Yes," said the smith, and looked at him, and thought, "That is a strong fellow who will strike out well, and earn his bread." So he asked, "How much wages dost thou want?"

"I don't want any at all," he replied, "only every fortnight, when the other journeymen are paid, I will give thee two blows, and thou must bear them." The miser was heartily satisfied, and thought he would thus save much money. Next morning, the strange journeyman was to begin to work, but when the master brought the glowing bar, and the youth struck his first blow, the iron flew asunder, and the anvil sank so deep into the earth, that there was no bringing it out again. Then the miser grew angry, and said, "Oh, but I can't make any use of you, you strike far too powerfully; what will you have for the one blow?"

Then said he, "I will only give you quite a small blow, that's all." And he raised his foot, and gave him such a kick that he flew away over four loads of hay. Then he sought out the thickest iron bar in the smithy for himself, took it as a stick in his hand and went onwards.

When he had walked for some time, he came to a small farm, and asked the bailiff if he did not require a head-servant. "Yes," said the bailiff, "I can make use of one; you look a strong fellow who can do something, how much a year do you want as wages?" He again replied that he wanted no wages at all, but that every year he would give him three blows, which he must bear. Then the bailiff was satisfied, for he, too, was a covetous fellow. Next morning all the servants were to go into the wood, and the others were already up, but the head-servant was still in bed. Then one of them called to him, "Get up, it is time; we are going into the wood, and thou must go with us."

"Ah," said he quite roughly and surlily, "you may just go, then; I shall be back again before any of you." Then the others went to the bailiff, and told him that the head-man was still lying in bed, and would not go into the wood with them. The bailiff said they were to awaken him again, and tell him to harness the horses. The head-man, however, said as before, "Just go there, I shall be back again before any of you." And then he stayed in bed two hours longer. At length he arose from the feathers, but first he got himself two bushels of peas from the loft, made himself some broth with them, ate it at his leisure, and when that was done, went and harnessed the horses, and drove into the wood. Not far from the wood was a ravine through which he had to pass, so he first drove the horses on, and then stopped them, and went behind the cart, took trees and brushwood, and made a great barricade, so that no horse could get through. When he was entering the wood, the others were just driving out of it with their loaded carts to go home; then said he to them, "Drive on, I will still get home before you do." He did not drive far into the wood, but at once tore two of the very largest trees of all out of the earth, threw them on his cart, and turned round. When he came to the barricade, the others were still standing there, not able to get through. "Don't you see," said he, "that if you had stayed with me, you would have got home just as quickly, and would have had another hour's sleep?" He now wanted to drive on, but his horeses could not work their way through, so he unharnessed them, laid them on the top of the cart, took the shafts in his own hands, and pulled it all through, and he did this just as easily as if it had been laden with feathers. When he was over, he said to the others, "There, you see, I have got over quicker than you," and drove on, and the others had to stay where they were. In the yard, however, he took a tree in his hand, showed it to the bailiff, and said, "Isn't that a fine bundle of wood?" Then said the bailiff to his wife, "The servant is a good one, if he does sleep long, he is still home before the others." So he served the bailiff for a year, and when that was over, and the other servants were getting their wages, he said it was time for him to take his too. The bailiff, however, was afraid of the blows which he was to receive, and earnestly entreated him to excuse him from having them; for rather than that, he himself would be head-servant, and the youth should be bailiff. "No," said he, "I will not be a bailiff, I am head-servant, and will remain so, but

I will administer that which we agreed on." The bailiff was willing to give him whatsoever he demanded, but it was of no use, the head-servant said no to everything. Then the bailiff did not know what to do, and begged for a fortnight's delay, for he wanted to find some way of escape. The head-servant consented to this delay. The bailiff summoned all his clerks together, and they were to think the matter over, and give him advice. The clerks pondered for a long time, but at last they said that no one was sure of his life with the head-servant, for he could kill a man as easily as a midge, and that the bailiff ought to make him get into the well and clean it, and when he was down below, they would roll up one of the mill-stones which was lying there, and throw it on his head; and then he would never return to daylight. The advice pleased the bailiff, and the head-servant was quite willing to go down the well. When he was standing down below at the bottom, they rolled down the largest mill-stone and thought they had broken his skull, but he cried, "Chase away those hens from the well, they are scratching in the sand up there, and throwing the grains into my eyes, so that I can't see." So the bailiff cried, "Sh-sh," and pretended to frighten the hens away. When the head-servant had finished his work, he climbed up and said, "Just look what a beautiful neck-tie I have on," and behold it was the mill-stone which he was wearing round his neck. The head-servant now wanted to take his reward, but the bailiff again begged for a fortnight's delay. The clerks met together and advised him to send the head-servant to the haunted mill to grind corn by night, for from thence as yet no man had ever returned in the morning alive. The proposal pleased the bailiff, he called the head-servant that very evening, and ordered him to take eight bushels of corn to the mill, and grind it that night, for it was wanted. So the head-servant went to the loft, and put two bushels in his right pocket, and two in his left, and took four in a wallet, half on his back, and half on his breast, and thus laden went to the haunted mill. The miller told him that he could grind there very well by day, but not by night, for the mill was haunted, and that up to the present time whosoever had gone into it at night had been found in the morning lying dead inside. He said, "I will manage it, just you go away to bed." Then he went into the mill, and poured out the corn.

About eleven o'clock he went into the miller's room, and sat down on the bench. When he had sat there a while, a door suddenly opened, and a large table came in, and on the table, wine and roasted meats placed themselves, and much good food besides, but everything came of itself, for no one was there to carry it. After this the chairs pushed themselves up, but no people came, until all at once he beheld fingers, which handled knives and forks, and laid food on the plates, but with this exception he saw nothing. As he was hungry, and saw the food, he, too, place himself at the table, ate with those who were eating and enjoyed it. When he had had enough, and the others also had quite emptied their dishes, he distinctly heard all the candles being suddenly snuffed out, and as it was now pitch dark, he felt something like a box on the ear. Then he said, "If anything of that kind comes again, I shall strike out in return." And when he had received a second box on the ear, he, too struck out. And so it continued the whole night. He took nothing without returning it, but repaid everything with interest, and did not lay about him in vain. At daybreak, however, everything ceased. When the miller had got up, he wanted to look after him, and wondered if he were still alive. Then the youth said, "I have eaten my fill, have received some boxes on the ears, but I have given some in return." The miller rejoiced, and said that the mill was now released from the spell, and wanted to give him much money as a reward. But he said, "Money, I will not have, I have enough of it." So he took his meal on his back, went home, and told the bailiff that he had done what he had been told to do, and would now have the reward agreed on. When the bailiff heard that, he was seriously alarmed and quite beside himself; he walked backwards and forwards in the room, and drops of perspiration ran down from his forehead. Then he opened the window to get some fresh air, but before he was aware, the head-servant had given him such a kick that he flew through the window out into the air, and so far away that no one ever saw him again. Then said the head-servant to the bailiff's wife, "If he does not come back, you must take the other blow." She cried, "No, no I cannot bear it," and opened the other window, because drops of perspiration were running down her forehead. Then he gave her such a kick that she, too, flew out, and as she was lighter she went much higher than her husband. Her husband cried, "Do come to me," but she replied, "Come thou to me, I cannot come to thee." And they hovered about there in the air, and could not get to each other, and whether they are still hovering about, or not, I do not know, but the young giant took up his iron bar, and went on his way.

44 The Gnome

There was once upon a time a rich King who had three daughters, who daily went to walk in the palace garden, and the King
was a great lover of all kinds of fine trees, but there was one for
which he had such an affection, that if anyone gathered an apple
from it he wished him a hundred fathoms underground. And
when harvest time came, the apples on this tree were all as red
as blood. The three daughters went every day beneath the tree,
and looked to see if the wind had not blown down an apple, but
they never by any chance found one, and the tree was so loaded
with them that it was almost breaking, and the branches hung
down to the ground. Then the King's youngest child had a great
desire for an apple, and said to her sisters, "Our father loves us
far too much to wish us underground, it is my belief that he
would only do that to people who were strangers." And while
she was speaking, the child plucked off quite a large apple, and
ran to her sisters, saying, "Just taste, my dear little sisters, for
never in my life have I tasted anything so delightful." Then the
two other sisters also ate some of the apple, whereupon all three
sank deep down into the earth, where they could hear no cock
crow.

When mid-day came, the King wished to call them to come
to dinner, but they were nowhere to be found. He sought them
everywhere in the palace and garden, but could not find them.
Then he was much troubled, and made known to the whole land
that whosoever brought his daughters back again should have
one of them for his wife. Hereupon so many young men went
about the country in search, that there was no counting them, for
every one loved the three children because they were so kind to
all, and so fair of face. Three young huntsmen also went out, and
when they had travelled about for eight days, they arrived at a
great castle, in which were beautiful apartments, and in one

room a table was laid on which were delicate dishes which were still so warm that they were smoking, but in the whole of the castle no human being was either to be seen or heard. They waited there for half a day, and the food still remained warm and smoking, and at length they were so hungry that they sat down and ate, and agreed with each other that they would stay and live in that castle, and that one of them, who should be chosen by casting lots, should remain in the house, and the two others seek the King's daughters. They cast lots, and the lot fell on the eldest; so next day the two younger went out to seek, and the eldest had to stay home. At mid-day came a small, mannikin and begged for a piece of bread, then the huntsman took the bread which he had found there, and cut a round off the loaf and was about to give it to him, but whilst he was giving it to the mannikin, the latter let it fall, and asked the huntsman to be so good as to give him that piece again. The huntsman was about to do so and stooped, on which the mannikin took a stick, seized him by the hair, and gave him a good beating. Next day, the second stayed at home, and he fared no better. When the two others returned in the evening, the eldest said, "Well, how have you got on?"

"Oh, very badly," said he, and then they lamented their misfortune together, but they said nothing about it to the youngest, for they did not like him at all, and always called him Stupid Hans, because he did not exactly belong to the forest. On the third day, the youngest stayed at home, and again the little mannikin came and begged for a piece of bread. When the youth gave it to him, the elf let it fall as before, and asked him to be so good as to give him that piece again. Then said Hans to the little mannikin, "What! Canst thou not pick up that piece thyself? If thou wilt not take as much trouble as that for thy daily bread, thou dost not deserve to have it." Then the mannikin grew very angry and said he was to do it, but the huntsman would not, and took the dear mannikin, and gave him a thorough beating. Then the mannikin screamed terribly, and cried, "Stop, stop, and

let me go, and I will tell thee where the King's daughters are."
When Hans heard that, he left off beating him and the mannikin
told him that he was an earth mannikin, and that there were
more than a thousand like him, and that if he would go with him
he would show him where the King's daughters were. Then he
showed him a deep well, but there was no water in it. And the
elf said that he knew well that the companions Hans had with
him did not intend to deal honourably with him, therefore if he
wished to deliver the King's children, he must do it alone. The
two other brothers would also be very glad to recover the King's
daughters, but they did not want to have any trouble or danger.
Hans was therefore to take a large basket, and he must seat himself in it with his hunting knife and a bell, and be let down.
Below were three rooms, and in each of them was a princess,
with a many-headed dragon, whose heads she was to comb and
trim, but he must cut them off. And having said all this, the elf
vanished. When it was evening the two brothers came and asked
how he had got on, and he said, "pretty well so far," and that he
had seen no one except at mid-day when a little mannikin had
come and begged for a piece of bread, that he had given some to
him, but that the mannikin had let it fall and had asked him to
pick it up again; but as he did not choose to do that, the elf had
begun to lose his temper, and that he had done what he ought
not, and had given the elf a beating, on which he had told him
where the King's daughters were. Then the two were so angry at
this that they grew green and yellow. Next morning they went to
the well together, and drew lots who should first seat himself in
the basket, and again the lot fell on the eldest, and he was to seat
himself in it, and take the bell with him. Then he said, "If I ring,
you must draw me up again immediately." When he had gone
down for a short distance, he rang, and they at once drew him
up again. Then the second seated himself in the basket, but he
did just the same as the first, and then it was the turn of the
youngest, but he let himself be lowered quite to the bottom.
When he had got out of the basket, he took his hunting knife,

and went and stood outside the first door and listened, and heard the dragon snoring quite loudly. He opened the door slowly, and one of the princesses was sitting there, and had nine dragon's heads lying upon her lap, and was combing them. Then he took his hunting knife and hewed at them, and the nine fell off. The princess sprang up, threw her arms round his neck, embraced and kissed him repeatedly, and took her necklace, which was made of pure gold, and hung it round his neck. Then he went to the second princess, who had a dragon with five heads to comb, and delivered her also, and to the youngest, who had a dragon with four heads, he went likewise. And they all rejoiced, and embraced him and kissed him without stopping. Then he rang very loud, so that those above heard him, and he placed the princesses one after the other in the basket, and had them all drawn up, but when it came to his own turn he remembered the words of the elf, who had told him that his comrades did not mean well by him. So he took a great stone which was lying there, and placed it in the basket, and when it was about half way up, his false brothers above cut the rope, so that the basket with the stone fell to the ground, and they thought that he was dead, and ran away with the three princesses, making them promise to tell their father that it was they who had delivered them, and then they went to the King, and each demanded a princess in marriage.

In the meantime the youngest huntsman was wandering about the three chambers in great trouble, fully expecting to have to end his days there, when he saw, hanging on the wall, a flute; then said he, "Why dost thou hang there, no one can be merry here?" He looked at the dragons heads likewise and said, "You too cannot help me now." He walked backwards and forwards for such a long time that he made the surface of the ground quite smooth. But at last other thoughts came to his mind, and he took the flute from the wall, and played a few notes on it, and suddenly a number of elves appeared, and with every note that he sounded one more came. Then he played until the room was entirely filled. They all asked what he desired, so he said he wished to get above ground back to daylight, on which they seized him by every hair that grew on his head, and thus they flew with him onto the earth again. When he was above ground, he at once went to the King's palace, just as the wedding of one princess was about to be celebrated, and he went to the room where the King and his three daughters were. When the princesses saw him they fainted. Hereupon the King was angry, and ordered him to be put in prison at once, because he thought he must have done some injury to the children. When the princesses came to themselves, however, they entreated the King to set him free again. The King asked why, and they said that they were not allowed to tell that, but their father said that they were to tell it to the stove. And he went out, listened at the door, and heard everything. Then he caused the two brothers to be hanged on the gallows, and to the third he gave his youngest daughter, and on that occasion I wore a pair of glass shoes, and I struck them against a stone, and it said, "Klink," and were broken.

45 The King of the Golden Mountain

There was a certain merchant who had two children, a boy and a girl; they were both young, and could not walk. And two rich-ly-laden ships of his sailed forth to sea with all his property on board, and just as he was expecting to win much money by them, news came that they had gone to the bottom, and now instead of being a rich man he was a poor one, and had nothing left but one field outside the town. In order to drive his misfortune a little out of his thoughts, he went out to this field, and as he was walking forwards and backwards in it, a little black mannikin stood suddenly by his side, and asked why he was so sad, and what he was taking so much to heart. Then said the merchant, "If thou couldst help me I would willingly tell thee."

"Who knows?" replied the black dwarf. "Perhaps, I can help thee." Then the merchant told him that all he possessed had gone to the bottom of the sea, and that he had nothing left but this field. "Do not trouble thyself," said the dwarf. "If thou wilt promise to give me the first thing that rubs itself against thy leg when thou art at home again, and to bring it here to this place in twelve years' time, thou shalt have as much money as thou wilt." The merchant thought, "What can that be but my dog?" and did not remember his little boy, so he said yes, gave the black man a written and sealed promise, and went home.

When he reached home, his little boy was so delighted that he held by a bench, tottered up to him and seized him fast by the legs. The father was shocked, for he remembered his promise, and now knew what he had pledged himself to do; as however, he still found no money in his chest, he thought the dwarf had only been jesting. A month afterwards he went up to the garret, intending to gather together some old tin and to sell it, and saw a great heap of money lying. Then he was happy again, made purchases, became a greater merchant than before, and felt that this world was well-governed. In the meantime the boy grew tall, and at the same time sharp and clever. But the nearer the twelfth year approached the more anxious grew the merchant, so that his distress might be seen in his face. One day his son asked what ailed him, but the father would not say. The boy, however, persisted so long, that at last he told him that without being aware of what he was doing, he had promised him to a black dwarf, and had received much money for doing so. He said likewise that he had set his hand and seal to this, and that now when twelve years had gone by he would have to give him up. Then said the son, "Oh, father, do not be uneasy, all will go well. The black man has no power over me." The son had himself blessed by the priest, and when the time came, father and son went together to the field, and the son made a circle and placed himself inside it with his father. Then came the black dwarf and said to the old man, "Hast thou brought with thee that which thou hast promised me?" He was silent, but the son asked, "What dost thou want here?" Then said the black dwarf, "I have to speak with thy father, and not with thee." The son replied, "Thou hast betrayed and misled my father, give back the writing."

"No," said the black dwarf, "I will not give up my rights." They spoke together for a long time after this, but at last they agreed that the son, as he did not belong to the enemy of mankind, nor yet to his father, should seat himself in a small boat, which should lie on water which was flowing away from them, and that the father should push it off with his own foot, and then the son should remain given up to the water. So he took leave of his father, placed himself in a little boat, and the father had to push it off with his own foot. The boat capsized so that the keel was uppermost, and the father believed his son was lost, and went home and mourned for him.

The boat, however, did not sink, but floated quietly away, and the boy sat safely inside it, and it floated thus for a long time, until at last it stopped by an unknown shore. Then he landed and saw a beautiful castle before him, and set out to go to it. But when he entered it, he found that it was bewitched. He went through every room, but all were empty until he reached the last, where a snake lay coiled in a ring. The snake, however, was an enchanted maiden, who rejoiced to see him, and said, "Hast thou come, oh, my deliverer? I have already waited twelve years for thee; this kingdom is bewitched, and thou must set it free."

"How can I do that?" he inquired. "Tonight come twelve black men, covered with chains who will ask what thou art doing here; keep silent; give them no answer, and let them do what they will with thee; they will torment thee, beat thee, stab thee; let everything pass, only do not speak; at twelve o'clock, they must go away again. On the second night twelve others will come; on the third, twenty-four, who will cut off thy head, but at twelve o'clock their power will be over, and then if thou hast endured all, and hast not spoken the slightest word, I shall be released. I will come to thee, and will have, in a bottle, some of the water of life. I will rub thee with that, and then thou wilt come to life again, and be as healthy as before." Then said he, "I will gladly set thee free." And everything happened just as she had said; the black men could not force a single word from him, and on the third night the snake became a beautiful princess, who came with the water of life and brought him back to life again. So she threw herself into his arms and kissed him, and there was joy and gladness in the whole castle. After this their marriage was celebrated, and he was King of the Golden Mountain.

They lived very happily together, and the Queen bore a fine boy. Eight years had already gone by, when the King bethought him of his father; his heart was moved, and he wished to visit him. The Queen, however, would not let him go away, and said, "I know beforehand that it will cause my unhappiness;" but he suffered her to have no rest until she consented. At their parting she gave him a wishing-ring, and said, "Take this ring and put it on thy finger, and then thou wilt immediately be transported whithersoever thou wouldst be, only thou must promise me not to use it in wishing me away from this place and with thy father."

That he promised her, put the ring on his finger, and wished himself at home, just outside the town where his father lived. Instantly he found himself there, and made for the town, but when he came to the gate, the sentries would not let him in, because he wore such strange and yet such rich and magnificent clothing. Then he went to a hill where a shepherd was watching his sheep, changed clothes with him, put on his old shepherd's-coat, and then entered the town without hindrance. When he came to his father, he made himself known to him, but he did not at all believe that the shepherd was his son, and said he certainly had had a son, but that he was dead long ago; however, as he saw he was a poor, needy shepherd, he would give him something to eat. Then the shepherd said to his parents, "I am verily your son. Do you know of no mark on my body by which you could recognise me?"

"Yes," said his mother, "our son had a raspberry mark under his right arm." He slipped back his shirt, and they saw the raspberry under his right arm, and no longer doubted that he was their son. Then he told them that he was King of the Golden Mountain, and a king's daughter was his wife, and that they had a fine son of seven years old. Then said the father, "That is certainly not true; it is a fine kind of a king who goes about in a ragged shepherd's-coat." On this the son fell in a passion, and without thinking of his promise, turned his ring round, and wished both his wife and child with him. They were there in a second, but the Queen wept, and reproached him, and said that he had broken his word, and had brought misfortune upon her. He said, "I have done it thoughtlessly, and not with evil intention," and tried to calm her, and she pretended to believe this; but she had mischief in her mind.

Then he led her out of the town into the field, and showed her the stream where the little boat had been pushed off, and then he said, "I am tired; sit down, I will sleep awhile on thy lap." And he laid his head on her lap, and fell asleep. When he was asleep, she first drew the ring from his finger, then she drew away the foot which was under him, leaving only the slipper behind her, and she took her child in her arms, and wished herself back in her own kingdom. When he awoke, there he lay quite deserted, and his wife and child were gone, and so was the ring from his finger, the slipper only was still there as a token. "Home to thy parents thou canst not return," thought he, "they would say that thou wast a wizard; thou must be off, and walk on until thou arrivest in thine own kingdom." So he went away and came at length to a hill by which three giants were standing, disputing with each other because they did not know how to divide their father's property. When they saw him passing by, they called to him and said little men had quick wits, and that he was to divide their inheritance for them. The inheritance, however, consisted of a sword, which had this property that if any one took it in his hand, and said, "All heads off but mine," every head would lie on the ground; secondly, of a cloak which made any one who put it on invisible; thirdly, of a pair of boots which could transport the wearer to any place he wished in a moment. He said, "Give me the three things that I may see if they are still in good condition." They gave him the cloak, and when he had put it on, he was invisible and changed into a fly. Then he resumed his own form and said, "The cloak is a good one, now give me the sword." They said, "No, we will not give thee that; if thou were to say, All heads off but mine,' all our heads would be off, and thou alone wouldst be left with thine." Nevertheless they gave it to him with the condition that he was only to try it against a tree. This he did, and the sword cut in two the trunk of a tree as if it had been a blade of straw. Then he wanted to have the boots likewise, but they said, "No, we will not give them; if thou hadst them on thy feet and wert to wish thyself at the top of the hill, we should be left down here with nothing."

"Oh, no," said he, "I will not do that." So they gave him the boots as well. And now when he had got all these things, he thought of nothing but his wife and his child, and said as though to himself, "Oh, if I were but on the Golden Mountain," and at the same moment he vanished from the sight of the giants, and thus their inheritance was divided. When he was near his palace, he heard sounds of joy, and fiddles, and flutes, and the people told him that his wife was celebrating her wedding with anoth-er. Then he fell into a rage, and said, "False woman, she betrayed and deserted me whilst I was asleep!" So he put on his cloak, and unseen by all went into the palace. When he entered the din-ing-hall a great table was spread with delicious food, and the guests were eating and drinking, and laughing, and jesting. She sat on a royal seat in the midst of them in splendid apparel, with a crown on her head. He placed himself behind her, and no one saw him. When she put a piece of meat on a plate for herself, he took it away and ate it, and when she poured out a glass of wine for herself, he took it away and drank it. She was always help-ing herself to something, and yet she never got anything, for plate and glass disappeared immediately. Then dismayed and ashamed, she arose and went to her chamber and wept, but he followed her there. She said, "Has the devil power over me, or did my deliverer never come?" Then he struck her in the face, and said, "Did thy deliverer never come? It is he who has thee in his power, thou traitor. Have I deserved this from thee?" Then he made himself visible, went into the hall, and cried, "The wed-ding is at an end, the true King has returned." The kings, princes, and councillors who were assembled there, ridiculed and mocked him, but he did not trouble to answer them, and said, "Will you go away, or not?" On this they tried to seize him and pressed upon him, but he drew his sword and said, "All heads off but mine," and all the heads rolled on the ground, and he alone was master, and once more King of the Golden Mountain.

46 The Raven

There was once upon a time a Queen who had a little daughter who was still so young that she had to be carried. One day the child was naughty, and the mother might say what she liked, but the child would not be quiet. Then she became impatient, and as the ravens were flying about the palace, she opened the window and said, "I wish you were a raven and would fly away, and then I should have some rest." Scarcely had she spoken the words, before the child was changed into a raven, and flew from her arms out of the window. It flew into a dark forest, and stayed in it a long time, and the parents heard nothing of their child. Then one day a man was on his way through this forest and heard the raven crying, and followed the voice, and when he came nearer, the bird said, "I am a king's daughter by birth, and am bewitched, but thou canst set me free."

"What am I to do," asked he. She said, "Go further into the forest, and thou wilt find a house, wherein sits an aged woman, who will offer thee meat and drink, but you must accept nothing, for if you eatest and drinkest anything, thou wilt fall into a sleep, and then thou wilt not be able to deliver me. In the garden behind the house there is a great heap of tan, and on this thou shalt stand and wait for me. For three days I will come every afternoon at two o'clock in a carriage. On the first day four white horses will be harnessed to it, then four chestnut horses, and lastly four black ones; but if thou art not awake, but sleeping, I shall not be set free." The man promised to do everything that she desired, but the raven said, "I know already that thou wilt not deliver me; thou wilt accept something from the woman." Then the man once more promised that he would certainly not touch anything either to eat or to drink. But when he entered the house the old woman came to him and said, "Poor man, how faint you are; come and refresh yourself; eat and drink."

"No," said the man, "I will not eat or drink." She, however, let him have no peace, and said, "If you will not eat, take one drink out of the glass; one is nothing." Then he let himself be persuaded, and drank. Shortly before two o'clock in the afternoon he went into the garden to the tan heap to wait for the raven. As he was standing there, his weariness all at once became so great that he could not struggle against it, and lay down for a short time, but he was determined not to go to sleep. Hardly, however, had he lain down, than his eyes closed of their own accord, and he fell asleep and slept so soundly that nothing in the world could have aroused him. At two o'clock the raven came driving up with four white horses, but she was already in deep grief and said, "I know he is asleep." And when she came into the garden, he was indeed lying there asleep on the heap of tan. She alighted from the carriage, went to him, shook him, and called him, but he did not awake. Next day about noon, the old woman came again and brought him food and drink, but he would not take any of it. But she let him have no rest and persuaded him until at length he again took one drink out of the glass. Towards two o'clock he went into the garden to the tan heap to wait for the raven, but all at once felt such a great weariness that his limbs would no longer support him. He could not help himself, and was forced to lie down, and fell into a heavy sleep. When the raven drove up with four brown horses, she was already full of grief, and said, "I know he is asleep." She went to him, but there he lay sleeping, and there was no wakening him. Next day the old woman asked what was the meaning of this? He was neither eating nor drinking anything; did he want to die? He replied, "I am not allowed to eat or drink, and will not do so." But she set a dish with food, and a glass with wine before him, and when he smelt it he could not resist, and swallowed a deep draught. When the time came, he went out into the garden to the heap of tan, and waited for the King's daughter; but he became still more weary than on the day before, and lay down and slept as soundly as if he had been a stone. At two o'clock the raven came with four black horses, and the coachman and everything else was black. She was already in the deepest grief, and said, "I know that he is asleep and cannot deliver me." When she came to him, there he was lying fast asleep. She shook him and called him, but she could not waken him. Then she laid a loaf beside him, and after that a piece of meat, and thirdly a bottle of wine, and he might consume as much of all of them as he liked, but they would never grow less. After this she took a gold ring from her finger, and put it on his, and her name was graven on it. Lastly, she laid a letter beside him wherein was written what she had given him, and that none of the things would ever grow less; and in it was also written, "I see right well that here you will never be able to deliver me, but if thou art still willing to deliver me, come to the golden castle of Stromberg; it lies in thy power, of that I am certain."

And when she had given him all these things, she seated herself in her carriage, and drove to the golden castle of Stromberg.

When the man awoke and saw that he had slept, he was sad at heart, and said, "She has certainly driven by, and I have not set her free." Then he perceived the things which were lying beside him, and read the letter wherein was written how everything had happened. So he arose and went away, intending to go to the golden castle of Stromberg, but he did not know where it was. After he had walked about the world for a long time, he entered into a dark forest, and walked for fourteen days, and still could not find his way out. Then it was once more evening, and he was so tired that he lay down in a thicket and fell asleep. Next day he went onwards, and in the evening, as he was again about to lie down beneath some bushes, he heard such a howling and crying that he could not go to sleep. And at the time when people light the candles, he saw one glimmering, and arose and went towards it. Then he came to a house which seemed very small, for in front of it a great giant was standing. He thought to himself, "If I go in, and the giant sees me, it will very likely cost me my life."

At length he ventured it and went in. When the giant saw him, he said, "It is well that thou comest, for it is long since I have eaten; I will at once eat thee for my supper."

"I'd rather you would leave that alone," said the man, "I do not like to be eaten; but if thou hast any desire to eat, I have quite enough here to satisfy thee."

"If that be true," said the giant, "thou mayst be easy, I was only going to devour thee because I had nothing else." Then they went, and sat down to the table, and the man took out the bread, wine, and meat which would never come to an end. "This pleases me well," said the giant, and ate to his heart's content. Then the man said to him, "Canst thou tell me where the golden castle of Stromberg is?" The giant said, "I will look at my map; all the towns, and villages, and houses are to be found on it." He brought out the map which he had in the room and looked for the castle, but it was not to be found on it. "It's no matter!" said he, "I have some still larger maps in my cupboard upstairs, and we will look in them." But there, too, it was in vain. The man now wanted to go onwards, but the giant begged him to wait a few days longer until his brother, who had gone out to bring some provisions, came home. When the brother came home they inquired about the golden castle of Stromberg. He replied, "When I have eaten and have had enough, I will look in the map." Then he went with them up to his chamber, and they searched in his map, but could not find it. Then he brought out still older maps, and they never rested until they found the golden castle of Stromberg, but it was many thousand miles away. "How am I to get there?" asked the man. The giant said, "I have two hours' time, during which I will carry you into the neighbourhood, but after that I must be at home to suckle the child that we have." So the giant carried the man to about a hundred leagues from the castle, and said, "Thou canst very well walk the rest of the way alone." And he turned back, but the man went onwards day and night, until at length he came to the golden castle of Stromberg. It stood on a glass-mountain, and the bewitched maiden drove in her carriage round the castle, and then went inside it. He rejoiced when he saw her and wanted to climb up to her, but when he began to do so he always slipped down the glass again. And when he saw that he could not reach her, he was filled with trouble, and said to himself, "I will stay down here below, and wait for her." So he built himself a hut and stayed in it for a whole year, and every day saw the King's daughter driving about above, but never could go to her. Then one day he saw from his hut three robbers who were beating each other, and cried to them, "God be with ye!" They stopped when they heard the cry, but as they saw no one, they once more began to beat each other, and that too most dangerously. So he again cried, "God be with ye!"

Again they stopped, looked round about, but as they saw no one they went on beating each other. Then he cried for the third time, "God be with ye," and thought, "I must see what these three are about," and went thither and asked why they were beating each other so furiously. One of them said that he found a stick, and that when he struck a door with it, that door would spring open. The next said that he had found a mantle, and that whenever he put it on, he was invisible, but the third said he had found a horse on which a man could ride everywhere, even up the glass-mountain. And now they did not know whether they ought to have these things in common, or whether they ought to divide them. Then the man said, "I will give you something in exchange for these three things. Money indeed have I not, but I have other things of more value; but first I must try yours to see if you have told the truth." Then they put him on the horse, threw the mantle round him, and gave him the stick in his hand, and when he had all these things they were no longer able to see him. So he gave them some vigorous blows and cried, "Now, vagabonds, you have got what you deserve, are you satisfied?" And he rode up the glass-mountain, but when he came in front of the castle at the top, it was shut. Then he struck the door with his stick, and it sprang open immediately. He went in and ascended the stairs until he came to the hall where the maiden was sitting with a golden cup full of wine before her. She, however, could not see him because he had the mantle on. And when he came up to her, he drew from his finger the ring which she had given him, and threw it into the cup so that it rang. Then she cried, "That is my ring, so the man who is to set me free must be here." They searched the whole castle and did not find him, but he had gone out, and had seated himself on the horse and thrown off the mantle. When they came to the door, they saw him and cried aloud in their delight. Then he alighted and took the King's daughter in his arms, but she kissed him and said, "Now hast thou set me free, and tomorrow we will celebrate our wedding."

47 The Water of Life

There was once a King who had an illness, and no one believed that he would come out of it with his life. He had three sons who were much distressed about it, and went down into the palace-garden and wept. There they met an old man who inquired as to the cause of their grief. They told him that their father was so ill that he would most certainly die, for nothing seemed to cure him. Then the old man said, "I know of one more remedy, and that is the water of life; if he drinks of it he will become well again; but it is hard to find." The eldest said, "I will manage to find it," and went to the sick King, and begged to be allowed to go forth in search of the water of life, for that alone could save him. "No," said the King, "the danger of it is too great. I would rather die." But he begged so long that the King consented. The prince thought in his heart, "If I bring the water, then I shall be best beloved of my father, and shall inherit the kingdom." So he set out, and when he had ridden forth a little distance, a dwarf stood there in the road who called to him and said, "Whither away so fast?"

"Silly shrimp," said the prince, very haughtily, "it is nothing to do with you," and rode on. But the little dwarf had grown angry, and had wished an evil wish. Soon after this the prince entered a ravine, and the further he rode the closer the mountains drew together, and at last the road became so narrow that he could not advance a step further; it was impossible either to turn his horse or to dismount from the saddle, and he was shut in there as if in prison. The sick King waited long for him, but he came not. Then the second son said, "Father, let me go forth to seek the water," and thought to himself, "If my brother is dead, then the kingdom will fall to me." At first the King would not allow him to go either, but at last he yielded, so the prince set out on the same road that his brother had taken, and he too met the dwarf, who stopped him to ask, whither he was going in such haste? "Little shrimp," said the prince, "that is nothing to thee," and rode on without giving him another look. But the dwarf bewitched him, and he, like the other, rode into a ravine, and could neither go forwards nor backwards. So fare haughty people.

As the second son also remained away, the youngest begged to be allowed to go forth to fetch the water, and at last the King was obliged to let him go. When he met the dwarf and the latter asked him whither he was going in such haste, he stopped, gave him an explanation, and said, "I am seeking the water of life, for my father is sick unto death."

"Dost thou know, then, where that is to be found?"

"No," said the prince. "As thou hast borne thyself as is seemly, and not haughtily like thy false brothers, I will give thee the information and tell thee how thou mayest obtain the water of life. It springs from a fountain in the courtyard of an enchanted castle, but thou wilt not be able to make thy way to it, if I do not give thee an iron wand and two small loaves of bread. Strike thrice with the wand on the iron door of the castle and it will spring open: inside lie two lions with gaping jaws, but if thou throwest a loaf to each of them, they will be quieted. Then hasten to fetch some of the water of life before the clock strikes twelve, else the door will shut again, and thou wilt be imprisoned." The prince thanked him, took the wand and the bread, and set out on his way. When he arrived, everything was as the dwarf had said. The door sprang open at the third stroke of the wand, and when he had appeased the lions with the bread, he entered the castle, and came to a large and splendid hall, wherein sat some enchanted princes whose rings he drew off their fingers. A sword and a loaf of bread were lying there, which he carried away. After this, he entered a chamber, in which was a beautiful maiden who rejoiced when she saw him, kissed him, and told him that he had delivered her, and should have the whole of her kingdom, and that if he would return in a year their wedding should be celebrated; likewise she told him where the spring of the water of life was, and that he was to hasten and draw some of it before the clock struck twelve. Then he went onwards, and at last entered a room where there was a beautiful newly-made bed, and as he was very weary, he felt inclined to rest a little. So he lay down and fell asleep. When he awoke, it was striking a quarter to twelve. He sprang up in a fright, ran to the spring, drew some water in a cup which stood near, and hastened away. But just as he was passing through the iron door, the clock struck twelve, and the door fell to with such violence that it carried away a piece of his heel. He, however, rejoicing at having obtained the water of life, went homewards, and again passed the dwarf. When the latter saw the sword and the loaf, he said, "With these thou hast won great wealth; with the sword thou canst slay whole armies, and the bread will never come to an end." But the prince would not go home to his father without his brothers, and said, "Dear dwarf, canst thou not tell me where my two brothers are? They went out before I did in search of the water of life, and have not returned."

"They are imprisoned between two mountains," said the dwarf. "I have condemned them to stay there, because they were so haughty." Then the prince begged until the dwarf released them; but he warned him, however, and said, "Beware of them, for they have bad hearts." When his brothers came, he rejoiced, and told them how things had gone with him, that he had found the water of life and had brought a cupful away with him, and had rescued a beautiful princess, who was willing to wait a year for him, and then their wedding was to be celebrated and he would obtain a great kingdom. After that they rode on together, and chanced upon a land where war and famine reigned, and the King already thought he must perish, for the scarcity was so great. Then the prince went to him and gave him the loaf, wherewith he fed and satisfied the whole of his kingdom, and then the prince gave him the sword also wherewith he slew the hosts of his enemies, and could now live in rest and peace. The prince then took back his loaf and his sword, and the three brothers rode on. But after this they entered two more countries where war and famine reigned and each time the prince gave his loaf and his sword to the Kings, and had now delivered three kingdoms, and after that they went on board a ship and sailed over the sea. During the passage, the two eldest conversed apart and said, "The youngest has found the water of life and not we, for that our father will give him the kingdom which belongs to us, and he will rob us of all our fortune." They then began to seek revenge, and plotted with each other to destroy him. They waited until they found him fast asleep, then they poured the water of life out of the cup, and took it for themselves, but into the cup they poured salt sea-water. Now therefore, when they arrived home, the youngest took his cup to the sick King in order that he might drink out of it, and be cured. But scarcely had he drunk a very little of the salt sea-water than he became still worse than before. And as he was lamenting over this, the two eldest brothers came, and accused the youngest of having intended to poison him, and said that they had brought him the true water of life, and handed it to him. He had scarcely tasted it, when he felt his sickness departing, and became strong and healthy as in the days of his youth. After that they both went to the youngest, mocked him, and said, "You certainly found the water of life, but you have had the pain, and we the gain; you should have been sharper, and should have kept your eyes open. We took it from you whilst you were asleep at sea, and when a year is over, one of us will go and fetch the beautiful princess. But beware that you do not disclose aught of this to our father; indeed he does not trust you, and if you say a single word, you shall lose your life into the bargain, but if you keep silent, you shall have it as a gift."

The old King was angry with his youngest son, and thought he had plotted against his life. So he summoned the court together and had sentence pronounced upon his son, that he should be secretly shot. And once when the prince was riding forth to the chase, suspecting no evil, the King's huntsman had to go with him, and when they were quite alone in the forest, the huntsman looked so sorrowful that the prince said to him, "Dear huntsman, what ails you?" The huntsman said, "I cannot tell you, and yet I ought." Then the prince said, "Say openly what it is, I will pardon you."

"Alas!" said the huntsman, "I am to shoot you dead, the King has ordered me to do it." Then the prince was shocked, and said, "Dear huntsman, let me live; there, I give you my royal garments; give me your common ones in their stead." The huntsman said, "I will willingly do that, indeed I should not have been able to shoot you." Then they exchanged clothes, and the huntsman returned home; the prince, however, went further into the forest. After a time three waggons of gold and precious stones came to the King for his youngest son, which were sent by the three Kings who had slain their enemies with the prince's sword, and maintained their people with his bread, and who wished to show their gratitude for it. The old King then thought, "Can my son have been innocent?" and said to his people, "Would that he were still alive, how it grieves me that I have suffered him to be killed!"

"He still lives," said the huntsman, "I could not find it in my heart to carry out your command," and told the King how it had happened. Then a stone fell from the King's heart, and he had it proclaimed in every country that his son might return and be taken into favour again.

The princess, however, had a road made up to her palace which was quite bright and golden, and told her people that whosoever came riding straight along it to her, would be the right wooer and was to be admitted, and whoever rode by the side of it, was not the right one, and was not to be admitted. As the time was now close at hand, the eldest thought he would hasten to go to the King's daughter, and give himself out as her deliverer, and thus win her for his bride, and the kingdom to boot. Therefore he rode forth, and when he arrived in front of the palace, and saw the splendid golden road, he thought, it would be a sin and a shame if he were to ride over that, and turned aside, and rode on the right side of it. But when he came to the door, the servants told him that he was not the right man, and was to go away again. Soon after this the second prince set out, and when he came to the golden road, and his horse had put one foot on it, he thought, it would be a sin and a shame to tread a piece of it off, and he turned aside and rode on the left side of it, and when he reached the door, the attendants told him he was not the right one, and he was to go away again. When at last the year had entirely expired, the third son likewise wished to ride out of the forest to his beloved, and with her forget his sorrows. So he set out and thought of her so incessantly, and wished to be with her so much, that he never noticed the golden road at all. So his horse rode onwards up the middle of it, and when he came to the door, it was opened and the princess received him with joy, and said he was her deliverer, and lord of the kingdom, and their wedding was celebrated with great rejoicing. When it was over she told him that his father invited him to come to him, and had forgiven him. So he rode thither, and told him everything; how his brothers had betrayed him, and how he had nevertheless kept silence. The old King wished to punish them, but they had put to sea, and never came back as long as they lived.

48 The Blue Light

There was once upon a time a soldier who for many years had served the King faithfully, but when the war came to an end could serve no longer because of the many wounds which he had received. The King said to him, "Thou mayst return to thy home, I need thee no longer, and thou wilt not receive any more money, for he only receives wages who renders me service for them." Then the soldier did not know how to earn a living, went away greatly troubled, and walked the whole day, until in the evening he entered a forest. When darkness came on, he saw a light, which he went up to, and came to a house wherein lived a witch.

"Do give me one night's lodging, and a little to eat and drink," said he to her, "or I shall starve."

"Oho!" she answered, "who gives anything to a run-away soldier? Yet will I be compassionate, and take you in, if you will do what I wish."

"What do you wish?" said the soldier. "That you should dig all round my garden for me, tomorrow." The soldier consented, and next day laboured with all his strength, but could not finish it by the evening. "I see well enough," said the witch, "that you can do no more today, but I will keep you yet another night, in payment for which you must tomorrow chop me a load of wood, and make it small." The soldier spent the whole day in doing it, and in the evening the witch proposed that he should stay one night more. "Tomorrow, you shall only do me a very trifling piece of work. Behind my house, there is an old dry well, into which my light has fallen, it burns blue, and never goes out, and you shall bring it up again for me." Next day the old woman took him to the well, and let him down in a basket. He found the blue light, and made her a signal to draw him up again. She did draw him up, but when he came near the edge, she stretched down her hand and wanted to take the blue light away from him. "No," said he, perceiving her evil intention, "I will not give thee the light until I am standing with both feet upon the ground." The witch fell into a passion, let him down again into the well, and went away.

The poor soldier fell without injury on the moist ground, and the blue light went on burning, but of what use was that to him? He saw very well that he could not escape death. He sat for a while very sorrowfully, then suddenly he felt in his pocket and found his tobacco pipe, which was still half full. "This shall be my last pleasure," thought he, pulled it out, lit it at the blue light and began to smoke. When the smoke had circled about the cavern, suddenly a little black dwarf stood before him, and said, "Lord, what are thy commands?"

"What commands have I to give thee?" replied the soldier, quite astonished. "I must do everything thou biddest me," said the little man. "Good," said the soldier; "then in the first place help me out of this well." The little man took him by the hand, and led him through an underground passage, but he did not forget to take the blue light with him. On the way the dwarf showed him the treasures which the witch had collected and hidden there, and the soldier took as much gold as he could carry. When he was above, he said to the little man, "Now go and bind the old witch, and carry her before the judge." In a short time she, with frightful cries, came riding by, as swift as the wind on a wild tom-cat, nor was it long after that before the little man reappeared. "It is all done," said he, "and the witch is already hanging on the gallows. What further commands has my lord?" inquired the dwarf. "At this moment, none," answered the soldier; "Thou canst return home, only be at hand immediately, if I summon thee."

"Nothing more is needed than that thou shouldst light thy pipe at the blue light, and I will appear before thee at once." Thereupon he vanished from his sight.

The soldier returned to the town from which he had come.

He went to the best inn, ordered himself handsome clothes, and then bade the landlord furnish him a room as handsomely as possible. When it was ready and the soldier had taken possession of it, he summoned the little black mannikin and said, "I have served the King faithfully, but he has dismissed me, and left me to hunger, and now I want to take my revenge."

"What am I to do?" asked the little man. "Late at night, when the King's daughter is in bed, bring her here in her sleep, she shall do servant's work for me." The mannikin said, "That is an easy thing for me to do, but a very dangerous thing for you, for if it is discovered, you will fare ill." When twelve o'clock had struck, the door sprang open, and the mannikin carried in the princess. "Aha! Art thou there?" cried the soldier, "get to thy work at once! Fetch the broom and sweep the chamber." When she had done this, he ordered her to come to his chair, and then he stretched out his feet and said, "Pull off my boots for me," and then he threw them in her face, and made her pick them up again, and clean and brighten them. She, however, did everything he bade her, without opposition, silently and with half-shut eyes. When the first cock crowed, the mannikin carried her back to the royal palace, and laid her in her bed.

Next morning when the princess arose, she went to her father, and told him that she had had a very strange dream. "I was carried through the streets with the rapidity of lightning," said she, "and taken into a soldier's room, and I had to wait upon him like a servant, sweep his room, clean his boots, and do all kinds of menial work. It was only a dream, and yet I am just as tired as if I really had done everything."

"The dream may have been true," said the King, "I will give thee a piece of advice. Fill thy pocket full of peas, and make a small hole in it, and then if thou art carried away again, they will fall out and leave a track in the streets." But unseen by the King, the mannikin was standing beside him when he said that, and heard all. At night when the sleeping princess was again carried through the streets, some peas certainly did fall out of her pocket, but they made no track, for the crafty mannikin had just before scattered peas in every street there was. And again the princess was compelled to do servant's work until cock-crow.

Next morning the King sent his people out to seek the track, but it was all in vain, for in every street poor children were sitting, picking up peas, and saying, "It must have rained peas, last night."

"We must think of something else," said the King; "keep thy shoes on when thou goest to bed, and before thou comest back from the place where thou art taken, hide one of them there, I will soon contrive to find it." The black mannikin heard this plot, and at night when the soldier again ordered him to bring the princess, revealed it to him, and told him that he knew of no expedient to counteract this stratagem, and that if the shoe were found in the soldier's house it would go badly with him. "Do what I bid thee," replied the soldier, and again this third night the princess was obliged to work like a servant, but before she went away, she hid her shoe under the bed.

Next morning the King had the entire town searched for his daughter's shoe. It was found at the soldier's, and the soldier himself, who at the entreaty of the dwarf had gone outside the gate, was soon brought back, and thrown into prison. In his flight he had forgotten the most valuable things he had, the blue light and the gold, and had only one ducat in his pocket. And now loaded with chains, he was standing at the window of his dungeon, when he chanced to see one of his comrades passing by. The soldier tapped at the pane of glass, and when this man came up, said to him, "Be so kind as to fetch me the small bundle I have left lying in the inn, and I will give you a ducat for doing it." His comrade ran thither and brought him what he wanted. As soon as the soldier was alone again, he lighted his pipe and summoned the black mannikin. "Have no fear," said the latter to his master. "Go wheresoever they take you, and let them do what they will, only take the blue light with you." Next day the soldier was tried, and though he had done nothing wicked, the judge condemned him to death. When he was led forth to die, he begged a last favor of the King. "What is it?" asked the King. "That I may smoke one more pipe on my way."

"Thou mayst smoke three," answered the King, "but do not imagine that I will spare thy life." Then the soldier pulled out his pipe and lighted it at the blue light, and as soon as a few wreaths of smoke had ascended, the mannikin was there with a small cudgel in his hand, and said, "What does my lord command?"

"Strike down to earth that false judge there, and his constable, and spare not the King who has treated me so ill." Then the mannikin fell on them like lightning, darting this way and that way, and whosoever was so much as touched by his cudgel fell to earth, and did not venture to stir again. The King was terrified; he threw himself on the soldier's mercy, and merely to be allowed to live at all, gave him his kingdom for his own, and the princess as his wife.

49 The Three Army-Surgeons

Three army-surgeons who thought they knew their art perfectly, were travelling about the world, and they came to an inn where they wanted to pass the night. The host asked whence they came, and whither they were going. "We are roaming about the world and practising our art."

"Just show me for once in a way what you can do," said the host. Then the first said he would cut off his hand, and put it on again early next morning; the second said he would tear out his heart, and replace it next morning; the third said he would cut out his eyes and heal them again next morning. "If you can do that," said the innkeeper, "you have learnt everything." They, however, had a salve, with which they rubbed themselves, which joined parts together, and they carried the little bottle in which it was, constantly with them. Then they cut the hand, heart and eyes from their bodies as they had said they would, and laid them all together on a plate, and gave it to the innkeeper. The innkeeper gave it to a servant who was to set it in the cupboard, and take good care of it. The girl, however, had a lover in secret, who was a soldier. When therefore the innkeeper, the three army-surgeons, and everyone else in the house were asleep, the soldier came and wanted something to eat. The girl opened the cupboard and brought him some food, and in her love forgot to shut the cupboard-door again; she seated herself at the table by her lover, and they chattered away together. While she sat so contentedly there, thinking of no ill luck, the cat came creeping in, found the cupboard open, took the hand and heart and eyes of the three army-surgeons, and ran off with them. When the soldier had done eating, and the girl was taking away the things and going to shut the cupboard she saw that the plate which the innkeeper had given her to take care of, was empty. Then she said in a fright to her lover, "Ah, miserable girl, what shall I do?

The hand is gone, the heart and the eyes are gone too, what will become of me in the morning?"

"Be easy," said he, "I will help thee out of thy trouble there is a thief hanging outside on the gallows, I will cut off his hand. Which hand was it?"

"The right one." Then the girl gave him a sharp knife, and he went and cut the poor sinner's right hand off, and brought it to her. After this he caught the cat and cut its eyes out, and now nothing but the heart was wanting. "Have you not been killing, and are not the dead pigs in the cellar?" said he. "Yes," said the girl. "That's well," said the soldier, and he went down and fetched a pig's heart. The girl placed all together on the plate, and put it in the cupboard, and when after this her lover took leave of her, she went quietly to bed.

In the morning when the three army-surgeons got up, they told the girl she was to bring them the plate on which the hand, heart, and eyes were lying. Then she brought it out of the cupboard, and the first fixed the thief's hand on and smeared it with his salve, and it grew to his arm directly. The second took the cat's eyes and put them in his own head. The third fixed the pig's heart firm in the place where his own had been, and the innkeeper stood by, admired their skill, and said he had never yet seen such a thing as that done, and would sing their praises and recommend them to everyone. Then they paid their bill, and travelled farther.

As they were on their way, the one with the pig's heart did not stay with them at all, but wherever there was a corner he ran to it, and rooted about in it with his nose as pigs do. The others wanted to hold him back by the tail of his coat, but that did no good; he tore himself loose, and ran wherever the dirt was thickest. The second also behaved very strangely; he rubbed his eyes, and said to the others, "Comrades, what is the matter? I don't see at all. Will one of you lead me, so that I do not fall." Then with difficulty they travelled on till evening, when they reached another inn. They went into the bar together, and there at a table in the corner sat a rich man counting money. The one with the thief's hand walked round about him, made a sudden movement twice with his arm, and at last when the stranger turned away, he snatched at the pile of money, and took a handful from it. One of them saw this, and said, "Comrade, what art thou about? Thou must not steal. Shame on thee!"

"Eh," said he, "but how can I stop myself? My hand twitches, and I am forced to snatch things whether I will or not."

After this, they lay down to sleep, and while they were lying there it was so dark that no one could see his own hand. All at once the one with the cat's eyes awoke, aroused the others, and said. "Brothers, just look up, do you see the white mice running about there?" The two sat up, but could see nothing. Then said he, "Things are not right with us, we have not got back again what is ours. We must return to the innkeeper, he has deceived us." They went back therefore, the next morning, and told the host they had not got what was their own again; that the first had a thief's hand, the second cat's eyes, and the third a pig's heart. The innkeeper said that the girl must be to blame for that, and was going to call her, but when she had seen the three coming, she had run out by the backdoor, and not come back. Then the three said he must give them a great deal of money, or they would set his house on fire. He gave them what he had, and whatever he could get together, and the three went away with it. It was enough for the rest of their lives, but they would rather have had their own proper organs.

50 The Seven Swabians

Seven Swabians were once together. The first was Master
Schulz; the second, Jackli; the third, Marli; the fourth, Jergli; the
fifth, Michal; the sixth, Hans; the seventh, Veitli: all seven had
made up their minds to travel about the world to seek adventures, and perform great deeds. But in order that they might go
in security and with arms in their hands, they thought it would
be advisable that they should have one solitary, but very strong,
and very long spear made for them. This spear all seven of them
took in their hands at once; in front walked the boldest and
bravest, and that was Master Schulz; all the others followed in a
row, and Veitli was the last. Then it came to pass one day in the
hay-making month (July), when they had walked a long distance, and still had a long way to go before they reached the village where they were to pass the night, that as they were in a
meadow in the twilight a great beetle or hornet flew by them
from behind a bush, and hummed in a menacing manner. Master
Schulz was so terrified that he all but dropped the spear, and a
cold perspiration broke out over his whole body. "Hark! Hark!"
cried he to his comrades, "Good heavens! I hear a drum." Jackli,
who was behind him holding the spear, and who perceived some
kind of a smell, said, "Something is most certainly going on, for
I taste powder and matches." At these words Master Schulz
began to take to flight, and in a trice jumped over a hedge, but
as he just happened to jump on to the teeth of a rake which had
been left lying there after the hay-making, the handle of it struck
against his face and gave him a tremendous blow. "Oh dear! Oh
dear!" screamed Master Schulz. "Take me prisoner; I surrender!
I surrender!" The other six all leapt over, one on the top of the
other, crying, "If you surrender, I surrender too! If you surrender, I surrender too!" At length, as no enemy was there to bind
and take them away, they saw that they had been mistaken, and

in order that the story might not be known, and they be treated as fools and ridiculed, they all swore to each other to hold their peace about it until one of them accidentally spoke of it. Then they journeyed onwards. The second danger which they survived cannot be compared with the first. Some days afterwards, their path led them through a fallow-field where a hare was sitting sleeping in the sun. Her ears were standing straight up, and her great glassy eyes were wide open. All of them were alarmed at the sight of the horrible wild beast, and they consulted together as to what it would be the least dangerous to do. For if they were to run away, they knew that the monster would pursue and swallow them whole. So they said, "We must go through a great and dangerous struggle. Boldly ventured, is half won," and all seven grasped the spear, Master Schulz in front, and Veitli behind. Master Schulz was always trying to keep the spear back, but Veitli had become quite brave while behind, and wanted to dash forward and cried:

> "Strike home, in every Swabian's name,
> Or else I wish ye may be lame."

But Hans knew how to meet this, and said:

> "Thunder and lightning, it's fine to prate,
> But for dragon-hunting thou'rt aye too late."

Michal cried:

> "Nothing is wanting, not even a hair,
> Be sure the Devil himself is there."

Then it was Jergli's turn to speak:

> "If it be not, it's at least his mother,
> Or else it's the Devil's own step-brother."

And now Marli had a bright thought, and said to Veitli:

> "Advance, Veitli, advance, advance,

And I behind will hold the lance."

Veitli, however, did not attend to that, and Jackli said:

"'Tis Schulz's place the first to be,
No one deserves that honour but he."

Then Master Schulz plucked up his courage, and said, gravely:

"Then let us boldly advance to the fight,
And thus we shall show our valour and might."

Hereupon they all together set on the dragon. Master Schulz crossed himself and prayed for God's assistance, but as all this was of no avail, and he was getting nearer and nearer to the enemy, he screamed "Oho! oho! ho! ho! ho!" in the greatest anguish. This awakened the hare, which in great alarm darted swiftly away. When Master Schulz saw her thus flying from the field of battle, he cried in his joy.

"Quick, Veitli, quick, look there, look there,
The monster's nothing but a hare!"

But the Swabian allies went in search of further adventures, and came to the Moselle, a mossy, quiet, deep river, over which there are few bridges, and which in many places people have to cross in boats. As the seven Swabians did not know this, they called to a man who was working on the opposite side of the river, to know how people contrived to get across. The distance and their way of speaking made the man unable to understand what they wanted, and he said "What? What?" in the way people speak in the neighborhood of Treves. Master Schulz thought he was saying, "Wade, wade through the water," and as he was the first, began to set out and went into the moselle. It was not long before he sank in the mud and the deep waves which drove against him, but his hat was blown on the opposite shore by the wind, and a frog sat down beside it, and croaked "Wat, wat, wat." The other six on the opposite side heard that, and said,

"Oho, comrades, Master Schulz is calling us; if he can wade across, why cannot we?" So they all jumped into the water together in a great hurry, and were drowned, and thus one frog took the lives of all six of them, and not one of the Swabian allies ever reached home again.

51 The King's Son Who Feared Nothing

There was once a King's son, who was no longer content to stay at home in his father's house, and as he had no fear of anything, he thought, "I will go forth into the wide world, there the time will not seem long to me, and I shall see wonders enough." So he took leave of his parents, and went forth, and on and on from morning till night, and whichever way his path led it was the same to him. It came to pass that he got to the house of a giant, and as he was so tired he sat down by the door and rested. And as he let his eyes roam here and there, he saw the giant's playthings lying in the yard. These were a couple of enormous balls, and nine-pins as tall as a man. After a while he had a fancy to set the nine-pins up and then rolled the balls at them, and screamed and cried out when the nine-pins fell, and had a merry time of it. The giant heard the noise, stretched his head out of the window, and saw a man who was not taller than other men, and yet played with his nine-pins. "Little worm," cried he, "why art thou playing with my balls? Who gave thee strength to do it?" The King's son looked up, saw the giant, and said, "Oh, thou blockhead, thou thinkest indeed that thou only hast strong arms, I can do everything I want to do." The giant came down and watched the bowling with great admiration, and said, "Child of man, if thou art one of that kind, go and bring me an apple of the tree of life."

"What dost thou want with it?" said the King's son. "I do not want the apple for myself," answered the giant, "but I have a betrothed bride who wishes for it. I have travelled far about the world and cannot find the tree."

"I will soon find it," said the King's son, "and I do not know what is to prevent me from getting the apple down." The giant said, "Thou really believest it to be so easy! The garden in which the tree stands is surrounded by an iron railing, and in front of the railing lie wild beasts, each close to the other, and they keep watch and let no man go in."

"They will be sure to let me in," said the King's son. "Yes, but even if thou dost get into the garden, and seest the apple hanging to the tree, it is still not thine; a ring hangs in front of it, through which any one who wants to reach the apple and break it off, must put his hand, and no one has yet had the luck to do it."

"That luck will be mine," said the King's son.

Then he took leave of the giant, and went forth over mountain and valley, and through plains and forests, until at length he came to the wondrous garden.

The beasts lay round about it, but they had put their heads down and were asleep. Moreover, they did not awake when he went up to them, so he stepped over them, climbed the fence, and got safely into the garden. There, in the very middle of it, stood the tree of life, and the red apples were shining upon the branches. He climbed up the trunk to the top, and as he was about to reach out for an apple, he saw a ring hanging before it; but he thrust his hand through that without any difficulty, and gathered the apple. The ring closed tightly on his arm, and all at once he felt a prodigious strength flowing through his veins. When he had come down again from the tree with the apple, he would not climb over the fence, but grasped the great gate, and had no need to shake it more than once before it sprang open with a loud crash. Then he went out, and the lion which had been lying down before, was awake and sprang after him, not in rage and fierceness, but following him humbly as its master.

The King's son took the giant the apple he had promised him, and said, "Seest thou, I have brought it without difficulty." The giant was glad that his desire had been so soon satisfied, hastened to his bride, and gave her the apple for which she had wished. She was a beautiful and wise maiden, and as she did not see the ring on his arm, she said, "I shall never believe that thou hast brought the apple, until I see the ring on thine arm." The giant said, "I have nothing to do but go home and fetch it," and thought it would be easy to take away by force from the weak man, what he would not give of his own free will. He therefore demanded the ring from him, but the King's son refused it. "Where the apple is, the ring must be also," said the giant; "if thou wilt not give it of thine own accord, thou must fight with me for it."

They wrestled with each other for a long time, but the giant could not get the better of the King's son, who was strengthened by the magical power of the ring. Then the giant thought of a stratagem, and said, "I have got warm with fighting, and so hast thou. We will bathe in the river, and cool ourselves before we begin again." The King's son, who knew nothing of falsehood, went with him to the water, and pulled off with his clothes the ring also from his arm, and sprang into the river. The giant instantly snatched the ring, and ran away with it, but the lion, which had observed the theft, pursued the giant, tore the ring out of his hand, and brought it back to its master. Then the giant placed himself behind an oak-tree, and while the King's son was busy putting on his clothes again, surprised him, and put both his eyes out.

And now the unhappy King's son stood there, and was blind and knew not how to help himself. Then the giant came back to him, took him by the hand as if he were someone who wanted to guide him, and led him to the top of a high rock. There he left him standing, and thought, "Just two steps more, and he will fall down and kill himself, and I can take the ring from him." But the faithful lion had not deserted its master; it held him fast by the clothes, and drew him gradually back again. When the giant came and wanted to rob the dead man, he saw that his cunning had been in vain. "Is there no way, then, of destroying a weak child of man like that?" said he angrily to himself, and seized the King's son and led him back again to the precipice by another way, but the lion which saw his evil design, helped its master out of danger here also. When they had got close to the edge, the giant let the blind man's hand drop, and was going to leave him behind alone, but the lion pushed the giant so that he was thrown down and fell, dashed to pieces, on the ground.

The faithful animal again drew its master back from the precipice, and guided him to a tree by which flowed a clear brook. The King's son sat down there, but the lion lay down, and sprinkled the water in his face with its paws. Scarcely had a couple of drops wetted the sockets of his eyes, than he was once more able to see something, and remarked a little bird flying quite close by, which wounded itself against the trunk of a tree. On this it went down to the water and bathed itself therein, and then it soared upwards and swept between the trees without touching them, as if it had recovered its sight again. Then the King's son recognised a sign from God and stooped down to the water, and washed and bathed his face in it. And when he arose he had his eyes once more, brighter and clearer than they had ever been.

The King's son thanked God for his great mercy, and travelled with his lion onwards through the world. And it came to pass that he arrived before a castle which was enchanted. In the gateway stood a maiden of beautiful form and fine face, but she was quite black. She spoke to him and said, "Ah, if thou couldst but deliver me from the evil spell which is thrown over me."

"What shall I do?" said the King's son. The maiden answered, "Thou must pass three nights in the great hall of this enchanted castle, but thou must let no fear enter thy heart. When they are doing their worst to torment thee, if thou bearest it without letting a sound escape thee, I shall be free. Thy life they dare not take." Then said the King's son, "I have no fear; with God's help I will try it." So he went gaily into the castle, and when it grew dark he seated himself in the large hall and waited. Everything was quiet, however, till midnight, when all at once a great tumult began, and out of every hole and corner came little devils. They behaved as if they did not see him, seated themselves in the middle of the room, lighted a fire, and began to gamble. When one of them lost, he said, "It is not right; some one is here who does not belong to us; it is his fault that I am losing."

"Wait, you fellow behind the stove, I am coming," said another. The screaming became still louder, so that no one could have heard it without terror. The King's son stayed sitting quite quietly, and was not afraid; but at last the devils jumped up from the ground, and fell on him, and there were so many of them that he could not defend himself from them. They dragged him about on the floor, pinched him, pricked him, beat him, and tormented him, but no sound escaped from him. Towards morning they disappeared, and he was so exhausted that he could scarcely move his limbs, but when day dawned the black maiden came to him. She bore in her hand a little bottle wherein was the water of life wherewith she washed him, and he at once felt all pain depart and new strength flow through his veins. She said, "Thou hast held out successfully for one night, but two more lie before thee." Then she went away again, and as she was going, he observed that her feet had become white. The next night the devils came and began their gambols anew. They fell on the King's son, and beat him much more severely than the night before, until his body was covered with wounds. But as he bore all quietly, they were forced to leave him, and when dawn appeared, the maiden came and healed him with the water of life. And when she went away, he saw with joy that she had already become white to the tips of her fingers. And now he had only one night more to go through, but it was the worst. The hob-goblins came again: "Art thou there still?" cried they, "thou shalt be tormented till thy breath stops." They pricked him and beat him, and threw him here and there, and pulled him by the arms and legs as if they wanted to tear him to pieces, but he bore everything, and never uttered a cry. At last the devils vanished, but he lay fainting there, and did not stir, nor could he raise his eyes to look at the maiden who came in, and sprinkled and bathed him with the water of life. But suddenly he was freed from all pain, and felt fresh and healthy as if he had awakened from sleep, and when he opened his eyes he saw the maiden standing by him, snow-white, and fair as day. "Rise," said she, "and swing thy sword three times over the stairs, and then all will be delivered." And when he had done that, the whole castle was released from enchantment, and the maiden was a rich King's daughter. The servants came and said that the table was already set in the great hall, and dinner served up. Then they sat down and ate and drank together, and in the evening the wedding was solemnised with great rejoicings.

52 Donkey Cabbages

There was once a young huntsman who went into the forest to lie in wait. He had a fresh and joyous heart, and as he was going thither, whistling upon a leaf, an ugly old crone came up, who spoke to him and said, "Good-day, dear huntsman, truly you are merry and contented, but I am suffering from hunger and thirst, do give me some alms." The huntsman had compassion on the poor old creature, felt in his pocket, and gave her what he could afford. He was then about to go further, but the old woman stopped him and said, "Listen, dear huntsman, to what I tell you; I will make you a present in return for your kindness. Go on your way now, but in a little while you will come to a tree, whereon nine birds are sitting which have a cloak in their claws, and are plucking at it; take your gun and shoot into the midst of them, they will let the cloak fall down to you, but one of the birds will be hurt, and will drop down dead. Carry away the cloak, it is a wishing-cloak; when you throw it over your shoulders, you only have to wish to be in a certain place, and you will be there in the twinkling of an eye. Take out the heart of the dead bird and swallow it whole, and every morning early, when you get up, you will find a gold piece under your pillow." The huntsman thanked the wise woman, and thought to himself, "Those are fine things that she has promised me, if all does but come true." And verily when he had walked about a hundred paces, he heard in the branches above him such a screaming and twittering that he looked up and saw there a crowd of birds who were tearing a piece of cloth about with their beaks and claws, and tugging and fighting as if each wanted to have it all to himself. "Well," said the huntsman, "this is wonderful, it has really come to pass just as the old wife foretold!" and he took the gun from his shoulder, aimed and fired right into the midst of them, so that the feathers flew about. The birds instantly took to flight with loud outcries, but one dropped down dead, and the cloak fell at the same time. Then the huntsman did as the old woman had directed him, cut open the bird, sought the heart, swallowed it down, and took the cloak home with him.

Next morning, when he awoke, the promise occurred to him, and he wished to see if it also had been fulfilled. When he lifted up the pillow, the gold piece shone in his eyes, and next day he found another, and so it went on, every time he got up. He gathered together a heap of gold, but at last he thought, "Of what use is all my gold to me if I stay at home? I will go forth and see the world."

He then took leave of his parents, buckled on his huntsman's pouch and gun, and went out into the world. It came to pass, that one day he travelled through a dense forest, and when he came to the end of it, in the plain before him stood a fine castle. An old woman was standing with a wonderfully beautiful maiden, looking out of one of the windows. The old woman, however, was a witch and said to the maiden, "There comes one out of the forest, who has a wonderful treasure in his body, we must filch it from him, my dear daughter, it is more suitable for us than for him. He has a bird's heart about him, by means of which a gold piece lies every morning under his pillow." She told her what she was to do to get it, and what part she had to play, and finally threatened her, and said with angry eyes, "And if you do not attend to what I say, it will be the worse for you." Now when the huntsman came nearer he descried the maiden, and said to himself, "I have travelled about for such a long time, I will take a rest for once, and enter that beautiful castle. I have certainly money enough." Nevertheless, the real reason was that he had caught sight of the pretty girl. He entered the house, and was well received and courteously entertained.

Before long he was so much in love with the young witch that he no longer thought of anything else, and only saw things as she saw them, and did what she desired. The old woman then said, "Now we must have the bird's heart, he will never miss it."

She prepared a drink, and when it was ready, poured it into a cup and gave it to the maiden, who was to present it to the huntsman. She did so, saying, "Now, my dearest, drink to me." So he took the cup, and when he had swallowed the draught, he brought up the heart of the bird. The girl had to take it away secretly and swallow it herself, for the old woman would have it so.

Thenceforward he found no more gold under his pillow, but it lay instead under that of the maiden, from whence the old woman fetched it away every morning; but he was so much in love and so befooled, that he thought of nothing else but of passing his time with the girl.

Then the old witch said, "We have the bird's heart, but we must also take the wishing-cloak away from him." The girl answered, "We will leave him that, he has lost his wealth." The old woman was angry and said, "Such a mantle is a wonderful thing, and is seldom to be found in this world. I must and will have it!" She gave the girl several blows, and said that if she did not obey, it should fare ill with her. So she did the old woman's bidding, placed herself at the window and looked on the distant country, as if she were very sorrowful. The huntsman asked, "Why dost thou stand there so sorrowfully?"

"Ah, my beloved," was her answer, "over yonder lies the Garnet Mountain, where the precious stones grow. I long for them so much that when I think of them, I feel quite sad, but who can get them? Only the birds; they fly and can reach them, but a man never."

"Hast thou nothing else to complain of?" said the huntsman. "I will soon remove that burden from thy heart." With that he drew her under his mantle, wished himself on the Garnet Mountain, and in the twinkling of an eye they were sitting on it together. Precious stones were glistening on every side so that it was a joy to see them, and together they gathered the finest and costliest of them. Now, the old woman had, through her sorceries, contrived that the eyes of the huntsman should become heavy. He said to the maiden, "We will sit down and rest awhile,

I am so tired that I can no longer stand on my feet." Then they sat down, and he laid his head in her lap, and fell asleep. When he was asleep, she unfastened the mantle from his shoulders, and wrapped herself in it, picked up the garnets and stones, and wished herself back at home with them.

But when the huntsman had had his sleep out and awoke, and perceived that his sweetheart had betrayed him, and left him alone on the wild mountain, he said, "Oh, what treachery there is in the world!" and sat down there in care and sorrow, not knowing what to do. But the mountain belonged to some wild and monstrous giants who dwelt thereon and lived their lives there, and he had not sat long before he saw three of them coming towards him, so he lay down as if he were sunk in a deep sleep. Then the giants came up, and the first kicked him with his foot and said, "What sort of an earth-worm is lying curled up here? The second said, "Step upon him and kill him." But the third said, "That would indeed be worth your while; just let him live, he cannot remain here; and when he climbs higher, toward the summit of of the mountain, the clouds will lay hold of him and bear him away." So saying they passed by. But the huntsman had paid heed to their words, and as soon as they were gone, he rose and climbed up to the summit of the mountain, and when he had sat there a while, a cloud floated towards him, caught him up, carried him away, and travelled about for a long time in the heavens. Then it sank lower, and let itself down on a great cabbage-garden, girt round by walls, so that he came softly to the ground on cabbages and vegetables.

Then the huntsman looked about him and said, "If I had but something to eat! I am so hungry, and my hunger will increase in course of time; but I see here neither apples nor pears, nor any other sort of fruit, everywhere nothing but cabbages," but at length he thought, "At a pinch I can eat some of the leaves, they do not taste particularly good, but they will refresh me." With that he picked himself out a fine head of cabbage, and ate it, but scarcely had he swallowed a couple of mouthfuls than he felt very strange and quite different.

Four legs grew on him, a large head and two thick ears, and he saw with horror that he was changed into an ass. Still as his hunger increased every minute, and as the juicy leaves were suitable to his present nature, he went on eating with great zest. At last he arrived at a different kind of cabbage, but as soon as he had swallowed it, he again felt a change, and reassumed his former human shape.

Then the huntsman lay down and slept off his fatigue. When he awoke next morning, he broke off one head of the bad cabbages and another of the good ones, and thought to himself, "This shall help me to get my own again and punish treachery." Then he took the cabbages with him, climbed over the wall, and went forth to seek for the castle of his sweetheart. After wandering about for a couple of days he was lucky enough to find it again. He dyed his face brown, so that his own mother would not have known him; and begged for shelter: "I am so tired," said he, "that I can go no further." The witch asked, "Who are you, countryman, and what is your business?"

"I am a King's messenger, and was sent out to seek the most delicious salad which grows beneath the sun. I have even been so fortunate as to find it, and am carrying it about with me; but the heat of the sun is so intense that the delicate cabbage threatens to wither, and I do not know if I can carry it any further."

When the old woman heard of the exquisite salad, she was greedy, and said, "Dear countryman, let me just taste this wonderful salad."

"Why not?" answered he, "I have brought two heads with me, and will give you one of them," and he opened his pouch and handed her the bad cabbage. The witch suspected nothing amiss, and her mouth watered so for this new dish that she herself went into the kitchen and dressed it. When it was prepared she could not wait until it was set on the table, but took a couple of leaves at once, and put them in her mouth, but hardly had she swallowed them than she was deprived of her human shape, and she ran out into the courtyard in the form of an ass. Presently the maid-servant entered the kitchen, saw the salad standing there ready prepared, and was about to carry it up; but on the way, according to habit, she was seized by the desire to taste, and she ate a couple of leaves. Instantly the magic power showed itself, and she likewise became an ass and ran out to the old woman, and the dish of salad fell to the ground. Meantime the messenger sat beside the beautiful girl, and as no one came with the salad and she also was longing for it, she said, "I don't know what has become of the salad." The huntsman thought, "The salad must have already taken effect," and said, "I will go to the kitchen and inquire about it." As he went down he saw the two asses running about in the courtyard; the salad, however, was lying on the ground. "All right," said he, "the two have taken their portion," and he picked up the other leaves, laid them on the dish, and carried them to the maiden. "I bring you the delicate food myself," said he, "in order that you may not have to wait longer." Then she ate of it, and was, like the others, immediately deprived of her human form, and ran out into the courtyard in the shape of an ass.

After the huntsman had washed his face, so that the trans-formed ones could recognize him, he went down into the court-yard, and said, "Now you shall receive the wages of your treach-ery," and bound them together, all three with one rope, and drove them along until he came to a mill. He knocked at the window, the miller put out his head, and asked what he wanted. "I have three unmanageable beasts," answered he, "which I don't want to keep any longer. Will you take them in, and give them food and stable room, and manage them as I tell you, and then I will pay you what you ask." The miller said, "Why not? But how am I to manage them?" The huntsman then said that he was to give three beatings and one meal daily to the old donkey, and that was the witch; one beating and three meals to the younger one, which was the servant-girl; and to the youngest, which was the maiden, no beatings and three meals, for he could not bring himself to have the maiden beaten. After that he went back into the castle, and found therein everything he needed.

After a couple of days, the miller came and said he must inform him that the old ass which had received three beatings and only one meal daily was dead; "the two others," he continued, "are certainly not dead, and are fed three times daily, but they are so sad that they cannot last much longer." The huntsman was moved to pity, put away his anger, and told the miller to drive them back again to him. And when they came, he gave them some of the good salad, so that they became human again. The beautiful girl fell on her knees before him, and said, "Ah, my beloved, forgive me for the evil I have done you; my mother drove me to it; it was done against my will, for I love you dearly. Your wishing-cloak hangs in a cupboard, and as for the bird's-heart I will take a vomiting potion." But he thought otherwise, and said, "Keep it; it is all the same, for I will take thee for my true wife." So the wedding was celebrated, and they lived happily together until their death.

53 The Old Woman in the Wood

A poor servant-girl was once travelling with the family with which she was in service, through a great forest, and when they were in the midst of it, robbers came out of the thicket, and murdered all they found. All perished together except the girl, who had jumped out of the carriage in a fright, and hidden herself behind a tree. When the robbers had gone away with their loot, she came out and beheld the great disaster. Then she began to weep bitterly, and said, "What can a poor girl like me do now? I do not know how to get out of the forest, no human being lives in it, so I must certainly starve." She walked about and looked for a road, but could find none. When it was evening she seated herself under a tree, gave herself into God's keeping, and resolved to sit waiting there and not go away, let what might happen. When, however, she had sat there for a while, a white dove came flying to her with a little golden key in its mouth. It put the little key in her hand, and said, "Dost thou see that great tree, therein is a little lock, it opens with the tiny key, and there thou wilt find food enough, and suffer no more hunger." Then she went to the tree and opened it, and found milk in a little dish, and white bread to break into it, so that she could eat her fill. When she was satisfied, she said, "It is now the time when the hens at home go to roost, I am so tired I could go to bed too." Then the dove flew to her again, and brought another golden key in its bill, and said, "Open that tree there, and thou willt find a bed." So she opened it, and found a beautiful white bed, and she prayed God to protect her during the night, and lay down and slept. In the morning the dove came for the third time, and again brought a little key, and said, "Open that tree there, and thou wilt find clothes." And when she opened it, she found garments beset with gold and with jewels, more splendid than those of any king's daughter.

So she lived there for some time, and the dove came every day and provided her with all she needed, and it was a quiet good life. Once, however, the dove came and said, "Wilt thou do something for my sake?"

"With all my heart," said the girl. Then said the little dove, "I will guide thee to a small house; enter it, and inside it, an old woman will be sitting by the fire and will say, 'Good-day.' But on thy life give her no answer, let her do what she will, but pass by her on the right side; further on, there is a door, open it, and thou wilt enter into a room where a quantity of rings of all kinds are lying, amongst which are some magnificent ones with shining stones; leave them, however, where they are, and seek out a plain one, which must likewise be amongst them, and bring it here to me as quickly as thou canst." The girl went to the little house, and came to the door. There sat an old woman who stared when she saw her, and said, "Good-day my child." The girl gave her no answer, and opened the door. "Whither away," cried the old woman, and seized her by the gown, and wanted to hold her fast, saying, "That is my house; no one can go in there if I choose not to allow it." But the girl was silent, got away from her, and went straight into the room. Now there lay on the table an enormous quantity of rings, which gleamed and glittered before her eyes. She turned them over and looked for the plain one, but could not find it. While she was seeking, she saw the old woman and how she was stealing away, and wanting to get off with a bird-cage which she had in her hand. So she went after her and took the cage out of her hand, and when she raised it up and looked into it, a bird was inside which had the plain ring in its bill. Then she took the ring, and ran quite joyously home with it, and thought the little white dove would come and get the ring, but it did not. Then she leant against a tree and determined to wait for the dove, and, as she thus stood, it seemed just as if the tree was soft and pliant, and was letting its branches down. And suddenly the branches twined around her, and were two arms, and when she looked round, the tree was a handsome man, who embraced and kissed her heartily, and said, "Thou hast delivered me from the power of the old woman, who is a wicked witch. She had changed me into a tree, and every day for two hours I was a white dove, and so long as she possessed the ring I could not regain my human form." Then his servants and his horses, who had likewise been changed into trees, were freed from the enchantment also, and stood beside him. And he led them forth to his kingdom, for he was a King's son, and they married, and lived happily.

54 The Devil and his Grandmother

There was a great war, and the King had many soldiers, but gave them small pay, so small that they could not live upon it, so three of them agreed among themselves to desert. One of them said to the others, "If we are caught we shall be hanged on the gallows; how shall we manage it?" Another said, "Look at that great cornfield, if we were to hide ourselves there, no one could find us; the troops are not allowed to enter it, and tomorrow they are to march away." They crept into the corn, only the troops did not march away, but remained lying all round about it. They stayed in the corn for two days and two nights, and were so hungry that they all but died, but if they had come out, their death would have been certain. Then said they, "What is the use of our deserting if we have to perish miserably here?" But now a fiery dragon came flying through the air, and it came down to them, and asked why they had concealed themselves there. They answered, "We are three soldiers who have deserted because the pay was so bad, and now we shall have to die of hunger if we stay here, or to dangle on the gallows if we go out."

"If you will serve me for seven years," said the dragon, "I will convey you through the army so that no one shall seize you."

"We have no choice and are compelled to accept," they replied. Then the dragon caught hold of them with his claws, and carried them away through the air over the army, and put them down again on the earth far from it; but the dragon was no other than the Devil. He gave them a small whip and said, "Whip with it and crack it, and then as much gold will spring up round about as you can wish for; then you can live like great lords, keep horses, and drive your carriages, but when the seven years have come to an end, you are my property." Then he put before them a book which they were all three forced to sign. "I will, however, then set you a riddle," said he, "and if you can guess that, you shall be free, and released from my power." Then the dragon flew away from them, and they went away with their whip, had gold in plenty, ordered themselves rich apparel, and travelled about the world. Wherever they were they lived in pleasure and magnificence, rode on horseback, drove in carriages, ate and drank, but did nothing wicked. The time slipped quickly away, and when the seven years were coming to an end, two of them were terribly anxious and alarmed; but the third took the affair easily, and said, "Brothers, fear nothing, my head is sharp enough, I shall guess the riddle. They went out into the open country and sat down, and the two pulled sorrowful faces. Then an aged woman came up to them who inquired why they were so sad? "Alas!" said they, "how can that concern you? After all, you cannot help us."

"Who knows?" said she. "confide your trouble to me." So they told her that they had been the Devil's servants for nearly seven years, and that he had provided them with gold as plentifully as if it had been blackberries, but that they had sold themselves to him, and were forfeited to him, if at the end of the seven years they could not guess a riddle." The old woman said, "If you are to be saved, one of you must go into the forest, there he will come to a fallen rock which looks like a little house, he must enter that, and then he will obtain help." The two melancholy ones thought to themselves, "That will still not save us," and stayed where they were, but the third, the merry one, got up and walked on in the forest until he found the rock-house. In the little house, however, a very aged woman was sitting, who was the Devil's grandmother, and asked the soldier where he came from, and what he wanted there? He told her everything that had happened, and as he pleased her well, she had pity on him, and said she would help him. She lifted up a great stone which lay above a cellar, and said, "Conceal thyself there, thou canst hear everything that is said here; only sit still, and do not stir. When the dragon comes, I will question him about the riddle, he tells everything to me, so listen carefully to his answer." At twelve o'clock at night, the dragon came flying thither, and asked for his dinner. The grandmother laid the table, and served up food and drink, so that he was pleased, and they ate and drank together. In the course of conversation, she asked him what kind of a day he had had, and how many souls he had got?

"Nothing went very well today," he answered, "but I have laid hold of three soldiers, I have them safe."

"Indeed! Three soldiers, that's something like, but they may escape you yet." The Devil said mockingly, "They are mine! I will set them a riddle, which they will never in this world be able to guess!"

"What riddle is that?" she inquired. "I will tell you. In the great North Sea lies a dead dog-fish, that shall be your roast meat, and the rib of a whale shall be your silver spoon, and a hollow old horse's hoof shall be your wine-glass." When the Devil had gone to bed, the old grandmother raised up the stone, and let out the soldier.

"Hast thou paid particular attention to everything?"

"Yes," said he, "I know enough, and will contrive to save myself." Then he had to go back another way, through the window, secretly and with all speed to his companions. He told them how the Devil had been overreached by the old grandmother, and how he had learned the answer to the riddle from him. Then they were all joyous, and of good cheer, and took the whip and whipped so much gold for themselves that it ran all over the ground. When the seven years had fully gone by, the Devil came with the book, showed the signatures, and said, "I will take you with me to hell. There you shall have a meal! If you can guess what kind of roast meat you will have to eat, you shall be free and released from your bargain, and may keep the whip as well." Then the first soldier began and said, "In the great North Sea lies a dead dog-fish, that no doubt is the roast meat." The Devil was angry, and began to mutter, "Hm! hm! hm!" And asked the second, "But what will your spoon be?"

"The rib of a whale, that is to be our silver spoon." The Devil made a wry face, again growled, "Hm! hm! hm!" and said to the third, "And do you also know what your wine-glass is to be?"

"An old horse's hoof is to be our wineglass." Then the Devil flew away with a loud cry, and had no more power over them, but the three kept the whip, whipped as much money for themselves with it as they wanted, and lived happily to their end.

55 The Turnip

There were once two brothers who both served as soldiers; one of them was rich, and the other poor. Then the poor one, to escape from his poverty, put off his soldier's coat, and turned farmer. He dug and hoed his bit of land, and sowed it with turnip-seed. The seed came up, and one turnip grew there which became large and vigorous, and visibly grew bigger and bigger, and seemed as if it would never stop growing, so that it might have been called the princess of turnips, for never was such an one seen before, and never will such a one be seen again.

At length it was so enormous that by itself it filled a whole cart, and two oxen were required to draw it, and the farmer had not the least idea what he was to do with the turnip, or whether it would be a fortune to him or a misfortune. At last he thought, "If thou sellest it, what wilt thou get for it that is of any importance, and if thou eatest it thyself, why, the small turnips would do thee just as much good; it would be better to take it to the King, and make him a present of it."

So he placed it on a cart, harnessed two oxen, took it to the palace, and presented it to the King. "What strange thing is this?" said the King. "Many wonderful things have come before my eyes, but never such a monster as this! From what seed can this have sprung, or are you a luck-child and have met with it by chance?"

"Ah, no!" said the farmer, "no luck-child am I. I am a poor soldier, who because he could no longer support himself hung his soldier's coat on a nail and took to farming land. I have a brother who is rich and well known to you, Lord King, but I, because I have nothing, am forgotten by every one."

Then the King felt compassion for him, and said, "Thou shalt be raised from thy poverty, and shalt have such gifts from me that thou shalt be equal to thy rich brother." Then he bestowed on him much gold, and lands, and meadows, and herds, and made him immensely rich, so that the wealth of the other brother could not be compared with his. When the rich brother heard what the poor one had gained for himself with one single turnip, he envied him, and thought in every way how he also could get hold of a similar piece of luck. He would, however, set about it in a much wiser way, and took gold and horses and carried them to the King, and made certain the King would give him a much larger present in return. If his brother had got so much for one turnip, what would he not carry away with him in return for such beautiful things as these? The King accepted his present, and said he had nothing to give him in return that was more rare and excellent than the great turnip. So the rich man was obliged to put his brother's turnip in a cart and have it taken to his home. When there he did not know on whom to vent his rage and anger, until bad thoughts came to him, and he resolved to kill his brother. He hired murderers, who were to lie in ambush, and then he went to his brother and said, "Dear brother, I know of a hidden treasure, we will dig it up together, and divide it between us." The other agreed to this, and accompanied him without suspicion. While they were on their way, however, the murderers fell on him, bound him, and would have hanged him to a tree. But just as they were doing this, loud singing and the sound of a horse's feet were heard in the distance. On this their hearts were filled with terror, and they pushed their prisoner head first into the sack, hung it on a branch, and took to flight. He, however, worked up there until he had made a hole in the sack through which he could put his head. The man who was coming by was no other than a travelling student, a young fellow who rode on his way through the wood joyously singing his song. When he who was aloft saw that someone was passing below him, he cried, "Good day! You have come at a lucky time." The student looked round on every side, but did not know whence the voice came. At last he said, "Who calls me?" Then an answer came from the top of the tree,

"Raise your eyes; here I sit aloft in the Sack of Wisdom. In a short time have I learnt great things; compared with this all schools are a jest; in a very short time I shall have learnt everything, and shall descend wiser than all other men. I understand the stars, and the signs of the Zodiac, and the tracks of the winds, the sand of the sea, the healing of illness, and the virtues of all herbs, birds, and stones. If you were once within it you would feel what noble things issue forth from the Sack of Knowledge."

The student, when he heard all this, was astonished, and said, "Blessed be the hour in which I have found thee! May not I also enter the sack for a while?" He who was above replied as if unwillingly, "For a short time I will let you get into it, if you reward me and give me good words; but you must wait an hour longer, for one thing remains which I must learn before I do it." When the student had waited a while he became impatient, and begged to be allowed to get in at once, his thirst for knowledge was so very great. So he who was above pretended at last to yield, and said, "In order that I may come forth from the house of knowledge you must let it down by the rope, and then you shall enter it." So the student let the sack down, untied it, and set him free, and then cried, "Now draw me up at once," and was about to get into the sack. "Halt!" said the other, "that won't do," and took him by the head and put him upside down into the sack, fastened it, and drew the disciple of wisdom up the tree by the rope. Then he swung him in the air and said, "How goes it with thee, my dear fellow? Behold, already thou feelest wisdom coming, and art gaining valuable experience. Keep perfectly quiet until thou becomest wiser." Thereupon he mounted the student's horse and rode away, but in an hour's time sent someone to let the student out again.

56 Snow White and Rose Red

There was once a poor widow who lived in a lonely cottage. In front of the cottage was a garden wherein stood two rose-trees, one of which bore white and the other red roses. She had two children who were like the two rose-trees, and one was called Snow White, and the other Rose Red. They were as good and happy, as busy and cheerful as ever two children in the world were, only Snow White was more quiet and gentle than Rose Red. Rose Red liked better to run about in the meadows and fields seeking flowers and catching butterflies; but Snow White sat at home with her mother, and helped her with her house-work, or read to her when there was nothing to do.

The two children were so fond of each another that they always held each other by the hand when they went out togeth-er, and when Snow White said, "We will not leave each other," Rose Red answered, "Never so long as we live," and their moth-er would add, "What one has she must share with the other."

They often ran about the forest alone and gathered red berries, and no beasts did them any harm, but came close to them trustfully. The little hare would eat a cabbage-leaf out of their hands, the roe grazed by their side, the stag leapt merrily by them, and the birds sat still upon the boughs, and sang what-ever they knew.

No mishap overtook them; if they had stayed too late in the forest, and night came on, they laid themselves down near one another upon the moss, and slept until morning came, and their mother knew this and had no distress on their account.

Once when they had spent the night in the wood and the dawn had roused them, they saw a beautiful child in a shining white dress sitting near their bed. He got up and looked quite kindly at them, but said nothing and went away into the forest. And when they looked round they found that they had been sleeping quite close to a precipice, and would certainly have fallen into it in the darkness if they had gone only a few paces further. And their mother told them that it must have been the angel who watches over good children.

Snow White and Rose Red kept their mother's little cottage so neat that it was a pleasure to look inside it. In the summer Rose Red took care of the house, and every morning laid a wreath of flowers by her mother's bed before she awoke, in which was a rose from each tree. In the winter Snow White lit the fire and hung the kettle over the hearth. The kettle was of copper and shone like gold, so brightly was it polished. In the evening, when the snowflakes fell, the mother said, "Go, Snow White, and bolt the door," and then they sat round the hearth, and the mother took her spectacles and read aloud out of a large book, and the two girls listened as they sat and span. And close by them lay a lamb upon the floor, and behind them upon a perch sat a white dove with its head hidden beneath its wings.

One evening, as they were thus sitting comfortably together, some one knocked at the door as if he wished to be let in. The mother said, "Quick, Rose Red, open the door, it must be a traveller who is seeking shelter." Rose Red went and pushed back the bolt, thinking that it was a poor man, but it was not; it was a bear that stretched his broad, black head within the door.

Rose Red screamed and sprang back, the lamb bleated, the dove fluttered, and Snow White hid herself behind her mother's bed. But the bear began to speak and said, "Do not be afraid, I will do you no harm! I am half-frozen, and only want to warm myself a little beside you."

"Poor bear," said the mother, "lie down by the fire, only take care that you do not burn your coat." Then she cried, "Snow White, Rose Red, come out, the bear will do you no harm, he means well." So they both came out, and by-and-by the lamb and dove came nearer, and were not afraid of him. The bear said, "Here, children, knock the snow out of my coat a little;" so they brought the broom and swept the bear's hide clean; and he stretched himself by the fire and growled contentedly and comfortably. It was not long before they grew quite at home, and played tricks with their clumsy guest. They tugged his hair with their hands, put their feet upon his back and rolled him about, or they took a hazel-switch and beat him, and when he growled they laughed. But the bear took it all in good part, only when they were too rough he called out,

"Leave me alive, children,
"Snowy-white, Rosy-red,
Will you beat your lover dead?"

When it was bed-time, and the others went to bed, the mother said to the bear, "You can lie there by the hearth, and then you will be safe from the cold and the bad weather." As soon as day dawned the two children let him out, and he trotted across the snow into the forest.

Henceforth the bear came every evening at the same time, laid himself down by the hearth, and let the children amuse themselves with him as much as they liked; and they got so used to him that the doors were never fastened until their black friend had arrived.

When spring had come and all outside was green, the bear said one morning to Snow White, "Now I must go away, and cannot come back for the whole summer."

"Where are you going, then, dear bear?" asked Snow White. "I must go into the forest and guard my treasures from the wicked dwarfs. In the winter, when the earth is frozen hard, they are obliged to stay below and cannot work their way through; but now, when the sun has thawed and warmed the earth, they break through it, and come out to pry and steal; and what once gets into their hands, and in their caves, does not easily see daylight again."

Snow White was quite sorry for his going away, and as she unbolted the door for him, and the bear was hurrying out, he caught against the bolt and a piece of his hairy coat was torn off, and it seemed to Snow White as if she had seen gold shining through it, but she was not sure about it. The bear ran away quickly, and was soon out of sight behind the trees.

A short time afterwards the mother sent her children into the forest to get firewood. There they found a big tree which lay felled on the ground, and close by the trunk something was jumping backwards and forwards in the grass, but they could not make out what it was. When they came nearer they saw a dwarf with an old withered face and a snow white beard a yard long. The end of the beard was caught in a crevice of the tree, and the little fellow was jumping backwards and forwards like a dog tied to a rope, and did not know what to do.

He glared at the girls with his fiery red eyes and cried, "Why do you stand there? Can you not come here and help me?"

"What are you about there, little man?" asked Rose Red. "You stupid, prying goose!" answered the dwarf; "I was going to split the tree to get a little wood for cooking. The little bit of food that one of us wants gets burnt up directly with thick logs; we do not swallow so much as you coarse, greedy folk. I had just driven the wedge safely in, and everything was going as I wished; but the wretched wood was too smooth and suddenly sprang asunder, and the tree closed so quickly that I could not pull out my beautiful white beard; so now it is tight in and I cannot get away, and the silly, sleek, milk-faced things laugh! Ugh! how odious you are!"

The children tried very hard, but they could not pull the beard out, it was caught too fast. "I will run and fetch some one," said Rose Red. "You senseless goose!" snarled the dwarf; why should you fetch someone? You are already two too many for me; can you not think of something better?"

"Don't be impatient," said Snow White, "I will help you," and she pulled her scissors out of her pocket, and cut off the end of the beard.

As soon as the dwarf felt himself free he laid hold of a bag which lay amongst the roots of the tree, and which was full of gold, and lifted it up, grumbling to himself, "Uncouth people, to cut off a piece of my fine beard. Bad luck to you!" and then he swung the bag upon his back, and went off without even once looking at the children.

Some time after that Snow White and Rose Red went to catch a dish of fish. As they came near the brook they saw something like a large grasshopper jumping towards the water, as if it were going to leap in. They ran to it and found it was the dwarf. "Where are you going?" said Rose Red; "you surely don't want to go into the water?"

"I am not such a fool!" cried the dwarf; don't you see that the accursed fish wants to pull me in?" The little man had been sitting there fishing, and unluckily the wind had twisted his beard with the fishing-line; just then a big fish bit, and the feeble creature had not strength to pull it out; the fish kept the upper hand and pulled the dwarf towards him. He held on to all the reeds and rushes, but it was of little good, he was forced to follow the movements of the fish, and was in urgent danger of being dragged into the water.

The girls came just in time; they held him fast and tried to free his beard from the line, but all in vain, beard and line were entangled fast together. Nothing was left but to bring out the scissors and cut the beard, whereby a small part of it was lost. When the dwarf saw that he screamed out, "Is that civil, you toad-stool, to disfigure one's face? Was it not enough to clip off the end of my beard? Now you have cut off the best part of it. I cannot let myself be seen by my people. I wish you had been made to run the soles off your shoes!" Then he took out a sack of pearls which lay in the rushes, and without saying a word more he dragged it away and disappeared behind a stone.

It happened that soon afterwards the mother sent the two children to the town to buy needles and thread, and laces and ribbons. The road led them across a heath upon which huge pieces of rock lay strewn here and there. Now they noticed a large bird hovering in the air, flying slowly round and round above them; it sank lower and lower, and at last settled near a rock not far off. Directly afterwards they heard a loud, piteous cry. They ran up and saw with horror that the eagle had seized their old acquaintance the dwarf, and was going to carry him off.

The children, full of pity, at once took tight hold of the little man, and pulled against the eagle so long that at last he let his loot go. As soon as the dwarf had recovered from his first fright he cried with his shrill voice, "Could you not have done it more carefully! You dragged at my brown coat so that it is all torn and full of holes, you helpless clumsy creatures!" Then he took up a sack full of precious stones, and slipped away again under the rock into his hole. The girls, who by this time were used to his thanklessness, went on their way and did their business in the town.

As they crossed the heath again on their way home they surprised the dwarf, who had emptied out his bag of precious stones in a clean spot, and had not thought that anyone would come there so late. The evening sun shone upon the brilliant stones; they glittered and sparkled with all colours so beautifully that the children stood still and looked at them. "Why do you stand gaping there?" cried the dwarf, and his ashen-grey face became copper-red with rage. He was going on with his bad words when a loud growling was heard, and a black bear came trotting towards them out of the forest. The dwarf sprang up in a fright, but he could not get to his cave, for the bear was already close. Then in the dread of his heart he cried, "Dear Mr. Bear, spare me, I will give you all my treasures; look, the beautiful jewels lying there! Grant me my life; what do you want with such a slender little fellow as I? You would not feel me between your teeth. Come, take these two wicked girls, they are tender morsels for you, fat as young quails; for mercy's sake eat them!" The bear took no heed of his words, but gave the wicked creature a single blow with his paw, and he did not move again.

The girls had run away, but the bear called to them, "Snow

White and Rose Red, do not be afraid; wait, I will come with you." Then they knew his voice and waited, and when he came up to them suddenly his bearskin fell off, and he stood there, a handsome man, clothed all in gold. "I am a King's son," he said, "and I was bewitched by that wicked dwarf, who had stolen my treasures; I have had to run about the forest as a savage bear until I was freed by his death. Now he has got his well-deserved punishment."

Snow White was married to him, and Rose Red to his brother, and they divided between them the great treasure which the dwarf had gathered together in his cave. The old mother lived peacefully and happily with her children for many years. She took the two rose-trees with her, and they stood before her window, and every year bore the most beautiful roses, white and red.

57 Strong Hans

There were once a man and a woman who had an only child, and lived quite alone in a solitary valley. It came to pass that the mother once went into the wood to gather branches of fir, and took with her little Hans, who was just two years old. As it was spring-time, and the child took pleasure in the many-coloured flowers, she went still further onwards with him into the forest. Suddenly two robbers sprang out of the thicket, seized the mother and child, and carried them far away into the black forest, where no one ever came from one year's end to another. The poor woman urgently begged the robbers to set her and her child free, but their hearts were made of stone, they would not listen to her prayers and entreaties, and drove her on farther by force. After they had worked their way through bushes and briars for about two miles, they came to a rock where there was a door, at which the robbers knocked and it opened at once. They had to go through a long dark passage, and at last came into a great cavern, which was lit by a fire which burnt on the hearth. On the wall hung swords, sabres, and other deadly weapons which gleamed in the light, and in the midst stood a black table at which four other robbers were sitting gambling, and the captain sat at the head of it. As soon as he saw the woman he came and spoke to her, and told her to be at ease and have no fear, they would do nothing to hurt her, but she must look after the house-keeping, and if she kept everything in order, she should not fare ill with them. Thereupon they gave her something to eat, and showed her a bed where she might sleep with her child.

The woman stayed many years with the robbers, and Hans grew tall and strong. His mother told him stories, and taught him to read an old book of tales about knights which she found in the cave. When Hans was nine years old, he made himself a strong club out of a branch of fir, hid it behind the bed, and then

JACOB AND WILHELM GRIMM

went to his mother and said, "Dear mother, pray tell me who is my father; I must and will know." His mother was silent and would not tell him, that he might not become home-sick; moreover she knew that the godless robbers would not let him go away, but it almost broke her heart that Hans should not go to his father. In the night, when the robbers came home from their robbing expedition, Hans brought out his club, stood before the captain, and said "I now wish to know who is my father, and if thou dost not at once tell me I will strike thee down." Then the captain laughed, and gave Hans such a box on the ear that he rolled under the table. Hans got up again, held his tongue, and thought, "I will wait another year and then try again, perhaps I shall do better then." When the year was over, he brought out his club again, rubbed the dust off it, looked at it well, and said, "It is a stout strong club." At night the robbers came home, drank one jug of wine after another, and their heads began to be heavy. Then Hans brought out his club, placed himself before the captain, and asked him who was his father. But the captain again gave him such a vigorous box on the ear that Hans rolled under the table, but it was not long before he was up again, and beat the captain and the robbers so with his club, that they could no longer move either their arms or their legs. His mother stood in a corner full of admiration of his bravery and strength. When Hans had done his work, he went to his mother, and said, "Now I have shown myself to be in earnest, but now I must also know who is my father."

"Dear Hans," answered the mother, "come, we will go and seek him until we find him." She took from the captain the key to the entrance-door, and Hans fetched a great meal-sack and packed into it gold and silver, and whatsoever else he could find that was beautiful, until it was full, and then he took it on his back. They left the cave, but how Hans did open his eyes when he came out of the darkness into daylight, and saw the green forest, and the flowers, and the birds, and the morning sun in the sky. He stood there and wondered at everything just as if he had not been very wise. His mother looked for the way home, and when they had walked for a couple of hours, they got safely into their lonely valley and to their little house. The father was sitting in the doorway. He wept for joy when he recognised his wife and heard that Hans was his son, for he had long regarded them both as dead. But Hans, although he was not twelve years old, was a head taller than his father. They went into the little room together, but Hans had scarcely put his sack on the bench by the stove, than the whole house began to crack the bench broke down and then the floor, and the heavy sack fell through into the cellar. "God save us!" cried the father, "What's that? Now thou hast broken our little house to pieces!"

"Don't grow any grey hairs about that, dear father," answered Hans; "there, in that sack, is more than is wanting for a new house." The father and Hans at once began to build a new house; to buy cattle and land, and to keep a farm. Hans ploughed the fields, and when he followed the plough and pushed it into the ground, the bullocks had scarcely any need to draw. The next spring, Hans said, "Keep all the money and get a walking-stick that weighs a hundred-weight made for me that I may go a-travelling." When the wished-for stick was ready, he left his father's house, went forth, and came to a deep, dark forest. There he heard something crunching and cracking, looked round, and saw a fir-tree which was wound round like a rope from the bottom to the top, and when he looked upwards he saw a great fellow who had laid hold of the tree and was twisting it like a willow-wand. "Hollo!" cried Hans, "What art thou doing up there?" the fellow replied, "I got some branches together yesterday and am twisting a rope for them."

"That is what I like," thought Hans, "he has some strength," and he called to him, "Leave that alone, and come with me." The fellow came down, and he was taller by a whole head than Hans, and Hans was not little. "Thy name is now Fir-twister," said Hans to him. Thereupon they went further and heard something knocking and hammering with such force that the ground shook at every stroke. Shortly afterwards they came to a mighty rock, before which a giant was standing and striking great pieces of it away with his fist. When Hans asked what he was about, he answered, "At night, when I want to sleep, bears, wolves, and other vermin of that kind come, which sniff and snuffle about me and won't let me rest; so I want to build myself a house and lay myself inside it, so that I may have some peace."

"Oh, indeed," thought Hans, "I can make use of this one also;" and said to him, "Leave thy house-building alone, and go with me; thou shalt be called Rock-splitter." The man consented, and they all three roamed through the forest, and wherever they went the wild beasts were terrified, and ran away from them. In the evening they came to an old deserted castle, went up into it, and laid themselves down in the hall to sleep. The next morning Hans went into the garden. It had run quite wild, and was full of thorns and bushes. And as he was thus walking round about, a wild boar rushed at him; he, however, gave it such a blow with his club that it fell directly. He took it on his shoulders and carried it in, and they put it on a spit, roasted it, and enjoyed themselves. Then they arranged that each day, in turn, two should go out hunting, and one should stay at home, and cook nine pounds of meat for each of them. Fir-twister stayed at home the first, and Hans and Rock-splitter went out hunting. When Fir-twister was busy cooking, a little shrivelled-up old mannikin came to him in the castle, and asked for some meat. "Be off, sly hypocrite," he answered, "thou needest no meat." But how astonished Fir-twister was when the little insignificant dwarf sprang up at him, and belaboured him so with his fists that he could not defend himself, but fell on the ground and gasped for breath! The dwarf did not go away until he had thoroughly vented his anger on him. When the two others came home from hunting, Fir-twister said nothing to them of the old mannikin and of the blows which he himself had received, and thought, "When they stay at home, they may just try their chance with the little scrubbing-brush;" and the mere thought of that gave him pleasure already.

The next day Rock-splitter stayed at home, and he fared just as Fir-twister had done, he was very ill-treated by the dwarf because he was not willing to give him any meat. When the others came home in the evening, Fir-twister easily saw what he had suffered, but both kept silence, and thought, "Hans also must taste some of that soup."

Hans, who had to stay at home the next day, did his work in the kitchen as it had to be done, and as he was standing skimming the pan, the dwarf came and without more ado demanded a bit of meat. Then Hans thought, "He is a poor wretch, I will give him some of my share, that the others may not run short," and handed him a bit. When the dwarf had devoured it, he again asked for some meat, and good-natured Hans gave it to him, and told him it was a handsome piece, and that he was to be content with it. But the dwarf begged again for the third time. "Thou art shameless!" said Hans, and gave him none. Then the malicious dwarf wanted to spring on him and treat him as he had treated Fir-twister and Rock-splitter, but he had got to the wrong man. Hans, without exerting himself much, gave him a couple of blows which made him jump down the castle steps. Hans was about to run after him, but fell right over him, for he was so tall. When he rose up again, the dwarf had got the start of him. Hans hurried after him as far as the forest, and saw him slip into a hole in the rock. Hans now went home, but he had marked the spot. When the two others came back, they were surprised that Hans was so well. He told them what had happened, and then they no longer concealed how it had fared with them. Hans laughed and said, "It served you quite right; why were you so greedy with your meat? It is a disgrace that you who are so big should have let yourselves be beaten by the dwarf." Thereupon they took a basket and a rope, and all three went to the hole in the rock into which the dwarf had slipped, and let Hans and his club down in the basket. When Hans had reached the bottom, he found a door, and when he opened it a maiden was sitting there who was lovely as any picture, nay, so beautiful that no words can express it, and by her side sat the dwarf and grinned at Hans like a sea-cat! She, however, was bound with chains, and looked so mournfully at him that Hans felt great pity for her, and thought to himself, "Thou must deliver her out of the power of the wicked dwarf," and gave him such a blow with his club that he fell down dead. Immediately the chains fell from the maiden, and Hans was enraptured with her beauty. She told him she was a King's daughter whom a savage count had stolen away from her home, and imprisoned there among the rocks, because she would have nothing to say to him. The count had, however, set the dwarf as a watchman, and he had made her bear misery and vexation enough. And now Hans placed the maiden in the basket and had her drawn up; the basket came down again, but Hans did not trust his two companions, and thought, "They have already shown themselves to be false, and told me nothing about the dwarf; who knows what design they may have against me?" So he put his club in the basket, and it was lucky he did; for when the basket was half-way up, they let it fall again, and if Hans had really been sitting in it he would have been killed. But now he did not know how he was to work his way out of the depths, and when he turned it over and over in his mind he found no counsel. "It is indeed sad," said he to himself, "that I have to waste away down here," and as he was thus walking backwards and forwards, he once more came to the little chamber where the maiden had been sitting, and saw that the dwarf had a ring on his finger which shone and sparkled. Then he drew it off and put it on, and when he turned it round on his finger, he suddenly heard something rustle over his head. He looked up and saw spirits of the air hovering above, who told him he was their master, and asked what his desire might be? Hans was at first dumbstruck, but afterwards he said that they were to carry him above again. They obeyed instantly, and it was just as if he had flown up himself. When, however, he was above again, he found no one in sight. Fir-twister and Rock-splitter had hurried away, and had taken the beautiful maiden with them. But Hans turned the ring, and the spirits of the air came and told him that the two were on the sea. Hans ran and ran without stopping, until he came to the sea-shore, and there far, far out on the water, he perceived a little boat in which his faithless comrades were sitting; and in fierce anger he leapt, without thinking what he was doing, club in hand into the water, and began to swim, but the club, which weighed a hundredweight, dragged him deep down until he was all but drowned. Then in the very nick of time he turned his ring, and immediately the spirits of the air came and bore him as swift as lightning into the boat. He swung his club and gave his wicked comrades the reward they merited and threw them into the water, and then he sailed with the beautiful maiden, who had been in the greatest alarm, and whom he delivered for the second time, home to her father and mother, and married her, and all rejoiced exceedingly.

58 The Moon

In days gone by there was a land where the nights were always dark, and the sky spread over it like a black cloth, for there the moon never rose, and no star shone in the obscurity. At the creation of the world, the light at night had been sufficient. Three young fellows once went out of this country on a travelling expedition, and arrived in another kingdom, where, in the evening when the sun had disappeared behind the mountains, a shining globe was placed on an oak-tree, which shed a soft light far and wide. By means of this, everything could very well be seen and distinguished, even though it was not so brilliant as the sun. The travellers stopped and asked a countryman who was driving past with his cart, what kind of a light that was. "That is the moon," answered he; our mayor bought it for three thalers, and fastened it to the oak-tree. He has to pour oil into it daily, and to keep it clean, so that it may always burn clearly. He receives a thaler a week from us for doing it."

When the countryman had driven away, one of them said, "We could make some use of this lamp, we have an oak-tree at home, which is just as big as this, and we could hang it on that. What a pleasure it would be not to have to feel about at night in the darkness!"

"I'll tell you what we'll do," said the second; "we will fetch a cart and horses and carry away the moon. The people here may buy themselves another."

"I'm a good climber," said the third, "I will bring it down." The fourth brought a cart and horses, and the third climbed the tree, bored a hole in the moon, passed a rope through it, and let it down. When the shining ball lay in the cart, they covered it over with a cloth, that no one might observe the theft. They conveyed it safely into their own country, and placed it on a high oak. Old and young rejoiced, when the new lamp let its light

shine over the whole land, and bed-rooms and sitting-rooms were filled with it. The dwarfs came forth from their caves in the rocks, and the tiny elves in their little red coats danced in rings on the meadows.

The four took care that the moon was provided with oil, cleaned the wick, and received their weekly thaler, but they became old men, and when one of them grew ill, and saw that he was about to die, he appointed that one quarter of the moon, should, as his property, be laid in the grave with him. When he died, the mayor climbed up the tree, and cut off a quarter with the hedge-shears, and this was placed in his coffin. The light of the moon decreased, but still not visibly. When the second died, the second quarter was buried with him, and the light diminished. It grew weaker still after the death of the third, who likewise took his part of it away with him; and when the fourth was borne to his grave, the old state of darkness recommenced, and whenever the people went out at night without their lanterns they knocked their heads together.

When, however, the pieces of the moon had united themselves together again in the world below, where darkness had always prevailed, it came to pass that the dead became restless and awoke from their sleep. They were astonished when they were able to see again; the moonlight was quite sufficient for them, for their eyes had become so weak that they could not have borne the brilliance of the sun. They rose up and were merry, and fell into their former ways of living. Some of them went to the play and to dance, others hastened to the public-houses, where they asked for wine, got drunk, brawled, quarreled, and at last took up cudgels, and belaboured each other. The noise became greater and greater, and at last reached even to heaven

Saint Peter who guards the gate of heaven thought the lower world had broken out in revolt and gathered together the heavenly troops, which are to drive back the Evil One when he and his associates storm the abode of the blessed. As these, however, did not come, he got on his horse and rode through the gate of heaven, down into the world below. There he reduced the dead to subjection, bade them lie down in their graves again, took the moon away with him, and hung it up in heaven.

59 The Goose-Girl at the Well

There was once upon a time a very old woman, who lived with her flock of geese in a waste place among the mountains, and there had a little house. The waste was surrounded by a large forest, and every morning the old woman took her crutch and hobbled into it. There, however, the dame was quite active, more so than any one would have thought, considering her age, and collected grass for her geese, picked all the wild fruit she could reach, and carried everything home on her back. Any one would have thought that the heavy load would have weighed her to the ground, but she always brought it safely home. If any one met her, she greeted him quite courteously. "Good day, dear countryman, it is a fine day. Ah! You wonder that I should drag grass about, but every one must take his burthen on his back." Nevertheless, people did not like to meet her if they could help it, and took by preference a round-about way, and when a father with his boys passed her, he whispered to them, "Beware of the old woman. She has claws beneath her gloves; she is a witch." One morning, a handsome young man was going through the forest. The sun shone bright, the birds sang, a cool breeze crept through the leaves, and he was full of joy and gladness. He had as yet met no one, when he suddenly perceived the old witch kneeling on the ground cutting grass with a sickle. She had already thrust a whole load into her cloth, and near it stood two baskets, which were filled with wild apples and pears. "But, good little mother," said he, "how canst thou carry all that away?"

"I must carry it, dear sir," answered she, "rich folk's children have no need to do such things, but with the peasant folk the saying goes, don't look behind you, you will only see how crooked your back is!"

"Will you help me?" she said, as he remained standing by

her. "You have still a straight back and young legs, it would be a trifle to you. Besides, my house is not so very far from here, it stands there on the heath behind the hill. How soon you would bound up thither." The young man took compassion on the old woman. "My father is certainly no peasant," replied he, "but a rich count; nevertheless, that you may see that it is not only peasants who can carry things, I will take your bundle."

"If you will try it," said she, "I shall be very glad. You will certainly have to walk for an hour, but what will that signify to you; only you must carry the apples and pears as well?" It now seemed to the young man just a little serious, when he heard of an hour's walk, but the old woman would not let him off, packed the bundle on his back, and hung the two baskets on his arm. "See, it is quite light," said she. "No, it is not light," answered the count, and pulled a rueful face. "Verily, the bundle weighs as heavily as if it were full of cobble stones, and the apples and pears are as heavy as lead! I can scarcely breathe." He had a mind to put everything down again, but the old woman would not allow it. "Just look," said she mockingly, "the young gentleman will not carry what I, an old woman, have so often dragged along. You are ready with fine words, but when it comes to be earnest, you want to take to your heels. Why are you standing loitering there?" she continued. "Step out. No one will take the bundle off again." As long as he walked on level ground, it was still bearable, but when they came to the hill and had to climb, and the stones rolled down under his feet as if they were alive, it was beyond his strength. The drops of perspiration stood on his forehead, and ran, hot and cold, down his back.

"Dame," said he, "I can go no farther. I want to rest a little."

"Not here," answered the old woman, "when we have arrived at our journey's end, you can rest; but now you must go forward. Who knows what good it may do you?"

"Old woman, thou art becoming shameless!" said the count, and tried to throw off the bundle, but he laboured in vain; it stuck as fast to his back as if it grew there. He turned and twisted, but he could not get rid of it. The old woman laughed at this, and sprang about quite delighted on her crutch. "Don't get angry, dear sir," said she, "you are growing as red in the face as a turkey-cock! Carry your bundle patiently. I will give you a good present when we get home."

What could he do. He was obliged to submit to his fate, and crawl along patiently behind the old woman. She seemed to grow more and more nimble, and his burden still heavier. All at once she made a spring, jumped on to the bundle and seated herself on the top of it; and however withered she might be, she was yet heavier than the stoutest country lass. The youth's knees trembled, but when he did not go on, the old woman hit him about the legs with a switch and with stinging-nettles. Groaning continually, he climbed the mountain, and at length reached the old woman's house, when he was just about to drop. When the geese perceived the old woman, they flapped their wings, stretched out their necks, ran to meet her, cackling all the while. Behind the flock walked, stick in hand, an old wench, strong and big, but ugly as night. "Good mother," said she to the old woman, "has anything happened to you, you have stayed away so long?"

"By no means, my dear daughter," answered she, "I have met with nothing bad, but, on the contrary, with this kind gentleman, who has carried my burden for me; only think, he even took me on his back when I was tired. The way, too, has not seemed long to us; we have been merry, and have been cracking jokes with each other all the time." At last the old woman slid down, took the bundle off the young man's back, and the baskets from his arm, looked at him quite kindly, and said, "Now seat yourself on the bench before the door, and rest. You have fairly earned your wages, and they shall not be wanting." Then she said to the goose-girl, "Go into the house, my dear daughter, it is not becoming for thee to be alone with a young gentleman; one must not pour oil on to the fire, he might fall in love with thee." The count knew not whether to laugh or to cry. "Such a sweetheart as that," thought he, "could not touch my heart, even if she were thirty years younger." In the meantime the old woman stroked and fondled her geese as if they were children, and then went into the house with her daughter. The youth lay down on the bench, under a wild apple-tree. The air was warm and mild; on all sides stretched a green meadow, which was set with cowslips, wild thyme, and a thousand other flowers; through the midst of it rippled a clear brook on which the sun sparkled, and the white geese went walking backwards and forwards, or paddled in the water. "It is quite delightful here," said he, "but I am so tired that I cannot keep my eyes open; I will sleep a little. If only a gust of wind does not come and blow my legs off my body, for they are as rotten as tinder."

When he had slept a little while, the old woman came and shook him till he awoke. "Sit up," said she, "thou canst not stay here; I have certainly treated thee hardly, still it has not cost thee thy life. Of money and land thou hast no need, here is something else for thee." Thereupon she thrust a little book into his hand, which was cut out of a single emerald. "Take great care of it," said she, "it will bring thee good fortune." The count sprang up, and as he felt that he was quite fresh, and had recovered his vigor, he thanked the old woman for her present, and set off without even once looking back at the beautiful daughter. When he was already some way off, he still heard in the distance the noisy cry of the geese.

For three days the count had to wander in the wilderness before he could find his way out. He then reached a large town, and as no one knew him, he was led into the royal palace, where the King and Queen were sitting on their throne. The count fell on one knee, drew the emerald book out of his pocket, and laid it at the Queen's feet. She bade him rise and hand her the little book. Hardly, however, had she opened it, and looked therein, than she fell as if dead to the ground. The count was seized by the King's servants, and was being led to prison, when the Queen opened her eyes, and ordered them to release him, and every one was to go out, as she wished to speak with him in private.

When the Queen was alone, she began to weep bitterly, and said, "Of what use to me are the splendours and honours with which I am surrounded; every morning I awake in pain and sorrow. I had three daughters, the youngest of whom was so beautiful that the whole world looked on her as a wonder. She was as white as snow, as rosy as apple-blossom, and her hair as radiant as sun-beams. When she cried, not tears fell from her eyes, but pearls and jewels only. When she was fifteen years old, the King summoned all three sisters to come before his throne. You should have seen how all the people gazed when the youngest entered, it was just as if the sun were rising! Then the King spoke, "My daughters, I know not when my last day may arrive; I will today decide what each shall receive at my death. You all love me, but the one of you who loves me best, shall fare the best." Each of them said she loved him best. "Can you not express to me," said the King, "how much you do love me, and thus I shall see what you mean?" The eldest spoke. "I love my father as dearly as the sweetest sugar." The second, "I love my father as dearly as my prettiest dress." But the youngest was silent. Then the father said, "And thou, my dearest child, how much dost thou love me?"

"I do not know, and can compare my love with nothing." But her father insisted that she should name something. So she said at last, "The best food does not please me without salt, therefore I love my father like salt." When the King heard that, he fell into a passion, and said, "If thou lovest me like salt, thy love shall also be repaid thee with salt." Then he divided the kingdom between the two elder, but caused a sack of salt to be bound on the back of the youngest, and two servants had to lead her forth into the wild forest. We all begged and prayed for her, said the Queen, "but the King's anger was not to be appeased. How she cried when she had to leave us! The whole road was strewn with the pearls which flowed from her eyes. The King soon afterwards repented of his great severity, and had the whole forest searched for the poor child, but no one could find her. When I think that the wild beasts have devoured her, I know not how to contain myself for sorrow; many a time I console myself with the hope that she is still alive, and may have hidden herself in a cave, or has found shelter with compassionate people. But picture to yourself, when I opened your little emerald book, a pearl lay therein, of exactly the same kind as those which used to fall from my daughter's eyes; and then you can also imagine how the sight of it stirred my heart. You must tell me how you came by that pearl." The count told her that he had received it from the old woman in the forest, who had appeared very strange to him, and must be a witch, but he had neither seen nor hear anything of the Queen's child. The King and the Queen resolved to seek out the old woman. They thought that there where the pearl had been, they would obtain news of their daughter.

The old woman was sitting in that lonely place at her spinning-wheel, spinning. It was already dusk, and a log which was burning on the hearth gave a scanty light. All at once there was a noise outside, the geese were coming home from the pasture, and uttering their hoarse cries. Soon afterwards the daughter also entered. But the old woman scarcely thanked her, and only shook her head a little. The daughter sat down beside her, took her spinning-wheel, and twisted the threads as nimbly as a young girl. Thus they both sat for two hours, and exchanged never a word. At last something rustled at the window, and two fiery eyes peered in. It was an old night-owl, which cried, "Uhu!" three times. The old woman looked up just a little, then she said, "Now, my little daughter, it is time for thee to go out and do thy work." She rose and went out, and where did she go? Over the meadows ever onward into the valley. At last she came to a well, with three old oak-trees standing beside it; meanwhile the moon had risen large and round over the mountain, and it was so light that one could have found a needle. She removed a skin which covered her face, then bent down to the well, and began to wash herself. When she had finished, she dipped the skin also in the water, and then laid it on the meadow, so that it should bleach in the moonlight, and dry again. But how the maiden was changed! Such a change as that was never seen before! When the grey mask fell off, her golden hair broke forth like sunbeams, and spread about like a mantle over her whole form. Her eyes shone out as brightly as the stars in heaven, and her cheeks bloomed a soft red like apple-blossom.

But the fair maiden was sad. She sat down and wept bitterly. One tear after another forced itself out of her eyes, and rolled through her long hair to the ground. There she sat, and would have remained sitting a long time, if there had not been a rustling and cracking in the boughs of the neighbouring tree. She sprang up like a roe which has been overtaken by the shot of the hunter. Just then the moon was obscured by a dark cloud, and in an instant the maiden had put on the old skin and vanished, like a light blown out by the wind.

She ran back home, trembling like an aspen-leaf. The old woman was standing on the threshold, and the girl was about to relate what had befallen her, but the old woman laughed kindly, and said, "I already know all." She led her into the room and lighted a new log. She did not, however, sit down to her spinning again, but fetched a broom and began to sweep and scour, "All must be clean and sweet," she said to the girl. "But, mother," said the maiden, "why do you begin work at so late an hour? What do you expect?"

"Dost thou know then what time it is?" asked the old woman. "Not yet midnight," answered the maiden, "but already past eleven o'clock."

"Dost thou not remember," continued the old woman, "that it is three years today since thou camest to me? Thy time is up, we can no longer remain together." The girl was terrified, and said, "Alas! Dear mother, will you cast me off? Where shall I go? I have no friends, and no home to which I can go. I have always done as you bade me, and you have always been satisfied

JACOB AND WILHELM GRIMM

with me; do not send me away." The old woman would not tell the maiden what lay before her. "My stay here is over," she said to her, "but when I depart, house and parlour must be clean: therefore do not hinder me in my work. Have no care for thyself, thou shalt find a roof to shelter thee, and the wages which I will give thee shall also content thee."

"But tell me what is about to happen," the maiden continued to entreat. "I tell thee again, do not hinder me in my work. Do not say a word more, go to thy chamber, take the skin off thy face, and put on the silken gown which thou hadst on when thou camest to me, and then wait in thy chamber until I call thee."

But I must once more tell of the King and Queen, who had journeyed forth with the count in order to seek out the old woman in the wilderness. The count had strayed away from them in the wood by night, and had to walk onwards alone. Next day it seemed to him that he was on the right track. He still went forward, until darkness came on, then he climbed a tree, intending to pass the night there, for he feared that he might lose his way. When the moon illumined the surrounding country he perceived a figure coming down the mountain. She had no stick in her hand, but yet he could see that it was the goose-girl, whom he had seen before in the house of the old woman. "Oho," cried he, "there she comes, and if I once get hold of one of the witches, the other shall not escape me!" But how astonished he was, when she went to the well, took off the skin and washed herself, when her golden hair fell down all about her, and she was more beautiful than any one whom he had ever seen in the whole world. He hardly dared to breathe, but stretched his head as far forward through the leaves as he dared, and stared at her. Either he bent over too far, or whatever the cause might be, the bough suddenly cracked, and that very moment the maiden slipped into the skin, sprang away like a roe, and as the moon was suddenly covered, disappeared from his eyes. Hardly had she disappeared, before the count descended from the tree, and hastened after her with nimble steps. He had not been gone long before he saw, in the twilight, two figures coming over the meadow. It was the King and Queen, who had perceived from a distance the light shining in the old woman's little house, and were going to it. The count told them what wonderful things he had seen by the well, and they did not doubt that it had been their lost daughter. They walked onwards full of joy, and soon came to the little house. The geese were sitting all round it, and had thrust their heads under their wings and were sleeping, and not one of them moved. The King and Queen looked in at the window, the old woman was sitting there quite quietly spinning, nodding her head and never looking round. The room was perfectly clean, as if the little mist men, who carry no dust on their feet, lived there. Their daughter, however, they did not see. They gazed at all this for a long time, at last they took heart, and knocked softly at the window. The old woman appeared to have been expecting them; she rose, and called out quite kindly, "Come in, I know you already." When they had entered the room, the old woman said, "You might have spared yourself the long walk, if you had not three years ago unjustly driven away your child, who is so good and lovable. No harm has come to her; for three years she has had to tend the geese; with them she has learnt no evil, but has preserved her purity of heart. You, however, have been suffi-ciently punished by the misery in which you have lived." Then she went to the chamber and called, "Come out, my little daugh-ter." Thereupon the door opened, and the princess stepped out in her silken garments, with her golden hair and her shining eyes, and it was as if an angel from heaven had entered.

She went up to her father and mother, fell on their necks and kissed them; there was no help for it, they all had to weep for joy. The young count stood near them, and when she perceived him she became as red in the face as a moss-rose, she herself did not know why. The King said, "My dear child, I have given away my kingdom, what shall I give thee?"

"She needs nothing," said the old woman. "I give her the tears that she has wept on your account; they are precious pearls, finer than those that are found in the sea, and worth more than your whole kingdom, and I give her my little house as payment for her services." When the old woman had said that, she disappeared from their sight. The walls rattled a little, and when the King and Queen looked round, the little house had changed into a splendid palace, a royal table had been spread, and the servants were running hither and thither.

The story goes still further, but my grandmother, who related it to me, had partly lost her memory, and had forgotten the rest. I shall always believe that the beautiful princess married the count, and that they remained together in the palace, and lived there in all happiness so long as God willed it. Whether the snow-white geese, which were kept near the little hut, were verily young maidens (no one need take offence) whom the old woman had taken under her protection, and whether they now received their human form again, and stayed as handmaids to the young Queen, I do not exactly know, but I suspect it. This much is certain, that the old woman was no witch, as people thought, but a wise woman, who meant well. Very likely it was she who, at the princess's birth, gave her the gift of weeping pearls instead of tears. That does not happen nowadays, or else the poor would soon become rich.

60 The Goose-Girl

There was once upon a time an old Queen whose husband had been dead for many years, and she had a beautiful daughter. When the princess grew up she was betrothed to a prince who lived at a great distance. When the time came for her to be married, and she had to journey forth into the distant kingdom, the aged Queen packed up for her many costly vessels of silver and gold, and trinkets also of gold and silver; and cups and jewels, in short, everything which appertained to a royal dowry, for she loved her child with all her heart. She likewise sent her maid in waiting, who was to ride with her, and hand her over to the bridegroom, and each had a horse for the journey, but the horse of the King's daughter was called Falada, and could speak. So when the hour of parting had come, the aged mother went into her bedroom, took a small knife and cut her finger with it until it bled, then she held a white handkerchief to it into which she let three drops of blood fall, gave it to her daughter and said, "Dear child, preserve this carefully, it will be of service to you on your way."

So they took a sorrowful leave of each other; the princess put the piece of cloth in her bosom, mounted her horse, and then went away to her bridegroom. After she had ridden for a while she felt a burning thirst, and said to her waiting-maid, "Dismount, and take my cup which thou hast brought with thee for me, and get me some water from the stream, for I should like to drink."

"If you are thirsty," said the waiting-maid, "get off your horse yourself, and lie down and drink out of the water, I don't choose to be your servant." So in her great thirst the princess alighted, bent down over the water in the stream and drank, and was not allowed to drink out of the golden cup.

Then she said, "Ah, Heaven!" and the three drops of blood

answered, "If thy mother knew, her heart would break."

But the King's daughter was humble, said nothing, and mounted her horse again. She rode some miles further, but the day was warm, the sun scorched her, and she was thirsty once more, and when they came to a stream of water, she again cried to her waiting-maid, "Dismount, and give me some water in my golden cup," for she had long ago forgotten the girl's ill words. But the waiting-maid said still more haughtily, "If you wish to drink, drink as you can, I don't choose to be your maid." Then in her great thirst the King's daughter alighted, bent over the flowing stream, wept and said, "Ah, Heaven!" and the drops of blood again replied, "If thy mother knew this, her heart would break." And as she was thus drinking and leaning right over the stream, the handkerchief with the three drops of blood fell out of her bosom, and floated away with the water without her observing it, so great was her trouble. The waiting-maid, however, had seen it, and she rejoiced to think that she had now power over the bride, for since the princess had lost the drops of blood, she had become weak and powerless. So now when she wanted to mount her horse again, the one that was called Falada, the waiting-maid said, "Falada is more suitable for me, and my nag will do for thee" and the princess had to be content with that. Then the waiting-maid, with many hard words, bade the princess exchange her royal apparel for her own shabby clothes; and at length she was compelled to swear by the clear sky above her, that she would not say one word of this to any one at the royal court, and if she had not taken this oath she would have been killed on the spot. But Falada saw all this, and observed it well.

The waiting-maid now mounted Falada, and the true bride the bad horse, and thus they travelled onwards, until at length they entered the royal palace. There were great rejoicings over her arrival, and the prince sprang forward to meet her, lifted the waiting-maid from her horse, and thought she was his consort. She was conducted upstairs, but the real princess was left standing below. Then the old King looked out of the window and saw her standing in the courtyard, and how dainty and delicate and beautiful she was, and instantly went to the royal apartment, and asked the bride about the girl she had with her who was standing down below in the courtyard, and who she was? "I picked her up on my way for a companion; give the girl something to work at, that she may not stand idle." But the old King had no work for her, and knew of none, so he said, "I have a little boy who tends the geese, she may help him." The boy was called Conrad, and the true bride had to help him to tend the geese. Soon afterwards the false bride said to the young King, "Dearest husband, I beg you to do me a favour." He answered, "I will do so most willingly."

"Then send for the knacker, and have the head of the horse on which I rode here cut off, for it vexed me on the way." In reality, she was afraid that the horse might tell how she had behaved to the King's daughter. Then she succeeded in making the King promise that it should be done, and the faithful Falada was to die; this came to the ears of the real princess, and she secretly promised to pay the knacker a piece of gold if he would perform a small service for her. There was a great dark-looking gateway in the town, through which morning and evening she had to pass with the geese: would he be so good as to nail up Falada's head on it, so that she might see him again, more than once. The knacker's man promised to do that, and cut off the head, and nailed it fast beneath the dark gateway.

Early in the morning, when she and Conrad drove out their flock beneath this gateway, she said in passing,

> "Alas, Falada, hanging there!"

Then the head answered,

> "Alas, young Queen, how ill you fare!
> If this your tender mother knew,
> Her heart would surely break in two."

Then they went still further out of the town, and drove their geese into the country. And when they had come to the meadow, she sat down and unbound her hair which was like pure gold, and Conrad saw it and delighted in its brightness, and wanted to pluck out a few hairs. Then she said,

> "Blow, blow, thou gentle wind, I say,
> Blow Conrad's little hat away,
> And make him chase it here and there,
> Until I have braided all my hair,
> And bound it up again."

And there came such a violent wind that it blew Conrad's hat far away across country, and he was forced to run after it. When he came back she had finished combing her hair and was putting it up again, and he could not get any of it. Then Conrad was angry, and would not speak to her, and thus they watched the geese until the evening, and then they went home.

Next day when they were driving the geese out through the dark gateway, the maiden said,

> "Alas, Falada, hanging there!"

Falada answered,

> "Alas, young Queen how ill you fare!
> If this your tender mother knew,
> Her heart would surely break in two."

And she sat down again in the field and began to comb out her hair, and Conrad ran and tried to clutch it, so she said in haste,

> "Blow, blow, thou gentle wind, I say,
> Blow Conrad's little hat away,
> And make him chase it here and there,
> Until I have braided all my hair,
> And bound it up again."

Then the wind blew, and blew his little hat off his head and far

305

away, and Conrad was forced to run after it, and when he came back, her hair had been put up a long time, and he could get none of it, and so they looked after their geese till evening came.

But in the evening after they had got home, Conrad went to the old King, and said, "I won't tend the geese with that girl any longer!"

"Why not?" inquired the aged King.

"Oh, because she vexes me the whole day long." Then the aged King commanded him to relate what it was that she did to him. And Conrad said, "In the morning when we pass beneath the dark gateway with the flock, there is a sorry horse's head on the wall, and she says to it,

"Alas, Falada, hanging there!"

And the head replies,

"Alas, young Queen how ill you fare!
If this your tender mother knew,
Her heart would surely break in two."

And Conrad went on to relate what happened on the goose pasture, and how when there he had to chase his hat.

The aged King commanded him to drive his flock out again next day, and as soon as morning came, he placed himself behind the dark gateway, and heard how the maiden spoke to the head of Falada, and then he too went into the country, and hid himself in the thicket in the meadow. There he soon saw with his own eyes the goose-girl and the goose-boy bringing their flock, and how after a while she sat down and unplaited her hair, which shone with radiance. And soon she said,

"Blow, blow, thou gentle wind, I say,
Blow Conrad's little hat away,
And make him chase it here and there,
Until I have braided all my hair,
And bound it up again."

Then came a blast of wind and carried off Conrad's hat, so that he had to run far away, while the maiden quietly went on combing and plaiting her hair, all of which the King observed. Then, quite unseen, he went away, and when the goose-girl came home in the evening, he called her aside, and asked why she did all these things. "I may not tell you that, and I dare not lament my sorrows to any human being, for I have sworn not to do so by the heaven which is above me; if I had not done that, I should have lost my life." He urged her and left her no peace, but he could draw nothing from her. Then said he, "If thou wilt not tell me anything, tell thy sorrows to the iron-stove there," and he went away. Then she crept into the iron-stove, and began to weep and lament, and emptied her whole heart, and said, "Here am I deserted by the whole world, and yet I am a King's daughter, and a false waiting-maid has by force brought me to such a pass that I have been compelled to put off my royal apparel, and she has taken my place with my bridegroom, and I have to perform menial service as a goose-girl. If my mother did but know that, her heart would break."

The aged King, however, was standing outside by the pipe of the stove, and was listening to what she said, and heard it. Then he came back again, and bade her come out of the stove. And royal garments were placed on her, and it was marvellous how beautiful she was! The aged King summoned his son, and revealed to him that he had got the false bride who was only a waiting-maid, but that the true one was standing there, as the sometime goose-girl. The young King rejoiced with all his heart when he saw her beauty and youth, and a great feast was made ready to which all the people and all good friends were invited. At the head of the table sat the bridegroom with the King's daughter at one side of him, and the waiting-maid on the other, but the waiting-maid was blinded, and did not recognise the princess in her dazzling array. When they had eaten and drunk, and were merry, the aged King asked the waiting-maid as a riddle, what a person deserved who had behaved in such and such a way to her master, and at the same time related the whole story, and asked what sentence such a person merited? Then the false bride said, "She deserves no better fate than to be stripped entirely naked, and put in a barrel which is studded inside with pointed nails, and two white horses should be harnessed to it, which will drag her along through one street after another, till she is dead."

"It is thou," said the aged King, "and thou hast pronounced thine own sentence, and thus shall it be done unto thee." And when the sentence had been carried out, the young King married his true bride, and both of them reigned over their kingdom in peace and happiness.

61 The WishingTable, the Gold Donkey, and the Cudgel in the Sack

There was once upon a time a tailor who had three sons, and only one goat. But as the goat supported the whole of them with her milk, she was obliged to have good food, and to be taken every day to pasture. The sons, therefore, did this, in turn. Once the eldest took her to the churchyard, where the finest herbs were to be found, and let her eat and run about there. At night when it was time to go home he asked, "Goat, hast thou had enough?" The goat answered:

"I have eaten so much, Not a leaf more I'll touch, meh! meh!"

"Come home, then," said the youth, and took hold of the cord round her neck, led her into the stable and tied her up securely. "Well," said the old tailor, "has the goat had as much food as she ought?"

"Oh," answered the son, "she has eaten so much, not a leaf more she'll touch." But the father wished to satisfy himself, and went down to the stable, stroked the dear animal and asked, "Goat, art thou satisfied?" The goat answered:

"Wherewithal should I be satisfied? Among the graves I leapt about, And found no food, so went without, meh! meh!"

"What do I hear?" cried the tailor, and ran upstairs and said to the youth, "Hollo, thou liar: thou saidest the goat had had enough, and hast let her hunger!" and in his anger he took the yard-measure from the wall, and drove him out with blows.

Next day it was the turn of the second son, who looked out for a place in the fence of the garden, where nothing but good herbs grew, and the goat cleared them all off. At night when he wanted to go home, he asked, "Goat, art thou satisfied?" The goat answered:

"I have eaten so much, Not a leaf more I'll touch, meh!

meh!"

"Come home, then," said the youth, and led her home, and tied her up in the stable. "Well," said the old tailor, "has the goat had as much food as she ought?" "Oh," answered the son, "she has eaten so much, not a leaf more she'll touch." The tailor would not rely on this, but went down to the stable and said, "Goat, hast thou had enough?" The goat answered:

"Wherewithal should I be satisfied? Among the graves I leapt about, And found no food, so went without, meh! meh!"

"The godless wretch!" cried the tailor, "to let such a good animal hunger," and he ran up and drove the youth out of doors with the yard-measure.

Now came the turn of the third son, who wanted to do the thing well, and sought out some bushes with the finest leaves, and let the goat devour them. In the evening when he wanted to go home, he asked, "Goat, hast thou had enough?" The goat answered,

"I have eaten so much, Not a leaf more I'll touch, meh! meh!"

"Come home, then," said the youth, and led her into the stable, and tied her up. "Well," said the old tailor, "has the goat had a proper amount of food?"

"She has eaten so much, not a leaf more she'll touch." The tailor did not trust to that, but went down and asked, "Goat, hast thou had enough?" The wicked beast answered:

"Wherewithal should I be satisfied? Among the graves I leapt about, And found no leaves, so went without, meh! meh!"

"Oh, the brood of liars!" cried the tailor, "each as wicked and forgetful of his duty as the other! Ye shall no longer make a fool of me," and quite beside himself with anger, he ran upstairs and belabored the poor young fellow so vigorously with the yard-measure that he sprang out of the house.

The old tailor was now alone with his goat. Next morning he went down into the stable, caressed the goat and said, "Come, my dear little animal, I will take thee to feed myself." He took her by the rope and conducted her to green hedges, and amongst milfoil, and whatever else goats like to eat. "There thou mayest for once eat to thy heart's content," said he to her, and let her browse till evening. Then he asked, "Goat, art thou satisfied?" She replied:

"I have eaten so much, Not a leaf more I'll touch, meh! meh!"

"Come home, then," said the tailor, and led her into the stable, and tied her fast. When he was going away, he turned round again and said, "Well, art thou satisfied for once?" But the goat did not behave the better to him, and cried:

"Wherewithal should I be satisfied? Among the graves I leapt about, And found no leaves, so went without, meh! meh!"

When the tailor heard that, he was shocked, and saw clearly that he had driven away his three sons without cause. "Wait, thou ungrateful creature," cried he, "it is not enough to drive thee forth, I will mark thee so that thou wilt no more dare to show thyself amongst honest tailors." In great haste he ran upstairs, fetched his razor, lathered the goat's head, and shaved her as clean as the palm of his hand. And as the yard-measure would have been too good for her, he brought the horsewhip, and gave her such cuts with it that she ran away in violent haste.

When the tailor was thus left quite alone in his house he fell into great grief, and would gladly have had his sons back again, but no one knew whither they were gone. The eldest had apprenticed himself to a joiner, and learnt industriously and indefatigably, and when the time came for him to go travelling, his master presented him with a little table which had no particular appearance, and was made of common wood, but it had one good property; if anyone set it out, and said, "Little table, spread thyself," the good little table was at once covered with a clean little cloth, and a plate was there, and a knife and fork beside it, and dishes with boiled meats and roasted meats, as many as there was room for, and a great glass of red wine shone so that it made the heart glad. The young journeyman thought, "With this thou hast enough for thy whole life," and went joyously about the world and never troubled himself at all whether an inn was good or bad, or if anything was to be found in it or not. When it suited him he did not enter an inn at all, but either on the plain, in a wood, a meadow, or wherever he fancied, he took his little table off his back, set it down before him, and said, "Cover thyself," and then everything appeared that his heart desired. At length he took it into his head to go back to his father, whose anger would now be appeased, and who would now willingly receive him with his wishing-table. It came to pass that on his way home, he came one evening to an inn which was filled with guests. They bade him welcome, and invited him to sit and eat with them, for otherwise he would have difficulty in getting anything. "No," answered the joiner, "I will not take the few bites out of your mouths; rather than that, you shall be my guests." They laughed, and thought he was jesting with them; he, however, placed his wooden table in the middle of the room, and said, "Little table, cover thyself." Instantly it was covered with food, so good that the host could never have procured it, and the smell of it ascended pleasantly to the nostrils of the guests. "Fall to, dear friends," said the joiner; and the guests when they saw that he meant it, did not need to be asked twice, but drew near, pulled out their knives and attacked it valiantly. And what surprised them the most was that when a dish became empty, a full one instantly took its place of its own accord. The innkeeper stood in one corner and watched the affair; he did not at all know what to say, but thought, "Thou couldst easily find a use for such a cook as that in thy kitchen." The joiner and his comrades made merry until late into the night; at length they lay down to sleep, and the young apprentice also went to bed, and set his magic table against the wall. The host's thoughts, however, let him have no rest; it occurred to him that there was a little old table in his lumber-room which looked just like the apprentice's and he brought it out quite softly, and exchanged it for the wishing-table. Next morning, the joiner paid for his bed, took up his table, never thinking that he had got a false one, and went his way. At mid-day he reached his father, who received him with great joy. "Well, my dear son, what hast thou learnt?" said he to him. "Father, I have become a joiner."

"A good trade," replied the old man; "but what hast thou brought back with thee from thy apprenticeship?"

"Father, the best thing which I have brought back with me is this little table." The tailor inspected it on all sides and said, "Thou didst not make a masterpiece when thou mad'st that; it is a bad old table."

"But it is a table which furnishes itself," replied the son. "When I set it out, and tell it to cover itself, the most beautiful dishes stand on it, and a wine also, which gladdens the heart. Just invite all our relations and friends, they shall refresh and enjoy themselves for once, for the table will give them all they require." When the company was assembled, he put his table in the middle of the room and said, "Little table, cover thyself," but the little table did not bestir itself, and remained just as bare as any other table which did not understand language. Then the poor apprentice became aware that his table had been changed, and was ashamed at having to stand there like a liar. The relations, however, mocked him, and were forced to go home without having eaten or drunk. The father brought out his patches again, and went on tailoring, but the son went to a master in the craft.

The second son had gone to a miller and had apprenticed himself to him. When his years were over, the master said, "As thou hast conducted thyself so well, I give thee an ass of a peculiar kind, which neither draws a cart nor carries a sack."

"To what use is he put, then?" asked the young apprentice. "He lets gold drop from his mouth," answered the miller. "If thou settest him on a cloth and sayest 'Bricklebrit,' the good animal will drop gold pieces for thee."

"That is a fine thing," said the apprentice, and thanked the master, and went out into the world. When he had need of gold, he had only to say "Bricklebrit" to his ass, and it rained gold pieces, and he had nothing to do but pick them off the ground. Wheresoever he went, the best of everything was good enough for him, and the dearer the better, for he had always a full purse. When he had looked about the world for some time, he thought, "Thou must seek out thy father; if thou goest to him with the gold-ass he will forget his anger, and receive thee well." It came to pass that he came to the same public-house in which his brother's table had been exchanged. He led his ass by the bridle, and the host was about to take the animal from him and tie him up, but the young apprentice said, "Don't trouble yourself, I will take my grey horse into the stable, and tie him up myself too, for I must know where he stands." This struck the host as odd, and he thought that a man who was forced to look after his ass himself, could not have much to spend; but when the stranger put his hand in his pocket and brought out two gold pieces, and said he was to provide something good for him, the host opened his eyes wide, and ran and sought out the best he could muster. After dinner the guest asked what he owed. The host did not see why he should not double the reckoning, and said the apprentice must give two more gold pieces. He felt in his pocket, but his gold was just at an end. "Wait an instant, sir host," said he, "I will go and fetch some money;" but he took the table-cloth with him. The host could not imagine what this could mean, and being curious, stole after him, and as the guest bolted the stable-door, he peeped through a hole left by a knot in the wood. The stranger spread out the cloth under the animal and cried, "Bricklebrit," and immediately the beast began to let gold pieces fall, so that it fairly rained down money on the ground. "Eh, my word," said the host, "ducats are quickly coined there! A purse like that is not amiss." The guest paid his score, and went to bed, but in the night the host stole down into the stable, led away the master of the mint, and tied up another ass in his place. Early next morning the apprentice travelled away with his ass, and thought that he had his gold-ass. At mid-day he reached his father, who rejoiced to see him again, and gladly took him in. "What hast thou made of thyself, my son?" asked the old man. "A miller," dear father, he answered. "What hast thou brought back with thee from thy travels?"

"Nothing else but an ass."

"There are asses enough here," said the father, "I would rather have had a good goat."

"Yes," replied the son, "but it is no common ass, but a gold-ass, when I say 'Bricklebrit,' the good beast opens its mouth and drops a whole sheetful of gold pieces. Just summon all our relations hither, and I will make them rich folks."

"That suits me well," said the tailor, "for then I shall have no need to torment myself any longer with the needle," and ran out himself and called the relations together. As soon as they were assembled, the miller bade them make way, spread out his cloth, and brought the ass into the room. "Now watch," said he, and cried, "Bricklebrit," but no gold pieces fell, and it was clear that the animal knew nothing of the art, for every ass does not attain such perfection. Then the poor miller pulled a long face, saw that he was betrayed, and begged pardon of the relatives, who went home as poor as they came. There was no help for it, the old man had to betake him to his needle once more, and the youth hired himself to a miller.

The third brother had apprenticed himself to a turner, and as that is skilled labour, he was the longest in learning. His brothers, however, told him in a letter how badly things had gone with them, and how the innkeeper had cheated them of their beautiful wishing-gifts on the last evening before they reached home. When the turner had served his time, and had to set out on his travels, as he had conducted himself so well, his master presented him with a sack and said, "There is a cudgel in it."

"I can put on the sack," said he, "and it may be of good service to me, but why should the cudgel be in it? It only makes it heavy."

"I will tell thee why," replied the master; "if any one has done anything to injure thee, do but say, 'Out of the sack, Cudgel!' and the cudgel will leap forth among the people, and play such a dance on their backs that they will not be able to stir or move for a week, and it will not leave off until thou sayest, "Into the sack, Cudgel!" The apprentice thanked him, and put the sack on his back, and when any one came too near him, and wished to attack him, he said, "Out of the sack, Cudgel!" and instantly the cudgel sprang out, and dusted the coat or jacket of one after the other on their backs, and never stopped until it had stripped it off them, and it was done so quickly, that before anyone was aware, it was already his own turn. In the evening the young turner reached the inn where his brothers had been cheated. He laid his sack on the table before him, and began to talk of all the wonderful things which he had seen in the world. "Yes," said he, "people may easily find a table which will cover itself, a gold-ass, and things of that kind—extremely good things which I by no means despise—but these are nothing in comparison with the treasure which I have won for myself, and am carrying about with me in my sack there." The inn-keeper

pricked up his ears, "What in the world can that be?" th
he; "the sack must be filled with nothing but jewels; I oug
get them cheap too, for all good things go in threeo." Wh
was time for sleep, the guest stretched himself on the bench,
laid his sack beneath him for a pillow. When the inn-keep
thought his guest was lying in a sound sleep, he went to him an
pushed and pulled quite gently and carefully at the sack to see i
he could possibly draw it away and lay another in its place. The
turner had, however, been waiting for this for a long time, and
now just as the inn-keeper was about to give a hearty tug, he
cried, "Out of the sack, Cudgel!" Instantly the little cudgel
came forth, and fell on the inn-keeper and gave him a sound
thrashing.

The host cried for mercy; but the louder he cried, so much
more heavily the cudgel beat the time on his back, until at length
he fell to the ground exhausted. Then the turner said, "If thou
dost not give back the table which covers itself, and the gold-
ass, the dance shall begin afresh."

"Oh, no," cried the host, quite humbly, "I will gladly produce
everything, only make the accursed kobold creep back into the
sack." Then said the apprentice, "I will let mercy take the place
of justice, but beware of getting into mischief again!" So he
cried, "Into the sack, Cudgel!" and let him have rest.

Next morning the turner went home to his father with the
wishing-table, and the gold-ass. The tailor rejoiced when he saw
him once more, and asked him likewise what he had learned in
foreign parts. "Dear father," said he, "I have become a turner."

"A skilled trade," said the father. "What hast thou brought
back with thee from thy travels?"

"A precious thing, dear father," replied the son, "a cudgel in
the sack."

"What!" cried the father, "a cudgel! That's worth thy trouble,
indeed! From every tree thou can cut thyself one."

"But not one like this, dear father. If I say, 'Out of the sack,
Cudgel!' the cudgel springs out and leads any one who means ill

ought
ht to
n it
nd
er
d

ce, and never stops until he lies on the
r fair weather. Look you, with this cudgel
ie wishing-table and the gold-ass which the
er took away from my brothers. Now let them
or, and invite all our kinsmen. I will give them to
rink, and will fill their pockets with gold into the
he old tailor would not quite believe, but nevertheless
relatives together. Then the turner spread a cloth in the
and led in the gold-ass, and said to his brother, "Now, dear
her, speak to him." The miller said, "Bricklebrit," and
stantly the gold pieces fell down on the cloth like a thunder-
shower, and the ass did not stop until every one of them had so
much that he could carry no more. (I can see in thy face that
thou also wouldst like to be there.)

Then the turner brought the little table, and said, "Now dear
brother, speak to it." And scarcely had the carpenter said,
"Table, cover thyself," than it was spread and amply covered
with the most exquisite dishes. Then such a meal took place as
the good tailor had never yet known in his house, and the whole
party of kinsmen stayed together till far in the night, and were
all merry and glad. The tailor locked away needle and thread,
yard-measure and goose, in a press, and lived with his three sons
in joy and splendour. (What, however, has become of the goat
who was to blame for the tailor driving out his three sons? That
I will tell thee. She was ashamed that she had a bald head, and
ran to a fox's hole and crept into it. When the fox came home,
he was met by two great eyes shining out of the darkness, and
was terrified and ran away. A bear met him, and as the fox
looked quite disturbed, he said, "What is the matter with thee,
brother fox, why dost thou look like that?"

"Ah," answered Redskin, "a fierce beast is in my cave and
stared at me with its fiery eyes."

"We will soon drive him out," said the bear, and went with
him to the cave and looked in, but when he saw the fiery eyes,
fear seized on him likewise; he would have nothing to do with

with me a weary dance, and never stops until he lies on the ground and prays for fair weather. Look you, with this cudgel have I got back the wishing-table and the gold-ass which the thievish inn-keeper took away from my brothers. Now let them both be sent for, and invite all our kinsmen. I will give them to eat and to drink, and will fill their pockets with gold into the bargain." The old tailor would not quite believe, but nevertheless got the relatives together. Then the turner spread a cloth in the room and led in the gold-ass, and said to his brother, "Now, dear brother, speak to him." The miller said, "Bricklebrit," and instantly the gold pieces fell down on the cloth like a thunder-shower, and the ass did not stop until every one of them had so much that he could carry no more. (I can see in thy face that thou also wouldst like to be there.)

Then the turner brought the little table, and said, "Now dear brother, speak to it." And scarcely had the carpenter said, "Table, cover thyself," than it was spread and amply covered with the most exquisite dishes. Then such a meal took place as the good tailor had never yet known in his house, and the whole party of kinsmen stayed together till far in the night, and were all merry and glad. The tailor locked away needle and thread, yard-measure and goose, in a press, and lived with his three sons in joy and splendour. (What, however, has become of the goat who was to blame for the tailor driving out his three sons? That I will tell thee. She was ashamed that she had a bald head, and ran to a fox's hole and crept into it. When the fox came home, he was met by two great eyes shining out of the darkness, and was terrified and ran away. A bear met him, and as the fox looked quite disturbed, he said, "What is the matter with thee, brother fox, why dost thou look like that?"

"Ah," answered Redskin, "a fierce beast is in my cave and stared at me with its fiery eyes."

"We will soon drive him out," said the bear, and went with him to the cave and looked in, but when he saw the fiery eyes, fear seized on him likewise; he would have nothing to do with pricked up his ears, "What in the world can that be?" thought he; "the sack must be filled with nothing but jewels; I ought to get them cheap too, for all good things go in threes." When it was time for sleep, the guest stretched himself on the bench, and laid his sack beneath him for a pillow. When the inn-keeper thought his guest was lying in a sound sleep, he went to him and pushed and pulled quite gently and carefully at the sack to see if he could possibly draw it away and lay another in its place. The turner had, however, been waiting for this for a long time, and now just as the inn-keeper was about to give a hearty tug, he cried, "Out of the sack, Cudgel!" Instantly the little cudgel came forth, and fell on the inn-keeper and gave him a sound thrashing.

The host cried for mercy; but the louder he cried, so much more heavily the cudgel beat the time on his back, until at length he fell to the ground exhausted. Then the turner said, "If thou dost not give back the table which covers itself, and the gold-ass, the dance shall begin afresh."

"Oh, no," cried the host, quite humbly, "I will gladly produce everything, only make the accursed kobold creep back into the sack." Then said the apprentice, "I will let mercy take the place of justice, but beware of getting into mischief again!" So he cried, "Into the sack, Cudgel!" and let him have rest.

Next morning the turner went home to his father with the wishing-table, and the gold-ass. The tailor rejoiced when he saw him once more, and asked him likewise what he had learned in foreign parts. "Dear father," said he, "I have become a turner."

"A skilled trade," said the father. "What hast thou brought back with thee from thy travels?"

"A precious thing, dear father," replied the son, "a cudgel in the sack."

"What!" cried the father, "a cudgel! That's worth thy trouble, indeed! From every tree thou can cut thyself one."

"But not one like this, dear father. If I say, 'Out of the sack, Cudgel!' the cudgel springs out and leads any one who means ill the furious beast, and took to his heels. The bee met him, and as she saw that he was ill at ease, she said, "Bear, thou art really pulling a very pitiful face; what has become of all thy gaiety?"

"It is all very well for thee to talk," replied the bear, "a furious beast with staring eyes is in Redskin's house, and we can't drive him out." The bee said, "Bear I pity thee, I am a poor weak creature whom thou wouldst not turn aside to look at, but still, I believe, I can help thee." She flew into the fox's cave, lighted on the goat's smoothly-shorn head, and stung her so violently, that she sprang up, crying "Meh, meh," and ran forth into the world as if mad, and to this hour no one knows where she has gone.)